Was she deliberately goading him?

What happened then, nobody but Diana saw. Philip Strang-Steele, still standing folded his arms and leaned back appraisingly. He looked at her without facial expression for a long moment. She was the only one then facing him. Everyone else was looking forward, at her. Eventually, he unlocked his arms, letting them hang loose at his sides. He raised the fingertips of his right hand and placed them against his mouth and then waved in a negligent salute.

A kiss? An insolent, arrogant kiss.

Also by Rosemary Enright
Published by Ivy Books:

ALEXA'S VINEYARD

PART ONE

CHAPTER
1

IN THE GROWN-UP world, virtue is not rewarded. Nor is innocence protected. And whilst beauty may deflect trifling annoyances, it is no armour against disaster.

These were the reflections which occupied the foremost part of Lord Justice Peake's much-admired brain as he prepared to pronounce sentence on the husband of one whom he considered, in his old-fashioned, romantic way, to be beautiful, innocent and virtuous. Diana Neville had behaved admirably. Unfortunately, she was married to a scoundrel and must take the consequences. Mr. Justice Peake rustled some papers, a pleasurable preliminary to the sound of his own voice.

"Since hearing the jury's verdict in this case which, I have no need to remind the court, was unanimous, I have considered the far reaching implications very thoroughly." The judge cleared his throat reedily, swinging his head from side to side, tortoise like, within the grey, blinkering wig. "And I have reached the conclusion that you, Michael Neville, must be punished with a severity that will serve as a caution to others who may be exposed to similar temptations."

Diana glanced covertly to where her husband stood in the dock. She saw, or thought she saw, his erect, stocky figure sway slightly and his hands tighten their grip on the rail. She averted her eyes quickly and looked down at her own interlaced fingers, whitening in her lap. She could hear the artist's crayon squealing in the silence as it raced to capture the tension of the moment, the conflicting expressions on the faces of judge, advocates, the prisoner and, no doubt, herself.

The press had made a good deal of the fact that she and Michael were a handsome couple. The reportage was littered with minute physical descriptions of the accused and his wife. Her neat, ballerina looks and his hair, faded from the colour of ripe wheat, as one fulsome caption had said, seemed somehow to sharpen the poignancy of their downfall in the public imagination. For this had been a very public trial.

Deliberately, Diana closed and smoothed her features so that they should give nothing away to the eagerly straining journalists in the press gallery. A year in the remorseless searchlight of public opprobrium had schooled her to apparent indifference. It was the only way to survive. And survive she must, for their daughter, and for the future. One day, the nightmare would be over and they would all be together again. Today was her fortieth birthday. Diana realised the fact with a faint shock. More than half her life was over and yet it must be rebuilt, from the ground up.

Some way in front of her, she was aware of the dark gowned forms of Michael's solicitor, Greville Goodwynne, Sir Eric Reith QC and his junior. They sat motionless, tautly awaiting the judge's next word as if even now they half expected some exploitable loophole to appear. But, of course, that was impossible. Michael had been found guilty of all eighteen charges under the Theft Act more than a week ago. This morning she had started to pack an overnight bag for him. But he had been unable to face the day's most probable ending.

"For God's sake, Diana! What an ignorant woman you are. Don't you ever read the newspapers? It's a first offence and the prisons are full to bursting with rapists and child fuckers. I'll get a ticking off, a bloody great fine and a suspended sentence. That's what Greville said."

Diana had put away the Jermyn Street shirts and socks resignedly. They probably wouldn't let him wear them, anyway. And she couldn't turn Michael into a realist by packing a few clothes. He was a dreamer of dreams. One of the few able to generate an ectoplasmic substance from ideas that gave them the illusions of solidity. Because of it she had lived in comfort for so long. But now reality was presenting the bill. She wondered if his trustees in bankruptcy would be empowered to pay a fine. She decided not to ask. It was not the moment. Probably not, anyway.

"Michael, Greville said he hoped that's what you'd get. I

think we should be prepared for . . . I mean, we mustn't be disappointed if it's worse."

"We? We?" Her husband's voice was querulous. "I don't see the *we* in this. It's me that's been hounded to hell and back again. And for what?" he added more quietly. "I've done no more than blokes in the City do every day. A deal here, a risk there—if there were no mistakes, the City of London would have ceased to exist long ago. That's business. It thrives on excitement, not safety."

"Yes, darling, I know."

It was useless to say more. Michael had wrenched open the lock on the full length window that gave on to the balcony overlooking the Boltons' oval gardens. The knob came off in his hand and he flung it backwards. It landed with a crash on Diana's dressing-table and sent a crystal perfume bottle flying. It shattered on the wood block floor. Silently she sat down and started to apply lavender coloured shadow to her eyes, mechanically painting the same picture on the same canvas, seeing nothing. Her own face had become an affair of newspaper photography. Surprising sometimes, impersonal always. Her face was now like her clothes. Something she put on in the morning to confront each day's new and terrible truths.

"You have enjoyed," the judge continued, his voice curling round each carefully enunciated syllable with leisurely perfectionism, "what the world calls a glittering career. Meteoric, in fact, if I may make use of that somewhat overworked metaphor. You have achieved abundant wealth and with that has come great power. Alas, the power to discriminate between the legitimate exercise of the authority vested in you by trusting investors and flagrant abuse of that trust deserted you as fast as success and influence were added to you.

"Let us make no mistake. Despite the complexity of your machinations, some would say their cleverness, to the plain man, you are a thief. A common thief."

Noted for his dramatic pauses since thespian triumphs at Winchester had led him to choose a legal career, Lord Justice Peake allowed the condemnation to hang in the air. For once he wished the coldness of the fluorescent strip lighting were not quite so effective. Mrs. Neville's pallor was not a thing he wished emphasised lest it distract him from his duty. He felt, rather than saw, her steady, serious regard. She was paying perfect attention, as usual. A remarkably well-chosen hat, too, the judge allowed himself the thought. Solemn but not crestfallen. A wise colour, grey.

"You had nothing further to wish for in life. You had more than an ordinary man dreams of owning. Several luxurious homes, a lovely, dignified wife," unconscious that he had just designated her a chattel, the judge nodded an acknowledgment in Diana's direction with dry gallantry, "the respect of your City colleagues . . . And a healthy child who just now, entering upon womanhood, must look with shame upon her father's record instead of rejoicing in the filial pride that should have been her truest and most valued heritage."

Diana turned her head sharply away. He might have spared them that. The hateful old man seemed to be enjoying himself. A ripple of sympathetic disapproval stirred the court room. This time Peake had gone too far. A scuffling noise and a short strangled cry made her look at the dock. Michael had stumbled and a man in a blue uniform was trying to support him. Michael shook him off roughly as he regained his footing.

"Would you care to be seated?" The judge enquired with eyebrows arched in mock ignorance of the cause of the prisoner's distress. "Sir Eric?"

Peake subsided as the barrister waved away the implied suggestion of a recess. The judge pursed his lips regretfully. He felt just a little ashamed of himself. He'd fallen into the trap of abusing his own power. But he'd wanted to put a dart through the fellow's arrogance. Sometimes Neville had come dangerously close to contempt. Mrs. Neville shared the punishment. A pity, he sighed with gloomy content, but that was the law of God and Nature.

Michael shook his head and, placing his feet apart, squared his shoulders and flung his head back defiantly. "I will stand," he announced harshly.

Throughout his long, tortuous trial, he had shown no emotion until now, when his daughter, Yolanda, had been dragged in to taunt him. For the first time he had tears to shed. Diana would know. He shrivelled inside, shrinking from the thought of her intolerable pity. She wouldn't be so crude as to let it show, but it would be there all the same.

Satisfied that the prisoner had recovered sufficient command of himself, the judge allowed his long, heavy eyelids to cover all but a glinting slit as he hastened the matter to a conclusion.

"Having regard to the privation you have callously inflicted on thousands of small investors, many of whom are elderly and must now face a retirement in straitened circumstances, I can find no appropriate alternative to a custodial sentence. And since men of your stamp are inclined to regard fraud as a peccadillo and being found out as mere 'bad luck,' I intend to make a contribution towards reducing the future incidence of pin-striped crime."

Peake ran the tip of his tongue over his upper lip, savouring the murmur of appreciation from the scribbling journalists. He looked on himself as something of a phrase maker.

"You will go to prison for eight years."

❦ DIANA ENTERED THE bleak basement room below the court to the sound of the tin ashtray rattling on the melamine surfaced table. Michael was stubbing out a half smoked cigar. Two already lay abandoned there.

Greville Goodwynne followed her closely, his hand resting reassuringly on the small of her back.

"We'll appeal, of course, Mike. This is just the first round."

"Get your hands off my wife, Goodwynne."

Patiently, the solicitor removed his hand, mouth compressed. Diana looked back at him, forming a slight *moue* of apology with her own lips. Michael was a difficult man under stress.

"We'll give notice of . . ."

"No point. That's it. Guilty as charged. I know it, you know it, now the sodding world knows it."

"Well, look . . . it'll be three years if you keep your nose clean." Goodwynne tried to restore some semblance of businesslike normality to the conversation.

"Stow it, Greville. Three years, eight years—what does it matter? I'm finished. I'm a marked man. On the scrap heap."

He stood up, kicking the tubular steel chair out of the way. Diana noticed that his fourth waistcoat button hung by a thread. Michael had put on a lot of weight in recent months. Every day there was another empty whisky bottle to dispose of. The Filipino valet had gone and the equipment in the apartment's small gymnasium hadn't been used for weeks.

"Darling, perhaps we should let Greville be the judge

of . . ." Diana took a step towards her husband, fighting down a feeling that she could not bring herself to recognise as fear. His mouth, that had always been so ready to smile in the past, had become a thin, mean line. This is what a year of accusations, enquiries and mountains of paper had done to him, Diana told herself miserably.

"Shut up, Diana. What do you know about it? I'm sorry. It's not your fault, any of it," he retracted awkwardly. Diana didn't understand business or accountancy, or the law. He'd always protected her from all that.

"It's your birthday today. You know, I always meant to give a surprise party for your fortieth birthday. Rivers of champagne and mountains of caviare and all the people you'd ever met and liked in your life . . ."

He stopped speaking, aware that the expressed wish sounded pathetic.

Michael dragged his fingers through his hair. He'd really never intended to do anything of the sort. There was no point. All Diana's friends were his friends. He'd have given her a piece of jewellery as usual. It was just that there was no money. They'd taken away his cheque book. He found that difficult to understand. How could there possibly be nothing where there had always been so much? And Diana stood there, the same as ever, pretending it didn't matter. He would have liked her better if she'd been hysterical. He wanted her to need something from him. It would have been some kind of relief to despise her. But he could not do that. Her containment during the past months and weeks had been absolute.

Diana stood still, uncertain now what to do or say that would seem natural and comforting. There was an embarrassing silence in the room, broken only by the dull roar of traffic outside. She heard the sound of footsteps in the corridor with relief.

"That's right, sir. He's in there."

The policeman on duty opened the door of the cell to admit Sir Eric with his black bag dangling over his lean shoulder, gown and wig stowed away.

"Well, I can't say how sorry I am about that. Peake's an unpredictable blighter," the tall barrister began, holding his hand out to Michael and looking searchingly at Diana. Up to now she'd done marvellously, of course, remarkably calm. But presumably she had her limits.

Sir Eric dropped his outstretched hand when it became painfully clear that his client intended to ignore it.

"Pull yourself together, Michael," Diana said, unexpectedly angry. "Sir Eric has done his best. Nobody could have done more. Without him and Greville it might have been a lot worse. Who else would have stood beside you with very little hope of getting paid in the foreseeable future? Ingratitude is so ugly. Haven't we had enough of ugliness?"

The three men stared incredulously at her. Michael's shock was the most acute. Diana was his wife. It was her place to defer to him, to depend on him, even for her opinions. Until this moment, she always had. Anger, from her, was unacceptable. His face darkened and his hands trembled. For a moment, it seemed as if he might actually hit her. But he turned on his heel and fell to staring out of the murky basement window, watching indifferent, disembodied feet pass by.

"Perhaps you and Diana would like to be alone for a few minutes?" Greville Goodwynne ventured smoothly.

"Not on your life, sport," Michael retorted vulgarly. "If it wasn't for that bitch and her expectations, we shouldn't be standing here right now. You wouldn't believe how much dosh a woman like that can consume in a year. You should see the jewels I've bought her . . ."

"Well, I'll be in touch, Goodwynne," Sir Eric interrupted hastily. He didn't want to witness the final disintegration of a personality which had drawn everything to itself in prosperity. The test of a man was fortitude in the face of a reverse of fortune. At the last, Neville had failed the test. And insulting his wife in public was an unpardonable lapse. "May I give you a lift, Mrs. Neville?"

Diana smiled her thanks and declined. Sir Eric laid his hand on her arm momentarily, a light, quick pressure. It conveyed his admiration and his sympathy. It was a shame she should be exposed to all this unpleasantness. Most women would have walked out on Neville months ago. But it seemed she was intent on remaining till the bitter end. On an impulse he raised her hand to his mouth and brushed her fingertips with his lips. Astonished, Diana did not resist.

Michael glowered from his station beside the barred win-

dow. He was more than half flattered by the distinguished barrister's interest in his wife. The *frisson* of possession. It was
the one pleasure that never failed. Diana was his and she
would never stray. Her faithfulness was dull until it was challenged and then he loved her passionately until the challenger
went away, defeated.

In twenty-two years of marriage, her slender figure had
never altered, except once, briefly, when she was carrying
Yolanda. Her honey toned complexion was still smooth and
fine and the delicate, precisely drawn features had never coars-
ened. Her looks had matured but not diminished. Her hair, almost black, had threads of silver in it now and occasionally
there were shadows under her deep set, violet tinged eyes. It
made no difference. She had a controlled vibrancy to which
Michael himself had long since become insensitive. But he enjoyed watching its effect on others.

It reminded him of when he had first known her and succeeded in detaching her from that untidy household where her
vague, shambling father and pretty, prattling mother had lived
from hand to mouth, from month to month. The tall redbrick
house had been smothered in musical scores, cat hairs and un-
paid bills. People with shabby clothes and obscurely famous
names had wandered in and out of the place, waving sheaves
of manuscript and expecting meals.

In the midst of it all, Diana's invincible neatness of face, figure and manner had a clean cut brilliance which he had cov-
eted and won. The Royal Ballet had not wanted her. She had
grown an inch too tall. Their loss had been his first, important
gain. Now he saw her only through the eyes of others. Her personality was less noticeable to him than oxygen. Something he
needed but never considered. She was a reliable woman.

"Transport's come, sir."

The duty policeman popped his head round the door
again. Curiously he looked from face to face. What did ex-
multimillionaires and their wives say to each other at times
like this? And with the lawyers hanging round? Didn't they
want any privacy? Ah well, he sighed inwardly, the rich
were different. Even here. Difficult to know how to tell a
bloke like Neville that there was a Black Maria outside and
not a chauffeur driven limousine awaiting his pleasure. It'd
be a bit of a shock. The constable congratulated himself on

"transport." A nice, tactful touch. Poor Mrs. Neville. Like everyone else on the duty roster, the constable thought she was a trooper. More'n done her bit, had Mrs. Neville. Always a smile for the little people. A special smile that told you she knew you just worked here.

"Thank you, officer. My husband will be ready in a moment." Diana closed the door firmly but gently on the policeman.

"I'll wait outside in the corridor. Goodbye for now, old man. Keep your spirits up and we'll see what we can do." The solicitor was rewarded with a grunt and a bare nod of the head. "I'll give Diana a lift home, so you've no need to worry about that." Goodwynne broke off. His client was well past worrying about anything but himself.

The door closed behind him and Diana and Michael were alone with a flat sea of despair oozing round the shipwreck of their life together.

"I will write, of course. As soon as I know where you are ..." Diana tried to keep her voice level, devoid of judgment. Michael had had enough of that.

"The Scrubs. At first, anyway. Look, I'm sorry. The things I said. I've got to hit out at something, you know. Chap like me. Can't just take it all lying down."

Diana was not even tempted to point out that the something he had swung blindly at was in fact her and that hurting her would not change anything. He knew all that. That material things actually meant very little to her, he had never known. She would have traded handfuls of pearls for his warm touch on her shoulder. It was a touch that never came and Diana accepted the jewels instead. They were his only caress and as such, she was grateful for them.

"Haven't got a handkerchief, have you?" Diana usually carried a spare for him, just one of the small wifely services he counted on without ever thinking about it. "My bloody nose is running. A cold. That's all I need."

"Of course, darling. Here."

Diana took a freshly laundered linen handkerchief from her handbag and held it out. He did not walk towards her and she heard her own heels clatter on the linoleum as she crossed the room. Michael took the folded handkerchief from her hand and pressed it to his eyes.

"Must have got a bad dose. My ruddy eyes are watering, too." Of course. Michael did not weep, ever. Knowing that was a household rule.

"You'd better take these. Screws will only swipe them if you don't." He fumbled at his cuffs, struggling with clumsy fingers to remove the gold and lapis lazuli cuff-links. "Sell them. Buy yourself something. It's your birthday."

Diana swallowed. He was only five foot nine inches tall. But to her he seemed as tall as an oak and less responsive. Why didn't they embrace in this last moment? She would have treasured the encircling pressure of his arms. But they remained stiffly at his sides. She understood, of course. If Michael showed any sign of human warmth now, he would break down. And then he would not be able to live with himself.

"Goodbye." She reached up and kissed his jaw. He did not bend to meet her but made a vague kissing sound into the empty air.

"I shan't sell the cuff-links. You'll need them again." Diana put everything she could of faith and resolution into her voice. It didn't matter that she'd bought them herself as a Christmas present for him, seven years ago. He'd forgotten. Diana had learned not to be wounded by such trivial oversights. She was just glad he'd liked them enough to wear them often.

She wanted to say something about their daughter. Michael must be worried sick about Yolanda—what she would think, how she would feel. But instinctively, Diana decided against it. The judge had guessed his Achilles' heel with cruel accuracy. Another touch on the smarting place and Michael would be unmanned.

She blew him a final, soundless kiss and smiled what he used to call her "slice of apple smile."

But Michael had already turned back to the window and was watching the disembodied feet, his hands thrust into his pockets. Life's more unpleasant moments were best ignored.

❦ OUTSIDE ON THE pavement, the September sunshine was hot and the flashlights of a dozen cameras dazzled her eyes.

"How's he taking it, Mrs. Neville?" A reporter standing near her asked, licking the tip of his pencil.

"Diana! Over here, love." Diana recognised the photographer. It was the man from the *Evening Standard*. Fervently, she hoped she would be front page news for the last time.

"What'll you do now, Mrs. Neville? Does your daughter know?"

Diana winced inwardly. Thank God Yolanda was in Somerset at school. She would be safe from all of this there. She would have to be told, of course. Tonight, before the morning papers.

"Love the suit. Armani, isn't it?" A female bystander turned brightly to her headscarfed companion.

Diana wished she could rip the garments from her body and trample them underfoot. She wanted to scream at them that she was wretched and alone. That they had taken her husband and the meaning of her life away. But of course, that was impossible.

She walked straight towards Greville Goodwynne's waiting Daimler, wearing the mild, abstracted smile that had made her seem inviolate and invulnerable. It also frustrated the curiosity and ingenuity of the press. They wanted to break down the reserve of this woman. The readers wanted to see, bewilderment, hope, grief, betrayal, despair. The rich impoverished, the mighty brought low. But they had been disappointed. All they had seen was a quiet self-assurance that went on day after day like a spell of cold weather, which in itself becomes a phenomenon. The public abuse heaped on Michael had been counterpointed by a growing fascination with his coolly indomitable wife.

"Let us pass, please. Mrs. Neville is very tired." Greville urged a path through the thronging reporters. "Come along now. Enough is enough. Yes, I'll be making a brief press statement tomorrow. No, not now."

Finally, they were in the car and the chauffeur began to slide it away from the kerb, pushing through the milling crowd and the gargoyle faces which stared in, their mouths moving ludicrously, lips, tongues and teeth, producing no words that could penetrate the tightly shut windows.

One man clung on to the car till the last minute. As it gathered speed, he stumbled back into the gutter but Diana understood the shape of the words he was speaking and the outline of a roof he was drawing in the air with his two forefingers. *Where are you going to live?* She really didn't know.

"Where to, Mr. Goodwynne, sir?"

"The Boltons. We're dropping Mrs. Neville and then back to the office."

❦ THERE WERE TWO men standing in the immaculately painted porch of number nine. They were carrying briefcases and although there were three large apartments in the house, Diana could not escape the conclusion that these men had something to do with her. One had his finger pressed to a bell. It looked like the middle one. And they were talking to each other intermittently, unsmilingly, as if they expected to conduct distasteful business.

She looked sideways at Greville who was already leaning forward, peering worriedly at the two men.

"Up-market double glazing salesmen, do you think?" Diana joked wanly, hopefully. Vulnerability showed in her face for the first time that day.

Goodwynne laughed. Diana Neville had a habit of puncturing balloons of suspense with random shafts of wry humour. Sudden beams of bright sunlight in a stormy sky.

" 'Fraid not," he answered her question. "You stay here with Hurst and I'll go and see what they want."

Diana sighed with relief. Soon, she knew, she would have to cope on her own. But Greville could do her this one last service. She couldn't talk to any more men in suits. Not today.

She watched the solicitor bound briskly up the steps of the house between the white columns of the porch. The men turned towards him, with the expression of those relieved to be dealing with a fellow professional. They shook hands and formed into a huddle. Diana looked away. Men talking in groups were like kettles. The one never broke up and the other never boiled if you watched them. She glanced upwards and saw the first floor casement swinging open in a sudden gust of wind. Michael had wrenched the knob off only three hours since. It seemed like an event that had occurred in a different lifetime. Silly to worry about an unlocked window now.

Lowering her eyes again, she saw Greville's head moving up and down as if on a short stiff spring, acknowledging the unheard statements of the other men, and then he moved it back and to one side, as men always did when they were appealing for reason and sure of receiving it.

Together, the group walked down the steps, still talking. The men with the briefcases met Diana's anxious gaze non-committally and walked off, absorbed in disgruntled conversation with each other.

"That's all right for the moment," Greville opened the car door and seated himself beside Diana. "Hurst, be a good fellow and go and see if you can find me a copy of *The Times*. I left mine at home this morning."

Hurst touched the peak of his cap and got out of the car obediently, understanding Mr. Goodwynne wanted a few moments alone with Mrs. Neville.

"You've got a week, Diana. That was somebody from the Official Receiver's office and an estate agent. The apartment here belonged to the Knightman Neville Trust, you know. I'm afraid it's part of the liquidation . . ."

Goodwynne looked at Diana steadily, hoping she was managing to grasp the fact that she was homeless. Brereton Park would have to go, and the house in Antibes, the yacht—everything. It was a pity Michael hadn't transferred some assets to her long ago. He should have seen the writing on the wall. Brereton was his personal property. He could have put that in her name before the bankruptcy proceedings started. Neville was a brilliant man in many ways. Piratical, adventurous, inventive—but stubborn. Against all advice he'd refused steadily to take avoiding action, to limit the damage and above all to protect his family. He'd believed to the end that he'd get away with it as others had in the past.

"Yes. I understand," Diana answered firmly. "What can I take?"

"Nothing unless it's your personal property. Your clothes, your jewellery, things you may have inherited from your own family, that sort of thing. The furniture will be auctioned. I'm afraid they want your car keys now. I promised I'd have them sent round to the Official Receiver's office this afternoon."

Diana glanced across the road to where the white Porsche was parked in the shade of a plane tree. She stirred the contents of her handbag until her fingers closed on the keys. It cost her no pain. She felt detached from the Porsche, anyway. It was just one more thing that Michael had thrust upon her. She would have liked a less splashy car. Now she had none.

"Here you are. The one with the plastic end is for the igni-

tion." Diana handed the keys over almost gaily. She felt sorry
for Greville Goodwynne. Telling her she was destitute must
have been his most unpleasant task of all.

"Since I have a roof over my head for a week, thanks to
you, Greville, I believe I'm still in a position to offer you a
cup of coffee after your morning's labours, or perhaps a drink.
I could even rustle up a sandwich. You must be hungry." The
instincts of the hostess rose automatically in her despite her
longing to be alone.

"No, really. I must get back to the office now." The solicitor
laid his hand over hers. "I'd like to stay but . . ."

"There's nothing more you can do. Quite. I must just get on
with it, mustn't I?"

Goodwynne did not attempt to deny the stark truth of what
she said. There was no way either of them could pretend that
the tidal wave held back so far, by legal argument and counter-
argument, was not about to close finally over her head.

"Diana, do you have any money at all?" He wished he had
not asked. It was tantamount to offering to open his purse to
her if she admitted to having no funds.

"Yes, please don't worry. I have a little because my parents
left me some. Just a few thousand. Musicians don't earn
enough to save much. And they never owned a house, you see.
Our Kensington house was rented. But Yolanda's school fees
are paid for the year, so there's somewhere for her to be, for
the moment anyway."

"What about you?" Goodwynne could not now draw back.
He had to know. The thought of this brave, exquisite woman
sleeping in some sleazy hotel or queuing up to collect the dole
was too horrible to contemplate. And yet, he would be powerless to prevent it. She would never accept his charity, nor
would his wife permit him to offer it. His partners were already baying about the seemingly irrecoverable costs of
Neville's defence.

"I've no relatives left alive. But actually, I do have somewhere to go. Somewhere of my own." Diana's face brightened
at the realisation. She had forgotten all about the letter and the
package which had come on the day Michael was first told he
would have to answer charges. She'd just put them away in a
drawer and forgotten about them. They were things from outside, on the fringe of her real life's intensity.

"Last November an old aunt died in Yorkshire. She was a great-aunt, really. I'd met her just once when I was about three. She came to see my parents when my father was first violin with the London Philharmonic. Apparently she was rather odd. Her clothes all reeked of mothballs. I remember that. Aunt Thea. Anyway, she left me her house because I was her only surviving relative, I suppose. Her solicitors sent me the deeds and a bunch of keys on an iron ring. I've never seen the place, it's probably a ruin. But it's mine, it seems, and it's somewhere to go. It's funny, I never thought about it till now. I'm not used to having things of my own."

Diana spoke in a rush, made conscious that every moment of the solicitor's time ought to be paid for.

Goodwynne breathed a sigh of relief. "Thank heaven. Well, Diana, keep in touch, won't you?"

Knowing herself to be dismissed, Diana touched him lightly on the cheek as he leaned across her to open the door on to the pavement. She smelled of lilacs and the perfume dizzied him momentarily. All at once Goodwynne realised how much he had come to count on seeing her every day. For him, the Neville trial had been Camelot because of her. The long faces had been only acting and in the last scene everything should have come right. The days would now be ordinary, paper shuffling, dictating, telephoning days with no performance to look forward to, no face in the audience to search for and find.

"No, indeed I shall not keep in touch. That would be too wearisome for you. I will let you have my address so that you can contact me if you need to. About Sir Eric's fee, I'll try to . . ."

Goodwynne shook his head forbidding her to speak of it. He was a rich man.

"But for now," gratefully, Diana acted on his signal, "I'm sure you've had more than enough of the Nevilles and their unprofitable affairs. Thank you, Greville. Thank you for everything."

❦ THE APARTMENT WAS warm from the sun streaming into the west facing windows. There was an odour of stale cigar smoke and wet, but unwashed, ashtrays in the kitchen sink. And newspapers. Diana usually threw them away as quickly as Michael would let her because she hated the smell. She wrinkled her nose with disgust.

Diana did not much care for this apartment. It was large and smart with magnificent plaster mouldings, parquet floors and mahogany doors. The white marble fireplaces were inanimate, unused, their empty mouths stuffed with stylised, unnourishing flower arrangements. The warm air ducted heating was efficient but soulless. Brutal modern furniture, black ash, chrome and steel, with hard, unwelcoming edges, stood in rigid, functional groups. Here and there, the huge blank walls were interrupted by a framed expanse of grey canvas, Post Impressionist paintings of the English school depicting windswept beaches and rainy streets. They were like the handwoven rugs on the floor, important, expensive, modernist and deeply depressing. There were mirrors too, reflecting the costly emptiness, but no curtains. All the windows had specially made louvred shutters so that there could be privacy without softness. It was Michael's taste. Masculine.

He had allowed her no hand in decorating the Boltons' apartment. It was a platform for entertaining, Michael had said. He wanted nothing competing with him. Nothing to take anybody's mind off what he said and nothing to take anybody's eyes away from her clothes.

"You're all the colour we need here," he had said. "I perform, she exists," he had told the decorator succinctly. "Make a stage for that." And the decorator, approving the austerity of his brief, had done as he was told.

Diana removed the felt toque wearily, inspecting her face in the console mirror in the hall. For the first time in a while, she saw a change in it. She was tired. There was nobody to be cheerful and energetic for any longer. No sooner had she thought it than she remembered about Yolanda. Another effort must be made. Reluctantly, she walked into the laboratory-like kitchen.

The Ansaphone showed that one person had telephoned during the morning. She touched the playback button and heard Michael's voice, grim and defensive, telling the unknown caller that he was out. Diana stifled an audible laugh. It seemed such a ludicrous understatement. He was very much out now. Out of the game. Would Michael have appreciated the joke? Diana doubted it. Michael's sense of humour did not extend to himself. I must be mad, she whispered to herself, ashamed of the sudden gust of laughter.

When the message was over, the machine whirred and Diana heard the fussy, officious tones of her daughter's headmaster, Mr. Laverack. All girls' schools seemed to have headmasters now.

"I really think we should talk at the earliest possible moment. I'd be glad if you'd respond by telephoning immediately on your return. I shall leave instructions that I may be disturbed even if teaching or in conference."

Mr. Laverack was often in conference. Anyone would think he was running General Motors. Irritated and nervous, Diana dialled the school's number.

The school secretary's voice intoned the usual formula coldly. In general, as Mrs. Neville knew, parents were advised to ring between 5:00 and 5:30 pm. But in the rather special circumstances, the secretary believed an exception might be made. Diana bore with the impudence. Laverack was some minutes in coming to the telephone. The delay had the feeling of an elaborate ploy.

"Yes, Mrs. Neville?"

Infuriated, Diana realised she was expected to explain the reason for her call. "If you remember, Mr. Laverack, I am returning *your* call."

"Ah, yes. I thought we should talk. The new situation . . . I want to make you aware of the school's position."

Diana held on to her temper, fidgeting with Michael's cufflinks in her pocket. Nervous tension.

"I am amazed, Mr. Laverack, that you should think I wish to discuss anything at the moment except my daughter. I'm afraid I have some rather bad news for her. May I speak to her?"

Yolanda, it seemed, was unavailable.

"What do you mean?" Diana asked sharply. "She's all right, isn't she?"

Laverack unburdened himself.

Yolanda had heard about her father on some pop station's midday news. A private study session. The senior girls worked in their own rooms, of course, and they all had wirelesses. Yolanda had been found by her house matron, crying wildly, uncontrollably, and beating her fists on a school wardrobe so as seriously to risk damaging it.

Diana noted that point with a faint smile, wishing that Yolanda had smashed the wretched wardrobe to matchsticks.

"Where is she now? What is she doing?" Diana cut into Laverack's further description of Yolanda's behaviour.

"She is in the sanatorium. The doctor was summoned and administered a mild tranquilliser. Yolanda is sleeping peacefully. Sister will keep her in overnight. As soon as you can collect her, I'll . . ."

Diana quickly disabused the headmaster of any notion that he was to be relieved of responsibility for Yolanda in the immediate future. He must cope. It was his job.

"Good. Mr. Laverack, please tell my daughter when she wakes that I am going up to Yorkshire tonight. Tell her also that I love her and will speak to her some time tomorrow. At the moment I'm unable to give you a telephone number. In the meantime, I should prefer her to remain quietly with Sister, in the sanatorium, until I am able to talk with her. Please convey my message. This is a difficult time."

Diana's voice was clipped, determined. It had a sound unfamiliar to her. It was like somebody else talking. And in the course of being firm with Laverack she had been firm with herself. She wasn't going to spend another night in this hideous apartment. A clean break, now.

She put the telephone receiver down with a bang on Laverack's outraged burblings. Sister was a good person, sensible. Yolanda was in safe, affectionate hands. Safer than mine, she murmured aloud.

The recording unit whirred back to zero. There were no other messages. The people Michael called their friends were only business acquaintances. Associates. Fair weather friends.

Diana wasn't sure how she was going to manage about Yolanda. She'd always been her father's child, accepting Diana with a vague, almost contemptuous tolerance. She was also aware that beneath her daughter's off-hand manner, "laid back" they called it, there was a passionate, forceful personality which sucked at Diana's energy and left her depleted in spirits. As a toddler, Yolanda had been able to keep up a temper tantrum all day and, after a night's angelic slumber, frown unforgettingly and unforgivingly over her bowl of Kiddybrek. No nanny had ever stayed longer than ten months and Diana had dreaded their days off.

Now she would have to be the stronger of the two. But she could not do it yet. Yolanda's grief and disbelief would spill like acid on whomever was near. And my metal, Diana thought to herself, will not take any more corrosion. I must build myself a rock, a wall, a safe place to be.

❦ THE LOCAL TRAIN from Leeds made a sudden, alarming lurch and Diana, who had been sleeping till then, was jerked into instant wakefulness. Coming quickly to herself, she peered through her cupped hands out of the black window. The train was flying through the air.

Far below she saw a narrow, deep gorge with a ribbon of black water at the bottom reflecting the myriad lights of houses with steeply pitched roofs clinging like limpets to the sides. Above, the sky was pricked with stars and a sickle moon swung like a fairground dreamboat. Fleetingly, she caught sight of some dimly silhouetted battlements. A toy town castle. It was only a moment and then the vision had gone as if a pantomime curtain had dropped.

Diana felt in her handbag for the umpteenth time. Yes, the bulky parchment deeds of Gilbert's Tower were there, together with the daunting collection of keys. Some were ancient and rusted, others were quite ordinary. There was nothing to say which was the front door, the back door ... or anything. All the way from King's Cross, in the orange plastic station buffet at Leeds where she had waited half an hour over two tasteless cups of coffee, and on this, the last leg of her journey, she had tried to prepare herself for what Gilbert's Tower might be. Neither the name, nor the incomprehensible documents, written in archaic English, gave the slightest clue. The house was old. Whether or not it would be habitable, she had no idea.

Aunt Thea's solicitor had written only the briefest of covering letters. He had said merely that since it was unlikely that she would ever wish to live in Nidcaster, he would be happy to handle the sale of the property. In her later years, he added, Miss FitzGilbert had allowed certain dilapidations to occur, although the house was basically weatherproof and structurally sound. As his firm had acted since its inception in the eighteenth century for the FitzGilbert family, he looked forward to being of service to its sole surviving member. And then there was a secretary's "pp" signature. Obviously she was not very important to the firm of Booth, Wilson & Meers.

She felt a sensation of rising panic. Perhaps she had missed Nidcaster and the train was rushing her through the dark, early autumn night to York. There was an old man, the only other occupant of the carriage, sitting on the opposite side of the aisle. He was shabbily dressed and fondling a long, lissome creature with shining dark eyes. Diana thought it might be a ferret. She had never seen one before. It added to her sense of having stumbled into an unmapped world, not connected by measurable miles or countable hours to real places. The ferret's owner had courteously ignored her since joining the train at a station called Starbeck.

"Excuse me. Will we soon be at Nidcaster?" Diana enquired hesitantly, looking apprehensively at the ferret. It had stopped its joyful squirming and studied her, whiskers twitching disdainfully.

"Aye. Next one." The man replied without elaboration or a smile.

It would be some time before Diana realised that the local people were sparing of words but generous in action. Nor did they waste muscular effort on smiling at strangers. Relationships were entered into cautiously and cultivated at leisure.

Chilled, Diana began to collect her things together. There were two large suitcases, a smaller one, her dressing-case and handbag. She prayed there would be a taxi at Nidcaster station. It was ten o'clock at night and she was coming to the end of her endurance. Perhaps her impulse to leave London without even ascertaining the whereabouts of Aunt Thea's house had been ridiculous. The train halted squeakingly.

"Nidcaster!" A man in the uniform of British Rail strode purposefully up and down the dimly lit platform, repeating his announcement on a note of triumph. The station itself had an optimistic look. Hanging baskets with trailing lobelia and geraniums depended from the lacy Victorian ironwork canopy. Nidcaster evidently took a pride in itself.

"Where you going, love?" the station master asked her once she and her luggage were safely deposited on the ground. "You'll have a job on with that lot tonight."

Diana could have melted with relief and gratitude. It was something that her predicament had been noticed.

"I'm going to a place called Gilbert's Tower, actually. I'm afraid I don't know how far it is, or if I'll need a taxi."

"Nah." The station master looked at her quizzically. "You're on t'doorstep. Put them cases in my cubby hole for tonight and I'll bring them down in t'morning."

"But where is the house?" Diana was bewildered. "Can I walk?"

"Aye. Go down that lane," he pointed airily across the single line and to the right. As Diana's eyes accustomed to the gloom she could see a steep cobbled street. "Go past my signal box, and keep on till you come to a right turn. Don't go up there, look to your left and you'll see a high brick wall with a white door in it. Go through there and you're at your old auntie's place. You've got a lot o' clothes on," he added matter of factly, examining Diana's cashmere overcoat and fur lined gloves with appreciative interest.

"I thought it would be cold up here." Somehow, Diana was not offended. Nor did it seem necessary to explain that she had come from London. He seemed to know everything without being told.

The station master let out a short, sharp bark of amusement. " 'S never cold here. You want Harrogate for that."

Giving up her ticket was the only formality. She was helped across the line and accompanied as far as the toy town signal box by the station master himself, who carried her small suitcase. He left her there, saying he must set signals for the last train from York.

"I do all t'jobs here, you know. Can't be everywhere at once."

That he seemed to know her identity was a mystery into which Diana was too disorientated by fatigue to enquire.

"Mind your feet on them cobbles. And think on, I'll be down wi' t'big cases tomorrer, after t'last Harrogate train's gone."

Diana waved and walked on, picking her way carefully down the starlit lane. On one side, silvered leaves fringed the top of a high wall. On the other, tall houses, no two alike, leaned inwards, their diamond-paned windows twinkling gold and rose in the warm darkness. Many had gable ends painted with a strange, geometrically exact, black and white chequerboard pattern.

An orange cat ran across her path. It froze, one paw raised and yellow eyes gleaming to appraise this stranger before it leaped noiselessly on to the high wall. Diana stopped to watch it prowl watchfully along the top before it disappeared with a whisk of its ringed tail into whatever mysterious territory lay beyond.

It was an absurd, through-the-looking-glass cat. An hallucination like the magic carpet scene on the train. A trick played, Diana thought as she tripped on a prominent stone, by a tired mind.

CHAPTER
2

❦ THE THUMB LATCH was smooth with age and yielded silkily to Diana's touch. Pushing open the heavy wooden door, her senses were instantly assaulted by an overwhelming fragrance. The surprise was complete.

Town bred, Diana had never yet encountered the concentrated scent of flowers. At Brereton, that stiffly formal house that Michael had bought for the sake of the shooting and weekend house parties, the garden was a flat affair of bare-legged roses and wide grass walks. No perfume had ever reached out to her there.

Startled, she put down the suitcase and waited to catch her breath after the steepness of the lane. The arched stone lintel of the doorway was bowered with a honeysuckle vine. Unpruned, its vagrant runners tapped her arm gently, dropping some late petals, cream and crimson on the sleeve of her coat.

From nowhere, the orange cat materialised and brushed lightly, experimentally, against her leg and then melted back into the shadows.

A sound of water, splashing and tinkling somewhere outside the arc of her clear perception, intrigued her ear. Before the abstract shapes of blues, blacks and greys could resolve themselves into any comprehensible image, Diana stood with the simplicity of a blind person, informed solely by the compelling musical and aromatic messages to her brain.

"Hello?" A male voice called peremptorily. "That you, Mrs. Neville?"

She said nothing but waited for the owner of the voice to reveal his whereabouts. He had her at a disadvantage. Standing

25

as she was, in a pool of light shed by the lantern affixed to the inner wall, he could perhaps already see her, but she could not see him. It no longer seemed odd that somebody should know her here. Diana had been less than fifteen minutes in Nidcaster, but already, all the ordinary rules of arrival in a strange place had been suspended.

"I'm here," she answered when nobody came. "By the door."

"Didn't waste any time, like, did you?"

Not used to the local intonation, Diana could not tell whether the question was friendly or sarcastic. She could see the speaker now as he crossed a gently sloping lawn, brushing his hands together as if there were soil on them. "Your aunt was right, then."

Dazed, Diana decided to deal with things in order because, even here, there had to be order. Of a sort.

"She was my father's aunt, actually. My great-aunt."

"Aye, I know."

Standing with her in the circle of light, she could see him clearly at last. He was short and wiry with neatly cropped hair and intelligent features. It was difficult to say how old he was. Not old, but not young either. His clothes were conventional, a collar and tie, jacket and trousers. He seemed vaguely uneasy in them, as if he were dressed up. There was an old-fashioned watch chain fixed in his buttonhole. He pulled up an enormous steel watch from his breast pocket and squinted at it, his head cocked on one side.

"Must have left London dead on five, then," he announced, in the tone of one who appreciates the mathematical beauty of cause and effect.

Diana was silent. The place was populated with warlocks and wizards. People who knew things without being told. She looked around her, trying to establish a geography for the fantasy because she was real and existed in time and space, even if her surroundings did not.

There was a dark mass on her right, blocking out the moon. It had many windows, not all the same. There were steps up to a pedimented porch some distance away, but there was another door at ground level nearer to hand. And then, where the perspective narrowed at the far limits of her vision, there was an uneven buttressed structure, taller than the rest with a crenellated top, cutting a sharp pattern against the sky. It was like the one she had seen from the train. It looked medieval. The tower. It had never occurred to her that there would really be a tower.

"This is Gilbert's Tower, isn't it?"

Diana heard herself ask the stupid question in a reasonable tone of voice, like Alice talking to the chaotic characters in her dream. The thing was, of course, that you cared for the good opinion of the Red Queen and the Caterpillar.

Albert Sedgely caught her before she fell.

"Look at me," she heard him say from across a void, "keeping you standing here. We'd best get you to bed, lass."

It was the last time Sedgely was to permit himself that much familiarity.

❧ DIANA NEVER KNEW by what route she had come to the small square room in the tower. She only remembered being there, sitting up in the crudely carved oak tester bed. It was very small, as if made for a child, but it fitted her perfectly. And like a child, she obediently drank some broth from a covered china cup, ate some cheese and part of a pear. She sipped a glass of oddly flavoured purple wine as she looked about her, accepting and unfearful.

Sedgely had gone, leaving her to herself and the soothing properties of his ten-year-old elderberry cordial.

The room's rough, unplastered walls were covered with faded cloths, painted to mimic tapestries. They enclosed a space not more than nine feet square. A window, large in comparison, was screened by a curtain which, like the bed-hangings, was embroidered all over with leaves and flowers, insects and birds in coloured wools. In the wall opposite the bed, logs burned fiercely in a square recess surmounted by a pointed stone canopy which seemed to pierce through the wooden ceiling. The beams had faint traces of painted foliage on them.

Drowsy with the wine and scent of burning applewood, Diana made a mental inventory of the furniture. Apart from the bed and the stool beside it, there was only an oak coffer which stood in the window embrasure, supporting her small suitcase. It looked restless there and Diana wished now that she had thought of pushing it under the bed. She watched passively as the flaming logs on the hearth filled the room with dancing shadows and made russet reflections on the bare floorboards, glossy with polish and use.

Leaning down to place the supper tray on the stool, Diana caught sight of a bulky white envelope lying on the top. She was sure it had not been there when she got into bed. Mr. Sedgely, who had proved so tactful an attendant she really couldn't remember what he had done for her, must have left it there before he said goodnight. She could make out her name on it. *Diana.* Just the one word, handwritten. She would look at it in the morning.

She was thankful there was no lamp to switch out. Even that small effort would have been an intolerable burden. Her toes flirted briefly with the stinging heat of the stone hot water bottle before she drifted into the dreamless, selfish sleep of exhaustion.

❧ "So you have come, as I said you would!"

Diana held the letter in one hand as she drew back the curtain on its clattering rings with the other.

The window was a bay, jutting out high above the river. Diana gasped as the jewel colours of stained glass splashed the little room. Stone mullions, crisply carved with pointed arches and trefoil lights, proclaimed the romantic fancy of some Victorian FitzGilbert. Warm sunshine filtered its rays through the clear parts of the glass. At once, Diana saw the reason for her odd illusion on the train, the previous night. A deep gorge was spanned by a soaring viaduct, its outermost feet firmly embedded on the rocky sides. The houses she had seen from the train clambered about, some casually leaning against the viaduct; others had clearly taken the rock itself for a rear wall. They were painted pink and lemon and white, a few had thatched roofs, the rest were lidded with pantiles and some showed the queer chequerboard design she had noticed in the lane.

In and amongst the clinging houses were terraced gardens with brilliant geraniums spilling over their walls into the next garden or on to the roof of some neighbouring cottage below. Fruit trees with ripening globes dotted the scene like the trees of legend, nursery rhyme and Christmas carol.

Diana wrinkled her brow. If she had been temporarily detached from her right mind yesterday, a night's sleep had not improved things greatly.

She could half believe the scene that met her eyes. She had seen such sights before. On the river Rhine, in Switzerland, but this was Yorkshire. Yorkshire, she knew by report, boasted moors, mills as fanciful as palaces, though dirtier and larger. It also had acre upon acre of rich, flat arable land punctuated by mansions which told of the fortunes that had been made here from wheat and wool and coal. She must be somewhere else. She felt mildly exasperated.

Opening a casement, Diana leaned out dangerously and saw that the tower itself plunged straight down into the still green water below. Upstream, a group of boats lay patiently moored near a little landing stage. Downstream, a handsome stone bridge carried red buses, motorbikes and cars roaring up a hill, out of the town. The buses were English enough.

She looked back to the letter and then to the window again, undecided as to which should first receive her attention. There was an area of forest on the far bank with a white path threading through it. The air from the open window was balmy, not cold but fresh and laden with an urgent, musky smell of ripeness. A breeze stirred the pages in her hand. Diana's nightgown was thin. She closed the casement and sat down on the bed to study the letter, drawing on her woollen robe.

Riffling through the sheets of paper, Diana's eye alighted on the signature. It sprang off the final page like a skeleton in a seaside ghost train. *Thea.* But Thea was dead. Disbelievingly, Diana stared at the signature. It was written in a bold, unwavering hand in royal blue fountain pen ink.

Feeling the temperature drop in the room, she got back into bed and began to examine the letter slowly. Her feet flinched away from the stone bottle. It was icy now.

"So you have come, as I said you would!" Diana read the words again, her eye travelling slowly along the line.

"My Dear Great-niece," the letter recommenced more formally.

This will seem a strange welcome because, by the time you read this, I shall have gone to what our Vicar quaintly calls my "eternal reward." I hope, therefore, you will excuse this posthumous greeting and not be afraid. I was always far too lazy to haunt anyone.

Picturing your arrival in this house of our common ancestors has lent both purpose and pleasure to my final days in this "vale of tears." (Again, I cannot resist quoting the Vicar. Personally, I've always been perfectly content in Nidcaster but I shouldn't dream of arguing with the poor man, he has enough on his plate with Series 1 and the Diocesan Synod.) Forgive an old woman's tendency to ramble. Let us get on.

Knowing of the terrible trouble which has befallen your husband and thinking you might, at the last, stand in need of a refuge, I have arrogantly taken unto myself the privilege of providing it. How did I know what the outcome would be, having regard to the notorious sensationalism and inaccuracies of the public prints? The prescience of the dying, perhaps, or just the pessimism of an old woman. Call it what you will.

Hard as I imagined things, I cannot predict at what time of day or night, or even on what day you will come. What, if anything, have you brought with you, Diana? What tasks relating to your old life must you still fulfil? I cannot say.

This is a long letter and you should not trouble to read it until you are rested. Go and do what you have to do and come back to me when your mind is settled. I have much to tell you.

The first page ended there and Diana lay back on the pillows, breathing deep, long breaths. She knew the first thing she must do was to find a telephone and speak to Yolanda. Nine o'clock showed accusingly on her watch face. It was uncanny to be reminded of her duty by a woman in her grave. But there was a warm, living vibration in Aunt Thea's words and as Diana began to dress, she felt surrounded by love.

❧ "OH, MUMMY, IT sounds out of this world." Yolanda's voice, the tears all spent now, was soft with wonderment at what her mother had told her.

The resilience of youth, a night's untroubled sleep and Sister's special sausage and marmalade treat, digestible only by convalescent teenage stomachs, had done their inevitable work.

It was not, Diana knew, that Yolanda's feelings for her father were shallow. Far from it, it was just that, being young, she had to move on to the next thing.

"Remember," Diana had told her, "men like your father take bigger risks than other people and have further to fall off the high wire. He may have done wrong. I think, quite frankly, darling, that he has. But I'm sure he honestly didn't realise it at the time."

"My friends have been really super about it," Yolanda replied, cheered. "They all said that everybody knows that eight years doesn't mean *eight* years. It means more like five, or even three, with time off for good behaviour."

Diana had repressed a chuckle. Right and wrong. The difference should not be joked over. Not in front of children, anyway. Good behaviour. A sudden image of Michael, unnaturally polite and deferential, rose in her imagination and faded instantly. It was an unsustainable idea.

"And Daddy's so clever and businesslike, he'll probably corner the cigarette racket too, and be rich again . . . in his own way," Yolanda added uncertainly. "The other inmates are bound to respect him."

Inmates. Evidently Yolanda had been boning up on the vocabulary. How quickly the young adapted to circumstances.

"Listen, darling. Don't worry too much about Daddy. As you say, he's a clever man and he'll be able to look after himself. You can be sure of that. I think what he'd like *us* to do is for you to concentrate on your 'A' Level work and for me to concentrate on taking care of both of us while he's away." Diana prayed that was true. True or not, it was the way things had to be.

"Yes, Mummy. All right."

"And another thing, darling. Things happen to people. It's part of life and can't be helped. But nothing ever stays the same in nature. People like your father and more famous ones too, politicians for instance, have done bad things, been punished for them and then come back and done something wonderful to make up. We must just go on loving Daddy and believing in him. Things will come right in the end. I know it."

"He'll rise from the ashes like a phoenix," Yolanda said dreamily. "That's what Iolanthe Thistlethwaite says."

"Does she?" Diana responded drily. "What a nice thought."

Iolanthe had inherited an unhealthily dramatic view of life

from her novelist mother. Her works were heavily and un-
originally symbolic.

And then the conversation had turned to Gilbert's Tower.
"When can I come and see it, Mummy?"

"At half-term, darling. I have a lot to do before then. However, I am coming down to see Mr. Laverack in a day or two
and I shall take you out to lunch. We can talk then."

As soon as the words were out of her mouth, Diana wished
she could recall them. The days of talking about taking people
out to lunch without a second thought were over. Money was
going to be a serious problem. But Yolanda musn't be allowed
to worry herself sick over that. Her own parents, never rich,
had kept all those things to themselves. So must she.

"Mummy, where are you actually, at this minute?"

Diana glanced around the lofty room in which she stood,
and shrugged. "I'm not exactly sure, to tell you the truth. I
think it might be the drawing-room. There's a grand piano and
a big mirror over the fireplace. There's a chandelier or something, but it's covered up in a sort of cotton bag. There are a
lot of framed sketches of people and animals. It's a lovely
room. Not really terribly grand. Full of light. There are three
windows right down to the floor. It's a bit dusty, though. Look,
darling, I've got to go. Mr. Sedgely is waiting for me. He's going to give me breakfast at his house. Isn't that kind? I'm terribly late already. I'll see you soon. Try not to worry. Bye. Oh,
by the way, the garden outside is incredible. There's a statue of
Mercury, and a fountain—all sorts of things. You'll love it."

Diana hung up. It couldn't last, of course. Yolanda would
start to brood and then the trouble would start. But for now,
just for now, Diana thought, I have a breathing space.

She gathered up her handbag and walked out of the room
into the hall. One of several spaces that might be given that description. Finding a room with a telephone in it had been an
adventure in itself. The house meandered, changing its levels
and architectural styles whimsically. It seemed to have grown,
naturally, casually, over the centuries, backwards into its large
walled garden from its starting point, the medieval tower
plunging into the gorge. Diana realised she didn't even know
the name of the river.

Since leaving the tower room she had descended by means
of a spiral staircase, its triangular steps awkward to her feet, to

a door in the masonry. That had let her into a part of the house that seemed to belong to another age. Charles II, perhaps. And then she had looked into room after room, panelled bedrooms with sheeted furniture and drawn holland blinds, a bathroom with a mahogany enclosed tub and a cylindrical iron contraption. A lavatory with a cracked willow pattern bowl, linen cupboards . . . The house led her on and on. Eventually, finding no telephone, she had drifted down a wide staircase with risers so shallow she had consciously to adjust her step to its leisurely downward progress.

The telephone, when she had found it, was perfectly ordinary and modern with push-button dialling. As soon as she saw it, resting on the piano, she had realised that it was probably cut off. What else? But it hadn't been. And once again, Diana's mind had flooded with thankfulness as she lifted the receiver and heard its cheerful purring. Aunt Thea had thought of everything.

Diana had not told Yolanda about Thea and the letter. It was still too close, too intimate—like a friendship which had only just begun, unadmitted, even between the parties.

❦ "YOU FOUND US, then."

Mr. Sedgely stood, shirt sleeved and relaxed, in the cart entrance to his little house. It was in an area of nineteenth century brick cottages, a place where small tradesmen and artisans had lived and worked. Finkle Street. Diana had had a stiff climb up the narrow, cobbled thoroughfares, but the distance had not been so great and everyone was happy to tell her where Albert Sedgely lived. Some had addressed her by name. This too must be the work of Aunt Thea, directly or indirectly.

"I'm sorry I'm so late."

Sedgely waved the apology away with a hint of impatience. "There's nowt to hurry for, is there? Come in and meet Mrs. Sedgely."

Diana stepped through the Judas gate in the entrance way and found herself in a tiny enclosed courtyard. It was a blaze of hot pinks, oranges and reds. Busy Lizzies in terracotta pots with translucent stems as thick as her own wrist stood on low walls and plinths. The surrounding walls of the place were trellised and covered with scarlet runner beans, yellow gourds and little marrows. There was a squat tree hung with furry green fruits which Diana could not identify. Almonds, she later discovered. Beneath the tree a table was laid with a white cloth, its edges frosted with crochet work. It was warm, very warm. Diana started to remove her jacket.

"Aye, you'll not be needing that," Sedgely commented. "Not for a month or so yet. Come in t'kitchen a minute. Mrs. Sedgely's bottling."

Down some steps and through a low door, Diana entered a spotless kitchen even smaller than the tower room. A coke fire glowed stiflingly in the tiled range and, before it, Mrs. Sedgely sat in a chair, leaning on a stick.

"Now then, Mrs. Sedgely," Albert Sedgely addressed his wife with old-fashioned formality. "Here's Mrs. Neville come for 'er breakfast."

Mrs. Sedgely rose painfully. She was taller than her husband and wore spectacles. Her smile was very sweet and her eyes, like her husband's, were sharp with intelligence.

"I'm right glad to see you, Mrs. Neville. Did Mr. Sedgely look after you all right? I thought I'd put you in t'tower room on t'first night because it's easy to heat. Did you eat your bit of supper? I didn't think you'd want much . . ."

The impulse to beg Mrs. Sedgely to sit down again died on Diana's lips.

"Please, how did you know?"

There was no immediate answer from either of them, but they exchanged a glance.

"Will you have coffee or tea, Mrs. Neville? I'm just finishing with Sedgely's tomatoes. Some on 'em came from the Tower so you must take all you like when they're done. Keep all winter, beautiful. Then I'll get on wi' t'red cabbages." Mrs. Sedgely shot a half severe, half affectionate look at her husband.

Diana shrugged helplessly. She was no match for the Sedgelys.

Over a breakfast of arcadian splendour with slices of rosy ham, home baked bread, bloomy skinned plums and tart raspberry jam, served under the almond tree in the courtyard, Sedgely made everything plain.

He and his wife had looked after Aunt Thea, gardening and cooking for many years. It wasn't a job they needed to do, Sedgely was particularly anxious to point out. It was just that

Miss FitzGilbert was one of a kind. Someone worth knowing. He was a miner by trade, but an accident below ground had resulted in an operation on his legs which made him unfit to return to the pit.

"Well, I didn't want no nancy boy surface job, did I? And I'd always been happy on my allotment. Main interest really, in them years. I got a fair bit of compensation money too, from t'Coal Board, so me and Mrs. Sedgely decided to come back here where she grew up. Her Dad was Irish, you know."

Seeing Diana's surprise, Sedgely explained as he refilled her cup with coffee and his own with tea. "Aye. You've seen t'viaduct, haven't you? Crossed over it last night, of course. Well, it were built in t'last century by Irish navvies. Lot of men died. But a lot stayed alive and they married Yorkshire girls. Their descendants are still here. Catholic, the lot of them. Chapel's just up from t'Tower. Full to bursting every Sunday. Course, it fitted in here all right on account of their being a fair number of *old* Catholics around. T'Reformation wasn't that popular round here. Guy Fawkes was born hereabouts, you know." The thought seemed to strike him suddenly. "And then there's your own family, the FitzGilberts ... mind, that dwindled off a bit in t'last generation or two. T'linen mills weren't doin' so well. Tried to marry into a bit o' Protestant brass."

Diana's mind whirled. Irishmen, linen mills, Guy Fawkes ... where would the surprises and the questions end?

"But Aunt Thea?" Diana bit into a plum, its scarlet flesh bled juice down her chin. Sedgely handed her a napkin, as if they had been friends for years. Diana noticed its thick, smooth texture and jacquard design of ivy leaves. "T'best is allus t'cheapest in t'end," was another local attitude she had yet to grasp.

"Yes, well," Sedgely took up the main thread of his story again, "Miss FitzGilbert thought she knew what was coming with all t'publicity before t'trial and all. She kept up with it like, in the newspapers and on t'wireless. 'Sedgely,' she said to me one day, 'that's my only living relation. My own flesh and blood.' She was pointing at your picture, see, in t'paper—right bonny." Sedgely swallowed the compliment, personal remarks being uncalled for. " 'And when all this is over, that child'll need a home, because there'll be a trial all right. Mark my words. She can have this one, as I shan't be needing it much longer. You're to keep it open for her, for a year from the verdict.' "

There were other directions too. Aunt Thea's will had provided that in exchange for a sum of money left to the Sedgelys expressly for the purpose, a room was to be prepared every evening for a year, a hot supper or other meal made available and somebody to greet Diana whenever she should appear.

"That weren't too difficult," Sedgely remarked with diffident satisfaction. "We can all read a train timetable and we none of us thought you'd drive t'motor car. Stands to reason." Diana didn't dare question the Byzantine logic of this statement. "And with Bob at t'station keeping an eye out, he could give us a ring and I could nip down i' t'van and get show on t'road, like."

"How terribly, terribly clever," Diana breathed.

Sedgely smiled slyly, pleased that Diana was impressed with his generalship. He pulled a pipe out and sucked it meditatively, unlit.

"Then we'd to keep t'garden tidy and t'ouse swept. Of course, Mrs. Sedgely's not been too clever with her hip lately, but we've done the best we could."

Diana shook her head wonderingly, a lump forming in her throat. Silently, she rehearsed several speeches of thanks but realised they all sounded artificial and stilted.

"Of course," Sedgely went on, "we haven't spent a penny of your aunt's money. That was right embarrassing. I tried to give it back but the lawyer wouldn't let me." He looked appealingly at Diana.

"But lighting fires and making meals costs money, surely?"

"Get away!" Sedgely was indignant. "We've usually an old apple tree come down in your orchard . . ."

Your orchard. Diana turned the words over in her mind. How quickly she had become the chatelaine of Gilbert's Tower. Before she knew its rooms, or had walked in its gardens, it was hers.

" . . . And there's always a bite for a friend to eat in this house," Sedgely finished on a note of outraged pride. "Any road, we've only done it a week. You came a week after the verdict . . ."

With a cold shiver, Diana realised she might have sold the house. It had been a pure matter of chance that she had not.

Aunt Thea's solicitor had expected her to. No doubt he knew all about her alternative plans but considered them to be too fanciful to be acted upon.

"Mr. Sedgely," Diana laid her fingertips on the back of his hand, tentatively. "You mustn't be afraid to use the money my aunt left you. No money in the world could repay what you and Mrs. Sedgely have done for me. It was just that my Aunt Thea was afraid to presume on your friendship, you see." Diana wondered at herself, daring to speak for Thea. "It's a lot to ask anyone to do ... carry on with your own projects when you're dead. Only it mattered so much to her ... and to me."

"Aye, well." Sedgely seemed a little easier in his mind, but Diana had no doubt that she would hear more of her aunt's well meant but unwelcome legacy to the Sedgelys. "Are you fit, Mrs. Neville?"

Diana saw that he meant to ask her if she had finished and was ready to go.

"Because if you are, let's get down to t'Tower and take a look at your peaches." He shrugged himself into an old jacket with the pipe sticking out of its pocket.

"Shall you be needing any red cabbages just yet, Mrs. Sedgely?" he called through the doorway of his kitchen.

Mrs. Sedgely appeared on the threshold, smoothing her apron.

"Not just yet awhile, Mr. Sedgely, if you please." She smiled conspiratorially at Diana, who returned the smile, thinking that in Nidcaster you reacted first and understood later.

𝕎 WALKING BACK DOWN the hill, in between the abrupt yet friendly greetings of passers-by, Sedgely continued to unfold a patchwork quilt of the history, geographic and climatic details of the extraordinary little town.

"Aye, it's a one-off is Nidcaster, and no mistake. Do y'know that on t'weather forecast, whatever they say about t'region in general doesn't apply to us? Weather men know all right, but they don't have time to talk about a square mile or so. But it's different here. What they call a micro-climate."

Nidcaster, it seemed, was situated in a deep fold at the foot of the Pennine moorland just before the land flattened out to the east and became the Vale of York where every acre was worth a mint of money for the grain it could produce. But

Nidcaster belonged to neither the heath nor the plain. It was itself. A pocket of warmth and plenty where rare, forgotten
fruits basked in the long summer sunshine and tender herbs
flourished in the rich, free-draining loam. The earth itself was
a happy caprice of nature.

"They've clay in t'west. Heavy stuff . . . waterlogged."
Sedgely was intent on his theme as he pushed open the garden
door and moved aside Diana's suitcases, duly delivered by Bob
the station master as promised. "And down on t'plain, they've
a sandy, light sort of soil. But here," he said gloatingly, "we've
a right sort of mixture, just right. Drains a treat, as well."

Looking around her in the daylight, even Diana, unused as
she was to considering these things, could see why. The whole
of the town, for the most part grouped on the eastern edge of
the river gorge, sloped in an ever steepening declivity to the
river bed until, like the tower which formed the western extremity of her own house, it hurtled vertically down the rock
canyon, into the water.

"There's no industry now. T'last linen mill closed a while
back. It was the FitzGilbert mill, up the river. By Royal Appointment, it was an' all. But bottom dropped out of t'market
for linen goods. All them synthetics."

Diana kept quiet, following Sedgely about the garden as he
talked. Without comment he led her from feature to feature,
gesturing with his empty pipe as if the things he showed her
needed no further explanation. They sat for a while on the low
stone parapet that surrounded the lily pond she had seen from
the house earlier in the morning. In its midst, the lead statue of
Mercury was patched with lichen and one of the wings on his
feet was missing. Perhaps it lay at the bottom of the pool. Diana promised herself she would try and find it. Mercury, messenger of the gods, must have all his wings. A jet of water
spurted from his mouth and Diana wondered if that was meant
to represent a bright stream of words.

"T'farmers hereabouts used to grow hemp in the fields for
t'coarse stuff. Flax for fine linen goods came from Ireland.
Phew!" Sedgely screwed up his face in memory. "It used to
pong something dreadful in them days when t'hemp was ret-
ting in t'fields. Like a privy it was."

They strolled on companionably, through a wrought iron
gate in a stone partition wall, lower than the outer, brick wall.

It marked a subdivision of the garden from its ornamental, smiling lawns and casually disposed beds, to a more serious area. Here was the orchard of which Sedgely had spoken, a group of dilapidated glasshouses, and regimented rows of cloches covering seedling lettuces and other edible plants. There was also a carefully cultivated area on which stood a quantity of large amethyst globes. Red cabbages. Sensing obscurely that the red cabbages were Sedgely's private affair, Diana forbore to make any remark concerning them. She asked him instead what the local people now did for a living since the linen mills had gone.

"Shops, cafés, boats an' all. There's tourists in the summer and a right mess they make. We're glad to see t'back on 'em, to be frank with you, Mrs. Neville." Sedgely shrugged a little crossly. "There's people who work in Harrogate in t'big hotels there and plenty as goes on t'train to Leeds to work. But tourists is t'main local thing. You see Nidcaster is . . ."

"Unique," Diana finished for him.

"Aye, that's right word. Unique." Sedgely regarded Diana with dawning respect. She was getting the hang of things.

Nearby a great bell rang out a peal. Sedgely stood still, his mouth still open on his next, unfinished word. Speech was impossible. Diana, although shaken by the sheer volume of this music, smiled with delight. The steeple of an old golden stoned church was visible over the top of the wall. She had passed it on her walk that morning. As its last glorious note died away, Sedgely was animated again.

"Aye. Dinner time. Best get at them peaches. They'll be t'last till next year, now."

Diana heard the word *peaches* but had not been able to absorb it. Peaches, in her experience, were either imported from places like Italy, or grown in the greenhouses of a few stately homes where the owners could still afford to heat the houses and employ gardeners to tend and prune the trees. She and Michael had never had anything of that sort at Brereton. They'd simply never thought of it. Of course, it hadn't been a home, Diana now realised. Just another location for business entertaining. Still, it was obvious that no peaches grew in the drunken, grimy glasshousing here. Nor did they.

The trees grew in the open air, snug in the south-west facing corner of the orchard. They were fan trained, as Sedgely described it, against the stone boundary wall. She watched, amazed, as he harvested a dozen or so into a basket which hung on his arm.

At the foot of the oldest tree's gnarled trunk, the orange cat was curled into a perfect circle, relaxed on the sun warmed soil. He opened a careful eye and shut it again, satisfied that the stranger in his garden had no intention of varying his personal programme of recreation.

" 'Course," Sedgely remarked, stepping round the cat, "Peregrine's an early. Comes in August mostly. We've had a good season with these. Now, will you eat all these, Mrs. Neville? Or shall I take them up to Mrs. Sedgely for bottling?"

Wordlessly, Diana took one of the fruits from the basket and examined its deep rose colour, feeling the smooth velvet texture of its skin as it lay sensuous and heavy in her hand. She bit into it and discovered that its flesh was white, its flavour and abundant juice were like no other peach she had ever tasted.

"Couldn't we sell these, Mr. Sedgely?" she asked carefully, the ghost of an idea forming in her brain.

Sedgely scratched his head, puzzled.

"Oh, aye. We do, when we've a glut, like. Little greengrocer in t'town'll take a few. But mostly your aunt just gave 'em away. There's been plenty this year, mind. But I didn't like to sell them with your aunt dead. Who'd take the money?"

Diana and the little man looked at each other unblinkingly. The thoughts of each, unexpressed but visible to the other.

"Your wages?" Diana spoke slowly, softly, afraid to give offence.

Sedgely was not offended. His gaze remained fixed on Diana's face.

"We didn't work like that, Mrs. Neville. Your aunt and I sort of shared the garden. We ate what we wanted, the both of us, bottled the rest and sold a bit now and again. A partnership, like. I looked after the place for her because she couldn't and I didn't have the room at my place and . . ."

His voice died away as their clamouring thoughts crowded the space between them.

"Used to be a market garden . . . during t'war, like. There's one of them aerial photographs up in t'post office."

"It could be again." Diana finished the peach and let the

stone drop on to the soil. She noticed there were many others there. Windfalls. The waste!

"Aye, I reckon!" Sedgely beamed. He tried to hand Diana the basket but she thrust it back at him, taking three of the precious fruits for herself.

"A partnership, Mr. Sedgely?"

"No reason why not, Mrs. Neville."

The clasp of Sedgely's palm as he squeezed her hand, in acknowledgment of their fledgling agreement, was dry and warm. The mark, Diana remembered Michael telling her, of a confident man.

CHAPTER

3

"I'M SORRY," SAID young Mr. Meers, son of Aunt Thea's old friend and solicitor, "very sorry to disappoint you, Mrs. Neville, but it scarcely seems a feasible proposition. I'm sure you understand, I should be failing you if I didn't speak as I find."

Mr. Meers was a nice young man. He was on the plump side and the plumpness seemed to have solidified into a permanent corpulence that would reassure the firm's clients for the rest of his professional life. His moon face was pink and bespectacled. He looked older than he probably was, Diana thought. His father, it seemed, had retired immediately after Aunt Thea's death.

There had been no trouble about allowing Diana a sight of Aunt Thea's will.

Booth, Wilson & Meers prided themselves on offering the sort of service that few firms now did. Families, old families, their ups and downs, their properties and trusts, their marriage settlements and wills, were still very much a part of their continuing business. A comfortably provincial practice, as Meers had put it. Of course the attics, which had been full of dusty buff files tied up in pink ribbon, had been cleared out now. The younger generation of partners had transferred all the centuries-long records on to microfilm during the past few months, as he had lost no time in informing Diana. The rows of clerks on high stools had all gone, too, and the accounts department was now run by one woman and an unsleeping computer that made no errors and wanted no time off to go to the dentist. That was "what progress was all about, wasn't it?" Mr. Meers had enquired of Diana, expecting no answer.

"I suppose so," she replied in as enthusiastic a tone as she could manage. Diana wondered what happened nowadays to people who perpetrated errors and needed dental treatment. Tempted to ask, she refrained. Too abrasive.

The offices of the firm were where they had always been, for the last hundred years, at any rate, in Princess Square in Harrogate. It had taken Diana just ten minutes to come on the train from Nidcaster. Bob had seen her off at the station. This time he complained at her light jacket and pleated skirt.

"Didn't I tell you, Mrs. Neville? Harrogate's a thousand feet above sea level—nasty cold place. You'll be glad to get back. How was your first day at t'Tower, then? All right?"

But walking to the premises of Booth, Wilson & Meers, whipped by the biting wind off the moors, Diana had marvelled at the town's wide, handsome thoroughfares and profusion of exclusive shops, restaurants, estate agents and antique dealers. The huge, expensive looking hotels must consume literally tons of fruit and vegetables between them every day. She and Sedgely had a market, ready made, right on the doorstep. Only Mr. Meers was being depressing about it now. She had listened to him very carefully. Advice, Michael had always said, should always be attended to. It need never be taken.

Young Mr. Meers took off his spectacles and put them down on his mahogany desk in a final sort of way. He'd reached the end of his ability to advise Mrs. Neville and time pressed. Not that he was indifferent to her, though. He admitted as much to himself. Her wide spaced eyes with their queer violet glimmer that came and went, the swallow's wing eyebrows and long lashes weren't easy to ignore. Nor was she. She had a way of getting your attention without saying much or even moving a great deal. She was alert, like a bird on a twig, watching for the opportunities, sensing the threats.

"So basically, Mrs. Neville," the young lawyer replaced his spectacles with a brisk, busy gesture, anxious to break the spell and get back to more productive affairs, "what we're saying is this . . ."

Diana shifted slightly on her chair, to show the young man that she knew the interview was nearing its close. He wouldn't want to send her a bill. It wasn't that sort of firm. As so often,

Diana was simply unaware that what reduced the normal expenses of her life was her own singular charm. She was what some acquaintances, unable to find an adequate English word, had called *simpatico*. People were intrigued by her stillness, warmed by her focused interest in them and what they were doing or saying. Mr. Meers was no exception. Modern clients, in his experience, were much too inclined to interrupt before they understood the issues.

"Miss FitzGilbert lived on an annuity for the last twenty years of her life. It diminished in value, of course, during that period, so she wasn't able to do much to the house except essential repairs. Most of her remaining liquid capital went to pay the estate duty on the house and contents. As I've told you, she was quite adamant that the house itself shouldn't be sold until you'd had a chance to decide whether or not you wanted it. At the end, she got some queer idea that you'd be bound to want it but it seemed both unnecessary and unwise to tie your hands or that of the estate by any inoperable codicils. And the rest, well . . . it went to pay our fee as executors. So, really, Mrs. Neville, your only asset is the house. It's a grand old place and worth quite a lot, even in its present state. Quite extraordinary. Quite."

"And you don't think the garden as a commercial enterprise is a workable idea?" Diana started to put her gloves on, her eyes fixed on his.

"No, I don't. We have a couple of market gardener clients in the practice. I have to tell you, Mrs. Neville, those concerns are cultivating areas between eight and twelve acres and you only have . . . what is it? One and a half? If you create a demand, you couldn't hope to satisfy it. No, it isn't on. Not viable. You'd be much better to sell Gilbert's Tower. You'd be quite well off then, you realise."

Mr. Meers' face was benevolent. He much preferred giving good news to bad.

"It's exactly the sort of place that so many people want, these days. Not too large, full of character, lovely garden, fabulous, yes fabulous views . . ." He was pleased with the felicity of his own phrase. "Yes, very desirable."

Diana considered for a moment, half-risen from her chair. There was no harm in knowing the facts.

"About how much do you think Gilbert's Tower is worth, Mr. Meers?"

"Well, I'm not an estate agent, of course, but . . ." He steepled his fingers and looked upwards to the corner of the room as he attempted to draw a figure out of the air. "But allowing something for replacement brickwork to the Carolean part of the house, a damp proof course in the Victorian wing . . . very shallow foundations that part . . . rewiring say, and a decent, modern kitchen . . . at today's values I doubt if it would realise a penny less than three hundred thousand pounds at auction. You see, it's what businessmen in Leeds, for instance, really go for. There just isn't enough of that sort of property around to satisfy the demand . . ."

Diana's brain had no difficulty in computing the figure. Over the years she had picked up some of Michael's quickness in these matters without ever being conscious of the fact.

With current interest rates standing at ten per cent, she could have an income of thirty thousand pounds a year before tax on top of the two thousand her parents' legacy produced. She wouldn't have to spend capital. She wouldn't have to work. They would be safe, she and Yolanda. Even modestly comfortable. Of course, she'd have to buy a smaller house, or a flat, perhaps, overlooking the manicured parkland that was Harrogate's greatest claim to fame—after it's evil-tasting therapeutic waters.

But the prospect failed to excite her. Rather, it saddened and deflated her. Mr. Sedgely would be disappointed. And it would be like breaking faith with Aunt Thea. Just sitting in a flat, month after month, waiting for Michael's sentence to be over and regretting the past, would be a living death. No. She must find another way. Diana was taking her leave of the solicitor as the thoughts rushed through her head.

"Don't take my word for it, Mrs. Neville. Go across the square here and ask for Brian Edgeworth at Vyne Edgeworth's—mention my name. We work together a good deal on property matters. They prefer to handle top end of the market stuff. Gilbert's Tower is just up their street."

"Thank you. I will. And thank you, Mr. Meers, for your time."

"A pleasure, Mrs. Neville. A pleasure."

With the conveyancing fee to think of, Diana was not above

realising that the solicitor's pleasure was at least partly in anticipation.

In the thick carpeted offices across the square, the estate agent more than confirmed Mr. Meers' view of the Tower's probable value. The property market was slow in general but there was always a sale for exceptional houses. And Gilbert's Tower was certainly in that bracket. Purchasers for that kind of house weren't usually much affected by mortgage rates and the hunger for something historic continued unabated, no matter how uncertain the economy.

Mr. Edgeworth had shown the greatest anxiety to usher Diana to an artfully designed negotiation area, with well-polished reproduction furniture and a bowl of early chrysanthemums on the desk. There was coffee too, rather speedily brought by a well-spoken girl in a thick velvet Alice band. Diana accepted these attentions with cynical equanimity, recognising the skills of hospitable persuasion. She had practiced them so often herself, to help Michael.

"It might make as much as four hundred and fifty thousand pounds, Mrs. Neville. All it takes is two determined bidders and relative values, recent precedents are just so much hot air."

Mr. Edgeworth, urbane in his grey flannel suit and maroon tie, regarded her keenly. Competition for important houses was tough in Harrogate. There were plenty of them, of course, in the town itself and outlying districts, but then, there were plenty of estate agents, too. And Gilbert's Tower—it would be a coup, even for Vyne Edgeworth. And the furniture—rumour had it that the Tower contained some rare and beautiful things. He began to assess the merits of auctioning the contents on site, in their original setting, or staging a sensational catalogue sale in their own, Harrogate premises. They'd have the sale in the evening, that was fashionable now.

"Of course," a light cloud appeared on the estate agent's eager face, "there's the easement to think of . . ."

Diana raised her eyebrows, puzzled. She was quite glad that Mr. Edgeworth had found a fly in his ointment. His enthusiasm was eating away at the happiness that Gilbert's Tower had already given her, narrowing its gracious, wide-armed welcome with a mean expediency. And yet, what choice did she have?

"The easement?" she prompted him quietly.

"Er, yes. It's an easement of way. You know—the lady chapel, at the bottom of the tower."

Mystified, Diana shook her head. She had not yet had time to read the rest of Aunt Thea's letter, or inspect every angle of Gilbert's Tower. She'd arrived only the day before yesterday. She knew her way now from the vast kitchen to the tower room and to the room where the telephone was. They had seemed quite enough of an achievement in the thirty-six hours that had passed since her first encounter with Mr. Sedgely in the garden.

"Well, yes, Mrs. Neville. The lady chapel's famous. One of the sights of Nidcaster."

Seeing no answering flicker in Diana's remarkable eyes, the estate agent remembered that she wasn't local. She was a Londoner and only a distant relative of Miss FitzGilbert's. She was going to sell, though. He recognised her. She was the woman whose husband had been convicted of fraud in the Knightman Neville Trust case. Bit of luck for her . . . well, most than a bit, she might get half a million for the place . . . stranger things had happened. And Vyne Edgeworth's commission at 1½ per cent . . . she wouldn't think of negotiating the percentage down . . .

The estate agent abandoned that train of thought abruptly. There was a rather disconcerting steadiness in Mrs. Neville's gaze. Like a child with a terribly high IQ. Of course, she had been the wife of one of the City's most legendary survivors. She might have some kind of business instinct, after all. Nothing in life, he sighed inwardly, was ever quite perfect. Not even a pretty woman.

"Yes," he went on. "The lady chapel . . . Well, let's see." He shuffled momentarily in a desk drawer. "I've got a copy of Potterton here," he said, producing a thick, well-thumbed reference book. "*Vernacular Houses in the West Riding of Yorkshire.* Let's see what he says about Gilbert's Tower." Edgeworth skimmed several pages of small type. Evidently the author considered Aunt Thea's house worthy of a substantial entry.

"Ah. Here we are. This is what he says about the tower itself: 'The lady chapel, otherwise known as St. Gilbert's Hermitage, is approachable only by boat from the river. It is situated in the base of the tower, which is twelfth century and partially hollowed out of the rock. Crudely apsidal in shape . . .' "

Diana's mind was already busy and she heard Mr.

Edgeworth's narrative only in snatches. He mentioned a bas-relief statue of the saint . . . polychrome . . . contemporary with the original construction . . . sizes, shapes, periods. Naturally, she had not seen the hermitage. She would have had to lean out very far indeed from the tower bedroom on that first morning to see all this detail. Too far. And although it would be visible from the bridge, she had come to Harrogate by train and at night. The door and the window . . . too small to notice from the viaduct. Not unless you knew they were there. Mr. Sedgely had had other things on his mind. Garden things.

"And the saint, Mr. Edgeworth," Diana asked when the estate agent stopped to catch his breath. "Who was he?"

"I'm no historian, Mrs. Neville," he shrugged. "But the legend is that he was the first FitzGilbert, a knight returned from the crusades. They say that he was sickened by what he had seen and decided to devote the rest of his life to . . . well, what you can only call prayer and contemplation . . . atonement, perhaps? I don't know."

"A medieval drop-out, in fact," Diana supplied with a smile. "Like those poor American ex-soldiers. Vietnam veterans. They've all got long hair and guitars now."

Mr. Edgeworth's mouth was slightly agape, Diana noticed with an amusement she politely concealed. She felt the crackle in the atmosphere as the estate agent grasped the aptness of her imagery. Soldiers seeking peace . . . progress hadn't made much difference to that. "And how does the chapel, the hermitage, affect the sale or value of the house as a whole, Mr. Edgeworth?"

"Um, yes. Well, as I was saying, the easement, as it's called, gives anyone who wants . . . actually that boils down to Catholics because nobody else would want, to make a yearly pilgrimage to the site . . . to the hermitage. In practice, once a year, in July, boatloads of them come from down the river, headed by an Abbot or somebody . . . No, it's a Monsignor . . . Some sort of Catholic brass hat . . . I say, I hope you're not . . ."

Diana shook her head. She wondered why he should *hope* she wasn't a Catholic, but it cost her nothing to reassure him on that point.

"Quite. Well, they say mass there, or whatever it is, and then they all go away again. It's not really a nuisance, it just means that one day a year there's somebody at your landing and on your property. I doubt that in fact it would reduce the value of the house. In a way, it's a feature, isn't it? Actually, in Miss FitzGilbert's time, she used to give them all lunch in the garden. Rather nice, but not a thing that binds a purchaser . . ."

No. Diana did not form the word with her lips. But it will bind me, I hope, for ever.

"As you say, Mr. Edgeworth, it is a feature."

"Oh, yes," the estate agent slapped his hand to his forehead. "There's something else I forgot. The Mummers' Play. Every Christmas. It happens at Gilbert's Tower. A sort of cross between Morris dancing and pantomime. Quite weird, they say, though I've never seen it myself. It's traditional but not compulsory. A sort of optional duty that hung on with the Lordship of the Manor . . . but John Meers will have put you in the picture there."

Mr. Meers had overlooked this point.

"Well, it's nothing really. A kind of legal appendix. A relic with no advantages or disadvantages attached. You can sell it if you want. Might fetch a couple of thousand. Quite a brisk trade in lordships in America, I understand. Not our style, though. If you take my advice you'll sell it with the house—goes down well with purchasers, a thing like that. A maintenance free feature," Edgeworth chuckled. "Like a ghost."

Diana digested these facts in silence.

"Well, then, Mrs. Neville," the estate agent went on swiftly, "let's firm up a date for me to come and measure up. We'll need photographs, too, for the particulars of sale . . ."

Diana rose decisively, all doubt removed from her mind. A refuge. A hermitage. A place to repair oneself.

"Thank you very much, Mr. Edgeworth, but I must take a little time to consider. About two weeks and then we'll speak again."

"Of course, Mrs. Neville." Diana was walking quickly to the door and he was having trouble ensuring that he arrived before her. "You'll need time to work out which pieces of furniture you're going to be able to keep. These family things, always difficult decisions to make."

The heavy plate glass door separated them at last and Diana smiled her final goodbyes through its thickness. The coffee

bringing girl in the Alice band waved from within. They all expected to see her again. But they won't. Diana said it aloud. She
turned her feet towards James Street and the direction of the station, shivering in the bitter wind. She only wanted to get back
to Nidcaster now, and the Tower, the FitzGilbert place of refuge.

Oh, Aunt Thea! How do we keep our house?

    AUNT THEA'S LETTER, although a mine of local information,
philosophy and observation, gave no clue. It had been beyond
her foresight to perceive that her descendant might not have
sufficient income to maintain a home like Gilbert's Tower. But
the letter's meandering, journal-like charm, peppered with
spurts of humour and sharp insights into character and motive,
provided Diana with odd moments of delight.

There was even a schedule of the stored preserves and country wines kept in the cellar, with notes concerning the seasons
and the garden crops which had produced them.

"Parsnip wine," she wrote, "sounds very nasty, I know. But in
fact it has a distinct flavour of *retsina* (that Greek stuff), a sort
of rustic distinction that marries well with the atmosphere here.
We made it because the parsnips that year were, in parsnip
terms, profoundly unlovely specimens. Sedgely miscalculated for
once and put the horse manure on before it was well rotted
down. My dear, they grew like mandrake roots. The only kind
thing to do was to consign their shape to oblivion and preserve
their taste and aroma in the wine. I hope you will enjoy it. I'm
afraid there's a great deal of it. Sedgely, you will discover,
thinks big."

It was that which led Diana to venture into the cellars beneath the Carolean house. It had been a matter of asking
Sedgely the way because the position of nothing in the house
was obvious or expected. The cellar steps in fact led down
from a small oak-panelled breakfast parlour, which must, before the Victorian wing was built, have been the kitchen; or so
Diana calculated.

Beneath was a sort of domestic catacomb with several semi-
subterranean rooms. The dimly lit spaces were barricaded with
cobwebs, tattered wedding veils, filmy and grey with age. On
the floors, chunks of damp, lime washed plaster lay, leaving
areas of naked brick exposed, their efflorescence of white salts
spongy and cold, like snow.

There were wine bins let into the walls and cupboards full of jams, pickles, chutneys, fruit cheeses and bottled fruits and vegetables. The jars were labelled in Thea's bold script, not only with the year and the ordinary name of the preserve, but also with exact details of the plant variety, a note on the harvest volume, average mean temperatures for the year and rainfall. The preserves glowed like jewels in their cupboards. Even the names—medlar, codlin, quince and mirabelle—piped the wraith like notes of distant music. Diana felt she had opened a treasure chest, full not only of beauty but also of a meaning which, for the moment, eluded her.

Later, she hired a boat from the landing stage up the river, picking her way down a flight of stone steps which zig-zagged down the sheer face of the gorge and snaked between the old cottages and houses. The boat place had a deserted café advertising hamburgers and fizzy drinks. Two ginger haired young men in waders and an elderly woman wearing a flowered pinafore came out to greet her.

"Now then, Mrs. Neville." By now Diana knew that this was the standard local greeting. It gave nothing away, it asked no questions. It merely stated a readiness to hold conversation or do business, whatever was required.

"I just wanted to go down the river a little way so that I can see the outside of the Tower."

"Nay, you've your own boat, Mrs. Neville," the old woman expostulated with perfect friendliness. "These is for tourists and such like."

"You see, I didn't even know that," Diana admitted. "Where is it? And anyway, I don't think I know how to row."

"Hop in and I'll take you down."

The younger of the two men rowed strongly upstream for a few minutes, saying nothing. The oars rattled in the rowlocks, warning a flotilla of mallard ducks of their approach. They flowed away, out of the path of the oncoming craft with scattered, unconcerned quacks. The season for rich pickings of bread, cake and biscuits was over. The holiday crowds were gone.

"There you are, Mrs. Neville. We shall have to get you rowing, though. I'll teach you, if you like. More time in t'winter. I'm Ned, by t'way."

Diana saw that it was all as the estate agent had said. The

carving of the knight was there guarding a low arch-headed door with steps that disappeared into the weed thickened depths. He sported a freshly painted white tunic with a red cross and brandished his sword with a sort of amateur cheeriness, like a small boy in a school play.

Ned manoeuvered in close, enabling Diana to peer through a lancet-shaped window. Its sill slanted crazily and the stone tracery, roughly repaired with clods of cement, crumbled at her touch.

"T'key's behind that loose stone there, if you want to go in." Ned shipped his oars. "Just by your hand. Go on. You can get out but steady, like."

Diana managed the door by herself and stepped into a green gloomed space little bigger than the room she slept in. The far wall glistened with moisture and had indeed been hacked out of the rock. An altar shaped slab, or votive surface as Mr. Edgeworth had called it, stood on the hard packed earthen floor. It too was of rock. There was nothing else to be seen and nothing to be felt but the cold. Diana stepped out into the leaf dappled sunshine again.

"Who paints him?" Diana indicated the knight.

"Dunno," Ned shrugged. "I expect some of t'left footers in t'town. Miss FitzGilbert would have known. He's allus done in t'spring. T'river generally gets up in t'winter and floods little chapel, like. So Gilbert needs doing regular. Look, there's your boat house."

She followed the direction of his finger and saw that a rickety corrugated iron roof projected low over the water on the bridge side of the tower. Ned poled the boat along so that she could see inside. There was a narrow mud bank there and an old boat, smaller than Ned's but painted green like his. It was drawn up above the water line.

"Doesn't it get flooded too?"

"Aye, it would. But we take it down with ours for the winter and fettle it a bit. Miss FitzGilbert used to like a spell on t'river in the summer. She was a fair rower too, for an old lady. Mind you, we didn't get round to it last winter, with 'er being dead and all. We'd better get it out now and take a look at it, now you've come."

Yolanda would love it, Diana was sure.

"You've a daughter, then?" Ned asked casually as he swung

the boat around midstream. "I wouldn't have thought you looked old enough."

Diana noticed the sparkle in his Viking's blue eyes and smiled secretly to herself. Ned was evidently one for the girls. He would flirt simultaneously with mother and daughter as easily as he synchronised both his oars. Hadn't Aunt Thea said as much in her dissertation on local characters?

"Ned Garvey," she had written, "gets the blarney from his father's side of the family and the overweening confidence in his own attractions from his mother's side—the red haired lot with the ice blue eyes whose ancestors undoubtedly came from Norway and sailed up the river, looting and pillaging . . ."

"What do I owe you, Ned?" Diana felt in her jacket pocket as Ned handed her out of the boat with a flourish worthy of Sir Walter Raleigh.

"Nowt, Mrs. Neville. We're neighbours, aren't we? Want a cup of tea? Gran allus has t'kettle on."

Diana refused, laughing at the kindness and the outrageous flattery in his glance.

"Mrs. Neville!" Ned's grandmother darted out of her café, holding a plastic supermarket bag. "Will you have some of my Golden Pippins? I've more'n we can eat this season."

Diana took the bag. It weighed heavily and looking in she saw it was full of amber coloured apples, some with leaves still attached to the stalks. It was hard to reject the gift, but she had an orchard full of apples at the Tower.

"Them's last Golden Pippins in England, they are," Ned's gran remarked with satisfaction. "They think at that research place down south, Surrey or somewhere, that there isn't so much as a pip left in whole of t'country. You taste these, Mrs. Neville. There's some as don't know what a good apple should taste like."

"I will. Thank you, Mrs. . . ." Diana hesitated deliberately. Aunt Thea's information had evened the score. A lot of people in Nidcaster might know who she was, but now she herself was quite well informed. Of course, there was no need to reveal the fact. The local people might take it amiss and hold it against Aunt Thea.

"Garvey, love. Cousin to Albert Sedgely's wife. Now you let me know what you think of them apples. Fit for a queen, they are."

Biting into one on her way up the steps, Diana was forced
to admit that they were. But *the last tree in England?* The
thought drifted like sediment to the bottom of her mind, along
with so many other hints and impressions.

At the end of the day, enclosed in the tower room once
more, Diana read more of Thea's letter sitting on the floor beside the medieval hearth. She read by the light of the flames
and three candles fixed in a pewter candelabrum she had found
in the kitchen. There were no electricity points in here. Obviously, the tower was maintained merely because it formed the
greater part of the house's western wall. It was like a withered
limb to which the blood supply was scant.

Once again, the letter supplied answers to questions that Diana had asked and some that she had not.

Father Murphy's choir boys from St. Mary the Virgin always freshen Gilbert's paintwork at Easter. Sometimes the
scamps give him a moustache, an adornment the sculptor
never intended, but I don't care to stand in the way of
youthful creativity. However, one year I did have to put my
food down about converting his tunic to a Leeds United
football strip. Actually, I think Father Murphy was in two
minds, being a fan himself, you see.

You'd do well to make yourself affable to Father Murphy,
incidentally. He is the guardian of an old damson tree, something rather rare these days. I'm sorry to say the specimen
in our orchard is only a bullace, which is not quite the same
thing. Catch the good Father in the right humour, around
September time, and he'll let you have a few pounds. Give
them to Sedgely and ask no questions. In the fullness of
time, a flask or two of liquid rubies will come back to you.
Sedgely, you see, has a still in his cellar, a fact we never al-
lude to ourselves for reasons not unconnected with the local
constabulary.

Aunt Thea went on to dilate on the town's policemen, calling them a "fresh faced bunch of innocents who appreciate a
glass of our 'cordial' when they call with a little summons or
something."

There was a fuller account, too, of Gilbert's career. Aunt
Thea's mind wandered from topic to topic, fertilising each pistil

of information with pollen from her previous subject. Buzzing randomly from place to place, she spun a lustrous thread of connection between the living and the dead, so that all seemed equally present to Diana as, absorbed, she turned page after page.

Sire Gilbert was a Norman who had fought against the Saracens with King Richard II in the Holy Land. He seems to have been a wandering, landless knight, with no property of his own to return to in Normandy. We must guess that he was close to the King because the Honour of Nidcaster was a Royal Manor held directly by the Crown since the Conqueror's time.

The King rewarded Gilbert's service with the Berewick of Leypoole which, being a dependent territory of his own Manor of Nidcaster, lay directly in his gift. And so Gilbert returned from the wars to take up residence here. He built the tower as a small fortified residence overlooking his bit of forest across the river, his fishery and his fields upstream, on either side of the river. Of course, the Leypoole Bridge was not built then and Harrogate was a bare, poverty stricken hamlet.

They say he was a hermit and holy man. Well, he may have been but he had a wife and children as the manorial records show. People *didn't* specialise quite so much in the Middle Ages. His son Hubert inherited the property and expanded it somewhat. I'm afraid, however, that by the late eighteenth century the last bit of FitzGilbert land had gone. The FitzGilberts cashed in on the linen boom. They preferred spinning and weaving hemp to growing it, or rather they were skilled at getting others to process it for them and in that way made a handsome fortune.

In the early years of the last century, they built Leighpole Hall and relegated this old place to the status of dumping ground for widows and redundant aunts . . . of which I trust I am the last.

Diana looked up from the page and hugged her knees. The flames from the fire reflected their *danse macabre* on the painted cloths and she realised that this room was the only possible place in which Sir Gilbert's family could have lived.

Its unthreatening walls were saturated with a past she had never known about, and yet it was in some sense her own history. The shadowy arms of an unknown family were drawing her in and bidding her welcome home.

And then, when the mills couldn't carry on with the competition from cotton and all these clever synthetics (we made sheets and glass cloths mostly), the Hall was sold as a private nursing home in the fifties and the FitzGilberts scattered all over. There was just me left here, in this house, where we began and where we belong.

Diana skimmed through the minutiae of recent history. *"So you see, my dear, in Nidcaster at least, we FitzGilberts are not without our modest importance ... which is pleasant, is it not?"*

Diana was touched by this delicate attempt to boost her self-esteem, which Aunt Thea had rightly guessed to be at a low ebb.

Cramped and rather cold, she got into bed. She would have to find herself another bedroom. There was no wardrobe here and the bathroom, let into the thickness of the walls, was the most primitive she had ever seen. But she was glad that she had first lodged here ... beginning, as it were, at the beginning. The auctioneer's hammer should not end it all yet.

Diana slept then, lullabied by the owls hooting across the river in Gilbert's old "bit of forest."

❦ THE FOLLOWING MORNING two letters arrived.

Diana was seated at the kitchen table, painfully calculating the effect of buying a small car on her slender finances when Sedgely, having collected the Tower's post from the box outside the garden door, delivered them personally.

"I'll be taking up t'red cabbages today, Mrs. Neville. Will you be wanting any?"

Diana knew two recipes for red cabbage. Both excellent but not ones that should be repeated more than once in the autumn season. Twice at the most.

"One small one, perhaps, Mr. Sedgely?"

Sedgely beamed mysterious relief and went off whistling, his empty pipe clamped energetically between his teeth. He'd come back to the house for his cup of tea later. Mrs. Sedgely, on the other hand, would come down further on in the week to help move Diana into her chosen bedroom. "She'll be tied up, like, today and tomorrow."

Diana examined the letters from the outside world with reluctance. Opening one, she found it was from Michael, forwarded by his solicitors. It was written on a lined form with Brixton Prison's address printed at the top. He said only that he was well, expected to be moved to an open prison within days and hoped the food there would be more palatable than it was at Brixton. Would she please let him have her address? That was all. Diana felt a pang of guilt. She had thought very little about him in the three days since she had last seen him. And when she thought about him, it was in the past tense, as if he had died. Aunt Thea had seemed more alive than her husband.

She put it aside with the intention of answering before the day was over. But what should she say? Would he want to think of her as happy, or desolate without him? There was no easy answer. In the past, Michael had been on many long business trips to distant parts of the world. Sometimes he had stayed away for many weeks at a time. But now, he had never been further away. Diana could not visualise his prison, guess at his feelings or imagine the things he saw and did each day. And she could never make him understand the world of Gilbert's Tower. They were separated by the watertight membrane of judicial guilt and innocence, torn bodily apart, with no communication between their minds. *Had there ever been?* What has he to do with me? Diana smothered the question before it could become one which demanded an answer.

The other letter was from Mr. Laverack. Diana found that Yolanda's headmaster foresaw difficulties for the school which he did not forbear to state in the plainest terms. Difficulties in continuing to "harbour," was the word he used, "a girl whose father was, to put it bluntly, detained at Her Majesty's pleasure." There had already been some attempted press intrusion, questions from parents and some registrations had been cancelled. And while he could not necessarily attribute the latter to the unhappy outcome of the Knightman Neville Trust case, he was bound to draw certain conclusions.

Yolanda, herself, Mr. Laverack felt, would almost certainly prefer to be with her mother at a time like this. Nidcaster, he happened to know, had one of the few remaining grammar schools in the country. It had a fine reputation and Yolanda could, with benefit, complete her "A" Level studies there. "Naturally," Mr. Laverack added, in the expectation of an early meeting with her mother, he had refrained from discussing the matter with Yolanda.

"I should hope so, too!"

Diana turned to the orange cat which now divided its time between the warm spot beneath the peach trees and a rag rug spread before the old solid fuel cooker in the kitchen. The cat raised itself on its front paws and, with its eyes still shut, yawned hugely and rolled over contentedly on its back, demanding to have its white belly stroked.

It was a cat of few words and fewer worldly concerns. It seemed to acknowledge no official home and answer to no name. It was just there.

"There's a few folks in Nidcaster thinks they own that cat, Mrs. Neville, and it's got a lot of silly names it don't care to answer to. It sleeps where it likes and eats where t'provender takes its fancy," Sedgely told her sagaciously as he drank his mug of thick, sweet tea.

Diana knew then that the orange cat's real name was its own secret. It did not prevent her from attempting to buy its favour with some tinned salmon and a dish of evaporated milk.

She moved quietly about the kitchen during the morning. It was in the Victorian part of the house, nearest to the garden door where Sedgely's frequent comings and goings could be seen from its windows. She was taking old blue and white dishes, copper jelly moulds and anything with colour or glint from cupboards and arranging them in the place of rusted graters and sieves. The kitchen needed colour. She made a golden pyramid of Mrs. Garvey's amber coloured apples and put them on the kitchen table, inhaling their pungent, sensuous perfume.

Large, with a stone flagged floor, white pot sink with a wooden draining board, the kitchen offered nothing in the way of modern convenience. The cooking utensils either stood on the open shelves of two great pine dressers, evidently made and plugged to the wall at the same time as the kitchen itself was built, or depended from hooks on a rack that hung from the dingy ceiling.

The uneven walls were gloss painted in cream and white-

tiled to waist height, finished with a line of black border tiles.
The sash windows gave a view of the garden up to the orchard
gate but the projecting side of the brick, Carolean house obscured the view to the western side, making it darker here than
in the rest of the house. When the stove was unlit, it felt dank.
But like any woman, Diana began her domination of the house
by imposing herself on the kitchen. Already, it looked friend-
lier. Unlike the lavish monuments to efficiency in her former
homes, this room needed to be used and occupied.

She and the cat were colonising it peacefully, hour by hour
while Diana's mind went steadily to work, uniting the things
she had always known with the new things she had learned at
Gilbert's Tower. The imagination works waywardly, by an independent, uncontrollable engine that scorns effort and timeta-
bles. Diana's body became progressively less active as her
brain's shuttle-like frenzy flew with ever increasing speed,
carrying a fine spun weft of speculation over and above the
stout warp threads of undeniable fact, meshing the two into a
firmly woven fabric.

After an hour during which she had sat more or less motionless, she bent down to stroke the cat again. Its pale lips were
stretched in the self-satisfied curve which in a feline looks so
extraordinarily like a smile.

"I shall have to buy that car today and go to Somerset tomorrow," she murmured to the cat. "When I get back, we'll
begin work on my idea."

The dread of venturing out of the safe enclosure of Gilbert's
Tower into the hostile world where, now it seemed, she and
her child were regarded as outcasts had receded like a spring
tide. A new and surprising vigour was coursing through her
veins. Suddenly she felt equal to the task of remaking her life
and Yolanda's—the world was new again and she viewed it
with appetite.

Rising, she continued to look down at the floor, no longer
seeing the cat. "There's no reason why a big scheme shouldn't
work as well as a small one. No reason at all."

CHAPTER
4

❦ THE LONG CASE clock in the hall had just begun to chime eleven o'clock when Diana stepped over the threshold of the main entrance to Tiverton Abbey School for Girls. Instantly, an odour of stewing meat, old shoes and beeswax assailed her nostrils, making her stomach lurch with untreasured memories of her own school days.

The last leg of her journey had been bedevilled with traffic cones and slow moving vehicles. Diana, who had left Nidcaster in the small hours, was glad she had allowed a broad margin for such delays. Lateness, discourteous in itself, would put her at a disadvantage. It was one she could not afford.

"Good morning, Mrs. Neville," the headmaster's secretary bustled forward, her spectacles, hung on a chain, bouncing importantly on her deep, hand-knitted bosom. "How was your journey?" The secretary slid an impersonal placard of welcome over her features. *Gestapo Gert,* Yolanda and her friends called her.

Not waiting to listen to Diana's murmured reply, the secretary hustled her across the parquet floored entrance hall. Since Mr. Laverack had taken over the headship an unspoken policy of ensuring that parents, whatever their worldly status, should be left with no illusions about which side their bread was buttered at Tiverton had been ruthlessly pursued. Bitterly, Diana read in every line of the secretary's stoutly corseted body, that Yolanda Neville's parents had no shred of dignity left.

"If you will take a seat in here," Diana was ushered into a room euphemistically called the "drawing-room" to mask its doom laden function as the antechamber where Tiverton miscreants awaited disciplinary interviews with the head. It was a room well known to every parent from details contained in artistically tear stained and frequently misspelled letters. Diana, despite her feeling of desolation, could not help smiling as she recognised the "yukky porridge coloured" curtains and "mushy pea" carpet of Yolanda's own adolescent ragings. Letters over which she and Michael had laughed and agonised by turns. She ached for the time in which such small, comfortable troubles had united them.

"Mr. Laverack should be available shortly."

The secretary snapped the door closed behind her, exasperated that the visitor declined to be seated. Vulnerable and touchy, Diana wondered why, since she herself was punctual, she should be obliged to wait for Mr. Laverack at all. Why was he not waiting to greet her? She watched the door, wondering what excuse he would make for his belated appearance.

After a pause of some minutes, in which Diana watched a group of running girls out of the window, their hair and school scarves flying, the secretary came back. She appeared this time, magician-like, at the other door, which communicated directly with the study. It had opened with cosmic speed and wideness betokening a portentous announcement.

"Mr. Laverack will see you now!" the secretary declaimed, her right arm outstretched, palm open, combining invitation with command.

"I am glad he is free, at last," Diana commented quietly, passing in front of her. "It is four minutes past eleven o'clock, you know." Her misgivings about this interview oppressed the sinking spirits she had striven so hard to keep up.

"Mrs. Neville, Headmaster," the secretary motioned Diana to advance into the study but found her gesture redundant as Diana had already taken possession of the middle of the room. She was glad now, as quite often before, of her ballerina's training. At least it had taught her how to occupy space. Mr. Laverack was seated at his desk and seemingly busy with some papers. He neither rose nor looked up.

The bracket clock on the wall ticked just five times before Diana's nervous antennae confirmed a suspicion that she was being subjected to some form of intimidation.

"Good morning, Mr. Laverack," Diana put her bag and

gloves down firmly on the nearest table, glad that although her hand trembled, her voice did not betray her.

"It is a long drive from Yorkshire and I had hoped we could begin this meeting promptly. I have a great deal to do. As a busy person yourself, I'm sure you will understand. If some emergency is preventing you from keeping our appointment, you had better let me be on my way and write our apologies in due course. If, on the other hand, your rudeness is some kind of sinister middle management technique learned from a book about putting people in their place, let me tell you, it falls far short of the sort of manners I hoped Yolanda would learn here."

The release of pent-up apprehension and hurt on her daughter's behalf burst from her like gun fire. Diana found herself collapsing without invitation on to a sofa, suddenly exhausted by her own temerity and a drive which had lasted seven hours. As she waited through the confused moments in which Laverack scrambled to his feet and attempted to recover from the defeat of his opening manoeuvre, Diana smiled with a fixed pleasantness. She nodded with mild impatience at his profuse apologies and excuses.

"I do assure you, Mrs. Neville . . ."

"Please, Mr. Laverack, may we just talk about Yolanda? It is the only reason I am here."

Laverack rang a bell for coffee. For once, Diana found him both frank and reasonable. She knew that he was so simply because she had surprised him as she had surprised herself. Anger, she was learning, was a positive impulse, a useful substance which did not improve with keeping.

"I must tell you, Mr. Laverack," Diana said as she refused the plate of biscuits he proffered, "that my own instinct is to leave Yolanda undisturbed if that is at all possible. The changes which have taken place in our life as a family are already sufficiently traumatic. If anything can be done to stabilise Yolanda and preserve what we can of the familiar and the reassuring, then I shall do it. The effect on your school is bound to be a secondary consideration as far as I am concerned. However, I will admit that if there *is* an effect, it cannot be to Yolanda's advantage and I shall remove her at once."

Laverack opened his mouth to reply, but Diana was determined to have her say whilst her argument was marshalled and ready at the forefront of her mind. It had been prepared and distilled over endless miles of unforgiving motorway.

"If you tell me, for example, that Yolanda is being victimised by any member of the staff, or the girls . . . blamed personally for events in which she has had no part . . . made to feel that she is a pariah . . . and of course, I shall ask her . . . in fact, I shall need to satisfy myself in considerable detail as to her treatment here in the last few days."

"There is absolutely no question of . . ." Laverack fingered his tie knot desperately. Diana's emphatic manner had unnerved him completely. It overturned every previous personal impression he had ever gained and contrasted quite shockingly with her monumental public silence. He, like others, had read the newspapers, as week had followed week.

Mrs. Neville had always been the kind of mother who confined her contacts with the school to correspondence about uniform and lost hockey sticks, cough medicine and domestic trivia. She was the sort of feminine, ornamental woman one was pleased to see eating strawberries and cream on Speech Day. In the past it was Neville himself, bluff and expansive, who had made all the running. And of course, his generous donations to the school building funds had been useful. An extraordinary meeting of the Board of Governors had confirmed the impracticability of returning those donations, whatever the implications. The money had been swallowed up by the new science block. The Nevilles had been what he called *good* parents. Laverack had never expected to find Diana Neville anything more than acquiescent, grateful for his advice, humbled by her situation. Now he half feared that she might stoop to reminding him of her husband's former benevolence. Inwardly, Laverack writhed.

The meeting was short, shorter even than Mr. Laverack had intended. Nor did it lead to the conclusion he had expected. Analysing the progress of their fifteen minute conversation later, he was staggered to find that he had awarded Yolanda Neville a valuable bursary. She was a clever girl, her mother said, producing every one of Yolanda's school reports for the past five years. Good marks, very creditable comments . . . they were all there, endorsed by his own signature.

Diana Neville had both finesse and method. She had learned her tactics, Laverack admitted ruefully to himself, at the feet of a master . . . picked his pocket with long, slim fingers. At the moment of her leave-taking, the headmaster felt a peculiar breathlessness. He had been mugged by a butterfly.

"So," Diana said, rising, "may I take it that subject to Yolanda's own agreement to stay here at Tiverton, we shall have your full support and, if necessary, a little fatherly guidance? I should be grateful, Mr. Laverack."

"Yolanda's a strong minded young woman," Laverack clasped Diana's hand weakly. "I'm sure she'll overcome this upset, and we shall do everything we can to help her, if she will let us."

"I was sure we could count on you," Diana celebrated her victory sweetly. She hadn't needed to mention the new science block at all, thank heaven. That would have been unpleasant.

Alone in the chilly hall, Diana felt every muscle relax and her eyelids weigh heavily as if sleep might overtake her where she stood. Michael had said it often enough in the early days. Fighting is the hardest work there is.

"Mummy!" Yolanda, tall and blond, detached herself from giggling companions in the corridor which led off the hall. "You look absolutely shattered."

🎇 "DISTRIBUTION," DIANA REPLIED to her daughter's question, observing anxiously that Yolanda had eaten six slices of toast and was now working on her second slice of chocolate cake with no sign of satiety. The teashop in Yeovil was the one most of the Tiverton parents favoured when visiting.

Yolanda's broad forehead with its downward swooping widow's peak was perplexed. The greenish eyes, so like her father's, narrowed.

"What's that?"

"It means making sure that shops and supermarkets, for instance, get just the right amount of the right products for their shelves at the right time."

Diana poured some hot water into the teapot and wondered just how much she ought to tell Yolanda. Would talking about it help to organize her thoughts, or would it somehow diffuse the concentrated vision she had nursed in her imagination? But she had begun now.

"There are companies who specialise in doing it, you see. Sometimes the stock is owned directly by the retail outlets themselves, the shops, you know, and just stored in the distributor's warehouse, and sometimes the distributor owns the stock and sells it to the retailer when it's needed. There are dozens of different permutations. Sometimes the shops own the trucks, or else the distributor rents them to the supermarket chain and paints their livery on them . . . or owns them himself."

Diana stopped, seeing the look of glassy eyed boredom on her daughter's face. Perhaps it did sound dull to somebody young like Yolanda, but then she didn't understand how different it was all going to be.

"Mummy, I thought you said we had hardly any money now? How can you afford warehouses and trucks and things? Could I possibly have some more cake?"

Diana succeeded in catching the eye of the waitress. Really, she should have said no. It would be awful if Yolanda got fat, not to mention the frightening cost of everything. But saying "no" to Yolanda invariably invited a fit of childish sulking. And Diana wanted what there was of happiness to be unspoiled. Mentally, she made a note to say "no" the next time. As the only child of a wealthy, indulgent father, Yolanda had never realised that every penny spent must be replaced with another penny earned. She must be made aware of it, painful as the learning process might be. Somebody had to teach her. They were lessons that Diana dreaded imparting but knew she must not shirk.

"Ah! That's the clever bit," Diana took up Yolanda's question about money. "Do you remember that saying of Daddy's: 'Always use other people's money'?"

It was an unfortunate thing to have said and Diana bit her lip with regret. Of course, Michael had never meant it that way, but would Yolanda realise the difference in the context?

"Don't look so worried, Mummy, I know what you mean."

"Well, that's the way I intend to do it. And the point is, it won't be an ordinary distribution business. Do you know what I mean by organic vegetables?"

Yolanda nodded, replacing the newly arrived slice of cake on the plate, untasted. She had not really wanted it.

"Oh, yes. Things grown without chemicals and things. Healthy food. People are terribly upright about pesticides and the awful diseases you can get now."

"Exactly. And if you've ever looked at the organic fruit and

vegetables in supermarkets, as I have, you'll know that they
cost twice as much as the ordinary produce and look too depressing for words. And the range is pretty limited too. I've
never bought the stuff although I'm basically in favour of the
theory . . . you know, of not messing up the planet or our bod-
ies with a lot of unnecessary chemicals that just make things
easier for big farmers and growers."

"So how are you going to change anything?"

Diana did not answer for a moment, half wishing that she
had resisted the temptation to talk to Yolanda yet. The words
were coming out slowly, like new shoots pushing through the
cold earth in the spring, risking the knife of sudden frost before
their leaves spread and flowers bloomed. It had all seemed so
brilliantly simple, so logical and neat at Gilbert's Tower. Now,
in this mundane teashop, confronting Yolanda's critically ex-
pectant expression, Diana couldn't help but fear her idea might
not survive even a schoolgirl's scrutiny.

"I am going to change things by buying stock from small
growers, *very* small growers indeed. Just people with gardens,
probably retired people with time and energy to spend on cultivating rather special, unusual things. You see, we already
know that there are enough people who will pay for organic
produce, otherwise the supermarkets wouldn't stock it at all.
There are always people who're prepared to pay for something
rare . . . something beautiful." Diana's voice softened as she remembered that first morning at Gilbert's Tower when the
dusky peach had lain warm, heavy and scented in her hand, its
quiet days of ripening on the brick wall perfectly accomplished. "And there are plenty of people who would buy things
grown at home rather than in some foreign place. You
know . . . apples from America, or France. Patriotism isn't
quite dead yet. And there are things we've forgotten about.
Have you the faintest idea what a Golden Pippin is or a Peregrine peach? Do you know what a mulberry is? Have you
ever tasted one?"

Diana continued to talk with growing enthusiasm. The ideas
worked as well in words as in thoughts. Yolanda watched her
mother in astonishment. She had never seen her like this,
caught up in herself rather than in others. It was as though she
was touched with a kind of gentle, benign madness. Her eyes
were shining and her face glowed with a vision that was invis-

ible to others, a place far beyond the low, mock beamed room with its gingham clothed tables, hurrying waitresses and cake laden trolleys.

Yolanda was not entirely comfortable. Her mother had become somebody else, not the predictable, reliable person she had been. And other people, customers at neighbouring tables, were turning round in their seats and staring. It wasn't that Diana was talking loudly, it was just the steady, intense bombardment of words and the way she looked. Transfigured.

"Oh, darling," Diana was remorseful, "you must think your mother has taken leave of her senses. I won't say any more. But all this is terribly important to me. I know I'm right. It will work and it will work for everyone who's involved. It's more than just money . . ."

"Mummy . . ."

"Oh, yes, darling. Yes. Let me just get the bill."

Driving through the winding lanes on the way back to the school, Yolanda asked no further questions about her mother's concerns, and chattered about Tiverton preoccupations. Sports fixtures, the school skiing trip planned for next March, the end of term play that was to be acted with boys from a neighbouring school—*A Midsummer Night's Dream*. The boy who was going to be Puck was brilliant and fantastic looking . . . his father was the British Consul in some South American place. Listening, Diana was only partially relieved. She told herself that all this was as it should be, as she had hoped. And yet, as she negotiated the high-hedged bends, she worried that Yolanda never once mentioned her own father.

The cherished hope that they might draw closer together, shielding and drawing strength from each other, faded. It had been unrealistic and selfish to expect it, Diana mused. Yolanda was still too young and if pushing the subject of her father away helped her to face her days and live her life, then *she* must say nothing to afflict the tender scar tissue which might already be healing. Swallowing her hurt and her doubts, Diana fed her maternal pride on Yolanda's achievements and her burgeoning beauty. She shall have everything, Diana vowed silently, even if I have to go out and scrub other people's floors to provide it.

"And so, darling," she said finally, stroking a shining lock away from the tall teenager's wide, smooth brow, "you are quite sure you will be all right at school and not worry about me or Daddy, or anything?"

Reassuring her mother for the umpteenth time, Yolanda watched her climb back into the little car and fasten the safety belt. Diana had explained that she must return on the same day, partly because she didn't want to spend money on a hotel bill and partly because she wanted to start work at once.

"Every day I grow older. Every hour, my name and my face are being forgotten. Ordinarily, I should be glad of that," she added, kissing the smooth young cheek Yolanda presented, "but life's a funny thing, even notoriety can have its uses when you want to get something done . . . and another thing, darling. Every week my clothes are getting a shade more out of fashion. When I go to talk to important gentlemen in London about finance, I want to look . . ."

"Rich." Yolanda finished for her.

"Yes. Even though I'm not and they will know I'm not. Silly, isn't it? But you know what they say . . . before you're successful, you've got to look successful."

"You mean Daddy says it."

Diana smiled. "Yes. I never realized how much he taught me. Isn't it lucky I paid attention?

"Write to him, darling, won't you? Just say . . . well, ordinary things. You'll know what to say. You've always been so close. He'll be longing to hear from you. After half-term you'll be able to tell him what you think of Gilbert's Tower."

"Why don't you tell him, Mummy? You've practically never stopped talking about the place."

Diana flushed. Yolanda had inherited Michael's ability to wound. As the little car's wheels crunched down Tiverton Abbey's gravel drive she glanced in the rear view mirror and saw Yolanda standing there, absurdly adult in her school uniform. She looked like her father, full of power.

I cannot be afraid of my own child.

❦ DIANA PICKED UP the telephone receiver and put it down again. To telephone a major London advertising agency and ask for an appointment seemed a small thing to do and yet so immensely difficult. She had been alone in the drawing room at Gilbert's Tower for two hours, trying to settle in her mind what she should say. She had tested her voice aloud, talking nonsense in tones that varied in her own ear between the hectoring and the breathlessly excited. None of them made music. And even if they had, could she reproduce precisely that tone when the flatness of a stranger's unsympathetic voice replied?

The church clock's melodious carillon reached into the room, spelling out the wasted quarters of precious, passing hours.

The trouble with telephoning was that you thought, Diana reflected, that you would be safe in your own stronghold amongst familiar things. But in fact, it was never like that. The minute an unknown voice answered, you were no longer at home, but transported in all but body to a strange place in which you were sightless, could not gauge reactions, see the half hidden sneer . . . the hand over the mouthpiece . . . the indifferent shrug and silently mouthed rejection. Faceless people, knowing nothing about you, judged with merciless blindness.

Outside it was drizzling greyly and a faint smell of damp earth penetrated the house. The orange cat had not been seen all day.

That morning, Diana had taken the dust covers from the furniture. This unveiling had revealed nothing as self-conscious as a colour scheme. Brocades and embroideries had been added to each other without thought and allowed to bleach in the flooding sunlight of many summers, until greens, blues, reds and violets had all the same value, like a bowl of pot pourri. A clutter of ebony plant stands, an oak settle, marquetry games and work tables, a mahogany framed sofa and curly, balloon back chairs lived together with the walnut cased piano as casual acquaintances, sharing the same faded, flower-strewn carpet, and enjoying each other's company thanks to the mutual tolerance of good breeding.

On the carved chimney piece, the collars of long dead dogs, each with its engraved nameplate, were lovingly preserved. Diana had stumbled over their poignant assembly of miniature gravestones in a corner of the orchard. On the walls, their pastel crayoned portraits smiled, soft eyed and devoted across at the answering gaze of forgotten, oil painted FitzGilberts who had owned and cared for them. The silence was full of their names, trilled or bellowed down the years in phantom voices whose timbre, like the yaps and barks which once responded, had been stilled in the oblivion of time.

Everything in this room was beautiful but nothing had been allowed the quality of specialness. No single item had ever been treated with more care and reverence than another. Scuffs and stains were evenly distributed and silver framed photographs jockeyed for position with curly-edged specimens which had none at all. Cheap Staffordshire plates stood in an inlaid credenza of ludicrous elaboration whilst what Diana recognised as a Sung dynasty vase did duty as a door stop. It was the kind of arrangement that no designer could achieve and would never wish to. It required an eye that was ignorant of value and indifferent to period. Aunt Thea had never been corrupted by a sale catalogue or a decorating magazine. Her room was a composition of uncalculating affection. It was nostalgic, ethereal even, but not stimulating.

Sighing, Diana leaned her forehead against the cool window pane and looked out over the garden. Mercury's flashing stream of sparkling water gushed from his mouth, mocking her dumbness. I must turn off the pump, Diana thought drearily. It looks pretty but it's wasting electricity. I must speak to them today.

"Mrs. Neville?"

Diana started at the sound of Sedgely's voice. He had gone home hours ago after their long talk. And he never, normally, came into this part of the house.

"Have you spoken to them advertising people yet?"

Sedgely's face appeared around the door, questioning and concerned.

"I was just going to." Diana moved away from the window, feeling she had been caught indulging a cowardly despondency. When she had talked about her master plan to Sedgely, his belief in her had buoyed her up. But later the emptiness of the house and the dripping rain outside had left her defenceless against the enormity of the thing she had conceived. Overwhelmed, she had thought and thought, but done nothing.

"Aye. I thought not. Would an audience help?" Sedgely came into the room tentatively as if he half feared a peremptory dismissal.

"I think, Mr. Sedgely, you must be the cleverest man alive."

"Nay, 'T weren't me," Sedgely deprecated the compliment. "It was Mrs. Sedgely. She said to me, 'Sedgely, I fancy Mrs. Neville might be needing a bit of company. Moral support, like. Why don't you go on down and see what she's doing? There's nowt for you to do round here in this weather.' She were just washing up the dinner things when she said it." Sedgely pointed at the empty grate with his pipe, "Why don't you light t'fire, Mrs. Neville?"

"It's not cold," Diana laughed, more pleased to see him than she could say, "and I didn't want to disturb Mrs. Sedgely's beautiful arrangement. I could never do it again."

Sedgely followed her glance at the tight packed newspaper spills and structure of kindling topped with a delicately balanced edifice of small coals. It was, in its fashion, a work of art. Newspaper roses in an iron basket.

"That's nowt. We don't have fires just because of t'weather. It's like having somebody in t'room with you . . . takes t'edge off solitude, like. I'll get it going for you while you ring those London types. Chimney's bound to be a bit cold."

He turned his back to her and, crouching down, busied himself with a box of matches and the old leather bellows. It was all easy now. Emboldened by Sedgely's comradeship, Diana dialled the number.

"Epoch Advertising. How may I help you?" a girl's voice chanted with sing-song insolence.

"I should like to speak to one of your directors." Diana wondered why she should have found that so difficult to say before. Sedgely, just by being there, had given her back a sense of solidity, of existing.

"Which one?" The girl sounded as if she was engaged in the classic occupation of receptionists and filing her nails.

"Any that happens to be free," Diana turned from the piano and looked at Sedgely's back; while he heard her, she would feel believable enough for anyone. "I think they all know me, or know of me."

"Whom shall I say is calling?" Diana could feel the girl's fingers hovering disdainfully over a switchboard. She told her the name. "My husband's company was a client of your agency. Mr. Olaff dealt with the account, I think."

The line was filled with a dreadful electronic rendering of "The Sting," intended, no doubt, to relax waiting callers and prevent them hearing the transactions which would now take place. "The Sting" stopped abruptly.

"What's it about, please?"

Diana had been prepared for this question. It was the one she did not wish to answer. An idea is an embryo, a foetus which cannot survive without the umbilical cord which joins it to the brain which has nourished it. It cannot be wrenched from the womb and sent alone into uncaring ears.

"A matter I shall be happy to discuss with Mr. Olaff, or any of his co-directors. That is why I have rung. To make an appointment," Diana defended sturdily.

"The Sting" intervened again, shutting her out.

"Hello, Mrs. Neville. Merlin Olaff speaking. What can we do for you?"

Diana had never, that she recalled, spoken to him before but his voice, light and fashionably cockneyfied, sounded friendly enough, if puzzled. And guarded.

"I don't think I've invented the wheel or anything," Diana started diffidently, "but I have had an idea that could . . ." She broke off. Never say anything conditional if you can say something positive. "*Will* make a big difference to the food retailing sector and generate an important trend. It's not complicated really, but I want an eye to eye meeting. Getting the promotion right is the key."

To Diana's relief, Olaff didn't press her to say more but began to leaf audibly through his diary, dismissing date after engagement packed date. He had met her once, at a large party for the launch of a pension fund. A vision of her came back to him. She had been small and composed but vivid, like a sharply cut jewel, dazzling the eye from a distance. Not an easy person to forget even if she hadn't decorated every front page for weeks past. He remembered too how her mauve coloured eyes had returned again and again to Neville, clothing him with the splendour of her admiration. No man could be less than princely if he had a woman like that to be proud of him. Talking to her now, as if nothing had happened, was like discovering somebody alive in the rubble of a collapsed building. Whatever she had to say, and it couldn't really be much, he would see her.

"October seventh suit you? At twelve o'clock. We could give you a bite of lunch . . . I'll see if Everard's free . . . if not, perhaps one of my other partners could come along. Another viewpoint . . . more if we can manage it on that day . . .

There's a fast train from York . . . Dean Street, yes. We're still here. Look forward to it."

Diana felt the constricting cork of self-doubt pop and a fizz of excitement bubble up inside her. Before the attack of stage fright had drained her courage, Diana herself had believed that curiosity, if nothing else, would win her a hearing. Little by little and step by step, she would prove to herself and others that she was right about everything. They would find she was more than a sideshow.

"Two weeks, Mr. Sedgely!" Diana put the telephone down. The billowing mousse of joyous relief flowed into every extremity of her body. The fire was crackling briskly now, causing small fragments of coal to spit on to the marble hearth. Sedgely continued his attentions to it without turning round, but from the way his ears twitched, Diana knew he was smiling. "I shall write a proposal. Just something brief for them all to read . . . to make sure I don't forget anything we've said. Do you want to come with me?"

Sedgely swung round from the hearth, squatting on his heels. Diana was half-walking, half-skipping round the room with her hands pressed together, trying to avoid breaking into an undignified, girlish dance.

"That I don't, Mrs. Neville. You're the one to do all t'talking. You'll not need me now you've broken t'ice."

Diana nodded, agreeing. "I feel like celebrating. What shall we do to celebrate, Mr. Sedgely?"

"T'parsnip wine, I reckon," Sedgely replied laconically. "Four year old now and there's plenty of it. Your aunt were a devil for t'parsnip wine. Swore by it, she did. I'll go down and get t'first bottle. You keep your eye on that fire, Mrs. Neville."

While he made his brief foray to the cellar, Diana studied the portrait of Aunt Thea painted by de Lazlo when she was a girl. A lace scarf was thrown coquettishly over the mass of dark, curly hair, falling on to creamy naked shoulders. In the lineaments of her face and the hyacinth eyes, Diana traced her own dim reflection. The painted lips curved at the corners, sweetly sardonic.

"You know, Aunt Thea," Diana whispered, "I've spent my life listening to other people. Now they're going to listen to *me*!"

By the time the great bells informed the townsfolk of

Nidcaster that it was six o'clock on a clear, fine evening, Sedgely and Diana were companionably and most agreeably drunk. Diana played the piano rather badly and Sedgely sang "The Surrey with the Fringe on Top" very well. He also smoked two full pipes of tobacco, a thing he never did, he told Diana, unless there were "something worth smoking about."

CHAPTER
5

❦ THE ELECTRIC ALARM clock shrieked, terrorizing the murky images moving behind Diana's fluttering eyelids. The goblins of unresolved conflict which prowled in her troubled, night-time mind, scuttled away from the snatch of wakefulness. But it was still dark. Beneath the half-tester of Aunt Thea's bed Diana sat bolt upright, shocked out of a fitful slumber. She groped clumsily for the clock. It was on the night table but the bed hangings got in the way and it was some moments before her hand could silence its mindless racket.

When it was stilled and she turned on the lamp, Diana tried to catch at the ragged coat tails of her dreams. Yolanda had been there somewhere. It had all been mixed up and miserable. Five o'clock. She must be at York City station by half past six. From the bell tower, the church clock began its harmonious confirmation of the hour. There was plenty of time.

Breathing easier, she checked the list of things she had to remember. The proposal, six copies. That should be enough. They were downstairs in a battered crocodile briefcase she'd found in the little book room or library she had taken for her study. Return ticket for the train with reserved seat. That was in her handbag which stood ready with her shoes on the threadbare carpet. Her clothes hung outside the cavernous old wardrobe.

The Valentino dress and coat were far from new, but it was still her favourite outfit. It had been bought the year Michael had rented a box at Epsom for the Derby. She remembered now, being wool, it had been much too warm, really. But an innate frugality had always stopped her spending extravagantly

75

on summer clothes. Impeccably cut, the garment's clean, elegant lines emphasised the spareness of her figure and followed her movements like a second skin. Once she had it on, she could forget it. Diana asked nothing more from clothes. The colour, a bright rust, coaxed the violet out of her eyes. She had decided to wear a hat because it would give her a little height and shade her face from the cruelty of tactless office lighting. Forty was very late for large undertakings.

Over the past few days, Diana had fought against the vertigo that attacks people in the crucial forty-first year. The pinnacle of her years had been reached. Looking back at the climb, she marvelled that she had done so little. More than two decades had gone by, full of motherhood and Michael. Serving his interests, his career and nursing Yolanda through the alarms of babyhood and childhood into adolescence. That is what she had done. No more.

Once that hated inch of growth had put an end to her dreams of a future with the ballet, Michael had been there. He was her total consolation and the only alternative future she had wanted. His positive, laughing confidence in life had carried her through. Within a year, they had been married. She had never even learned to type.

She had worked once, very briefly, helping out in the offices of a music publisher her father knew. It hadn't been much of a job, but she had loved it. Going off every day to a place where she was known and welcome. She'd even had a little money to spend. Money for birthday and Christmas presents, so that the presents were really from her and not from Michael. It was absurd to give your husband a present paid for out of his own money. But Michael had soon put a stop to all that.

"Real men don't have wives who work," he had said bitterly. "All these womens' lib harridans and the poor downtrodden sods who wash dishes and do laundry because they're too shit scared of being out of step to put their bloody feet down . . . they can say what they like. It's degrading. A man should work for his wife and a woman should look after her husband. What's so wrong with that? It was good enough for my parents. Don't I give you everything? Why do you want to waste your time on some tuppenny halfpenny firm who pay you peanuts and make me feel like the sort of silly cunt who can't earn enough to support his own woman?"

"But Michael, darling," she had pleaded reasonably, "nobody thinks like that any more. A lot of wives work. Lots of people I know . . . look at Mummy."

He had shouted her down. His big voice always reduced her to quivering silence.

"You're *my* wife!"

No more had been said just then, but later when she reached for him in bed, he had turned away and said he couldn't make love to a woman who despised him. He had sounded so desperately hurt. She had tried once more to reassure him but he wouldn't listen. He got out of bed saying he was going to fetch a glass of water. But he never came back that night.

It hadn't seemed worth risking her marriage over. It was true. She did earn only a few pounds. Sometimes the tubes were so full that train after train went by and she would be late home. Then she would find Michael there at their pretty Battersea cottage waiting for her in the dark in silent, enraged protest. She gave it up because she loved him. His joy and relief had been her reward. And then there was Yolanda.

The ancient tea making machine on the other side of the bed clattered and gurgled into belated life. One of those unreliable gadgets which only the rich could afford.

Perhaps, Diana mused as she sipped from the china mug of beige, leaf-speckled fluid, it was already too late. When you are forty, she thought, you know far too much about what can go wrong. Far too much. The steep escarpment of years she had not yet lived yawned at her feet. Would she totter weakly down those years, dragged by gravity until she fell into her grave?

Belief in her idea, its truth and viability, was as powerful as ever. But had she the strength to see it through? You are only one person, a small insidious voice taunted. Not rich, not clever and no longer young. Will they listen? Will you be able to make them listen?

Many times lately, sitting in the book-lined room where the unpruned spurs of an espalier pear rapped at the window panes, she had chased the same doubts fiercely from her mind. Then she had bent over the proposal again, cutting, pruning and refining the outpouring of her thoughts. When at last they were reduced to a crisp, coherent text, she typed them painfully with two fingers on a manual typewriter, her fingers plunging between the keys with tiresome frequency. There were three whole pages. Michael had always said he never liked to see a rambling screed. "If it's worth saying, it will fit into half a page." This time she had trusted her own judgment. Three pages. It could not be said in less.

Diana swung her legs over the edge of the high bed. Her legs stuck straight out in front of her so that she could see her feet. She hated the sight of her feet. The toes, bunched and misshapen by blocks, were a constant reminder of wasted pain. Effort that need never have been made. Quickly, Diana thrust them into her slippers. None of that mattered now.

Padding quietly across the room, she drew the heavy damask curtains back. Outside the street lamps in the lane dropped cones of yellow light over the east wall into the sombre garden. Beyond them a fringe of grey was stealing over the massed shapes of the town roofs. This was the day on which she would begin walking, strong and straight, down that slope of years. And on the way, she would do something. Nobody, she told herself, is going to stop me this time.

❦ ON SALISBURY PLAIN, in a corrective institution so experimentally liberal the Home Office was anxious to protect it from publicity, Michael Neville woke early on the same day. The morning of October 7th. In the twenty-one days since his arrival a reliable internal clock had ensured that he was aware of the prison before its staff and other inmates were aware of him. To be alert in advance of the opposition had been a lifelong habit. He had no intention of abandoning the practice now. Opening his eyes before the prison's corporate awakening was the sole, major pre-emptive option left to him. Clinging to the habit was a conscious decision.

His morning erection was a sullen, short lived affair. As his eyes adjusted to the darkness, diluted by a dim light in the corridor leaking through the clear pane of glass above the locked door, Michael could make out the geography of Room 91. He had it to himself, thank God.

There was no talk of cells here. The Governor, a reformer, had sanitised the vocabulary of incarceration to the point where even locks were designated "security components." The already euphemistic "inmates" had been replaced with the cumbersome phrase, "programme participants." That had been the best the Governor could do.

Michael was "PP Neville (203/91)." Only the number was never mentioned. They called him by his first name in tones of relentless understanding. Michael detested it. By taking away the staple foods of resentment, they inflicted a more subtle torture. They had hated him enough to lock him up. Indecently, they were depriving him of the right to hate back. But Michael had not given up.

He refused to respond with overt relief that the nightmare noises, stenches and enforced camaraderie of Brixton had been left behind. They could stuff their compassion. And their curiosity. Room 91, like its inhabitant, was mute. It had acquired none of the personal touches the prison authorities here were so keen to encourage.

Michael propped himself up in bed with his hands behind his head. He looked around in the gloom, his eyes traversing every surface like a geiger counter, checking that no article not supplied by the prison was visible and that none of the furniture had acquired an unguarded, idiosyncratic slant. It was Michael's protest to reveal nothing of himself, to give no clue to his personality. No handles.

The sheet steel furniture was battleship grey. A clothes locker, a desk with some drawers of the type used in the forces, a bed, chair and some stacking shelves were the standard issue. There was a flush lavatory in the corner near the window and a hand basin. It was an improvement on the chamber pots and slimy communal wash-rooms of Brixton. But he wasn't tempted to make himself at home. Even his toothbrush was hidden in a drawer. There were no books, no photographs, no calendars. Letters—there had only been two, both from Diana—he read and destroyed. There was nothing in them anyway. Just platitudes about some ramshackle old ruin in Yorkshire where she was living. He didn't know whether he missed her or not. An unacknowledged shame prevented him from thinking of her. The shame of failure. Sexually, he was numb.

Yolanda hadn't written yet. Michael's mind shrunk from thinking about his daughter. She would be all right. She was like him. Resilient. A tough little nut.

A dull rivulet of light gleamed on the polished linoleum floor.

"Bit stark in here, isn't it, Mike? You should get the wife to send you some rugs and stuff," the young deputy governor in charge of the wing had advised matily in his first week. "Might as well be comfortable. How about some music making gear? We've got a great tape library."

Rewarded with an arctic stare, the deputy had made a note on his pad to arrange an interview with the prison psychologist for PP Neville. *Dangerously withdrawn.* Michael, with his well-developed facility for reading upside down, looked forward to the confrontation. He wasn't in the business of providing job satisfaction for do-gooders and progressives.

He got up to relieve his bladder, shooting the stream into the blue tinted water with maximum force, a small, impotent expression of anger. Shaking his penis in the dark, he drew the cheap green curtain back from the window so that he could watch the weak, yellowish bubbles of urine pop and disappear. Life had reduced to very small things. Michael washed his hands, then cleaned his teeth in the semi-darkness and shaved with rapid, predetermined strokes. He dried his hands on the government issue towel and refolded it with meticulous neatness.

Every morning when the warder opened the door of Room 91, PP Neville was found already dressed and his bed made with hospital precision. He stood in the same position, with his back to the door, arms folded, looking out of the window across the prison compound and its lightly guarded boundary fence to the lightening plain. So far, the daily reports told the Governor, this behavior had never varied.

The warders did not know what to make of him. Their cheerful morning greetings grew more strained as day followed day. PP Neville's response remained mildly contemptuous. "Good morning, sir," he said.

"Tell him to drop the 'sir'. The Governor doesn't like it," the deputy admonished his staff at their weekly meeting.

"He's a model PP," one recently joined probationer ventured innocently.

"He's a bloody menace and he's making monkeys out of all of us." The young man's naive assessment was drowned in a storm of derision.

The officers were the carefully skimmed cream of the prison service. Working with high grade, white collar offenders was a plum job. There was optimism, hope for the future. Their charges would do their bird quietly and never darken the doors of a prison again. First timers, the lot of them, they were usually depressed when they arrived. That was to be expected.

None of them, as the deputy pointed out for the benefit of his probationer, had ever believed that they would one day find themselves in the dock. And when the unthinkable did happen, they had unwavering faith in their legal representatives. There was always a way round things. That was the thing they had in common, a sort of culture. Professional men stuck together, dug each other out of holes. For them, the law was not something to fear. It was there to control others and help them. The betrayal of that belief must have shaken Neville, of all people, to his foundations. In his case, the catastrophe had been of titanic proportions.

The group argued these points back and forth, expounding them to the probationer.

"It's the same for all of them. Can you imagine what it's like to have your bath in the 'en-suite' one night, kiss the wife goodbye in the morning, like always, tell her you'll be home by six. And then, bingo. It all goes wrong and you're carted off to the nick and told to strip naked, given a shower you don't need and banged up with a lot of blokes in for armed robbery and rape? Neville's used to saying, 'Come here, go there and lick my bloody arse' . . . then all of a sudden the boot's on the other foot. He'll take longer to get over it than the rest."

It sounded reasonable, but the prison psychologist was not so sure. He'd found Neville depressed, all right. But he was tough, obstructive. Fighting it every inch of the way. It was as if he was trying to make something out his depression. Something usable. Remorse? He hadn't seen much sign of it. Asked how he felt about his conviction, Neville had just said it was "unfortunate." Trying to explore the degree of guilt he felt, the psychologist had asked him about the trial. Neville had shrugged. "Get a transcript and read it for yourself," had been his only reply. He was polite, just—but monosyllabic and unsmiling.

"How's he getting on with the other guys?" the deputy asked. "Anyone?"

The junior staff each contributed a snippet of information. But it was thin. Nothing much to go on.

The other PPs seemed to like him in a nervous sort of way. Touch of hero worship, perhaps. After all, he'd been a big shot in a world most of them understood. More or less. But he had no special friends. In the common room he read the *Financial Times* and played billiards. He had mastered the computerised lathe in the small engineering workshop in record time. He worked quietly, with intense concentration, discouraging conversation. At meal times in the canteen he ate moderate amounts, always sitting at the nearest empty table to the self-service area. The psychologist had watched it all and drawn no real conclusions.

"What about his family?" The deputy probed. "Isn't he worried about them? They usually are." He looked directly at the social counsellor.

"Nope. Says his wife has 'retired to her own property in Yorkshire.' *Very* posh. I asked him if she was OK for money and offered to get on to social services. Gordon Bennett! If looks could kill. Won't say a word about his daughter. Just glares."

The deputy sighed. An ex-multimillionaire *would* be prickly about social security payments. He looked at his watch. This meeting had gone on long enough. It was time for the shift change and a pint of bitter with the lads down at the Ancient Briton.

"Well, then," he appealed to the psychologist, "what's the bottom line?"

"He's deliberately repressing his own personality and that's all I can tell you at this stage," the psychologist snapped, thrusting his hands into the pockets of his leather jacket. His brush with Neville had done nothing to improve his professional self-esteem. "Maybe he thinks if he turns himself into a non-person he won't actually be here. That could be dangerous."

Reading the minutes of the meeting later, the Governor was reassuring.

"I shouldn't worry too much about Neville. He's a smart bastard." The Governor stopped speaking and frowned. That was exactly the sort of language he disapproved of in connection with programme participants. Neville was certainly having a disruptive effect. The Governor didn't like admitting to failure. And it was too early yet to be sure. "Look, he's old soldiering. He's like me ... old enough to have done National Service. Working his ticket. He may even have figured out I can recommend an early release on mental health grounds. Just keep an eye on him."

Prison walls may be thick, but as in any tight packed community, they are not impermeable. Michael found the gossip about himself and his future interesting. The idea that stepping up his campaign could be the means of tunnelling a way out of the mind deadening environment of the open prison appealed to him. He had no desire to assume the leadership of a bunch of bent accountants and building society clerks. He wanted the real world, where pissing in the pot wasn't a major event and battered cod wasn't the gastronomic highlight of the week.

He was immersed in these thoughts later on in the morning as he readjusted the lathe's parameters for a new metal component spec when the warder on duty came up to him. Programme leaders, they preferred to call themselves. Michael regarded him with careful blankness.

"You'd better drop that now, Mike," the programme leader, dressed in the same overalls as himself, shouted above the din of the engineering shop. "The Governor wants to see you right away. Your kid's showed up."

Michael's face registered a kaleidoscope of emotions.

"Yolanda! Here?" He grasped the programme leader's arm, acutely anxious, unaware of what he was doing.

Gotcher! The programme leader smiled to himself. So bloody Neville was flesh and blood, after all.

❧ WISELY, THE GOVERNOR left them together in his office. They stared at each other wordlessly for a minute. Yolanda was shocked to see her father in an overall. A workman's overall. He had always been so dapper. Even on holiday he never wore anything but a suit and tie. On a trip to the Pyramids once, he'd flatly refused to do so much as loosen his collar. She remembered because her mother had joked that Daddy was prudish about necks. Daddy had said it was a feeble joke.

But they had all laughed just the same. It had been a happy time.

Michael had never felt so helpless, so powerless to comfort or protect. She would have done better to stay away. And yet he longed for her. In her, he saw himself reborn. The strong gene carried forward, like a credit balance. Something nobody could argue with. Proof positive of potency. His only, beautiful child.

She was wearing the Tiverton track suit and anorak with her long blond hair scraped back into a scruffy pony tail with an elastic band. Had she come from school? But how and with whom?

"You look a bit of a mess, Landa." He tried out his voice cautiously.

"Speak for yourself," Yolanda shot back surlily. And then she broke down in noisy tears. The sort that only children can cry, angry and accusing. Grief that their world, their safe world had turned out to be a house of cards. She howled with the piteousness of those who have been lied to, betrayed. The fortress of her father's invincibility had crumbled around her. The tears coursed down her cheeks, making channels through a layer of grime.

She must have hitch-hiked, Michael realised. Bloody dangerous. Laverack would get his balls screwed off for this. He went to her, perilously close to tears himself. But she pushed him away, furiously. How very much she was his own child. He grabbed her, with an equal tender fury at the rejection, and held her in a vice-like grip against his chest. Gradually, her convulsions calmed and she laid her head against him. He lowered his own head till his chin rested on the top of hers.

"Do you hate me, Landa?" His voice was now a croaked whisper.

Yolanda nodded vigorously and then shook her head slowly.

"Why did you come?"

"To see you," Yolanda stated in a small voice.

"And now you have, do you feel any better?" Michael asked her, brushing her hair with his lips.

"A bit."

They talked then, about what Michael was doing. Did he like it? she asked.

"It was quite interesting at first. But once you've done it, you've done it. One component type's much like another and the lathe's never any different. Good machine, though."

He had been about to say he'd buy shares in the company that manufactured the lathe. The reflex was still there although the muscle was gone. He could buy nothing.

"Will they let you do anything else, Daddy?" Unconsciously, both Yolanda and her father were coming to terms with what had happened to him.

"Oh yes, they'll let me breed pigs here if I want to."

"Oh! But that *does* sound fun. Don't you want . . . ?"

"No!" Michael cut her off. He wanted to do what he had always done. That and nothing else. He wanted to feel the balance of the economic world tip beneath his feet when he moved. But Yolanda was too young to understand that. And the wrong sex.

"I think I might have a bash at financial journalism."

The thought had come, unbidden, like a ray of sunshine piercing the leaden dullness in his mind.

"You know, all those articles in my pink newspaper you say is so boring. And there are other journals too. I could stir the pudding without having to get my hands dirty."

Michael was smiling. Yolanda saw it was the old crocodile grin he used to tease her with in her bath when she was small. Mummy had always made a fuss about over-stimulation at bedtime. And a futile protest it had been. When Michael wanted to play with Yolanda, he played with her, no matter what anybody else said. Sometimes he would get her out of bed, late at night, to show to his friends. She would perch on his shoulders, pyjama'd and pretty, loving the attention and enjoying the sips of wine. How *cross* it had all made Mummy. Part of the fun.

"Oh, Daddy," Yolanda replied to her father's proposal, "that's an absolutely brilliant idea! You could have a byline. How about . . ."

"Jailbird?"

They were both laughing, Yolanda sitting in the Governor's big swivel chair with her legs over the arm, when the Governor himself came in, beaming. Neville was going to be all right. This handsome, arrogant little minx of a daughter of his had done the trick. It had made an interesting variation in the routine to be told by a pony-tailed teenager, none too clean either, that she'd come to see her father and if she wasn't allowed to, she'd tear his prison brick from brick. A chip off the old block—which might be a good thing, and might not, the Governor thought ruefully.

"Well now, young woman. We must do something about sending you back where you came from. The Home Office will be on my tail if I start a ladies' wing without so much as a by your leave."

The Governor observed Yolanda's dirty, tear streaked face with a combination of pity and detachment. He had daughters of his own.

"Come on," he said kindly, "why don't you just pop in there and wash your face? I think you'll find everything you need." He indicated the door of the private wash-room which led off his bright, modern office. "Your father can just give me a few details."

When Yolanda emerged, Michael had supplied the Governor with the telephone numbers of the school and Gilbert's Tower.

"Now then, Neville. Why don't you and Yolanda here walk down to the Ancient Briton for a bite while I make some arrangements? Pick up some money at reception on the way out." The Governor eyed Michael meaningfully and lifted the telephone on his desk. "We'll square it up later. And when you come back, Yolanda, if there's time, you can go and have a look at the farm we have here."

The Governor was gratified by the stupefaction in Neville's face and the joy in his daughter's. Trust was the basis of his method. It had never failed yet. His programme participants left the unit not only reformed, but transformed. They had never really been bad men in the first place. Misguided at worst. Several had gone into welfare work, one had even been ordained. He had hopes, now, of Neville.

When contacted, Laverack's obvious, overwhelming relief touched a nerve in the Governor. They were both in the caring business, after all. They had a mutual interest in the affairs of this very troubled family. The two men talked, communicating their interlocking anxieties with ease and confidence.

"I've tried talking to Yolanda," Mr. Laverack told the Governor. "She's closed up like a clam. I honestly believe she'd feel more secure at home. I gather there's somewhere suitable for her to go and in my judgment, now is the right moment. If it's left another year or even two, as her mother seems to want, does want, this family may never achieve any cohesion again. The effects on the child could be profoundly and permanently demoralising."

The Governor did not reply immediately. He sucked his teeth meditatively.

"Have you tried talking to the mother?"

"Mrs. Neville? Yes, I have. It didn't go well. She was on the offensive from the start. I think she's afraid she won't be able to cope with Yolanda without Neville's support. You've got to understand, this young woman has an exceptionally powerful personality."

The Governor did understand that completely. "What did Yolanda say about going home herself?"

"She says her mother and she have nothing in common, never have had and her mother doesn't want her, anyway. Too wrapped up in her own concerns. That's unlikely though I do think both Yolanda and Mrs. Neville are backing away from each other."

Speaking with a warmth which would have surprised Diana, the headmaster described her skill and courage in protecting her daughter's practical interests as she saw them. "More than a match for a simple schoolmaster . . .

"But frankly," he concluded, "I think she's got to confront the emotional problems. It's as if she didn't realise there are any. Yolanda's always been closest to her father and Mrs. Neville may feel inadequate in this context."

The two men agreed that Laverack should keep trying the Nidcaster number.

"And whatever you do, don't take up any hard and fast positions. You're reporting an incident, that's all. These two have got to come together on their *own* initiative. I'll have a word with Neville, too. We must get this family pulling in the same direction."

The Governor put the telephone down and frowned. He'd done it again. Stuck his neck out. Still, that was all part of his job. Making sure the programme participants had a warm, supportive family to go back to.

The Governor drove Yolanda back to Somerset himself. On the way there, Yolanda asked him what he thought of her father taking up financial journalism.

"You know, writing about business and money. Daddy knows more about that sort of thing than anybody," she affirmed proudly.

The Governor had thought it an excellent proposition. First rate. Nothing would be gained by allowing a top flight mind like her father's to rot. Mentally, the Governor congratulated himself. Neville had worked out his own salvation. Patience had paid off. He looked sideways at Yolanda in the car. Without her irregular intervention, it would never have happened. Judging by what Laverack had said, they made quite a pair, Diana Neville and her daughter.

As the Governor's car swung between the gateposts of Tiverton Abbey Yolanda told him that in a strange sort of way, it had been one of the nicest days of her life. Was that crazy?

No, it wasn't, the Governor replied. But he thought she should go home.

"And Daddy's idea . . . about writing. You will let him do it, won't you?"

"With your permission, young lady," the Governor smiled gravely at Yolanda's earnest entreaty, "I'll *make* him do it."

Yolanda was jubilant. Daddy was still *Daddy*. He always would be, wherever he went.

❧ DIANA, TOO, HAD reason to celebrate. All her fears had proved groundless. In the end, the Epoch partnership had endorsed her idea with enthusiasm.

She had been kindly received in the Dean Street agency. At first it had only been Mr. Olaff but after reading her three-page proposal he'd soon gone and fetched his partners. In the end, they were all there sitting round the smoked glass table in the conference room, poring over the typed sheets. When they looked up, there had been respect in their eyes. Suddenly, Diana had been entirely at ease.

"So what you're saying," the one in the eccentrically thin tie with rimless spectacles said, "is that the organic factor is only a part of it? That environmentally friendly produce won't attract a market unless a tangible luxury factor is built in?"

Diana had amplified the point confidently for the benefit of the meeting.

"Now if you add an element of genuine, self-indulgent self-interest ... rarity, luxury, and positive individual identification ..."

They stopped her there. They didn't know what she meant.

"Well, look at wine labels. People like hallmarks. Something to tell them where the commodity they've paid a stiff price for comes from. Snobbery comes into it too. We've got to make it so that a Peregrine peach from my orchard, for example ... Garden No. 1, Gilbert's Tower, Nidcaster, Yorkshire ... Proprietor, Diana Neville ... is seen as being infinitely more glamorous than some anonymous peach from somewhere in Italy, nobody knows where."

The partners had nodded sagely and conferred in muttered voices amongst themselves.

"We've understood your point about supply coming from domestic gardens to ensure variety," Mr. Olaff had been elected spokesman for this query, "but could you tell us how you see the commercial significance of retired people?"

At that point they had been interrupted by the appearance of a tray of sandwiches and two bottles of wine. They were brought in by a girl of devastatingly trendy appearance. She was the girl Diana had spoken to on the telephone. The receptionist. Diana watched entranced while she struggled to recover a crumb which had fallen on the carpet. The astonishing length of her fingernails made it difficult. Eventually, Diana did it for her.

"It must be like using chopsticks," she told the girl.

The girl laughed and the air of relaxation in the room encouraged the men to loosen their ties and take off their jackets. Diana removed her hat. Height had not been necessary. They were on her side.

Later she had returned to the point made about retired people.

"It's a double-edged benefit. Retired people these days are often vigorous, with many years of active life in front of them. They have the energy to engage in a new, small scale project. Many of them already have the means—a small garden. Not that we're ruling out bigger ones, of course. Also, this is the first generation of widely distributed affluence among the elderly. Pension schemes are responsible. As a result, garden centres have sold gardening to them. The next logical step is for them to sell the results back into the marketplace. That feeling of usefulness will appeal to them, boosting their incomes and ensuring us a supply.

"For the consumer," Diana went on without a pause, a half finished glass of wine at her elbow, "well, who would you rather buy from? Somebody you can relate to with only a small axe to grind, or a nameless, faceless power farmer with a big axe to grind? And remember, we've got an awful lot of retired people in this country."

They had been convinced and charmed. Diana's lucidity and glowing conviction had fascinated these sophisticated men from a world where original thinking was the raw material of success. Only ideas were very hard to come by. New ones were like gold dust. And, as Olaff later pointed out to his partners, this whole project was one which was going to need a high degree of personal leadership. Diana, he said, had the charisma to carry it through.

"Remember, she made a big impact during the trial and she said nothing then. Imagine how our Diana will come over with a voice!"

They talked until long after the staff had gone home.

Even the financial section of Diana's proposal, the one which had given her most uneasiness, was accepted readily. She had no money. Epoch's first job was to make a full speculative presentation to a merchant bank. If they succeeded in winning her the support of a bank, they would recover the cost of the presentation *and* get the account on a guaranteed five-year contract. It was a risk. About ten thousand pounds' worth of risk. But it was well worth it. Epoch, they told Diana, was sure they had another client. They hoped the association would be long and happy.

❦ SITTING NOW IN the first class dining car of the York train from King's Cross, she felt only the tiniest pang of guilt. After all, the promised lunch had never materialised. They had been too busy talking. Six hours, even six hours of enthusiasm, was exhausting.

Idly, she flipped open the back number of *The Grower* which had been dug out of the agency's library and lent to her. All around her tired businessmen were engaged in similar pursuits. Reading trade journals, examining figures, looking through the evening papers. They had all given their orders. Smoked trout or oxtail soup. Diana had chosen the trout, but as a harassed steward had explained to her, service would not begin before Peterborough. They were short staffed. Diana's faint scowl of disgruntlement had amused a man who sat in the corner seat diagonally opposite. She was hungry.

"When you've been on this ruddy train as often as I have, dear," he consoled, "you'll be resigned to it."

They chatted then, desultorily. He travelled in fertilisers. Chemical fertilisers. Grantham was his home base. Noticing that Diana was reading *The Grower*, he asked her what her own involvement in the world of arable agriculture was. Diana was wary. It was too early to answer that sort of question. She was grateful when the man prevented any reply by seizing the magazine and pointing at its cover. There was a large colour photograph of a man whose features Diana herself had thought arresting.

"That's one of our biggest customers. Philip Strang-Steele. Got a big spread in East Anglia. Property abroad, too. Buys tons from us every year."

Diana looked more closely at the photograph. It was strange to think that this man, with his crisply curling grey hair, light, penetrating blue eyes and expression of amused cynicism, was now a rival. An opponent. He stood for everything she and Mr. Sedgely were against. Uniformity, damaging bio-chemical technology and above all, the drabness of mass produced food. He was one of those whose profits were leaching the soil of any natural fecundity and depriving the world of poetry.

Opening the magazine to read the article about him, Diana gently withdrew from any further conversation with the fertiliser man. She was weary and preoccupied with her own thoughts.

The article was by Strang-Steele himself. In it he assured fellow large-scale growers that the organic movement posed no threat to conventional producers. The organic movement was a fringe thing, he said, fraught with commercial risks for the growers themselves, the wholesalers and retailers. Because of that, the supply was uneven, the produce when available was unsightly and too costly to be attractive to all but the most

committed consumer. Packaging and presentation was bad. The
vast majority of consumers liked their fruit and vegetables to
look good.

I entirely agree with you, Mr. Strang-Steele, Diana
thought contentedly. You are so absolutely right. But what if
organic produce did look good? What if packaging and
presentation were professional, stimulating? What if the
consumer was weaned off the idea of a year round unfaltering supply of the same old thing? What if the consumer began to see shopping for fruit and vegetables as an exciting,
creative experience? And that's just what we're going to
achieve. So you'd better watch out, Mr. Big. The little people are on the march!

Diana closed her eyes, smiling.

A jolt as the train halted clumsily forced her to open her
eyes again. The door of the carriage opened, letting in a blast
of cold air. She heard a man's voice taking leave of somebody
on the platform. Her musical ear identified the strands running
through its subdued, cultivated resonance. A distant throb of
Scottish rhythm, a metallic brightness to the vowels which
might almost be French . . . Latin, anyway. It was unusual,
compelling.

Diana was again perusing the magazine, looking at small advertisements for machinery, when she became aware of a large
man in a well-tailored grey flannel suit settling himself into the
reserved seat directly in front of her. He exchanged greetings
easily with the fertiliser salesman in the corner seat. Evidently
they knew each other. It was a natural reflex to look up.

Recognition was instant. Philip Strang-Steele's eyes met her
own and held her gaze.

"This lady's in the agro-chemical trade . . . or the growing
business, she hasn't said which . . ." The salesman attempted to
effect an introduction.

Strang-Steele waited, his left eyebrow cocked quizzically,
waiting for Diana to declare herself. Her face interested him.
But it stirred no recollection in his memory. Diana smiled
briefly, close lipped, and looked down again. Involuntarily, she
shuddered. Like a cat shaking raindrops from its fur. No man
had a right to look at her like that.

The moment passed and the man in the window seat engaged Strang-Steele in talk. The meal came, the steward's banter covering the inept service.

"What'll you be having then, Mr. Strang-Steele, sir?"

Diana's eyes were lowered. She felt rather than saw the grey head lean across the table, courteously confidential.

"Would you recommend the smoked trout?" The voice simmered in her nerve ends.

Diana indicated with the minimum of gesture and no words that the trout was passable. Quietly, Strang-Steele gave his order.

Throughout the meal, Diana ate mechanically. She watched Strang-Steele's large, well-manicured hands deal decisively with first the trout and then the guinea fowl, conveying the food from his plate to his unseen mouth. She herself ate little, pushing most of the food to the side of her plate.

The steward removed the dishes, plaguing her with mock reproaches. Strang-Steele watched, his expression withdrawn. The salesman looked from Diana to the steward, his face alight with hope. He kept leaning forward to read Strang-Steel's features too, willing his companions' reserve to break down.

She refused the pudding, as did Strang-Steele. The salesman ate Black Forest gâteau on his own, clashing his cutlery in disappointment. He was naturally gregarious.

The two men got off at Grantham, to Diana's infinite relief.

Strang-Steele recovered a furled umbrella from the parcel shelf, apologising to Diana for disturbing her. He nodded, almost curtly, wishing her a good night and safe journey. Empty, formal words. There was no smile on his pale, chiselled mouth but his eyes stroked like warm fingertips on cool piano keys.

She read his article again. This time she heard the rich, complex tones of his voice. They came to her ear as her eye struck each written syllable. It was the same way her father had read a musical score. Every note vivid and alive in the mind.

Diana had no doubt that the text came from Strang-Steele's own hand. It was cogently expressed, logical—but wrong.

She drank her coffee, more disturbed by the encounter than she would allow herself to admit.

At Gilbert's Tower, the telephone shrilled through the empty house. Ten rings, every thirty minutes.

CHAPTER
6

❦ GILBERT'S TOWER WAS now a busy place. Its pulse quickened to the infusion of new life which Diana brought back with her from London. Yolanda's youthful presence too, her questions, laughter, demands and door slamming, pushed the shades of previous occupants back to the margins. The telephone rang incessantly, dislodging the silences as the old floorboards grumbled under the pressure of running feet. The house stretched and creaked, awaking to the next phase of its existence. Outside, the vernal equinox shortened the days while the soil steamed in the cooling sunshine, preparing to sleep away the winter.

At first, Yolanda claimed the lion's share of Diana's attention. She gave it unstintingly. And although a taut forty-eight-hour period passed in which Yolanda oscillated between a sullen, monosyllabic lumpishness and volcanic explosions of opinion on every topic from British justice to the stupidity of parents, Diana kept her temper. Her reward was not long in coming. Soon, Yolanda had talked herself out. And if she was not purged of every last drop of bitterness, at least she had discovered that her mother would listen. Now that Diana received many letters through the post with typewritten envelopes, her attention had a measurable value.

This fine pointer to her mother's new importance in the world led Yolanda to confide her father's plans. It was market day in Nidcaster and they talked whilst threading their way among the crowded stalls in the town's medieval square. Aunt Thea advised buying butter from a certain trader stationed near

95

the market cross. "If you like your dairy goods from cows with names, not numbers."

"He calls it 'financial journalism.' He thought of it whilst I was there." Yolanda's voice penetrated Diana's absorbed contemplation of the array of buttercup yellow sculptures.

"But that's quite marvellous, darling! What a resourceful man your father is! We must make an album of every single thing he gets printed. By the time he comes home, he'll have a brand new career ready made."

The stallholder, a mountainous woman in a flowered overall with a brick red face, placed her hands on her hips.

"Now, what'll you have, Mrs. Neville?"

"Does everybody here know you, Mummy?" Yolanda asked on the way back down the lane.

Diana only smiled in reply. Already she had caught something of her neighbour's reticence.

Inevitably, Yolanda was subject to mood swings.

"Of course, this is only temporary, isn't it?" she said at the end of her second day. "Nidcaster isn't a serious place to live. Not very practical for someone like Daddy. We'll have to go back to London eventually."

Diana said nothing, allowing Gilbert's Tower to disarm Yolanda by stealth. And in the hours that Diana was forced to spend at her desk, her daughter explored the domain, opening doors and pursuing shadows. Indoors and out, the orange cat walked before her, its tail held rigidly aloft like a wand of office.

"He's like a museum curator, isn't he?" Yolanda smiled broadly, clearly enchanted by her guide.

Leaving them to themselves, Diana turned back to the queries and proposals that had followed her from Epoch. There were many questions which had been overlooked at the meeting. Some were beyond her own or Sedgely's competence to answer. It would also, Merlin Olaff pointed out in a long letter, materially assist Epoch to generate interest in the right quarter, if Diana's own property were shipshape and sample figures could be quoted for the yield of every tree.

There was much more and a great deal to be done. It was only fair, Diana allowed, that she should first commit her own time and resources to making the walled garden at Gilbert's Tower the example which could be quoted and copied. It was an act of faith that would cost more money than she actually had. Reserving the problem of raising it to herself, she sought Sedgely's views on other matters.

"Nay, Mrs. Neville," Sedgely demurred as he sat with her in his own, personalised area of the third glasshouse. "Some of these old trees will come down this autumn if they're not pruned. They've too much up top. Wind catches 'em and loosens t'roots. Some of them are that neglected it would take half a dozen men to straighten 'em out before t'gales hit us. They're old-fashioned standards, you see. Not grown on dwarfing stocks like these modern trees."

"But do you know what to do yourself, Mr. Sedgely?"

Diana resisted any temptation to tap her toe on the quarry tiled floor whilst Sedgely drew on his empty pipe, meditating his answer. He was not a man to be hurried.

"Aye," he admitted finally. "I do, up to a point, but there's always improved methods to take into t'account. And there's nowt I can do with these steel pins in me legs. I've tidied some of them up wi' t'long shears for a few years past. But it's got beyond that. We need some smart young feller from one of these 'ere agricultural colleges to give advice, like . . . and then there's t'labour to think of."

Diana left Sedgely to his work of classifying herbaceous seed and went back to the house to look up the name of the nearest agricultural or horticultural college. Thorpe Overblow Manor. The principal of the horticultural wing was helpful. He said he had a number of young men and women in their final year, several of whom were interested in top fruit. He was sure one or more of them would be glad to give advice on Mrs. Neville's property in exchange for a modest fee. One, a research student, had completed a special project on organic methods. It was an expanding market. Was that of any interest? Diana assured him it was of quite particular interest. The principal rang off with a promise that he would contact her soon with the young man's name and telephone number.

"This is quite off the record, you see, as far as the college is concerned. You must come to your own arrangement."

Straining her eyes to read the thickening pile of correspondence in the westering sun's magenta rays, Diana was seated at her desk in the book room when the newly installed telephone extension rang. She lifted it absently, expecting to hear again from the agricultural college.

"Gilbert's Tower, Diana Neville speaking."

"Hello, Diana. How are things in the frozen north?"

She was perplexed for a moment, recognising the voice but not remembering to whom it belonged. It came to her.

"Greville! How delightful to hear from you!" Diana lied expertly, "How are you?"

Her voice shook slightly. She brushed an imaginary hair from her tweed skirt, quelling the butterfly flutters inside. Her peace and concentration were shattered by this affable invasion from the past. What could he want? Oh please, not money, Diana prayed inwardly, not now!

"I shall be in your neck of the woods next week, Diana. We've a client who's a big security printer ... cheques and share certificates, things like that," he explained patiently in response to her quick question. "They're taking over two smaller companies in Bradford ... quite complicated. If you could fit it in, I'd love to take you out to dinner."

Diana protested. Like the vast majority of those Sedgely serenely referred to as "bloody southerners," Greville Goodwynne could not have realised the distance which separated the West Riding city from little Nidcaster. She herself, had already acquired the local cast of mind which equated the psychological distance with physical mileage. Bradford was a strange, disputed territory where mosques and mills jostled and two populations seethed in dark streets. It was far away. She laughed with relief.

"But Greville, that's miles!"

"No, it isn't," he argued. "It's an hour and a quarter at most, driving at a relaxed pace. I could come on to you after my completion meeting, pick you up about sevenish and then we could go on to the Tsaritsa in Harrogate for dinner. It's had a terrific write-up in one of those so called 'top people's' magazines."

Yolanda appeared in the doorway of the book room and sniffed appreciatively. The scent of the old leather bindings and pearwood prunings burning in the tiny Edwardian grate filled the air.

She was wearing a plain kilt, diamond patterned sweater and knee socks, the few items of uniform demanded by the King

Henry Grammar School. A duffle bag dangled from her hand, overflowing with exercise books and all the untidy clutter from which schoolgirls are inseparable. She began to mouth something unintelligible. Diana placed her hand over the receiver and motioned her to sit down on the horsehair sofa before the fire.

"I'd like to see for myself how you are and there's lots to talk over," Goodwynne's voice went on persuasively.

A host of possibilities crowded into Diana's mind. Something to do with Michael? Grounds for an appeal? Anxious to end the conversation before it could take a turn which, even half heard, might have an unsettling effect on Yolanda, Diana agreed.

"I'll send you a sketch map. The house is in the middle of the town but it's very secluded, you'd never find it on your own ... Yes. Lovely. I'll look forward to it."

"Who was that?" Yolanda asked suspiciously. She had picked up the copy of *The Grower* and was studying the photograph of Philip Strang-Steele.

"Greville Goodwynne. Nobody you know."

"Yes, I do. I know his name, anyway. Isn't he Daddy's solicitor? Has he come up with something ... an appeal?"

"No, darling, no," Diana soothed away the futility of hope. "He's coming up to Yorkshire shortly and wants to take me out to dinner. He just wants to fill in an evening, that's all. He did so much for your father that it would be churlish of me to refuse."

She heard the element of self-justification in her own voice. It had not occurred to her previously that Yolanda might be watchful for any sign that her father's place in their lives might be offered to another. Children could upset themselves terribly over that kind of thing. Perhaps it was her imagination.

"Don't you think he's handsome?" Yolanda challenged, holding up the magazine for her mother to see.

"Oh, I suppose so," Diana replied casually, "in an obvious sort of way." She averted her eyes quickly from Strang-Steele's image.

"Hm. *I* think he's fabulous looking," Yolanda commented, reassured in some unacknowledged part of herself that her mother had neither the power to attract or be attracted. That

would be disgusting. "I love these super grooves running down
from his nostrils to the corners of his mouth. Terribly sexy."

Diana took the magazine from Yolanda's hand making a
conscious effort not to snatch. She still needed it for the article.
Obscurely, she felt Yolanda was trespassing in a place where
she had no business. Strang-Steele's living presence still ad-
hered to the walls of her recent memory. Every time she turned
her inner eye towards that day, he was there. An absurd quirk,
like the cobweb in the corner of the drawing-room ceiling.
Something she meant to get rid of but kept forgetting.

"Sedgely says I can help with the bonfire." Yolanda changed
the subject restlessly.

Diana observed her daughter coolly.

"What did you say, Landa?" Diana hardened herself against
the nerve-wearing pettishness with which Yolanda invariably
met the gentlest reproof.

"I said, Sedgely says I . . ."

"I think you mean *Mr.* Sedgely, don't you?"

Yolanda's beautiful mouth pushed itself into a childish pout.
"OK, OK. *Mr.* Sedgely, then . . . but Daddy always says . . ."

Diana got up and turned on a lamp, her mouth firmed into
a determined line whilst she listened to the parroted litany of
her husband's rather questionable rules of address. *Daddy's not
a lady* was the instant, neat riposte that came to her lips. But
she did not let it escape. The time for such nanny-like, nursery
equivocations had come to an end. There was even a hint of
implied criticism in the easy phrase that Yolanda was old
enough to identify. And that was one of Diana's unfaltering
principles. One parent should not criticise the other. Just now,
the temptation was severe.

"Hush, Landa. Please understand that Gilbert's Tower is my
house and everything we do here will be done according to my
rules."

Yolanda's jaw dropped slightly. She slumped on the sofa and
folded her arms defensively. She had not actually meant to hurt
or annoy. It was just that her mother, in the role of law giver,
a person of independent substance, was an entirely new phenomenon.

"Mr. Sedgely," Diana went on, "is the kindest friend to me,
to *us* . . . and I could not bear him to be offended. And I need
him very much more than he needs me. Please remember that.

Now, I'm going to get some tea and then we'll both go and look at the bonfire."

While she was gone, Yolanda slipped off a shoe and advanced her toe flirtatiously to where the orange cat lay stretched out on the hearth rug. Its alarmingly extensible body was attenuated to the point where it looked less like a four-legged creature than a fluffy snake. At the touch of Yolanda's stockinged toe it opened one yellow eye warningly. It, too, demanded respect.

"You're all such touchy old things," Yolanda sighed.

Shabby as it was, Gilbert's Tower had quickly wound its tendrils around Yolanda's heart. It was home now, in a way that no other place had ever been. There was nothing temporary about it. The future would happen here, in Nidcaster.

Unknown to either Yolanda or Diana, the headmaster of the grammar school had addressed the morning assembly before her arrival. Yolanda, he had said, was a Nidcaster girl by family association. She was in a special and very sad situation. He told the gawping youth of Nidcaster what he knew of her father's position in the briefest possible terms ... and a great deal less than he knew about the Nevilles' former lifestyle. Yolanda, he stressed, would need all the support, friendship and understanding they could give her. He was confident that King Henry's would do its part in making her at home.

His words had borne fruit. Yolanda had sunk into the nest of kindness prepared for her and sustained no bruises. If she was occasionally accused of "talking posh" or being a "bloody southerner," she gave as good as she got and was soon liked for herself. Her looks did her no harm with the boys, and her apparent lack of interest in them consoled the girls. The written work she had done and the class contributions she had made drew moderate expressions of satisfaction from her teachers. She had, they agreed guardedly, "twelve pence to the shilling." Effusiveness was not the Nidcaster way.

The telephone rang again and Yolanda answered it. This time it was the agricultural college. The principal's secretary spoke, leaving a brief message for Diana. Just a name and number. Yolanda wrote it down.

"Yes, thank you. I'll tell her."

When Diana came back into the room bearing a tea tray, she forestalled Yolanda with a small sheaf of newspaper cuttings.

Each was stapled to the printed docket of a cutting agency employed by large companies and their advertising agencies. They had arrived with a stark covering letter from Epoch that morning. It had said simply, "This is not helpful," and was signed by Merlin Olaff.

Yolanda examined the cuttings with mild interest. They were just dull little paragraphs from provincial weeklies and one, a line or two, from the *Daily Mail*. They concerned her unauthorised visit to her father in Wiltshire.

"How did anybody know about it? Mr. Laverack wouldn't have told anyone and I don't think . . ."

"Darling, don't you see? That isn't important. What is important is this." Diana reached across to her desk and handed Yolanda the covering letter.

Yolanda read the bare line and looked up, plainly puzzled.

"Look. I'm trying to borrow a great deal of money from a bank. This gentleman, the one who wrote that letter, and his partners, are trying to help me. They are also risking a lot of their money. They are naturally concerned that we shouldn't do anything to make a bank think that the situation here is unstable . . . or do anything to remind everyone that . . ."

"Daddy's in prison?" Yolanda interrupted sharply. "You can't just sweep him under the carpet."

Diana leaned forward towards the fire, cradling the tea cup in both her hands. There were things Yolanda couldn't understand and shouldn't know.

"No, of course not. It's more subtle than that. It's to do with minimising any appearance of . . . just keeping things . . ."

Abruptly, Diana gave up the attempt to explain such concepts as public and market perception to Yolanda. There had to be a clean break in everybody's mind between the Diana Neville who had been Michael Neville's wife and the Diana Neville who was the initiator of a new company . . . a whole new direction for . . . not that that prevented her from *being* Michael Neville's wife, of course. Diana found she was quite confused herself.

"Landa, let me ask you one question. Do you like it at Gilbert's Tower?"

Yolanda's eyebrows arched in surprise.

"You know I do, it's the most marvellous place I've ever lived in. It's just that . . ."

"Well, if you want us to stay here and if you want Daddy

to come and live with us here eventually and have all the things he must be missing now, you must trust me. Don't do anything unusual or anything the press might consider interesting. If you're in doubt, please ask me. Because, if anything goes wrong, I will have to sell this house."

Alarmed, Yolanda gave her sincere promise and kissed her mother with unusual fervour. Gilbert's Tower was a treasure to be guarded and Diana held it in her hand.

"Oh, look, Mummy. This person rang. Thorpe Overblow Manor. They said it was about your enquiry to the horticultural wing. Somebody's coming to see you about organic stuff unless you tell them not to. You have to ring him anyway."

Yolanda handed her mother the piece of paper on which she had scribbled the name. Alisdair Strang-Steele. Diana looked at it, feeling the tide of her own blood ebb a little. Whoever he was, whatever he cost, *this* Mr. Strang-Steele was needed.

A tap on the door was followed by Sedgely's face surmounted by his flat cap.

"Fire's going now, Miss Yolanda." He looked over her head as he spoke into Diana's eyes. "If you've t'goblets handy, Mrs. Neville, I've brought a bottle of t'damson cordial down with me. First bonfire of t'season needs doing right by."

No autumn pleasure can compare with the primitive excitement of feeding a wild, hot fire, thundering up into the starlight and drinking a wild, strong spirit, distilled outside the law.

Diana leaned against the orchard wall, watching Sedgely and Yolanda nourish the leaping, hungry flames, their faces ageless, sexless and darkly intent. Druidical.

Goodwynne, Michael, this other Strang-Steele . . . they would all come sooner or later, planting their unthinking feet on her sacred soil. The fortress drawbridge was down.

"That's given me an appetite for my tea, that has," Sedgely announced prosaically. "You tell me when this young lad's coming from t'college. We'll need to get t'measure of him."

THE MEASURE OF Alisdair Strang-Steele was taken two days later.

Sedgely dressed formally for the occasion in his blue serge, British Legion suit, gold watch chain and dazzling toe caps. Mrs. Sedgely accompanied him that afternoon, bringing with her an enveloping white apron which crackled with starch. She would answer the front door bell and bring in the tea, she announced firmly, when Mrs. Neville should choose to call for it.

"Aye," Sedgely confirmed sternly. Diana did not argue. She understood that the Sedgelys had advanced in force to ensure that she was not taken lightly.

"I'll be saying nowt," Sedgely reassured Diana needlessly as they left the kitchen, "I'll just see t'lad knows what he's talking about. Begging your pardon, Mrs. Neville, you don't know a right lot about t'nitty gritty, do you?"

Humbly, Diana admitted that she knew next to nothing about the mysteries of cultivation.

"Not like your Aunt Thea," Sedgely grunted in sour approval. "Still, that's no matter. Not while I'm alive."

Diana had never seen Sedgely quite so edgily protective before. She guessed correctly that what was ruffling Mr. Sedgely's feathers was a deep-seated fear that he might be supplanted in the scant acre and a half where he had held sway. And there was something else, more difficult to define. There was something in the air at Gilbert's Tower. A fragile ecology of past and present, of spirit and organism, of growth and decay that would need an artist's hand to preserve. But they were not things which could be discussed or described.

"Don't worry, Mr. Sedgely," Diana comforted. "If he's not right for us, we shan't have him."

Alisdair Strang-Steele was shown into the book room. He was about twenty-five, tall and well made with the long skull, firm chin and penetrating hazel-eyed glance that betrays the man of Scottish descent all over the world. His dark hair waved thickly back from a brow which already showed signs of creasing. Diana liked him at once.

The introductions made, Diana sketched the outlines of their project. Sedgely produced his pipe from a waistcoat pocket and clamped it between his teeth, removing it at the end of every statement made by Diana. Watching, Alisdair quickly interpreted the code. Pipe *in* stood for reserved judgment, whilst pipe *out* indicated total endorsement. There was, of course, no smoke to confuse the message.

"You cannot help us, Mr. Strang-Steele, unless you know the objectives. But I hope you will treat them in the strictest confidence at the moment. And if this gentlemen is any connection of yours," Diana showed him the photograph of the grey haired Strang-Steele on the cover of *The Grower*, "you may think it wrong to involve yourself in a scheme such as ours."

Alisdair took the periodical from her hand and examined it for a moment before replacing it on the desk. A faint smile livened his long, mobile mouth.

"Yes, he is a connection of mine. Anyone called Strang-Steele is bound to be a kinsman. There are an awful lot of us in the Tayside area. Philip Strang-Steele's a very big commercial grower. A mass market supplier. With respect, he has little to fear from small scale operations or organic competitors . . . I'm sorry to say."

Satisfied, Diana told him everything she had told Epoch. Alisdair listened with unwavering attention whilst Sedgely subjected him to the most intense observation. The young Scotsman bore the Yorkshireman's inspection with equanimity. Partner, friend and neighbour he may be to Mrs. Neville, but Alisdair knew a self-appointed liegeman when he saw one.

"What we need you to do, Mr. Strang-Steele, is to help us maximise the potential of this property, tell us what we can expect from it in terms of volume production, advise where we should concentrate our efforts and let us have an estimate for the necessary work."

Diana closed the file which contained the list of topics to be covered. She handed him a folder with a summary of the brief.

"One final thing," she kept her hand on the file. "This isn't a farm any more than the many other gardens I expect to involve. It's my home. Charm is not to be sacrificed to productivity. I hope it's not asking too much."

Alisdair's face gave nothing away. In spite of his English education, some residue of Scottish dourness prevented him from admitting to excitement. But he was impressed. He had eked out his allowance whilst doing his post-graduate work with various small horticultural commissions. Crop trials for market gardeners and even a few domestic design projects. But this was the most original and stimulating assignment he had yet been given.

And as for its size . . . he regretted now speaking of "small scale operations." There was nothing small about the thinking here. The thing could snowball. Diana Neville was preparing to hand on a torch which could light fires in the imagination from Penzance to Perth. But it was complicated, very. He didn't envy her the colossal logistical problems of distribution.

"Where did you get the idea for this, Mrs. Neville?" he asked unwisely.

"She's a head on her shoulders, has Mrs. Neville," Sedgely growled.

He was mollified when Strang-Steele asked him to help in the collection of soil samples and measurements.

"I took a few snaps from various angles as I came in . . . before the light went," Alisdair produced a pocket camera from his tweed jacket pocket. "But I'd be glad of Mr. Sedgely's help in assessing the overall capabilities here."

They were gone over an hour and it was dark before they returned to a late tea. It was served in the panelled breakfast parlour at the round table there. Yolanda was home from school and joined them, warned by Diana to confine her sociability to answering questions and passing plates.

Any former tension between the two men had evaporated. There was now a mutual cordiality which proved that Sedgely had tried Strang-Steele and not found him wanting. He had asked perceptive questions and was gratifyingly amazed by all he was shown. The old grapevine in the third glasshouse could be rejuvenated, he said, and would justify an entirely new structure to be built around it. In fact, he said a great deal and none of it had antagonised Sedgely. For one thing, he was "sound" on red cabbages.

The tea was a mountainous meal of cucumber sandwiches, curry puffs, cheese scones and fruit cake. Mrs. Sedgely admitted to having expanded the menu, thinking the items suggested by Diana inadequate to the nutritional needs of this "strapping young gentleman." It was a fulsome compliment by Nidcaster standards and even Diana was shocked. Of course, it was intended as a clear signal from Mrs. Sedgely that young Mr. Strang-Steele would, in local parlance "do," and there was to be no nonsense.

Yolanda signalled her agreement with an immodest grin and offered the visitor more cake. Nothing can eradicate the Scots sweet tooth and Alisdair accepted gratefully. There were too many households in England where afternoon tea was treated with a lack of seriousness. He dropped his eyes shyly.

Alisdair combined the hot blood of his race with its native caution.

He could not help knowing that experienced women found him attractive. But this innocent girl's imperious challenge to his masculinity rocked him. A single smile had openly invited and contemptuously taunted. The effect, he decided, had been quite unintentional. Miss Yolanda Neville was too young to know her own power. Just as well. The schoolgirl daughter of a client was an impossible object.

"Broadly speaking," he recovered himself, "I think Mr. Sedgely and I are in agreement. We believe you should focus on four main crops. The peaches, without a doubt . . . open air peaches from Yorkshire will give the foreign exotics some competition. You might try Rochester as well. They bear after Peregrine and would keep your season going. Asparagus . . . because the fresher it is, the better it tastes. That will give French and Spanish exporters something to think about. Miniature strawberries . . . I'm conducting a trial of a new climbing variety at the moment . . . and unusual salads. But I will need some details of your packaging plans because you already have some opposition in that area."

He looked up from his plate. "There are a few special things, horticultural curios you could call them, that ought to be retained for their own sake. We might find a use for them. We might not. And then of course you will need various companion plantings to keep off pests and contribute soil nutrients. I'll let you have my detailed plans and costings in ten days' time."

"And your fee, Mr. Strang-Steele?" Diana prompted.

"Five percent of the construction and planting costs if the plan is implemented and I supervise it. If not, a thousand pounds."

It was reasonable. Alisdair badly wanted the job.

"I know it's hardly fair to ask you," Diana said diffidently, "but how much, very roughly, do you think it would cost to put it all in hand?"

"Don't hold me to it, Mrs. Neville, there are a lot of sums to do. I'm afraid I can't see you having much change out of forty thousand pounds."

Yolanda looked from Sedgely to her mother and back again.

"We shall find it," Diana rose from her chair. "Somehow."

As he took his leave at the garden door, Alisdair knew he had arrived a suspect stranger and was departing a friend. He would do everything he could to ensure a continuing welcome. Diana Neville had put the things he dreamed of into words. It was his own truth. Alisdair did not ask himself what part Yolanda played in his desire to return to Gilbert's Tower. He did not dare.

They all congregated round his old Rover to say goodbye.

As he backed the car away from the garden door, the orange cat's eyes flashed round and yellow in the headlamps. It was stationed on top of the arched lintel. Alisdair could almost believe that if he came looking for this place in daylight, it would have disappeared. Loath to leave them all, he wound down his window to say a final goodbye, his breath billowing in the light of a street lamp.

"Touch of frost, I wouldn't wonder," Sedgely said equably, lighting his pipe. " 'T won't last."

❦ THE TSARITSA, NAMED for the ill-fated last Empress of Russia, was established in a tall Edwardian terrace where she had once lodged fleetingly on a visit to Harrogate. Philip Strang-Steele waited at the window table of the third floor *salle* for his son.

His eye took in the red damask walls, aspidistras in brass *jardinières* and framed facsimiles of sepia tinted European royalties enjoying the health giving rigours of Harrogate at the turn of the century. Philip had no opinions on interior decor but piped balalaika music displeased him. He half wished that he had submitted to the offer of a microwaved pizza at Alisdair's rented cottage near the college.

But Philip's sense of propriety had baulked at the notion of taking an adult child to task over his own kitchen table. He had spent the weekend shooting on a friend's grouse moor, and lingered in the area today with the specific object of entering into plain speech with Alisdair. The Tsaritsa was the agreed neutral territory.

Philip eyed the waiter austerely and ordered a whisky and soda. Alisdair was late.

His son's consultancy activities were expanding and beginning to bring in some respectable sums of money. Not that Philip was concerned about that. As his only child, Alisdair would be very rich some day. He could be rich now. It was Philip's intention to tell him this evening that as soon as he abandoned his fringe interests and put his shoulder to the Strang-Steele Group's commercial wheel, the quicker Philip could start transferring assets to him. It was something he very much wanted to do. After all, at fifty-three there was no knowing how much longer he might live. Although in magnificent health, Philip had an inordinate fear of untimely death. The prospect of the Inland Revenue getting its thieving hands on the proceeds of twenty years' honest toil outraged his sense of decency. Tax avoidance, particularly inheritance tax, was no more than simple duty.

Philip's mother, a formidable old French lady, heartily concurred in these strictures. Her grandson, she said, was an 'ippie with no thought for his family. Why was he not married? she wanted to know. What would be the ultimate fate of her own small family properties in Normandy and Provence? Was she not entitled to set eyes on her great-grandchildren before death should claim her?

There was no point in telling Louise Strang-Steele that there were limits to her entitlements. She would simply stage an alarming collapse which would bring her maid, almost as old as she was, clucking reproachfully on to the scene with her own view of Monsieur Alisdair's outrageous neglect of responsibility.

Alisdair's mother had died twenty years before, leaving Philip alone with a small boy, a four hundred acre mixed farm in the fertile Tay valley and a grief which had immobilised him for over a year. Pulling himself together, trying to go forward and make a life for himself and their son, he had found that many of the pieces were missing. The colours of life were irretrievably dimmed.

Things that had interested him before no longer did so. Food meant little to him; he locked his piano and threw the key into the back of a cabinet. The faces of friends looked grotesque, like quacking puppet heads. The farm suffered because he could not love it any longer. Its undulating green fields and copses dotted with cattle and sheep became flat celluloid images. They could be turned off like a television programme. The stockman and the shepherd took over from their master. There were no plans and no developments.

Four years went by in which his neighbours tried with ceaseless good will to introduce him to a potential bride. A sensible girl, with an interest in music to match his own and a love of country life, would be the best thing for him and little Alisdair. Kind hearts set eagerly to work to fill the empty place.

They worked in vain. To a range of frustrated hostesses, it seemed incredible that a personable man of thirty-two with a well-appointed house should not wish to share it with any of their tactfully promoted candidates.

Philip did try for a time. He took a number of impeccably qualified girls out to dinner and to concerts. These evenings always ended with him refusing the customary offer of a nightcap at the door of some Edinburgh flat. A chaste kiss and hurried departure were sometimes followed by a bouquet of flowers but never by a telephone call. *Shallow*, was the unjust, if understandable, verdict.

The reverse was true. Philip's emotions were intense and powerful. Having invested all of himself once and lost so completely, he felt himself bankrupt of any honest currency. In the first years of his bereavement, his occasional sexual needs had been satisfied by a pricey call girl. He made love to her in hotel rooms with a straight-forward magnificence that astonished her. Each time, he thanked her gravely and rewarded her lavishly. The call girl fell in love with him to his great sorrow and embarrassment. Once she had told him, they did not meet again.

On the advice of his doctor, Philip sold his farm. Louise took her six-year-old grandson with her to France and Philip bought a small arable property in Lincolnshire. It had been no more than a hundred and fifty acres of flat, dull ploughland with a hideous little redbrick house on it. The place, as forlorn as he was, was blessedly free of memories.

Knowing little, he had imitated his predecessor on the land and planted potatoes. A stock of seed potatoes had been included in the purchase price, fertiliser and pesticides had come from a nearby agricultural merchant. Following the practices of the region and driving his own machinery, he had raised a crop without trouble. It was harvested by contracted labour from distant industrial towns. The Hogarthian ganger who brought these grey faced men and women to his fields each dawn suggested he sell the crop to a packer not five miles distant. That first year, the profit had been good, the labour small and the procedures uncomplicated. Philip was fascinated.

He bought more of this biddable, uncomplaining soil and more machinery with which to work it. He tried other crops and prospered. Some years were better than others but when the crops in the fields rotted from rain, smaller men than Strang-Steele went under. He was always there to buy their land before the banks foreclosed. One such purchase included a gabled mansion, complete with contents. Standing in an extensive park and well provided with ancillary buildings, Philip made the place his company headquarters and called it his home.

When Alisdair went to prep school and later to a public school in England, he spent some of his holidays there in the Lincolnshire house. The rest he spent with his grandmother. The summer holidays in Provence were best. There, his grandmother's untidy little estate grew lavender, a few rows of straggling vines, olives and apricots. Philip came too for a few weeks. He had once wanted to put the entire acreage to melons. But the fourteen-year-old Alisdair had begged him to leave it alone for the sake of the old couple who worked the land.

"Henri and Mathilde live here. It's their home. They need the trees to shade their goats and they drink the wine from those grapes."

"You're a funny chap," Philip had ruffled his hair affectionately. "Well, keep your toy farm for the present. But once the Bouffes are gone, I can't deprive your grandmother of the income she could have in this property. I'm afraid the melons must come."

Telling his grandmother of this conversation later, Louise had shrugged her thin shoulders with resignation. She too loved the olive groves where the gnarled trees threw patches of black shade on the burning white earth. The lavender fields were lakes to the eye in June. But the small crop brought little profit.

"I'm afraid your father is right, *chéri*. I and my forebears have lived in the countryside all our lives. It is not, as townspeople think, a garden for pleasure. It is a factory where food is made. The factory grows no bigger but the number of people who need the food increase in numbers every year. We cannot enlarge the factory, so we must modernise it. That is the pitiful truth. We must face it."

The land as a factory had been his father's great idea. There is perhaps room for only one idea of power in any lifetime. It did not occur to Philip Strang-Steele that his vision could be superseded by a new one.

Between the Humber and the Wash, the name of Strang-Steele loomed large. Philip ceased to look on himself as a farmer. He had become a businessman. That part of his mind that was not occupied by his growing son and ageing mother was filled with the cleanliness of arithmetic. What had begun as little more than occupational therapy had grown into an empire. Alisdair was the thankless heir.

He had gone, willingly enough, to agricultural college. There, the prevailing fashion for placing illusory moral burdens on farmers and growers of all kinds had ensnared Alisdair, or so it seemed to Philip.

During his second and third years there had been differences of opinion in the holidays about crop spraying and grubbing up hedges. When Philip had rationalised his mother's Normandy cider orchards by planting disease resistant, universally marketable and easily shipped varieties, his son had accused him of vandalism. There had been angry words and raised voices. Hating to see her son and grandson, both equally dear, at odds with each other, Louise had simulated a heart attack to devastatingly good effect. But the truce had not lasted.

Alisdair had gone his own way and refused to involve himself with the Strang-Steele Group until his own ideas were listened to. His maggot liberation theories, as Philip called them. But neither ridicule nor reason had yet unseated Alisdair's intractable idealism. Time and steady pressure, Philip believed, would wear it away. A firm pressure on his shoulder told him Alisdair had arrived.

"I'm sorry to be late, Father. I had to take a plan to a client in Nidcaster. How are you?"

The two men shook hands. Neither could conceal his pleasure in seeing the other. A waiter with dolorous moustaches and an apron down to his feet placed large menu cards in their hands.

"The Beluga caviare . . . she is good," the waiter kissed his bunched fingertips.

"At thirty pounds a portion I am content to believe you," Philip flashed back in French.

A Yorkshire-born Pole, the waiter looked hurt. This was not playing the game. Philip glanced apologetically at his son. Sometimes, he knew, he was testy without reason.

They talked for a few moments of indifferent things, skirting the disputed issues, sporting with dead ones.

While his father talked, Alisdair continued reading the menu. It was a pity, he reflected, that he would taste nothing he ate. The painful subject of the company would come up. There would be proposals, conditions, counter-proposals, rejections . . . and finally an angry silence. Alisdair loved his father but at the end of the day, the Strang-Steele Group could go to hell. Turning East Anglia into a polluted dust bowl was not a project, however profitable, in which he could share. Philip's *résumé* of family affairs ceased abruptly.

Looking up, Alisdair followed the direction of his father's gaze. He saw a handsome middle-aged couple talking with the commissionaire just beyond the awning which covered the entrance below. They were laughing. The woman threw her head back so that her face, foreshortened before, was fully visible in the light of lamps hidden among the laurel bushes. It was Diana Neville. He had delivered the plans for her garden only this afternoon. She had been happy. She looked happy now. He didn't know who the man was. Her husband? Did she have a husband? Alisdair realised he didn't know. But the source of his unease was not Diana or her companion but his father's state of peculiar paralysis.

Diana disappeared under the awning and Philip sat back in his chair. He blew air down his nostrils forcefully and flicked an upward glance at his son.

"Do you know those people?" Alisdair asked. His father so rarely looked at other people and never with interest.

"No," Philip replied brusquely.

She was there, she was real and she was somewhere in the building now. She might even come into this room. But she was married. Of course, she would be. He did not know her name or anything else about her. He had spoken to her . . .

twice, he recalled. She had not replied. Philip said nothing. There was no story worth telling.

Alisdair too dismissed the small coincidence of seeing her. He did not believe his father and Mrs. Neville would have anything in common. He had forgotten that he had been a little less than frank about his relationship with Philip Strang-Steele. But the four tables in the third floor *salle* were occupied. Diana and her escort were shown into the room below.

Philip and Alisdair began to talk of compromise, both knowing that none was possible.

❦ DIANA'S OWN EVENING began uncomfortably and ended disagreeably.

Greville Goodwynne had little to say about Michael. He had visited him once, it seemed, receiving only the most perfunctory welcome from his client.

"I tried to let him down lightly. There's no fresh evidence and no grounds for an appeal that I can scratch together," Greville told Diana as he scanned the Tsaritsa's encyclopaedic wine list. "You know, he just looked through me as if I was some sort of sub-efficient office boy. It's a hell of a drive from London to Wiltshire ... not that I'm looking for gratitude but ..."

Diana's acute embarrassment worked like a tonic on Goodwynne. Instantly he became brisk and smiling.

"Sorry, Diana. Shouldn't say these things to you. God knows you've done everything a wife could and you've enough on your plate ... oysters OK? Or caviare?"

There was nothing very much Diana felt it wise to tell Greville and their conversation was soon forced down the narrow alley of their shared memories. As they were few in number and all dominated by Michael, this material quickly failed them.

"Pretty swish, this place," Greville said in a pause as he looked around. "You don't imagine this sort of thing in the provinces ... What does this place live on? Harrogate, I mean. Old ladies with constipation and carpet salesmen. I mean, nobody comes here, do they?"

"Oh yes, they do. It's a noted rallying centre for nobodies like you and me and even better known nobodies than us. You can go down and look at the register of newly arrived nobodies at the *Harrogate Advertiser*'s office any day of the week. It says so outside."

Diana kept this tongue twisting banter up for as long as she could, waiting for better inspired conversational material to occur to her. They talked a little about Gilbert's Tower and Greville speculated delicately on its value.

"Quite a rarity, I'd say. You ought to tout it round the property editors on the big Sundays. They'd lap it up and an article would push up its market price . . . no harm in having a go." He bent over his soup plate and did not see Diana's pained expression. "Then you could have a smaller property, nice and clean with low running costs . . . that place must *eat* money."

"Greville," she stopped him. "Every house I lived in with Michael was automatically understood to be on the market . . . as long as the price was right. Gilbert's Tower is mine and not for sale."

During the rest of the meal Diana covered the painful absence of any common ground between them by questioning the solicitor closely about his clients in the printing trade. There were things she would need to know about this subject. Her questions bore an intimate relationship to those which Epoch was daily asking her about her detailed distribution plans.

Greville concealed his irritation at this catechism with only partial success. He could not know that Diana's interest in the distinction between letterpress and offset litho, photo typesetting and hot lead, the economics of short runs and the cost of machinery was genuine. To him it seemed like an hysterical attempt to avoid the personal.

"I'm so sorry, Greville," she said. "You want to relax and I'm boring you to distraction."

"You could never bore me, Diana. But I really don't know much about printing. I can't imagine why you should want to know anything about it, either. All I can tell you is that it's highly technical, capital intensive and competitive. And there are as many different kinds of printers as there are customers . . . you surely don't want to go into printing . . ."

Quickly, Diana feinted away.

"It never crossed my mind. I suppose I just miss learning something new once in a while. When Michael and I lived together there was always something to learn about. Do you know, I once sat next to a man at dinner who assured me he'd told me everything there was to know about industrial filling and capping machinery."

"How has it been, Diana? I mean, with you, since Michael went away."

Confused by the question, Diana merely shrugged. He had seen her house. He knew that Yolanda was now at home. There was no further description of herself she could give that was prudent.

"Oh, you know, life goes on. I cook and I clean. I've no help, of course, but I've made one or two friends."

Greville applied his napkin to his mouth to hide a wince. *Cooking and cleaning* . . . what a fate for the incandescent Diana. The words themselves sounded unseemly on her lips. Diana placed her knife and fork together with little girl politeness. She wished she might be allowed to "get down," like a child in whom the grown-ups are no longer interested.

"Any boyfriends?" Greville's eyes slid sideways to the hovering waiter.

"Of course not! Of *course* not. How could you ask?" She laughed, sorry for Greville that what was so obviously intended as a joke hadn't really been funny at all.

Later she realised her mistake. When he drove her back to Gilbert's Tower she was surprised that he accepted her automatic invitation to drink a final cup of coffee with her. They had nothing left to talk about. She was even more surprised when he rejected the chair he was offered in the drawing-room and elected instead to sit beside her on a sofa clearly designed to accommodate one Edwardian lady and her lapdog. It was unavoidable that the full skirt of her frock should spill on to his trouser leg. The counterfeit nature of this closeness troubled her.

Diana poured the coffee, keeping up a stream of nervous inconsequentialities until he took the cup from her hand and embraced her. Shocked and repelled by the uninvited approach, she evaded his attempt to place a wet, open mouthed kiss on her lips. It all felt so gauche. Her overwhelming instinct was to cover the error . . . to turn it into something else . . . some mere affectionate exchange which Greville himself could remember without shame. A light, sisterly peck on the cheek was the only kind response. But he held her tight and would not let her resume pouring the coffee.

"Be generous, Diana," he muttered thickly, brushing aside her face-saving gesture. "I didn't expect ingratitude from you. I thought you liked me."

Panic-stricken thoughts fled through her mind. She ought to hit him. Most women would. He would be humiliated . . . she would be humiliated. She remembered how she touched his face fleetingly in his car, that last day, outside the flat in the Boltons. Was that what she had done wrong? It was such a grotesque way to lose a friend.

"Oh, Greville, please!" Diana pushed hard at him. "You must know I'm far too inexperienced to slap your face. It's sweet of you to flatter me like this but I do want to drink my coffee."

It was neat, the gentlest of reproofs but woefully inadequate. The only proper dismissal would involve a thick wad of high denomination bank notes which she did not have.

His departure was hastened by Yolanda's voice outside in the hall.

The next day Diana sent, in coldly formal terms, for the account in respect of services rendered to Michael Neville. There was no reply. And that, Diana admitted to herself, was fortunate. The cost of pride would, in any case, have been too high.

The incident recurred in Diana's memory daily for weeks and months afterwards. She turned it over like a stray foreign coin found in a pocket. What was it that she had been expected to pay for? A meal or Michael's legal expenses? She should have been much, much angrier. She had thought that Goodwynne valued her for herself. Michael's possessiveness had been a protection. One that she never knew she needed. Now she would have to protect herself. At times, Philip Strang-Steele's face and the look he had given her materialised in her mind. Had he seen her as a kind of recyclable debris? The flotsam and jetsam of some other man's life?

❦ To raise the capital necessary to execute Alisdair's radical plan for the garden at Gilbert's Tower, Diana sold all the jewellery she had that was of noticeable worth.

Acting on Mr. Meers' advice, she summoned the appropriate valuers from Harrogate's own two local auctioneers, one from Sotheby's office in Harrogate and the gentleman from Christie's in York. The youthful head of a court jewellers of fabulous discretion also came in his turn, followed by a wisp of a man from Hull wearing a loud pin-stripe suit and renowned for his dealings in antique jewellery.

What she had to sell was of undoubted interest. A gold and enamel Giuliano necklace which she had inherited from her mother was instantly admired by the antique jeweller. He showed her how, by the insertion of gold rivets kept in the necklace's case, it could be converted to a tiara. He offered a price for it which the Sotheby's man believed could be bettered at auction.

The other items, a four carat, pear shaped diamond which Michael had bought for the double celebration of his fifth wedding anniversary and second million, an opera length of lustrous Bahraini pearls with diamond clasp, a choker of South African amethysts with green garnets and tiny yellow diamonds, had all been gifts from her husband. Their value and interest was not disputed by any of the gentlemen who viewed them. However, Diana's ownership, her competence to sell them *was*.

"You do realise, I hope, Mrs. Neville," one man apologised, "that I don't in any way doubt that these were quite honestly purchased—this bill and valuation from Bulgar in Rome are perfectly authentic—or that it is your husband who purchased them." He inserted the loupe in his eye and examined the great diamond, while Diana's heartbeat slowed. What could he mean?

Outside, the lawns had already been taken up, leaving Mercury stranded in a sea of earth. Barrow loads of fresh topsoil were being wheeled noisily along the terrace and an electric saw whined in the orchard. Ned Garvey, helping in the garden now that he was not needed for the boats, glanced in at the drawing-room windows as he passed with another load. He winked and grinned impudently, tossing his carroty forelock out of his eyes. Diana waved.

"You see," the valuer withdrew the loupe from his eye, "with items of this quality, given as gifts by a husband to his spouse, there is some question as to the underlying intention of the gift."

Diana's eyes widened while the man extracted a gauge from his pocket and began to measure her pearls.

"I'm so sorry, I don't follow you."

"Mrs. Neville, your husband may have acquired these jewels for the use of his wife, whilst she remained his wife. You do see, don't you? To have any confidence in offering these for sale, I should need your husband's express permission. The Giuliano necklace, of course, is yours."

Diana absorbed what had been said slowly. The other jewels might not be hers in any useful sense at all. But Greville Goodwynne had said she might take them on the day they took Michael away. But she had quarrelled with Greville Goodwynne. There were no witnesses to her conversation with him in the car because, she remembered, he had dismissed the chauffeur.

Without analysing why she did so, Diana moved closer to the valuer so that he should feel his height when she looked up at him. There was a needle of logic she could insert between the plates of his armour.

"If I tell you that my husband was made bankrupt and all his assets were forfeit, wouldn't you say that these things *are* mine, otherwise they would have gone along with my car and our home . . . other things my husband owned . . ."

The valuer looked down at Diana and felt professional caution dissolve. He saw now why the extraordinarily garish Roman piece, the African amethysts, had been chosen for this slight, childlike woman. Her eyes made perfect sense of their colour. It struck him too that this was almost certainly *the* Mrs. Neville. It was awkward.

"That would certainly make a difference, Mrs. Neville. In the circumstances, I should still like some sort of confirmation—perhaps your husband's legal advisers?"

Diana got him Greville Goodwynne's card from her desk. She was now in his hands.

Three weeks later, the entire collection was sold at a special sale in Tokyo. On the following Saturday, the *Financial Times* carried a long piece on Japanese collectors. Diana's amethyst necklace was shown in full colour round the neck of a kimono'd model under the headline: "The Spoils of Economic Imperialism." The sum realised was large, far larger than the auctioneer's estimate and way above the reserve. Michael read the article.

"Screw you, Diana," he twisted the newspaper violently and threw it into the common room wastepaper basket.

Diana did not take the *Financial Times*. She paid Alisdair's bills for work completed and materials supplied on time, wondering bitterly what Greville Goodwynne might expect in the way of gratitude for telling the truth.

Early December brought wild weather and an expensive mischance. The new glasshouse raised around the muscat vine was circular in shape and designed to serve, in addition, as a summer dining-room. The construction was only just completed when an old standard apple, still awaiting the attentions of a tree surgeon, shed a heavy branch during the night, crashing through the glasshouse's domed roof. The damage, although sickening to look at, was insured. The insurers claimed contributory negligence and Diana was left with a bill for repairs which absorbed the whole of the sum raised by her mother's necklace.

Worriedly, Diana examined the effect on her finances. There was no possibility now of defraying any of Michael's legal expenses if she were to have enough money to see her and Yolanda through what promised to be a very lean year.

PART TWO

CHAPTER
7

❦ THAT YEAR, WINTER broke with convention and came when she was welcome. Ten days before Christmas, Nidcaster woke to swirling blizzards. The town's Gothic angles were all plumped with snow.

Of Nidcaster's principal residents, Diana alone chafed at the enforced confinement. Her last meeting with Epoch before the list of banks to be approached was finalised, was cancelled.

All that Epoch could do in putting the campaign together had been done. Every practical detail of execution had been thoroughly explored by Diana. The garden, re-laid, reformed and made ready by Alisdair and Sedgely, now waited only for the spring. The avalanche of daily post had slowed to a trickle. Telephones rang less frequently now. The meetings and talks which Diana had had with potential suppliers and contractors were all over. Now that so much had been invested, it made her deeply anxious that there should be the smallest delay in the planned programme.

"You'll not be going to London today," Bob from the station told her with undisguised glee when Diana telephoned him early. "York and Leeds lines is blocked solid. There's nothing getting through." Like all his kind, Bob relished disruption. "Nay, Mrs. Neville. We'll have to see, like. They might put a train or two on tomorrer, but I doubt it."

As there was no prospect of driving her little car on the motorways in what the television weather men termed "white out" conditions, Diana resigned herself to enjoying Nidcaster's embattled beauty.

For days a pleasurable chaos reigned. The lane outside the

Tower's walls, too narrow for any snow plough, lay in deep drifts. The red pillar box and the stone cross had the market square to themselves. The headmaster of the King Henry Grammar School informed parents in a gravely worded note that the school's central heating boiler had broken down and that pupils should stay away. Instructions for private study would be communicated by individual teachers on the telephone . . . unless, by any mischance, the weather should effect the wires.

Reading the note, Diana could not resist the thought that the headmaster was a man who had seen a delightful opportunity for an extended Christmas holiday. Certainly, he was to be seen about the town in a sheepskin coat accessorised with red bobble hat and mittens, distributing marked essays and homework assignments like an academic Father Christmas. He called at Gilbert's Tower and eagerly accepted a glass of damson cordial. He seemed surprised to find Yolanda at home.

"You want to get out and enjoy it while it lasts," he said. "Sparkles up the brain does this, you know."

Sedgely was narrowly prevented from digging paths from the Tower's kitchen and front entrances to the garden door.

"Please, Mr. Sedgely, don't. I love the feel of snow under my feet," Diana begged, "and it never lasted in London."

But Sedgely felt the need of some specialised duties. With his snow shovel despised, he turned to rummaging in the cellar, emerging triumphant after a good two hours with a Victorian toboggan as big as himself. Its rusted iron runners curled up exuberantly at the front and horse hair burst from the red plush of the upholstered seat.

"Your aunt Thea said she were too old for tobogganing but I reckon Miss Yolanda's not. I'll just fettle this a bit."

The toboggan was declared fit for service when Alisdair arrived at the Tower, stamping the snow from his boots. Diana was pleased to see him but surprised as she had been told the Broughton Road was closed. Alisdair had borrowed a four-wheel-drive vehicle and defied the police bollards. His purpose was to discuss a volume discount for rosemary bushes supplied for edging the new parterres. It seemed a hazardous journey to undertake on so thin a pretext.

"I suppose I came to see how it would all look under snow," he grinned engagingly.

"We can see how *you* look under snow now," Yolanda cut in. "Mr. Sedgely and I are going sledging in a minute. Are you going to come?"

Alisdair looked from Yolanda to Diana, uncertain what to do. He knew that Diana was unimpressed by his excuse for coming. With the college closed for the Christmas holidays, he was short of company and missing the household at Gilbert's Tower since his work there was done. Looking out of the cottage window, the flat, white countryside taunted him with his loneliness. He wanted to share the snow with somebody. Instinct had drawn him to a place where, on a day like this, there would be enchantment.

"We will all go," Diana solved the difficulty, "on the understanding that Alisdair stays for dinner and breakfast, too."

"How lucky I packed," Alisdair pulled an electric razor from the pocket of his riding mac. He smiled the elusive, half shy, half cocksure smile that had made more than a few pairs of knees weaken.

"You exploitive bum," Yolanda punched him playfully. "I bet you brought a toothbrush, too."

"No, I thought that would be just a little *too* pushy. I always have a woody cutting about my person—twig to you—and that does just as well in a social emergency."

Sedgely led his troop across the Leighpole Bridge and into the woods opposite Gilbert's Tower on the other side of the river. Alisdair and Yolanda pulled the toboggan together, laughing and talking. There were steep slopes rising through the trees, already uproarious with brightly clad children sliding joyously on every kind of contrivance. Their parents and various of Nidcaster's notable citizens were equally engrossed. The headmaster whizzed past, spreadeagled on a lethal bobsleigh, and Father Murphy, rotund in his clerical overcoat and battered Homburg, slalomed reflectively on a pair of ancient wooden skis.

He swished to a halt, tipping his hat before Diana's party, still toiling up the hill.

"I've been neglecting ye, Mrs. Neville. I had meant to pay me respects to Miss FitzGilbert's successor as guardian of our local shrine," he began in a brogue which owed more to theatrical talent than Irish birth. "Will you be wanting any damsons now? Because ye know it is far too late," the priest steamrollered imperturbably over Diana's reciprocal pleasantries. "I'd not the heart to harvest the tree with herself cold in her heathen grave. Time was when I thought it should woo her back to the faith of her fathers with those blessed damsons. But she was only after what she could get out of a fellow. Aye," he sighed, "she'd a black, black heart on her, had Theadosia FitzGilbert. Good day to ye, Mrs. Neville. I'll be calling on ye in due course." And, with a nod to Sedgely, he continued his downward path, his breath steaming behind him like a vapour trail.

"The old bugger," Sedgely muttered, more or less benevolently.

There were many such encounters that afternoon and some alarm when the momentum of the headmaster's bobsleigh carried him straight over the forest path and into the coagulating waters of the river. Attempts to rescue him were clumsy and slow. Eventually, assisted by Alisdair, Ned Garvey hauled him aboard a punt and poled the sodden pedagogue downstream in the direction of a hot bath and a warm scolding from his wife.

By four o'clock the light was all but gone and it had begun to snow again. Lighted windows sent shivering reflections across the river and even Yolanda admitted it was time to go home.

"If we light a fire in there now, we can put Alisdair in the tower room," she suggested. "It's much the most fun place to be and ideal for a tramp with no luggage."

"Next time," Alisdair answered her mildly, "I'll come with a steamer trunk and you can put me in the suite reserved for visiting royalty, can't you? Is it haunted, your tower?"

"Must be. Mummy slept in there a couple of nights and came out a fruit and nut case."

"Fruit and veg case," Diana amended absently, unoffended.

The verbal horseplay continued all the way back to the house. A few paces ahead, the twitch of Sedgely's ears indicated the presence of a reluctant smile on his unseen face. Miss Landa was a cheeky young monkey. Too clever by half.

After an evening passed in playing three-handed bridge by the drawing-room fire, the Nevilles and their guest retired to bed. Noting as she undressed that Alisdair was her first house guest at Gilbert's Tower, Diana thought how fitting that was since he was its co-rejuvenator.

The easy friendship between the young Scotsman and her daughter pleased her, too. He handled Yolanda's alternating moods of callow flirtatiousness and aggression with a sure footed, gently humorous touch. And whereas it would be absurd to think of such a young man in the role of father, he supplied something that Yolanda's own father never had. A kind of security, tranquillity perhaps, that no hammer blow of worldly fortune could ever take away.

In the tower room, Alisdair was watching the flickering shadows play over the painted cloths and falling into sleep. His eyes were already closed when he was roused by a soft tap on the door. At first he did not respond, thinking it just one of the old house's many night-time coughs and groans. Investigation was also ruled out by the fact that Alisdair lay naked in the bed with three hot water bottles for company. There had been no masculine night attire in the house for Diana to offer him. But the tap was repeated, louder and more insistent.

"Yes? Who is it?"

"It's me! Yolanda."

In some consternation, Alisdair draped himself in the counterpane and opened the door to find her standing on the threshold, clad in a towelling bathrobe with her hair spread over her shoulders. Alisdair felt himself on treacherous ground.

"Is anything wrong, Yolanda?"

"No," she shrugged with infuriating nonchalance and walked past him into the room. "You've no idea how silly you look in that thing."

"Yolanda!" Alisdair's exasperation was plain, "It's past midnight. What's the matter? Do you feel ill . . . is your mother all right?"

"No. I just wanted to talk. For instance," she tossed her hair back challengingly, provocatively, "have you the least idea who we are?"

Alisdair looked down at her, still clutching the counterpane around his shoulders, wryly conscious that he must cut a ridiculous figure.

"Yolanda! Do you really think this is the time and place to discuss your family tree? And as you so penetratingly point out, I'm hardly dressed for genealogical discussions . . . or discussions of any kind, for that matter."

"My mother keeps it quiet," Yolanda cut across him, "but my father's in prison."

There was a moment's silence in which nothing could be heard but the logs collapsing on the stone hearth and a dog barking in the distance.

"I thought you ought to know, that's all," Yolanda said finally.

Alisdair regarded her despairingly. Discretion does not suit some natures. Secrets are irksome to them. Unlike those to whom secrecy is a stored effervescence, Yolanda could not be easy until everyone around her knew the worst she had to tell of herself.

"Do you want to talk about it?" he asked her.

"That's why I came, stupid."

They talked, crouched by the fire, until the church's bell sounded a quarter past three in the morning. Yolanda, with the extreme, healthy selfishness of the very young, told Alisdair her life's story. It began with fleeting impressions of nurses and prams and ended with the confrontation between herself and her father in the prison.

"So now you know," Yolanda said in the end.

"Yes. I do. I remember reading about it in the newspapers but I didn't make the connection. If I had, did you think I should feel any differently about you, Landa?" It was the first time he had used her pet name. He did it without thinking. "Or your mother," Alisdair added prudently after an imperceptible pause.

"I had to be certain. It might have made a difference. It would to some people."

"Tell me something. Have you actually met anyone like that yet?" Alisdair grimaced. The difficulties of retaining both modesty and dignity were causing unbearable cramp.

"No, I haven't, but I know I'm going to."

"Don't pull things down on yourself, sweetheart. Now I think you should go back to your own room very quietly. I don't want your mother calling me a vile seducer and forbidding me to darken her doors ever again."

Yolanda leaned across and kissed him on the cheek. He drew her to himself and held her close, the counterpane slipping from his shoulders.

"Go on," he pushed her away gently.

As she slipped through the door, Alisdair thought how very simple it would have been to seduce Yolanda Neville. But he wanted to go on being welcome in her home for the rest of time, because one day, he told himself, she would be his wife.

🌿 LAFONTAINE FRÈRES WERE small as merchant banks go. A family affair with Huguenot links, the partnership still retained directors on its board who bore the old name. With an unimpeachable reputation in the City and more than sufficient reserves, they had resisted flotation on the stock market.

"We can still afford our privacy, I'm happy to tell you," one white haired elder was to tell Diana much later. "It allows us the privilege of occasional eccentricity, my dear Mrs. Neville. Personally, I look on the old firm as a gentleman's gambling club. We win some, we lose some . . . and when we do, we can blush in private."

LF, as the bank was now more commonly called, was first on Epoch's list of prospects. The reasons were simple. The bank was itself a client of Epoch's although, as Merlin Olaff pointed out acidly in the taxi which collected her from King's Cross on the day of the presentation, "They pay us an annual retainer in case they want any publicity except they never do. The retainer is just a seigneurial gesture. The only thing we've ever persuaded them to do is alter their name so it sounds a bit more user friendly. And there's another thing," he added as he paid the cabbie off, "we didn't tell you when we first met you, but we've a food retail chain that's desperate for a new idea." The name of the high street giant made Diana's eyebrows take wing.

The discussion continued in Epoch's Dean Street premises whilst vast blow-ups of artwork on melamine panels were loaded into a box van on the narrow street below.

"You know the story yourself, Diana, because you've probably shopped there yourself like everybody else. This retailer commanded the high ground in terms of quality and originality, virtually from the beginning. They were the first large-scale reaction against the "pile 'em high and sell 'em cheap" theory of supermarket strategy. Trouble is, the consumers liked it so much that the cut price baked bean merchants took a leaf out of their book and left our client with nothing much to mark them out from the crowd."

Diana knew a sensation of rising panic. Where was all this leading? It was all too much, too soon. How could she possibly supply a chain like the one Merlin was talking about in her first year, or even her second? While he talked, people kept coming in and out of the conference room with folders and files, leaving some and removing others. The Creative Director put his pony-tailed head round the door.

"We on schedule?" He addressed Olaff over Diana's head. She had met him before and seen his work as a stream of beautifully executed creative ideas had been submitted for her comments. Under his hand, her vision had begun to take solid, three dimensional shape.

"Yep, we're fine. Diana'll want to powder her nose but we've plenty of time. How's your circus coming on?"

The Creative Director admitted that there had been a cessation of work on the truck loading owing to some altercation with a traffic warden. There had also been a last minute hitch with the editing of the sample promotional video. The hair on the back of Diana's neck rose.

"Relax, Diana," Olaff grinned. "This is situation normal for the advertising industry. Don't worry, we'll get you to the bank on time. Have a cup of coffee and a fag. Put your feet up. You're the star of the show."

Diana, of course, neither accepted a cigarette from the box Olaff pushed at her across the glass table, nor did she put her feet up on it. But she laughed.

"Great to see you, Diana," the Creative Director addressed her directly. "I'll let you know when its wagons-roll time. No panic." The door swung behind him with a decided air of haste.

"In fact," Olaff said, "who wants coffee at a time like this? I always keep a little something cool and calming in the fridge here for prepresentation nerves."

Once he had provided Diana with a glass of admirable Chablis, Olaff shot is cuffs and resumed his former topic.

"Where was I? Oh, yes. Our supermarket client with the USP problem . . . that means unique selling point. They haven't got one any more, that's the problem. Well, listen up because here comes the good bit. This supermarket chain is not only our client but LF's as well. Get it?"

Rapidly as Diana's mind worked through the labyrinth of information with which she had been bombarded, after a moment she had to confess that she did not entirely *get it*.

"Keeping it in the family doesn't sound like the most motivating reason for Lafontaine Frères to lend me money. They might think it all a bit incestuous . . . faintly unhealthy."

"Aha! I forgot to tell you the punch line," Olaff poured himself another mouthful of Chablis and offered the bottle to Diana. She shook her head.

"Don't be drunk but do be cheerful, that's what I tell my youngsters about presentation technique. Yes, our supermarket client owes our banker client money. Not doing too well, you see? Now, if LF can see that you . . . we have an idea that can rescue our mutual client . . . by the simple expedient of making you a mutual client this very day . . ."

"How do you know that they owe money to the bank? I thought these things were kept quiet."

Olaff gave Diana a long look. As so often, she had put her finger on the grey area with unerring accuracy. She was never satisfied with half the story. And she always knew when she had not heard it all. The business world had already encountered two or three of these housewife superstars. Here was another with her tidy mental cupboard and evasion-proof "turn out your pockets" mode of information gathering. Not that Olaff had anything to hide.

"Very simple. LF are not our supermarket client's only source of financial support. They're not big enough. But that supermarket client owes money to other banks . . . clearing banks . . . so it's a reasonable assumption that . . ."

Diana admitted it was a possibility.

"Anyway. Forget about it. That's just background. Stuff I would have told you if you'd been able to get down before Christmas. The great thing is to go in there and bowl 'em over."

❦ A TINY STONE building cowering beside a steel and glass skyscraper in St. Mary's Axe bore a polished brass plate with the cryptic initials LF. The plate did not even inform passers-by that here were bankers. Either you knew, Olaff explained on a slight note of hysteria, or LF did not want to know *you*.

Amongst the Epoch cavalcade, it seemed that Diana alone

was outwardly serene. Despite incessant admonitions to each other to "stay cool," the presentation team appeared to be breathing like blown horses by the time they stood in the bank's minute, mahogany lined reception hall. They were not kept waiting.

The board of directors greeted Diana with old world courtesy and, to her embarrassment, gave her pride of place in the centre of a half circle of chairs arranged around a podium erected in their library. The eighteenth century furniture, richly tooled and gilded books, oriental rugs and portraits of founding fathers formed an odd background for the casually dressed young men from Epoch. But they fitted the LF directors in their world weary Savile Row elegance like a glove.

While some arrangements were made with video screens and other things, the directors scrutinised Diana. They did so with complete openness. They had been asked to back the wife of a fraudster. It was a risk they were entitled to look at very closely and from every angle.

Anticipating this, Diana had gone to considerable trouble and expense over her appearance. The name of a couture dressmaker serving Harrogate ladies who lunched in good causes had been passed to her by the first dressmaker she had approached. She wanted an old dress copied. Eyeing the garments her prospective customer showed her, the good Nidcaster woman had said, "Ee lass, I can't mek owt like that you've got on. Why don't ye buy summut?"

"Because," Diana told her, "I'm a size eight and there aren't many things on the rack for people like me. It's terribly important, every single stitch has to be right. And also it has to be a specific colour. I have to fit in with things, you see."

"Then you'd best go to Bessie Brown. She meks for all t'fussy flibbertygibbets in 'arrogate. She'll be right glad to get 'er 'ands on you and she'll do you a grand job. Cost you, mind."

Bessie Brown had not only copied the dress and coat accurately but subtly updated it, adding original and expensive detail of her own. The bill was large, but not as large as it would have been in London and Diana was well satisfied. Bessie Brown was a local treasure.

"You'll wear short black gloves if you've any sense, Mrs. Neville. Get some shoes dyed to match the fabric and you don't need any jewellery with that hair and those eyes. Maybe some ear-rings and a bracelet. Nothing else, mind. That'll be just four hundred pounds and thirty pounds for fittings in your own home." The dressmaker presented her handwritten bill briskly. Evidently she didn't believe in the nonsense of sending accounts.

"And the very best of luck to you. That apricot really does something for you. Gives you a lift. You'll look a treat."

"I bet you say that to all the ladies," Diana joked as she wrote the cheque.

"Indeed, I do not," Bessie Brown fumed. "Some people are just plain unfortunate. You could have been a mannequin if you weren't so pipsqueak . . . not that you'd know it to look at you. Tall looking you are. Like the Queen in her portraits."

Leaving that barrage of compliments, seasoned with subtle criticism for honour's sake, behind her, Bessie Brown went on her way.

The presentation began with an exposition of Diana's business aims and a breakdown of what action she would take to achieve them. Now that he had begun, Merlin Olaff appeared relaxed and confident, taking the bankers through the headings quickly. He used a flip chart which showed the regional development planned, the strategic deployment of printing and packaging units, the location of distribution centres and the systems for transport to those centres. De-centralised packing stations were covered, together with recycled materials and related topics. There were questions at the end of this section of the presentation.

"Will you appoint existing printers in the relevant areas, Mrs. Neville?" The question came from the back of the room and Diana had to crane her neck. Olaff motioned her to step up on the podium.

"No. I shall set up independent dedicated units. Most printers are struggling for survival. Their chief interest is in long runs to amortise the capital cost of new offset litho machinery. Changeover between one run and the next is time consuming and therefore expensive. With low individual product volumes, my runs are likely to be short but numerous. I shall, wherever possible, use secondhand Heidelberg letterpress machinery and recruit skilled men already retired from the mainstream industry. Young men have not been trained on letterpress."

Diana found she was enjoying herself. The arcane vocabulary of the printing industry and many others now came as naturally to her lips as a nursery rhyme. The weeks of research had left her more thoroughly informed in every area of her great endeavour than she realised. It was only now, when she was being questioned as at a *viva voce* examination, that she began to realize how much she knew, and about how much.

"Is there any reason apart from low cost to prefer letterpress?" an elderly gentleman with a *pince nez* probed.

"Yes, in fact, there is. It's not apparent to the unpractised eye, but letterpress print work has a slightly softer look. It also embosses the paper very slightly which gives a subliminal impression of texture and quality appropriate to the style of our merchandise."

There were a few more questions about the rival merits of cellophane and polyethylene and Diana was soon aware that she knew more than anyone in the room about the subject, Epoch's Creative Director included. He caught her eye and mimed an enraged strangulation. It made her smile again, the one thing which she sometimes forgot to do when absorbed in her subject.

Passing on to distribution itself, the bankers asked how she would handle such an immensely complex procedure on a national scale from a standing start and with no experience. It was the key to everything.

"Gentlemen, I shan't do it at all," she paused for dramatic effect. It came off. The room was pin-drop quiet and Merlin Olaff hugged himself. She was a natural.

"The world is full of large distributors who claim that they will distribute any product or product range in any area for any producer. The complications will be their problem. These people have computerised systems and battalions of transport. For a consideration, they will equip trucks or vans of appropriate size, paint them in our livery and deliver up and down the country direct to both wholesalers and retailers. They can and will collect the money, deduct their own expenses and deliver the balance to me. I shall have to set up a central computer to identify the individual growers to whom that money is owed ... or rather, some of it. Of course, the price of the goods allows a profit for the company."

Diana's face was sweetly distressed that she should have left this vital point so late in the speech. The bankers laughed indulgently but she was afraid she had made a fool of herself. A glance at Merlin Olaff reassured her. He gave her a discreet thumbs up sign. She was doing all right.

The second phase of the presentation belonged to the Creative Director. There was a rustle of repressed anticipation as the blinds were lowered and all lights extinguished except some specially positioned spots fixed earlier in the day.

The creative presentation fell into three distinct parts and in each case the approach was startlingly different.

"The first step," the Creative Director said, "is to get gardeners to garden . . . for the company. And, by the way, as this logo shows, the company will be called 'English Gardens.' "

The logo represented a simple wrought iron garden gate with the initials EG incorporated and "English Gardens" in small upper case letters beneath. It was a one-glance statement of the company's business designed to look good on packaging, letterheads and transport.

"What happens if you move into Scotland and Wales?" The question arrowed through the dimness.

"Simple. Operations in those areas will be called Scottish or Welsh Gardens as appropriate. It's a matter of striking a balance between the parochial and the national. Mrs. Neville herself is the expert on this aspect of perception. She'll be glad to address any questions later, gentlemen." The objection was fielded smoothly from the floor by Olaff.

A blow-up of a black and white advertisement headlined simply, "Your Garden could earn you Money," was brought on to the podium.

The treatment was what Olaff had called "folksy," showing everyday people, past their first youth, harvesting garden fruits and vegetables. The body copy, or small print, would give details. There were six more of these advertisements, refining the message and expanding it. The advertisements were all friendly, unpatronising and factual. They were to be printed in a range of magazines, some aimed at the retired, some gardening hobby magazines. A short video showing a low budget television commercial followed the same homespun theme. A tape of a radio commercial rounded off the section.

"Nothing tricksy here, gentlemen, just a straightforward proposition designed for maximum exposure at minimum cost.

Mrs. Neville insisted on a non-exploitive approach to potential producers and we thought she was right."

Diana smiled a little grimly to herself in the darkness. In fact, it was the only aspect of the promotional material over which she had fought Epoch. At first, the disagreement had been sharp. Their ideas for appealing to greed and dangling the hope of big profits had been hopelessly out of tune with her own views. "Remember," she had told them in one letter, "these people will be our partners in a very real sense. I don't want to start with a confidence trick." Sedgely's opinion of the drafts and sample layouts she had been sent had proved of inestimable value here.

"I've never thought much about advertisements, Mrs. Neville. But I suppose if I read them at all, I want to know what's on offer and how to get it. If it's owt flashy like, I feel suspicious."

The layouts shown to the bankers all had Sedgely's seal of approval.

Next the trade advertising was shown. Here Epoch's creative men had concentrated on the commercial viability factor. High value goods have fatter profit margins. The illustrative content was made subordinate to persuasive copy. This was routine stuff. It was a fact of shopkeeping life that to stay ahead, new attractions in tune with the times were essential. "Take the Gamble out of Organic," one headline said. The advertisements were full colour and full page. They were workmanlike, effective and expensive. Designed to give the businessman confidence in the company.

"Once again, we have resisted the temptation to do anything unusual. Proposition, explanation and, as you'll see from the cut-out coupons, a call to immediate action." The Creative Director used a kind of outsize conductor's baton to point out the working features of the advertisements.

"Research shows that response to coupon advertising can be as high as sixty per cent and conversion in the food sector is conservatively estimated at seventeen per cent."

There were murmurs of approval from the bankers. They were on home ground here. So far so good.

"To give retailers and wholesalers a better insight into English Gardens and the profits they can expect, we have prepared a sales video. You'll find it juxtaposes hard facts with emotive visual images. Diana, Mrs. Neville, that is, constantly reminds us that everybody's human ... vulnerable to charm ..."

The Chairman of the bank, sitting next to Diana, tapped her on the back of the hand and nodded.

"Very acute of you, my dear."

The video ran for five minutes and commanded complete attention.

The *pièce de résistance* of the creative presentation was, of course the consumer advertising. Unconsciously, Diana held her breath. The purely practical played a large part in her plan, but at the end of the day, everything would disintegrate if the imagination of the shopper was not caught and held. No holds had been barred to create the crucial demand at street level. In very large measure, the pictures and the words reflected what Diana had conveyed to Epoch about Gilbert's Tower ... its air of legend and unpolluted virtue. The press ads and the television commercials were lavish and evocative ... works of art with which Epoch hoped to win one of the big advertising awards.

To the disappointment of Epoch and Diana herself, the Chairman waved away the pack shots and dummies.

"I'm happy, gentleman. Are you?" He turned around in his chair to look at his colleagues.

There were grunts of agreement and the Creative Director gave way to media buyers and account planners. They were heard politely but by the time the blinds had been raised and the spotlights switched off, the bankers' concentration was unfocused. Diana's female antennae picked up the tension of decision in the men sitting around her. They crossed and uncrossed their legs restlessly. Everything else was just going through the motions. She answered a few more questions. None of them seemed very sensible to her. It was as if the bank had withdrawn into its own mind. Their answer, she felt sure, would probably be "no."

"Thank you, Mrs. Neville, and you gentlemen, for the presentation." The chairman rose. "I'm sure we have all been very much interested in your, if I may say so, unique vision. I hope you will understand if we leave you for a little while to consider the elements of your proposal."

Diana was not optimistic. The latter part of the presentation had gone too quickly, as if the bank was keen to get it over. The directors had retired for courtesy's sake. They were going out like a jury which was already unanimous in condemning the prisoner at the bar. They would come back with a refusal. If it were otherwise there would have been much more talk. She lifted her chin in a small, unconscious gesture of defiance. There were other banks.

When the Lafontaine team had left the room, Diana thanked Epoch and they thanked her. Everyone had done their best and done well. The chatter of mutual congratulation covered the nervousness like a ragged garment.

"I don't really understand this," Diana confided to Olaff. "I thought they'd send us away and write to us later." She did not dare express her own gloom concerning the likely outcome.

After a few minutes had elapsed the party in the library had become silent. Further speech was futile. A messenger in a neat, shiny suit popped his oil slicked head round the door.

"Chairman'd like a word with you, Mr. Olaff, sir."

He was not away long and came back surrounded by the bank's beaming directors.

"Well, Mrs. Neville," the white haired chairman began, "we like your proposal and to be frank, we like you. If you'll pardon me for saying so, it might have been a different story if your husband had been in a position to influence you, but since this is entirely your own show, we'll give you five million pounds to kick off with a pilot in Yorkshire and the North East. What do you say?"

"I say thank you," Diana responded weakly. The allusion to Michael pricked her conscience faintly. Of course she would be influenced by him. She had been already. She had consulted the best of his example . . . emulated his energy, his daring . . . and would go on doing so. Now was not the time to explain, if ever.

Conflicting tides of emotion swept over her, feelings of relief and unbelief. She had been willing to pit her strength against obstacles. She had been prepared to sit out a long, nerve testing wait. To Diana, success had seemed to come simply and unexpectedly, like the visit of a rare bird to the window sill. The months of work and worry were forgotten in the miracle of fruition.

"Here, get the poor girl a chair," somebody else's voice

reached her ear as if from a separate continent. Funny that people should think of her as a girl. She heard a spontaneous burst of hand clapping and a glass of champagne was thrust into her hand. Five months. It had taken five months to come from nowhere to somewhere.

The Chairman sat down beside her.

"Drink up, my dear girl. You're as white as a sheet. Tell me now, who have you in mind for co-directors? You'll have to have at least one, you know. Companies Act. At any rate, we shall put one of our directors on your board. But don't worry. Watching brief only. No interference unless you want it. Who's going to do the donkey work, though?"

Diana had known for a long time whom she would need at her side. The moment of shock had passed and adrenalin began to course through her veins. There were so many new things to think about now. The planning was over and the doing was imminent.

She never replied to the query about her directors. Another man came over to them to refill their glasses. He was introduced to her as Cedric Lafontaine, the Chairman's nephew.

"When you're ready, Mrs. Neville, we can put you in the way of a large retailer." The young man tapped his nose conspiratorially, glancing at his uncle. "We're in a position to use some strong arm tactics so . . ."

The Chairman cleared his throat significantly. Disliking the role of hatchet man himself, he had assigned the chore of acquainting Mrs. Neville with the less agreeable features of her triumph to his nephew. He intended that the message should be conveyed without delay and in his absence. Bidding Diana a gallant adieu, the Chairman withdrew suavely. A less interesting, though nonetheless urgent affair claimed his attention. Regretfully, he must leave her in Cedric's charge. They would all meet again soon, no doubt . . . perhaps to discuss the supermarket. But, his parting glance at his nephew stressed, first things first.

"Oh, Mrs. Neville," Cedric spoke as soon as his uncle was out of earshot. "There's a small formality to be observed. We'll need the deeds to your house. Could you have your solicitors forward them to us here?"

Evidence of commitment. Diana did not need to ask. Her jewellery had been sold in that cause and now the Tower itself was at risk. But there was no other way. Gilbert's Tower was hostage for a five million pound ransom. Old Mr. Lafontaine had eschewed the task of telling her so himself, she noted. That was his privilege.

SEDGELY'S FACE FLUSHED darkly when he was invited to become a director of English Gardens.

"Do you remember us shaking hands in the orchard near the peach trees all those months ago?" Diana asked him.

"Aye, I do. But that were for something a lot smaller'n this."

"Albert," Diana used his Christian name for the first time, "I like to think it was for whatever might have happened to us and our garden."

Sedgely was visibly moved. Tears formed in his eyes and he wiped them away with the sleeve of his potting shed jacket. Diana made herself busy with some papers on the desk. He was not the sort of man who would like a woman to see him weep. It was the only thing he and Michael had in common. Sedgely accepted on condition that he be allowed to buy shares in the company with the three thousand pound legacy which Aunt Thea had left him and his wife. There was some trouble over his salary since he flatly refused to take one. In the end, Diana and he compromised. He would accept a token director's fee of a thousand a year. She could push him no further.

With Alisdair it was different. He accepted the directorship with alacrity. Diana mentioned the minimum salary with which she felt she could hope to buy his undivided attention and loyalty. She need not have worried. Alisdair would have given his all for far less.

"You'll be travelling a lot to give individual producers advise, so you'll need a good car. Get what you want up to fifteen thousand pounds."

Alisdair felt no compunction in accepting the post. He now knew who Yolanda's father was but Diana did not know the identity of his own. Nor was it relevant. Alisdair did not believe in burdening situations with facts which might make them unclear. His own mind was very clear. He would do everything he could to make English Gardens a success and then he would marry the boss's daughter. Reconciling his father and

Grandmère to these realities was not today's problem. In the meantime, Yolanda should be watched over with care. She still had some growing up to do before she became romantically involved. A year, perhaps a little longer ... when she had left school at any rate, and then he would speak.

Grilling six sausages and preparing a large quantity of mashed potato, Alisdair contemplated his future with complete satisfaction. He was not so vain as to imagine that Yolanda would necessarily fall into his arms. But as he told himself, sheer persistence had won the battle for blokes in the past. Persistence was his strong suit. He sneaked a covert glance at himself between the lettering on the old pub mirror in his kitchen. He'd never have the kind of looks his father had but, on the other hand, Landa could do worse.

Epoch began the media campaign to recruit gardeners immediately. The response was overwhelming. Alisdair and Sedgely were soon fully occupied, visiting plots that varied in size and type from cramped backyards to spacious but neglected kitchen gardens attached to country houses. Everywhere they were welcomed with the same query. "Why has nobody thought of it before?" The list of suppliers committed to the aims of English Gardens lengthened rapidly.

It put pressure on Diana to set up her centralised computer system since much preparatory work must be done before the growing season started. She rented a small unit in a light industrial estate on the outer fringes of Nidcaster.

For suitable hardware and a tailor-made software package she had to go to Leeds. Compatibility with the software used by any of several sub-contracted distributors she might appoint was a key requirement. The computer specialists also agreed to recruit an operator for her.

A Bradford dealer in second-hand printing machinery was alerted to look out for any presses coming on the market which corresponded with Diana's specification. They were to be bought subject to inspection by the dealer himself and stored.

"Remember, I know what to look for because you taught me yourself, Mr. Holmroyd. No bent rollers. If you manage to get ten together, stop at that for the time being. Oh, and any metal type. Times and Palace Script. Buy it. Can I leave it with you?"

Mr. Holmroyd scratched his head. He'd been impressed with

Mrs. Neville when she'd first come to ask his advise. At least she knew the difference between a platen and a double crown, and that was something for a woman. Now she was buying.

"You've t'brass, Mrs. Neville?"

"I have that, Mr. Holmroyd," Diana found herself falling naturally into the idiom of the place.

He didn't doubt her. She'd a handshake as firm and true as any man's. Didn't go slack on you at the wrist. Funny thing for such a little scrap of a woman. Mr. Holmroyd had confidence. So had everyone else.

Also in Bradford, there were companies who dealt in packaging machinery. Diana had visited them before. Now she was able to go back to them and advise them to stand by to fill orders quickly.

"I can't wait weeks and months for the German manufacturers to get round to delivering. When I want a machine, I'll want it within seven days. If you can't supply from stock or get it from Germany, buy in Italy or Spain . . . anywhere you can. As long as it's a good machine and simple to operate with rapid change-over. It'll do if you say it will. I trust your judgment."

At Excelpak, they didn't really like people trusting them. It wasn't good commercial policy. But they reconciled themselves to being trusted by Diana. "You couldn't," as the partners agreed bitterly between themselves, "refuse a lady."

Back in Leeds a major industrial estate agent was set on to scour the area for suitable print and packing workshops. Between two and three thousand square feet, all on one level, with vehicular access, loading bay and turning space.

"To rent or buy, Mrs. Neville?" a startled negotiator asked her.

"Ideally, to rent with enfranchisable leases."

It was the same everywhere. In Whitelocks and other city watering holes, the name of Diana Neville was much bandied about. In Leeds, if not in Bradford, the new businesswoman was a familiar phenomenon. But where was the big, brand new briefcase and the square-shouldered suit? Diana darted about like a humming bird. One moment she was there, vibrant and needle sharp, whirring with energy, and then she was gone. Who was she? The editor of the *Yorkshire Business Pages* was intrigued.

When he got back to his office he sorted through his waste-paper basket. Ah, yes. There it was. A press release on pale green paper. Now he came to look at it again, it seemed to come from a London agency. The company it was rabbiting on about was English Gardens. Due for launch on March 1st. "The inspiration of Diana Neville," it said, and "heavily under-pinned financially by LF." Bit of a turn up for the books, that. LF usually liked to keep their business quiet. They must have taken a fancy to this lady.

"Here," he slung the crumpled press release on a junior's desk. "Clean the superlatives out of this and send it down."

A few moments later he was reading an article submitted by a freelance. It was about pension fund investments. The guy seemed to know what he was talking about. When he read the name typed at the bottom, the editor was not surprised. Michael Neville. He took a swig of cold coffee from a plastic cup. The pieces fell into place at once.

"Oi! Sling that press release. Send a stringer round to see this Mrs. Neville. Bit of a story there."

❦ THE *FINANCIAL TIMES* had also received a press release from Epoch. The paper devoted a bare column centimetre to Diana's new venture. It was enough to catch not only Michael's vigilant eye but also those of some of his fellows.

"You'll be riding the hog's back when you get out, Neville," one chaffed him at breakfast. "Your missus will have made you a brand new fortune to go home to. You're lucky you don't have to worry."

The man, a disgraced stockbroker, went on to talk about his own wife who was barely coping without him. She'd gone to Cornwall to stay with his parents. There was friction. Michael did not listen but went on eating.

What sort of fools would back Diana to set up and run a company of any size? In response to his furious enquiry about the sale of her jewellery, she had told him that she was starting a business based on organic produce. She hadn't said much more than that. It sounded like the kind of half-baked, roman-tic idea that a woman would get herself mixed up in. Michael hadn't taken it very seriously.

He felt angry that Diana considered herself free to dispose of valuable assets to pay for a whim of her own without consulting him. That's what he said, anyway. He would never forget the shock of seeing those amethysts round the flat faced Japanese girl's neck. It was as if he himself had been discarded. Sold for hard cash.

"Michael, darling," he remembered her voice, maddeningly patient, "I just have to do this to secure our future. I know you'd like to be involved and I wish you could. But let's face facts, you can't . . . at least not yet. Do try and be supportive. Tell me what you're doing. You haven't written for weeks."

The words had rung discordantly in his ear. It was not his business to be supportive. It was hers. Diana violated him with her liberty of action.

Although the programme participants were allowed to telephone their families as often as they wished, most agreed that this was a privilege spiked with pain. There were long silences while the separated spouses racked their brains for anything to say. The wives would talk about bills and burst pipes, mortgage repayments . . . managing or not managing. The children were well or not well . . . the weather was good or bad. In the end, the inability to describe a world that the other could not imagine; the inability of the imprisoned to solve the problems which made the other's freedom a mockery, would bring down a cloud of silence.

The telephones were in a corridor outside the canteen. The only privacy was afforded by a bubble of perspex. Every programme participant got used to seeing others doing what he himself did. Leaning against the wall with the receiver held to his ear, saying nothing and listening to silence.

"I want Yolanda to come and see me," Michael had said at length. "If you're such a prime mover these days, you can get stuck into organising that."

Michael knew it was not an easy request to fulfil. The train journey from York or Leeds to Salisbury took eight hours and she would have to change twice. The carriages were full of quarrelsome youths swilling lager and terrorising other passengers. But he did not think of it. He was beginning to forget things like that. The details of life outside the prison's enclosure had grown indistinct.

Yolanda was determined to go. In the end Alisdair volunteered to take her, saying that he could visit a nursery in the area whilst she was at the prison. Diana was only mildly surprised that Alisdair should know about Michael. Yolanda would have told him.

Michael, by the Governor's grace, was allowed to keep some of the money he earned from writing articles. The rest was placed on deposit for him. What he had left enabled him to take Yolanda on a bus to a film in Salisbury that neither of them really wanted to see and later to a hamburger joint. It was simply a matter of finding somewhere warm. He questioned his daughter closely.

"Your mother seems to have got herself pretty heavily involved. What on earth does she think she's up to?"

She told him as well as she was able. The information was patchy but sufficiently coherent to allow Michael to form an idea of the scale of his wife's activities.

"Who's that fellow who brought you down here? Not a boyfriend, is he, Landa?"

"No! He's Mummy's new Horticultural Director. He offered to drive me down here to save me going on the train. I do like him, though." Yolanda crumpled a paper napkin and threw it on her plate. She could not define her relationship with Alisdair.

"How much is she paying him?" Michael started singeing the napkin with the end of his cigar, avoiding Yolanda's eye.

"*I* don't know. Quite a lot, I think. He's rather well qualified."

"Around much, is he?" Michael asked, taking a long drag on the cigar.

Yolanda caught the nuance in the question. Her own reactions told her more about her feelings for Alisdair than any other incident had yet done.

"Yes. An awful lot. But he's certainly not Mummy's boyfriend, if that's what you're worried about, Daddy. He's far too young for her. And anyway, you know you're the only person in her life and always will be. It's just business, that's all."

Michael was satisfied. Whoever he was, he was no threat. Landa would see to that. He changed the subject.

"Has she, your mother, I mean," Michael corrected himself, "fixed herself up with some sub-contracted distributors yet?"

He wasn't really interested. It was just something to say.

"Yes, she says she's got to now. I think she said she's going with some people called Fernley Distribution. I think that's right, anyway. I don't suppose it means any more to you than to me. I hear so many names. There seem to be dozens of firms and companies involved. The whole thing's so awfully complicated. It's amazing Mummy thought of it."

"Fernley?"

Michael stubbed out his cigar and looked at the incomprehensible, faintly printed bill. He started to summon the waitress, anxious now to go back to the prison, away from the head-splitting pop music and gimcrack jollity of the place. They would go back in a taxi. Michael had felt Yolanda's sense of vicarious humiliation on the bus. She'd said it was fun. But it wasn't, not for either of them.

"They're a good little company, Fernley. Done very nicely for themselves, too. There's a bit of talk about a take-over by the Strang-Steele Group. Does she know that?"

❦ THE STRANG-STEELE conglomerate's absorption of Fernley was more than talk and Diana was thoroughly up to date with the details by the middle of March. Although the coincidence seemed relatively unimportant, she was sufficiently struck by it to carry the mass of glossy literature which Fernley had sent concerning the take-over, out of the house and into the orchard where Sedgely was mounted on a step ladder.

"It will make no difference to the way this business is run," Diana read the covering letter aloud to Sedgely, who was pollinating each single star of peach blossom spangling the naked spurs, ". . . except that customers will now experience an enhanced level of service owing to the joint resources available to Fernley through membership of the Strang-Steele Group . . ." It was the usual corporate mumbo jumbo and Sedgely, absorbed in his work with a sable brush, evinced little interest in it.

"Aye well, aye. I 'spect it'll do, Mrs. Neville, if you say it will," he dismounted from the ladder and moved the improvised frost shield aside from the neighbouring tree. "What does Mr. Alisdair think to it?"

Diana didn't know. She had not yet tested Alisdair's reactions.

Sedgely grunted unhelpfully. He knew Mr. Strang-Steele in a manner of speaking, having once, during a period of unemployment, found work in a ganger's team harvesting the great man's pea fields. And he'd a fair idea who Mr. Alisdair was, too. Inessential information on which Sedgely's lips were firmly closed. 'T weren't neither here nor there, he told himself.

The orange cat which lay along the top of the wall in an attitude of imperial supervision closed its eyes slowly. It, too, had nothing to communicate.

There was no more to be got out of either of them and Diana stood for a moment in silence, enjoying the oven like heat of the orchard's south-west corner.

"Well," she said finally, because to a person of nervous, metropolitan culture, it seemed necessary to say something, "I'll go and get on with my salesmanship."

It was too late to change horses now, anyway, she mused, walking back to the house through the formal parterres. By signing the contract with Fernley she would become Philip Strang-Steele's customer at one remove. A tick bird riding on the rhinoceros's back. Strang-Steele himself would never feel her claws or be aware that English Gardens was there at all.

Business had a way of making bed fellows of people with nothing whatever in common. Michael had often said so. A routine irony.

CHAPTER
8

❧ Diana's life was now bedevilled with computer print-outs and summaries. Not naturally numerate, her eyes ached with the effort of reading figures in the correct columns. They were apt to wander all over the page. And sometimes she would stare and stare at what she knew perfectly well to be an eight, but only the quality of *fiveness* would lodge in her brain. It was a strain and an effort. But she would do it. She was determined to understand everything herself, however long it took. Often enough, it took till the small hours of the morning.

By the end of June, the accountants appointed by the bank were able to say that English Gardens was staying neck and neck with the projections. Only a rise in the cost of petrol prevented the company from outperforming expectations. On the credit side, soaring temperatures in May and June boosted the demand for salads and early soft fruits.

The endless sunny days induced a free-spending optimism. Every enterprising restaurateur in Yorkshire with a few square feet of concrete to call his own filled it with tables. Those who did not encroached on the public highways. It seemed the pleasure of eating an omelette out of doors outweighed any fear of fatal injury from a juggernaut. Many a burly Yorkshireman unbuttoned his shirt to the waist and garnished his chest hair with a gold medallion.

"Inside every Yorkshireman," Diana joked with Alisdair, "there seems to be an Italian trying to get out."

The spirit of hedonism was rife.

The Confederation of British Industry did its best to restore order. Factual, finger-wagging talk of coming recession, inflation and unemployment was pumped out of television studios. The presenters were talking to switched-off sets in empty living-rooms. Life was lived out of doors.

In these freak conditions, Diana's theories illustrated themselves beyond denial. Once the British have good weather, then they have everything. A cheerful, self-satisfied chauvinism took over. "You can't get a good bottle of wine as cheap in France as you can in England," said the Dordogne set. "There's nowhere as nice as this when it *is* nice," was the way they expressed it in Nidcaster marketplace. "We shouldn't go abroad, should we, Mrs. Neville, if it were like this all t'time?" Self-approval breeds generosity. English Gardens satisfied an impulse to buy British and offered opportunities for discovery.

No product was sold without a full, anecdotal description. Very often a proprietor's recipe was included in the pack. Individual names became known. As far away as Barnsley and Redcar, they were comparing Diana Neville's Little Ruby strawberries from Gilbert's Tower with Dick Garside's Mini Sovereigns from The Mill House, Mytholmroyd. It was becoming a cult.

Up and down the motorways and in the baking town centres, the cream vans with the English Garden gate logo were seen scurrying through the traffic. Independent greengrocer stockists allotted little shelf space at first but found themselves sold out of the sparkling, intriguing, high-priced packages before many hours had gone by. They scratched their heads and ordered again. There was something in this organic business.

Not everything went on oiled wheels. There were administrative hitches.

Gholam Khan, who had made a modest fortune in anoraks, hadn't been paid for his green coriander. Diana herself went to his stone villa in Heaton, with its lordly, panoramic view of Bradford. The house thronged with children, grandchildren and remoter, collateral descendants. Diana's apology and explanation were graciously received. Her personal cheque was waved aside.

"You and I, Begum Sahiba . . . we are good Yorkshiremen. Our word is our bond."

And then Gholam, hindered by a posse of huge-eyed children, showed her how he made his fresh green chutney.

"I am a liberated fellow, a new man."

Diana wrote the recipe down and stayed for supper. Mrs. Khan did not speak English and would not sit down at the table. Not so liberated and half hidden by a veil, she smiled delightedly through the whole colourful episode. The next day, Diana sent her flowers. Mrs. Khan threw them away only when the blooms were dried to a crisp and the water stank.

Less easily solved were teething problems with packing machinery, which led in one instance to the ruination of one gardener's entire delivery of lamb's lettuce and an angry, disaffected retailer. Both were compensated. The gardener was soothed, the retailer was not. The first lost customer.

A generalised power cut in the Nidcaster area caused forty-eight hours' worth of havoc with the central computer. To guard against future chaos, a permanent battery stand-by power pack was installed.

As Diana said, for every milk tooth her infant organisation shed, she had to produce a silver sixpence to give immediate comfort. But in the sore places, adult replacement systems always grew, rooted in the healthy bone of experience.

❧ ALISDAIR, TOO, WAS fully stretched, balancing an expanding market with the recruitment and encouragement of new suppliers.

Diana had made him aware of the connection now existing between Fernley and English Gardens. He had, he considered, no personal interest in the matter to declare. Not to Diana, at least. An inconvenient visit from his grandmother, however, shook a few facts loose—atoms of information that began to dart and flow into unpredictable patterns.

Louise had announced her intention of coming in a letter. She treated the telephone, whenever possible, as if it had not been invented. Where its use was unavoidable, she blamed it for every unscheduled change in her own plans.

"You see," she would say, "it is impossible to get anything right on the telephone. You mishear, you forget . . . with a telegram, there can be no confusion. Always, there is clarity."

Therein lay her preference for the written word. It did not invite immediate argument. Rapid and decisive action could not be easily forestalled. Approaching her eightieth birthday, this was the style of action which Louise preferred. Accordingly, her maid posted the letter on the day they both set out from Boulogne. Aircraft, too, were disdained. They allowed insufficient time for the recipients of such a letter as she had sent Alisdair to prepare for her reception.

"We must be considerate, no?" she demanded of Marie.

Marie had once pronounced her name with a long a in the Gaelic fashion. Both the vowel and the identity had long been dazzled into submission by her mistress's lapidary Frenchness.

As it was impossible either to prevent his grandmother from coming or to accommodate two elderly ladies of luxurious habits in his cottage, Alisdair arranged to put them up at a nearby coaching inn. A suite, the only one, was reserved. Alas, the bathroom boasted no bidet. *Grandmère* would have to rough it.

Louise was undaunted by this or any other deficiency. She declared her rooms "most convenient" and tipped the dumbfounded manager handsomely in French francs. She was too vain to wear the pebble thick spectacles without which she had only the vaguest notion of her surroundings. Marie followed her, hung about like a yak with the various contraptions considered essential for their travels abroad. "Nothing," Louise often said, "can be relied upon *en voyage*. A *caravanserai* of some sort is all I ask. Marie and I are accustomed to be the boy scouts."

Marie, overcome by the rigours of the journey, was urged to retire early.

"She 'as not my constitution," her mistress observed sadly, whilst selecting digestible items from the dinner menu to be sent up on a tray. Alisdair was reading them out to her in the cocktail bar, as Louise swore she had mislaid her spectacles.

"Please ensure," she addressed a fellow diner before her grandson could intervene, "that the cabbage has no element of stalk and is very thoroughly cooked. My poor companion is much enfeebled, you understand. Also her teeth are entirely false."

Later, over their own meal, Louise admired the elegant, rose coloured stalks of rhubarb she took for desert. They were served just warm in a tansy flavoured syrup with whipped cream. She so far forgot herself as to discover her spectacles at the bottom of her bag.

"Quite extraordinary," she muttered to herself in French. "So beautiful, so simple and so delicious."

"You must tell the waiter," Alisdair smiled. "Whilst you can still see which one he is."

Louise proceeded to do so at some length.

The rhubarb had been supplied by English Gardens. Garden 12, to be precise. Alisdair congratulated himself. A patch of reclaimed bombsite in a slum area of Leeds. It was presided over by a retired trouser cutter and his brother. Allotments were no good, they said. You got "had up" if you so much as sold a lettuce to a neighbour. Squatting suited the entrepreneurial instincts of the brothers better. Passionate about their rhubarb, they had supplied the recipe for its preparation themselves. Their compost heap was exemplary. Listening to his grandmother's unstinting praise of the product, Alisdair felt confident of further orders. He looked forward to telling Diana.

It was not until he had shepherded Louise into the hotel lounge where they were to drink coffee, that they were able to get down to what Louise called "hard nails."

"Brass tacks," Alisdair corrected automatically. Louise ignored him.

"You may think I am here solely in pursuit of pleasure . . ."

Alisdair was quick to point out that he laboured under no such delusion.

"No, *Grandmère*. You are here to conduct your biennial audit of my behaviour, daily employment and domestic circumstances. And as usual, you are very, very welcome. Why you didn't wait till . . . ?"

Louise cut across him impatiently. She had come to explain that now that his father had, by means of acquiring two sizeable distribution businesses, including Fernley, and a further two or three of lesser account, expanded his activities, he was entitled to expect some family support.

"Did he say that?" Alisdair was in time to prevent Louise from tapping the ash from one of the small cheroots in which she sometimes indulged into the cream jug.

"Certainly not. He said he would not ask you again. The plans are laid. When he dies, the family shareholding . . . which amounts to sixty-four per cent, will be sold. I shall, I trust, predecease your father. It is the usual arrangement . . . *You*, you worthless boy, will cop the lot." Louise was rather proud of that expression. She had learned it when associating with British airmen during her years in the resistance. "And my little properties will pass out of our family's hands for ever. As you know, they were incorporated into the Group holdings a long time ago. Something to do with tax."

Spikily mascara'd and bravely painted, Louise's crinkled old eyes glittered with anger. And then, fleetingly, they were clouded.

That, of course, was the nub of the matter. *Grandmère* had sometimes regretted the well-meaning manoeuvre by which her son had robbed her of undisputed suzerainty over her fair French acres. "My family," she was fond of telling anyone who would listen, "have drawn honour and sustenance from this land since long before the Bonaparte upstarts were heard of." That was the farm in Provence. The Normandy property had been acquired by her Scottish husband. The Manoir des Evêques and its dependencies were dear for that reason.

"Alisdair, I wish my great-grandchildren to inherit my land. I cannot conclude my end until I know my posterity is safe."

Alisdair always felt a disgraceful urge to laugh when Louise began to talk of her death. She spoke of it as if it were some bureaucratic annoyance. A thing to be dealt with in due course, like a tax return. Her "posterity" was a thing she discussed with a stock breeder's proprietary enthusiasm. The drive for continuance. In her, it was unfaded.

"There is a simple solution, *Grandmère*. Why does my father not buy your property back from the Group?"

"It is you that are simple!" Louise smacked her coffee cup down, accurately for once. "Your father is a Scotsman," she ran the thumb of her right hand across the fingertips expressively, "and he does not care to buy what is by nature his own."

It all became very involved. In the end, Alisdair was obliged to tell his grandmother that he was unable to take over his father's new distribution business, even if he had wished to. He had a three-year service contract with another company. There would be a conflict of interest. He could not sit on the boards of both supplier and customer. Nor would he have the time. English Gardens was in its infancy and required his undivided attention.

The name slipped out unawares. Louise sprang on it like a delighted cat with a hapless mouse.

It was not long before her grandson had "spilled the peas,"

or most of them, anyway. By way of compensation, there was the small pleasure of telling Louise that the rhubarb she had eaten had arrived on her plate via English Gardens and Fernley.

"*Estimable!* But for you, not a priority. No doubt you can come to some arrangement . . ."

It was then that Yolanda's name was drawn into the conversation.

"So you see, *Grandmère* . . . I couldn't let her mother down and then expect to . . . Yolanda will be of age, but only just."

The effect on Louise was galvanising.

"Cognac! I must have Cognac immediately."

"Why, are you going to have a heart attack?" Alisdair asked with an unflattering lack of alarm. Louise looked at him sharply.

"Why should I? For once I have heard something to please me. It is grief that has been shortening my life."

"You do realise, don't you," Alisdair blocked the start of a monologue on the mysterious inconsistencies of his grandmother's health, "that Yolanda knows nothing about this? She's very young . . . she may not want . . ."

Louise understood perfectly. Alisdair was her own flesh and blood, after all. The same talent for benevolent manipulation that flourished in her was detectable in him. It was, of course, inconceivable that this young girl would reject her grandson's hand. Louise was also aware of his charming modesty. Like her son's, it was never allowed to assume disabling proportions.

"But naturally, *cheri*. It is most unwise—unkind, I would say—to distract a young girl's mind with the plans that are being made for her future by older and wiser heads. She has her studies to think of. It is enough."

Louise did not ask Alisdair for any description of Yolanda. It would be unreliable. She intended to see for herself. It was the work of a moment to extract Diana's name from Alisdair. These details, she said reasonably, were a matter of public record, as would be the address of the company's registered office.

"I shall call on Mrs. Neville tomorrow," Louise announced as, helped by Alisdair, she made her way rather unsteadily up the inn's staircase. "I have a claim on her attention." Another of *Grandmère's* stupefying assumptions.

"She may not be in," Alisdair countered. This was a worrying development. Nor would it be of any use to explain the difference between business and social acquaintance. *Grandmère* would play *gaga* . . . as she did whenever total incomprehension suited her best.

"Then I shall leave my card," Louise replied equably.

"Don't you think you should telephone first?" Alisdair suggested, and instantly regretted it. Louise raised her pencilled eyebrows in cool surprise.

"Then that would not be a 'call' in the proper sense at all, would it? It would be mere pestering. Very ill bred."

Louise had learned the social customs of the British in prewar Edinburgh, her husband's native place. That the system of exchanging formal calls had been old-fashioned then and had since been entirely dropped was, to Louise, supremely irrelevant.

"You say Mrs. Neville is . . . alone?"

"Yes," Alisdair confirmed shortly. It was difficult to say more. He was already wondering if he should warn Diana of the impending outrage and advise her to be "not at home." Tactfully, of course. It was inconvenient when people you loved insisted on getting mixed up with each other prematurely.

"If you do meet Mrs. Neville, and I must say, *Grandmère*, I think you will have a wasted trip, please keep my father out of the conversation. The Neville's are rather hard pressed and it would embarrass Diana, Mrs. Neville, to know she was employing a millionaire's son."

A pitiful argument, Alisdair berated himself, but to his relief it seemed to do the trick. Why was it that *Grandmère* always involved him in such intolerable intricacies?

Louise tapped him on the cheek affectionately. There was still so much of the anxious schoolboy about Alisdair. He partitioned his world into watertight compartments, afraid that the dye from one would leak into the next and muddy the colours. Clear divisions. Each cell of experience simple and unsullied. A boyish illusion. One day he would come to terms with his subtle, southern inheritance.

"You may rely on me, *cheri*, to exclude your father from any discourse. I visit Mrs. Neville not to inform, but to learn."

❦ LOUISE ARRIVED AT Gilbert's Tower by taxi the following morning. It was Saturday.

The interview between herself and Diana lasted fifteen minutes and was conducted in an atmosphere of astonishment on the one side and guarded approval on the other.

Card case in hand, Louise was ushered from the front door to the drawing-room by Yolanda. A blurry impression of the girl's goldness, a warm radiance of body heat and scent of good English soap impinged on her senses. Alisdair's basic instincts, at least, were sound.

"Please do sit in Mummy's chair," Yolanda said ingenuously. "It's the only one that doesn't wobble. I'll get her, shall I?"

While Yolanda was out of the room, Louise whipped out her spectacles and appraised her surroundings swiftly. Everything was in that ramshackle English style which is no style at all and is so much copied. Like the child's manners, Louise thought as she closed her smart little handbag with a snap. Endearing. But no respect for form.

"Alisdair's granny's come. She's French! You should see her feet! They're *minute* and she's got *fantastic* shoes!" Yolanda's voice carried from more distant parts of the house. Louise was not displeased. She was proud of her feet.

As it was eleven o'clock, Diana offered her visitor "something stronger" in accordance with the custom of the house established by Aunt Thea.

"I'm afraid you would be disgusted by our coffee." Diana herself felt in need of some fortification. The authoritative figure which had so calmly taken command of her drawing-room communicated a volatile energy. She sat, erect on the sofa, in the manner of an unexploded bomb. Fascinating and dangerous.

"Ah! You have a contact, I see," Louise sipped from the cut glass thimble with one eyebrow raised. "In France. An excellent *marc*, Madame. I congratulate you."

Smiling, Diana held her peace. Praise that denied an English origin to any drink of superior quality was the highest that a French person, a patriot, could offer.

"I trust I don't incommode you, *Madame*? My grandson, an inattentive boy, you understand, could not remember your *jour* . . ."

Diana emitted a gurgle of laughter. "All my days are *jours, Madame*. I haven't so many friends that I'm not overjoyed to see them at any time. New ones are especially welcome."

Louise was disconcerted by the smoothness of her reception. Mrs. Neville and her daughter were, perhaps unconsciously, a formidable duo. Yolanda had articulated all the attractive surprise that an older woman might have been expected to repress. Diana, therefore, appeared almost disappointingly unflustered. Such a very distinguished simplicity. So far, it would appear, Alisdair planned to connect himself admirably. Miss Yolanda and her mother might do very well. In thinking along these lines, Louise had no consciousness of either snobbery or absurdity.

Keeping up a rippling stream of uninterruptible pleasantries, Louise amassed and conveyed as much information as she could.

She had noticed the rather fine piano . . . a Bechstein . . . quite the best. Was it much used? It should be removed from its present position where the sun would damage the case. Her grandson spoke with so much respect of her hostess. The paintings on the walls . . . she had not her *distance* glasses with her . . . would Mrs. Neville be kind enough to name their subjects to her? How interesting. She had never been into Yorkshire before. It was full of history, no? Lincolnshire was much more dull. Her son had a fine house there. Yes . . . of course. The same. The widowed husband of Alisdair's mother. Alisdair was touchingly attached to Mrs. Neville's daughter. These young people . . . The miniature gazebos in the garden . . . that *is* what they were . . . ten of them? To support climbing strawberries . . . How charming. Alisdair had derived much pleasure from the project . . . The design resembled Villandry in France . . . Did Mrs. Neville know it? So many happy interludes in that region before her daughter-in-law had died. A misfortune . . . yes. Her son . . . such a lonely man. Working himself to death. All for his son, of course.

In this way, Louise more or less kept her promise. It was her "son," not Alisdair's "father" that featured in the conversation. References to his business and its recent strategic extension

were delicately introduced. A small world, was it not, in which
the employer of one Strang-Steele should find herself the trading partner of another? Nature was full of such exquisite patterns, Louise tinkled. "From honeycomb to spider's web,"
Diana illustrated her guest's point drily.

She found that the missing pieces in her jig-saw puzzle,
pieces whose absence she had never noticed, had been slotted
into place.

Musing on the matter later, Diana found it impossible to be
angry. Alisdair had not been untruthful. Not exactly. He had
told the truth but not the whole truth. And with a grandmother
like that, it was not surprising. It must be difficult to reserve
ownership of anything, even one's thoughts, in the face of
Mme. Strang-Steele's expansionist policies.

Diana had to stop herself from moving the piano.

Louise was equally impressed. She had not *seen* Mrs.
Neville, or only indistinctly. Nor had she heard much of her.
After all, the fifteen minutes allotted by tradition to a first call
does not allow for time wasting. But Louise had felt her. She
was not one of those who leach their surroundings of significance. On the contrary, she celebrated them. How many English people would have dispensed with their never-ending,
repellent coffee and served an excellent glass of spirits instead?
And French, too. It showed a proper respect . . . a sense of occasion.

As they took leave of each other at the garden door, Diana
and Louise clasped hands with a pressure that conveyed
amused, mutual appreciation.

"It was wondrously kind of you to treat me as a friend. I do
so love people to just . . . drop in," Diana said meltingly.
"Please come again."

"Next time I warn. Yes? A telegram is best. Then you
know."

With the rear windscreen of the taxi safely between them,
both felt it safe to smile broadly. Diana felt she had drawn in
a strenuous tournament. But what on earth was the game?
Louise had spoken of patterns. Obscurely, Diana sensed de-
signs.

"My son," Louise told Marie that night as she brushed her
mistress's abundant white hair, "would do well to acquaint
himself with that lady. I feel a certain inevitability in the air."

"And ye'd do well, ma'am," Marie replied sourly, "to leave well alone."

"And what would that achieve?" Louise regarded the woman who had been her alter ego since both had been in their twenties. "You don't seem to realise, Marie, I have very little time."

🐾 PRIOR TO HER annual departure for Provence, Louise spent a few days in Lincolnshire.

The stone gateposts of her son's house were inset with costly but unlovely brass plates. *The Strang-Steel Group.* Additional notices exhorted visitors to report to reception in the old stables and warned of sleepless electronic security devices. Contemptuously, Louise called the place "The Depot."

Her son, Philip, was not so preoccupied with business as it pleased his mother to suppose. Delegation was his strength. It enabled him to maintain a skimming, roving eye on any aspect of the agrobusiness, as it was now called, that caught his attention. His attention was increasingly disengaged. He was, as he admitted to himself, beginning to get stale.

Spring had come and gone yet again. It was not a season he liked. It made him feel his age ... produced a readiness for change that was always disappointed. Now it was late in June and those vague, uncomfortable springtime inflammations of the spirit were quieted.

The face he had glimpsed twice in the winter, the one which had produced such extraordinary moments of exhilaration, of possibility, had flattened out of recognition. An image faded by too much handling. You could not, he admonished himself sternly, grieve over a face in the crowd.

As ever, he remained inside the armour of contented isolation he showed to the world and went in search of a fresh interest. It was merely a matter of identifying something worthy of his attention. An annual quest.

The year before last he had thought of taking up racing. He went to a yearling sale at Tattersalls once or twice and talked to a handful of trainers. He concluded that you could waste of lot of money on horses and never see a profit.

For a time he had thought of buying an ocean-going yacht and circumnavigating the world single handed. And then, he considered, to make the enterprise pay, he'd have to write a book. Far too self revealing. Philip shuddered with distaste.

More recently, he had wondered if he might involve himself in the theatre as an "angel." Supporting the arts was an appropriate pastime for a wealthy man. He was sent a few scripts, even saw a couple of underfunded plays already in production. He found them neurotic or banal. Further study revealed the financial risks to be suicidal.

"I can afford to waste money," as he told one shocked producer in a wellington boot tone of voice, "but I cannot pretend to enjoy it. Your best chance of shoring this show up is to trawl every private lunatic asylum in the land. Maybe they'd cough up."

It was on the return journey from that particular *débâcle* that Philip had first encountered Diana. A lady who did not strike up casual acquaintances with strange men on trains.

It seemed to Philip that the world was forcing misanthropy upon him.

This mood of quiet desperation made Louise's visit all the more welcome. His mother supplied the essential womanly ingredient in his life. To her, he displayed a limitless chivalry. Her extreme, aggressive femininity was powerless to irritate him. When she was with him, they dressed for dinner and Philip held out her chair for her with a courtier's deference. He enjoyed her unquenchable zest for stratagem and plot. In her hands, the most lacklustre facts and probabilities assumed sensational perspectives. Beside his matchless mother, the few other women with whom he came into contact were just shapes in frocks, married to men he knew ... or unperfected office equipment.

Philip was not blind to Louise's faults, however. In his well-staffed, tax allowable household, poor Marie was allowed to do nothing for herself and as little as possible for Louise. Marie was sent out on pleasant, time consuming errands for his housekeeper. There was always a chauffeur-driven car and a list of congenial people on whom to call with thoughtfully provided pretexts. A brace of pheasants, a misdirected letter, a pot of jam, some message about a dyke or a gate. Very reposeful. Mister Philip was a hero to Marie.

As for the insidious quality of Louise's mind, Philip had been armed against it by his own father.

"Always remember," Professor Strang-Steele had said, "your mother is a fascinating phenomenon. Her intellect can be compared to a slide rule. Its processes are rational in proportion to its information. It conclusions are therefore entertaining but ludicrous."

It was in that spirit that Philip listened to Louise's vivid account of Gilbert's Tower and its inhabitants.

"So you see, my darling boy, there is much to interest you there. This English Gardens . . . perhaps you should buy it? That way . . ."

"I encircle Alisdair," Philip only partially caught her drift, "and draw him into the Group in spite of himself?" His mouth was compressed with the effort not to roar with laughter. Louise could not see the spark of mirth in his eyes but she sensed she was not being taken as seriously as she deserved.

"Does every woman have this experience? One proposes a solution to a problem that a slow-witted man finds insoluble . . . a solution that is elegant, symmetrical, logical . . . quite out of the common British way of cobbling and compromise . . . and one is laughed to scorn!"

"*Madam*, you are ingenious. Beside yours, my brain is a clod of earth . . . anything you like. But I must tell you that this Mrs. Neville, whoever she is, is travelling the road to ruin. And I'm not going along for the ride."

Emptying his dinner jacket pockets that night in his dressing-room, Philip scribbled a note. Before many days had gone by, the Fernley management had produced a full report on English Gardens . . . whatever was known of its policies, internal structures and, most importantly, the state of its account with Fernley.

The report was interesting. Mrs. Neville's company was a model customer, it seemed. The only cause for concern, read a gloss on the figures, was the *speed* of growth. Quite, Philip thought. Unhealthily rapid expansion. Before too long, English Gardens would be overtrading. Its inevitable collapse would have a sobering effect on Alisdair.

It was shortly after laying the report aside that he allowed his secretary to accept an invitation on his behalf. He was to record a television interview for a programme purporting to weed the fact from the fiction circulated about organic growing. An outside broadcasting unit would be sent. They wanted pictures of big fields. He wrote the date in his diary irritably. The whole subject was beginning to get on his nerves.

🕱 IGNORANT OF PHILIP Strang-Steele's doom laden forecasts concerning her future, Diana was indeed suffering the penalties of early success. The books were hard to balance. Small suppliers had to be paid long before any settlement could be expected from a customer. The larger the customer, the longer payment was delayed . . . and those same customers expected exacting volume and delivery requirements fulfilled without hesitation or demur.

In May, in order to pay Fernley up to date, Diana had sacrificed her own salary. Neither Sedgely nor Alisdair knew.

It was hard. But, as she argued with Cedric Lafontaine on the telephone, many very powerful companies, as he well knew, had faced similar problems and survived. She would go on juggling.

🕱 DIANA HAD LOOKED forward to the Pilgrims' Lunch on St. Gilbert's Day as a break in the routine of hurry and worry. She had been told by Father Murphy that she might expect around fifty to stay for lunch in her garden after the mass. Between Mrs. Sedgely and a firm of caterers, enough iced soup, cold chicken, salads and puddings were prepared.

The day dawned like every other that summer, with a shimmering haze destined to harden into a brazen, hammering heat. Diana was proud of the garden and looked forward to showing it to so many new friends. For a day, Gilbert's Tower was to be as it ought to be, a *pleasaunce* . . . a citadel proof against any trouble.

A large round table was set up in the vine conservatory. Other smaller ones were dotted around the orchard and in the blocks of shade created by the strawberry clad gazebos. Everybody would have something pretty to look at and nobody would get too hot.

A lethal punch was concocted by Sedgely in the house . . . ominously, he called it "summut a bit special." Outside, in the shade, what looked like a coal bunker full of ice was chilling eight dozen bottles of rosé. Mercury's wing had been repaired and he spurted water from his mouth with abandon. Half a dozen slim young golden orfe, Alisdair's gift, leaped and sported in the spray.

It was extravagant. But to Diana, just to carry on the tradition was a privilege and a luxury worth paying for. Out of the little she took from the company for her own living expenses, she had budgeted for this event with care.

She and Yolanda watched the mass, or what they could see of it, from the top of the west wall, looking down into the cool green canyon of the gorge. The pilgrims, mostly middle-aged women with sunburnt arms, sat in Ned Garvey's boats and punts making the responses from printed sheets. There was no room for more than a half dozen clergy and laity in the hermitage itself. The Monsignor's address boomed over the water assisted by a megaphone while a surreptitious rustle of paper bags brought ducks bustling across from the forest bank.

"I was beginning to think they'd all brought a picnic with them," Diana whispered of the plastic shopping bags. "But I expect the ducks have Gilbert's Day down in their diaries."

As there was no longer any safe access direct from the hermitage to the house, the pilgrims paddled back downstream after the mass was over and approached the garden by climbing from Garvey's landing stage. Many of Diana's guests had seen the Tower's gardens before and there were mixed reactions to the changes. Some liked it, some mourned the lawns. All spoke with affection and genuine regret of Aunt Thea. Many wished Diana good fortune in her aunt's place. Others, knowing about English Gardens, congratulated her on its success.

"Did you see *Grub n' Stuff* on the telly, last night, Mrs. Neville?" Diana admitted she had missed this influential consumer food programme. She had been too busy, understandably.

"They did a test or something on organic produce. They were very down on it. Still, I don't suppose that'll bother you."

Somebody else said something about her husband having written a book . . . did it worry her? Diana had no time to enquire further. Father Murphy stepped in promptly and moved the speaker aside. Tact. Nobody mentioned Michael Neville at Gilbert's Tower unless it was Diana herself. An unwritten rule.

Perplexed, thrilled and curious, she hardly dared believe the stray remark was true. A mistake, surely. But he would have told her anything so exciting. A book! How clever he was.

Yolanda would be so proud of him. Diana hugged the hope to herself for the rest of the day. Like a crumpled raffle ticket, it was something to keep till later.

Her hands were full for the next few hours. And whilst a party of grey haired ladies with a bee in the bonnet about an obscure medieval saint might not seem the ideal basis for a party, it went with a noticeable swing.

The arrival of a motorbike messenger in the late afternoon, bearing a video tape recording of the *Grub 'n Stuff* programme, was unnoticed by anyone but Diana herself. She read the accompanying note from Merlin Olaff hurriedly before returning to her guests.

"Look at this as soon as you can then let's talk."

It would certainly have to wait, she thought. She might get to it later in the evening when the by now distinctly squiffy "pilgrims" and their gaitered leader had gone home. When that would be, their hostess had no idea.

The church clock carolled out seven o'clock before the Monsignor rose, with evident regret.

"We're indebted to the rival organisation for the time, Mrs. Neville. And we're indebted to yourself. A day of wine and roses, indeed."

Within half an hour the last stragglers had gone, leaving the garden littered with the detritus of pleasure that is past. At least they had taken their plastic bags and duck-feeding rubbish with them. Nice, dotty people.

Diana, Sedgely and Yolanda started to clear up. The kitchen door stood open and the clink of dishes in the pot sink harmonised with Mrs. Sedgely's murmured propitiations of the orange cat. A sliver of smoked salmon, a forgotten shrimp . . . the acceptable residue of a monstrous invasion offered on a china saucer. The cat did not care for plastic.

Father Murphy sat on benignly, watching Diana and her helpers from a vantage point on the terrace as the shadows lengthened. Mrs. Neville had done right by her aunt's memory and the local saint's dignity. He approved of her, cool and active in her sleeveless beige linen. She was a credit to the place. He closed his eyes contentedly. He opened them again directly.

"Oh, no! I don't believe it! How could they?" Diana's anguished voice floated across the parterres. "Oh, Father Murphy, tell me it isn't true!"

Every strawberry from every gazebo trellis had been removed. The crop destined to be picked and packed on the following morning had disappeared.

Sedgely laughed sardonically. "They'll be having 'em to their teas, Mrs. Neville, love. That's another tradition for you. Plastic bags and large handbags. They're the very devil. In your aunt's time it was cuttings from t'herbaceous borders . . . and a lettuce apiece if I didn't look sharp."

Father Murphy melted tactfully away. A sermon on the virtue of resignation would not be well received just now. All good things under heaven came to a sorry end. He sighed luxuriously over the melancholy truth as he walked, soft soled up the lane.

Alisdair was contacted and arrangements were made with other strawberry growers. It took till have past ten to weather the crisis and the video tape was forgotten. Diana remembered it only as she fell into bed that night. It was hardly uppermost in her mind. The next Gilbert's Day lunch, she vowed, would be an exercise in high density, low profile policing.

The last thing that occurred to her before she fell asleep was the extraordinary assertion that Michael had written a book. How lovely. Why should it worry her?

❧ THE FOLLOWING MORNING, a harassed telephone call from Merlin Olaff reminded Diana about the video tape which had arrived so inopportunely the day before. Yes, she promised, the three of them would watch it that evening without fail.

Sedgely, Alisdair and Diana saw it together in the book room on the equipment lent by Epoch for viewing rushes of promotional footage made earlier. Diana had really outgrown the book room and it was necessary to move piles of papers and files from the sofa and chairs. Her hackles rose as Alisdair took charge of the remote control device without asking. Even the nicest men did it.

He accelerated the signature tune of the programme and all the familiar, preliminary frames until the affable, porcine features of the chief presenter in his striped butcher's apron were recognised.

"Tonight we examine the claims made for organic fruit and vegetables," he beamed. "Are they really better for your health? Are they really better for the environment? A biochemist and a food scientist will help us here in the studio, and you at home, to make our minds up. Also with us this evening is Philip Strang-Steele, Chairman and Managing Director of the mighty Strang-Steele Group, which grows and now distributes a significant percentage of the fresh produce for sale on high streets the length and breadth of Britain."

Diana glanced at Alisdair. Paler? Perhaps. But definitely slumped. Should she rescue him now or later? Sedgely's face was grim. He knew nothing, of course. Diana decided to leave it until the end of the programme before straightening accounts. Let dear Alisdair suffer just a little. That would teach him to be economical with the truth! Poor Alisdair.

They watched in silence for another fifteen minutes.

The scientists said they could find no evidence for higher nutritional value in the organic specimens presented for their analysis compared with the conventionally grown controls. After all, the whole of nature was essentially chemical in its make-up. On purely nutritional grounds, there was no justification whatever for the higher price.

Then the studio team took over. Brightly, they scooped up spoonfuls of this and dollops of that and slotted them between spanking white teeth. Critically, fair mindedly, they munched whilst eyebrows samaphored. Nooo. They couldn't taste any difference ... perhaps these peas were ... Oh? They were a different variety. Not really fair. No, on balance, no difference at all. Not worth paying a premium for taste. Appearance? Conventional produce won hands down.

Back to the scientists. Yes, there was no doubt that organic methods were ecologically preferable. Waterways in the East Anglian arable region were found to have unacceptable nitrate levels. But could the public be relied upon to vote with their housekeeping money? No. A nice idea. But sadly, no. An imperfect world ... and all that.

Diana reached over and took the control unit from Alisdair's slackened hand and stopped the tape.

"Well, that's all right. Nothing too dreadful there. That's the attitude we went into business to combat, isn't it? The nutritional and taste factors don't affect us either because we don't do bread and butter items."

The other two nodded slowly. It might be worse, they supposed. Diana released the stop button. In the curtained gloom, Alisdair was feeling very uncomfortable.

Philip Strang-Steele's face swam into view. For the first moment or two Diana heard nothing he said. He looked weary, detached. He gave the impression of listening to the presenter's questions with a schoolmaster's irascibility.

"My position has never altered . . ."

"Mummy?" Yolanda came into the room and Diana pushed the stop button. She had been a million miles away. Her daughter was wearing a tennis dress. She looked bronzed and eager. The exams were over for the term.

"Yes, darling? What is it? We're just busy in here for the moment."

"Can I go on the river with Ned Garvey? We're going to go round the bend at the top . . . going on towards Broughton and stop for a drink."

Yolanda stopped, her eyes resting on the screen. For once, she ignored Alisdair. A shadow passed over his face.

"Isn't that the gorgeous chap on the front of that magazine you had before?"

"Yes. All right. You may." Diana interrupted her daughter swiftly. The cross-currents in the room were confused and enmeshing. "Put some proper clothes on, though. And don't let Ned encourage you to drink too much. A glass of cider, or lager. *One*, remember. And be back by ten o'clock. Do you understand . . ."

Yolanda was gone, interested only in her mother's bare permission. Alisdair looked after her and there was something in his glance to puzzle Diana. In love with her? It was hardly possible. She was little more than a child.

Diana released Philip Strang-Steele from his state of suspended animation.

His voice with its peculiarly attractive intonation, fused with her fading recollection of him. There was another layer to her knowledge of him now. The slow, half reluctant smile he had bequeathed to Alisdair . . . the seamless self-assurance he had inherited from his mother. She found herself searching his face for detail she remembered or recognised. It was like doing one of those puzzles . . . comparing two identical pictures, one of which has some obscure, unimportant features missing. His eyebrows, bushing and curling up into two engagingly demonic horns, the diamond shaped cleft in his chin . . . the long upper lip, drawn down in judgment. What a nuisance he was, with his experience, his money and his certainties.

"If the public want cheap food, and it seems they do, then it cannot be produced without effect. Whether or not that effect is actually damaging, is still imperfectly understood."

"But surely, Philip . . ." Diana thought she detected the smallest wince. No more, perhaps, than a flicker in those fjord cold eyes. Mr. Strang-Steele was not at home with the breezy, trendy familiarity of the young studio team. "You won't deny that the reduction in the number of freshwater fish in East Anglian rivers *is* damage?"

"In a purely local sense, of course I don't deny it. But the British peoples' consumption of fish overall has reduced dramatically since the war. It is a commodity for which there is a restricted sale. Frozen peas and instant potato powder, on the other hand . . . It is a question of supplying existing demands."

Oh, how clever you are, Alisdair's father.

There was not much more of interest until the very end of the programme.

"Next week we take a look at English Gardens. For those of you outside the north-eastern area, this is a new organic enterprise which has been operating successfully, flying in the face of the reasoning we have heard tonight."

Diana arrested the presenter in mid-flow.

"I'm sorry, I did know about this. Epoch were trying to get us on. The programme must have dropped an item and slotted us in at short notice. They may only have told Merlin today."

The others nodded as Diana released the button again. To get television exposure after little more than four months was phenomenal good fortune. The news was hard to take in, but not as difficult as the presenter's concluding words.

"We shall also be examining its unique marketing approach and high priced products in the light of an article to be published in the *Sunday Times* colour supplement this week. 'Eating for Solvency' is an extract from a book, *The Folly of Fashion*, due for publication next year. Michael Neville, whom some of you may remember as the Chairman of the Knightman Neville Trust which foundered so spectacularly last year, is the author. And, quite coincidentally, he is married to the founder of English Gardens . . ."

"Coincidentally!" Diana spluttered angrily. "Did they dig that out for themselves, do you think, or did he tell them himself?"

Alisdair froze the tape again. Sedgely ground his teeth on the pipe stem. Neither felt entitled to comment on Diana's vehement outburst. It had sounded like a repudiation. Flushed with annoyance and embarrassment, Diana motioned Alisdair to start the recording again. No wonder Merlin Olaff had wanted her to see this. They had always agreed that Michael's presence in her life should be minimised. For business purposes.

"In this article Michael Neville contends that we could all halve our expenditure on food if we learned to identify and ignore the blandishments of marketing experts. It's new, persuasive thinking. How will it affect his wife's company, English Gardens, and others who not only cater for, but actually create food fads?

"To find out, join us next week."

Inwardly, Diana reeled. Alisdair's father had defended his own business. There had been no overt or focused hostility in what he said. It was unfortunate, unhelpful ... but not malicious. But Michael ... did he *know* what he was doing?

Diana was the first to speak.

"They're not invincible, you know. Your father and my husband. We can fight back and we shall.".

Alisdair did not look very surprised that he was found out. *Grandmère*. She was never to be trusted. It was a relief, in a way. Better out than in ...

"Diana, I'm sorry ..." Alisdair half rose in his chair.

"It's all right, Alisdair, you're entitled to your privacy." She forgave him easily, distracted by the far greater treachery. She wanted to be alone to absorb the impact of the blow. Sedgely and Alisdair understood. There was nothing either of them dared to say. Neither had had time to assess the potential damage, internal and external. Both felt the distress and confusion that Diana was holding in check. Her pride repelled sympathy. They felt helpless.

"Aye. Well, I'll be off now, Mrs. Neville. I'll just run t'van up Broughton Road and make sure young Garvey's not getting into mischief with Miss Yolanda."

"No." Alisdair got up and put his hand on Sedgely's shoulder. "It's all right, Albert. I'll go. It's on my way. You go home."

They went, talking together about the time when Sedgely had worked for a ganger in Strang-Steele fields. Diana heard them in the hall.

"Hard graft, that were."

Alisdair's voice apologised miserably.

"Don't be so soft, lad . . ."

The realisation that Sedgely had known something about the connection between the Strang-Steele Group and Fernley all along barely stirred the fringes of Diana's mind. It was typical. Sedgely always deployed his knowledge of affairs warily. What else did he and Alisdair know that she didn't? Probably nothing. Her nerves were on edge.

Diana heard the front door close and, for the first time since she had come to Gilbert's Tower, felt like crying. Now she could not talk to her friends nor they to her. Neither distance nor isolation had prevented Michael from shouting her down again. Drowning her out. She still could not believe that he meant to do it . . . to be deliberately destructive of her work, of *her*.

Although it was late, Diana rang Merlin Olaff at home.

Yes, he had considered every conceivable angle. There was nothing to be done. Michael Neville was entitled to state that he was married to Diana Neville in whatever context. Merlin had obtained a photocopy of his article from the television company. He would fax her a copy but he could see no libellous matter that might enable them to obtain an injunction on publication. Yes, it was bad. Couldn't Diana talk to her husband? It was really too late to do anything effective. Lafontaine Frères? It depended what view they took of publicity squalls . . . but English Gardens was really too fragile to withstand a buffeting like this.

"You started a trend, Diana, but it looks as though your husband's going to put it into reverse. Believe me, this book of his is going to cause a hell of a shake-up."

❦ THE BANK'S REACTION was not precipitate. It was eight days later, the day following the broadcasted review of Michael's book and publication of the extract when Cedric Lafontaine called an extraordinary meeting of the Directors of English

Gardens. Would Mrs. Neville name a time and a day next week which suited everyone? The bank wished to re-schedule its loan. Diana recognised the euphemism for what it was. Lafontaine Frères wanted their money back . . . and fast.

❦ THE MEETING WAS to take place in London. The natural location would have been the company's registered offices, Gilbert's Tower. Diana objected. She was not, she told Mr. Meers, inviting Cedric Lafontaine up to gloat over his security. Let him get round and tot up the re-sale value of second-hand printing and packing machines. That should keep him busy.

Albert Sedgely had never been to London before. Diana did not suppose he would wish to favour the capital with a visit on this occasion, either. She was wrong.

"I've your aunt's brass to think of. If it's to be chucked away, then I'll be there at t'chucking ceremony," he rebuked Diana. Indeed, Sedgely had invested all of Aunt Thea's legacy in English Gardens. And whereas the money had previously been a sore trial to him, it was now a symbol of solidarity.

Mrs. Sedgely sent his British Legion suit to the cleaners immediately. Re-texturing and everything. A proper do.

"Gettin' a medal, is he, then? Your Albert?" the manageress at Ramsbottom's Dry Cleaners enquired.

"Aye, 'appen," Mrs. Sedgely replied glacially. There was enough trouble without letting on to folk.

Alisdair possessed two identical tweed suits. One was older than the other and therefore automatically preferred. His overriding concern was for Yolanda. How were they going to tell her that she had lost her home? Alternative funding was the only straw Alisdair could cling to.

Mr. Meers spent an evening searching for his bowler hat. He was resigned. In spite of his advice, Mrs. Neville had gone her own way. He would try to save Gilbert's Tower for her if he could. Perhaps the bank would allow English Gardens to wind down slowly, an orderly retreat.

Fernley Distribution pressed for payment a week early. English Gardens, they assured Diana, was not the only victim of this tightened credit policy. Michael Neville's article was the writing on the wall for premium foods. Had she read it? When the book was published there would be mayhem right across the entire retailing sector. A spectacular consumer backlash.

From now on shoppers would turn up their noses at anything that wasn't rock bottom and basic. Everyone would suffer. Fernley Distribution was battening down the hatches. A directive from the main board. They were part of the Strang-Steele Group now.

Philip Strang-Steele did not involve himself personally in the day to day decisions made by senior personnel in his organisation. It would have made no difference if he had. English Gardens was not and never had been a sound trading partner. A will o' the wisp, like its boss. Diana Neville was a name with no face . . . someone who had given Alisdair a job he didn't need and, very soon, would not have. A sad but salutary lesson.

❦ DIANA EXERCISED THE privilege of the unreformed female and changed her mind unilaterally. She would not, she decided, submit to any cumbersome meeting with men in suits. No agendas, no preordained dialogue, no confrontation. The art of the morning call could always, as Louise Strang-Steele had so ably demonstrated, be revived.

She extracted an old dress from the back of her wardrobe. A foamy, filmy, spindrift sort of garment, it had proved suitable for no appointment in Diana's calendar to date. Lavender blue. Ideal, she told herself grittily, for an occasion when nothing had been planned.

CHAPTER
9

🌸 DIANA CHEATED LAFONTAINE Frères of the meeting they had instigated and spared her co-directors the duty of attending it. She went to London alone on a day of her own choosing, arriving unannounced. She was, of course, fortunate to find old Mr. Lafontaine at liberty to see her, but then she had backed some shrewd hunches.

Of the three days available to her before the scheduled meeting, Monday was rejected. It was a day on which, she calculated, elderly gentlemen of substance in senior positions often absented themselves from their offices. A messy, bad tempered sort of day in any organisation. A man with Mr. Lafontaine's *savoir faire* would be bound to spend it at home, preparing at leisure to appear on Tuesday when corporate poise would be restored. On Wednesday, she believed, the dapper, silver haired chairman would almost certainly quit the City early in order to play the first of the two weekly games of golf that undoubtedly preserved his svelte appearance. Wednesdays and Saturdays, very probably. An educated guess, no more.

It was a little after quarter past twelve on Tuesday, therefore, that Cedric Lafontaine was startled to recognise Diana's ethereally clad figure emerging from a taxi on St. Mary's Axe. Wrongly suspecting that he was about to be the targeted object of a personal, feminine appeal, he moved away from the window and rang reception immediately. He would leave a little earlier than usual for his luncheon appointment by a rear exit. Was his uncle still in the building? The receptionist, who was new and confused as to who was who, did not know. She would try to find out. Making a cat's cradle of the bank's

switchboard communication lines, the receptionist handed
Diana a few valuable seconds on a plate.

Diana tripped past her with the warmest of smiles and a gesture that indicated her complete understanding of the receptionist's preoccupation with baffling technology. There was no
need to break off to assist one who was so clearly here on a
purely personal visit and knew her way about. Leaving two
very recognisable Bond Street carrier bags on a hall chair, Diana ascended the thickly carpeted staircase without opposition.

Struggling with the switchboard, the receptionist thought
fleetingly how pleasant it must be to have been born a
Lafontaine lady . . . as Diana had hoped she would.

Of the three closed walnut doors on the deserted first floor
landing, Diana knew which led into the library. She judged that
the room adjacent, also commanding a view of the street below, would belong to the Chairman. She knocked once.

"Come in."

Mr. Lafontaine had a secretary seated before him, pen
poised over a shorthand pad. She turned and her mouth formed
a roundel of horror. For a split second, Mr. Lafontaine senior's
face was blank, then it was wreathed in smiles. Diana knew
how to evaluate those smiles. As a woman she was welcomed.
As a customer of the bank, her surprise visit could not have
been more provoking.

The Chairman rose as Diana walked towards him, hand extended. The secretary executed a kind of ducking movement
and walked out of the room stiffly. An irregularity had occurred.

"My dear Mrs. Neville, what a refreshing sight you are. I
must confess I thought we were to have the pleasure of seeing
you on Thursday."

Mr. Lafontaine went on to make some hollow, chaffing remarks about his age and the inevitability of failing memory.

There was no mistake, of course, they both knew that. Stra-
tegically speaking, Mr. Lafontaine found himself boxed in.
Where, in God's name, he asked himself, was Cedric? The
transaction of this unpleasant business had been delegated to
him.

"I would so value your advice," Diana stated demurely seating herself in the chair the secretary had vacated. She did so
uninvited, aware that a gentleman of Mr. Lafontaine's suscep-

tibility would find it impossible to ask her to rise. "I was passing," Diana lied shamelessly, "and hoped you might just be able to spare me a little of your time."

The Chairman found himself looking down into those confiding, compelling violet eyes. He resumed his chair slowly . . . a doomed man.

Cedric succeeded in interrupting the first moments that he and Diana spent together. A telephoned warning that came too late. Should he, Cedric asked in a voice clearly audible to Diana, come and rescue his uncle? He couldn't think what had gone wrong at reception. The Chairman looked questioningly at Diana. She shook her head.

"No. Kind of you, my dear fellow, but I think Mrs. Neville and I will let you lunch in peace while we have our little conference. Perhaps we shall see you later?"

Mr. Lafontaine spared somewhat over an hour to listen to Diana. Nor did he recall giving any advice or being asked for it. On the contrary, it was he who learned for the first time of some very fine distinctions.

At the conclusion of Diana's fluent account of English Gardens' trading platform, he was barely conscious that there had been a shift of emphasis between what he now heard and what had been conveyed to him at Epoch's presentation many months since. The article written by Mrs. Neville's husband which had been brought to his attention (as was all written matter which might affect clients of the bank), was, in Mr. Lafontaine's mind, set at nought. He had over reacted. Missed the point.

It was a curious fact, as Diana pointed out, that although their points of reference were different, she and her husband were on the same side. Advertising had a lot to answer for. Mr. Lafontaine found himself nodding. That, indeed, was what Michael Neville had said. Or something like it.

Later, he guided Diana chivalrously by the elbow to his nephew's office where Cedric was found pacing the carpet, having eaten no lunch at all.

"Well," the Chairman addressed the younger man guilelessly. "Mrs. Neville and I have had a most illuminating chat and I think we can assure her of the bank's continued support. As she rightly says, English Gardens is not so much selling organic produce or fashion as *values*. Preserving . . . ah, reviving a kinder, purer past. Isn't that right, Mrs. Neville? It's an expanding market, I fancy. I'm sure you won't argue with that, Cedric."

Diana could not, she said, looking up at the genial old gentleman, have put it better herself.

"And we are providing quite a lot of work in the late career sector."

"Indeed, you *are*, my dear. Values again, you see, Cedric. Idealism. Very marketable commodity in the near future. I can't think why you didn't spot it, Cedric. We really must try and think ahead of the trend. Scrub round Thursday's meeting, shall we?"

Cedric Lafontaine looked stunned. Diana sympathised with him sincerely. She was quite certain that whatever his cancelled orders had been, they had proceeded directly from his uncle. Which was why she had undertaken to deal with the fireman and not the shovel . . . a picturesque way of describing the chain of command favoured by Sedgely.

As Diana bade Mr. Lafontaine farewell in the hall, making at the same time a forceful, pre-emptive defence of the unfortunate receptionist on whom, she admitted, she had played a really rather dreadful trick, Cedric Lafontaine tore up his brief.

What were long range economic forecasts, adverse consumer trends or Michael Neville's power packed prose compared with the guerrilla tactics of *Diana* Neville? His uncle would claim to have been overcome by sweet reason. Cedric knew he had been outgunned by altogether less rational weapons.

Diana caught the five o'clock train from King's Cross and was moderately satisfied with her exploit. It had, at least, and at long last, justified the purchase of a most impractical dress.

Agreeing with Michael, more or less, had been a spur of the moment inspiration. Taking the fax copy of his article from her handbag, she read it again. The last, damning paragraph summed it all up.

"Branded and packaged food is offered to the public as being of superior quality, as having what is called 'added value,' whereas in fact, nothing is added but profit for distributor, retailer and advertiser. It is the most daring of confidence tricks and one for which the public falls time and time again."

Diana felt equal to defending the quality of her goods. They were unique. But the promotional method would have to change. There could be no more up-front, obvious advertising. She would have to think of something else. Subtle persuasion.

🐾 PERSUASION HAD NO effect on Michael. He was on his guard against any conciliatory moves that Diana could make. Could he not soften, amend or retract any of what he had already said before the book itself was published? Although there was merit in his arguments, he must realise her position.

"Don't come whining to me about your business," he snarled at her on the telephone when she questioned him. "I haven't set out to ruin it. It never entered my head. I've got a publisher and a chance to make some worthwhile money. I'm going to do it. You wanted to be a tycoon ... so now you've got the headaches. You said it yourself," he reminded her unfairly, "I'm in no position to help you. It's not my affair. How's my daughter?"

Yolanda was always "my" daughter to Michael.

The Folly of Fashion was due out in less than six months' time. Over and over again, Diana strangled suspicions that its true target was her own company. The bank had stopped short of claiming that outright. It was *she* who had squared up to the issue. Not them. But unless the book's expected impact was detonated, English Gardens would be badly mauled. Nor did Philip Strang-Steele's prosing about practicalities help. Both were problems she must confront. The bank had been clear about that. Correct reflexes, fast reactions.

🐾 THE PROMOTIONAL CHANGES meant harder work for Diana and less money for Epoch Advertising. Epoch, unsurprisingly, were against it.

"I'm sorry but I can't take time out to discuss it just now. I've been to London already this week and we're very busy here. For the moment, just cancel all the advertising space we've booked, as far as you can."

Merlin Olaff took the telephone from his ear and looked at it. She did not sound like herself. Nor was she. Acutely conscious that her written contract with Epoch was couched in very elastic terms, Diana knew she was reneging on a gentleman's agreement. She would find a way through it, a way of compensating them somehow. But for now, English Gardens must come first.

Epoch's conference was brief but heated. Jackets were stripped off. Ties were run down at half mast and top collar buttons undone. The signal for tough action.

"Someone will have to go and see her . . . stop her panicking. Calm her down. A spot of bad publicity and a rocky passage with the bank . . . no big deal. No! For God's sake. I can't take any calls now," the Finance Director screeched at the receptionist. "We've got a crisis on our hands."

"And a hundred and fifty thousand grand for five years is the sort of budget we don't give up without a fight. Public relations? That's what she's talking about, you realise. What makes her think it will be better?"

"Talk her out of it, Merlin. It may be cost effective for her but it's too dicey for us. We don't have the resources. Clients! Christ, how I hate them."

Merlin Olaff came up to Gilbert's Tower. Diana was happy to conduct this interview on her own ground, an environment she could control. She greeted him at the station in person. Bob, knowing a little of what was afoot, having been warned privately by Sedgely that Mrs. Neville was expecting a "tricky" visitor from London, treated the advertising man to a full display of his skills. No sooner had the train halted than a kind of dismounting block had been placed before the door of the first class carriage.

"Just nicely on time, sir. Mind the step. Nidcaster!" The versatile station master bellowed for the benefit of less favoured travellers. "Nidcaster! We've been expecting you. Orders from Gilbert's Tower. Mrs. Neville's walked up to meet you." Bob managed to make this sound like a rare compliment. "She's in my office now, if you'll come this way. Nidcaster!"

By the time Merlin Olaff was seated in the vine conservatory, where Diana had spread an impressive array of notes, he had stepped through the looking glass. Sedgely snipped away on a step-ladder, thinning the pendulous cones of purple grapes, a bumble bee droned languorously and Olaff was as powerless as any dreamer. What a place!

Diana's voice splashed in his ear, as cool as a waterfall. He heard the words but in the soporific atmosphere, Olaff's reactions were sluggish. His advertising budget was cut by more than three-quarters and he never raised a single objection. Something to do with the heat and Diana's deliberately domesticated prettiness robbed him of anxiety or protest. The orange cat twirled around his legs. Merlin liked cats.

"The only advertising I want to see in future is the church noticeboard, parish magazine type of thing. You concentrate on getting articles written and included in every one of the journals we used to advertise in ... the editors don't charge for that, do they?"

Olaff nodded in confirmation.

"No. It's at their discretion. Editorial submissions, if they accept them, are printed without charge and have the editor's authority behind them ..."

"That's what I thought," Diana said. "So we have to get the editors in all sectors on our side. Cultivate them. I'll keep feeding you with new stories about the company and new activities."

"We'll need to spend something on photography," Olaff interrupted. "Editors feel more inclined to print something if there's a pretty picture to go with the story."

"Fine. People and places. Perfect." Diana was jubilant. It seemed that what she wanted was possible, after all. It would be both cheaper and better. People believed what they read in the editorial columns of any journal. Advertisements got noticed quicker, but they were taken with a pinch of salt.

"And I'll give lectures to every Women's Institute, Townswomen's Guild and retired people's club I can get to invite me. Chat shows on television, local interest programmes, I want you to try them all. We have to get right away from any taint of commercialism without losing the look of professionalism. What we save on advertising will be passed on to the consumer and producer alike. Lower prices for one, higher rewards for the other."

"Look, Diana," Olaff stirred himself with an effort. "Frankly, what you say makes a lot of sense but my partners are going to haul me over the coals. You're taking a lot of money off us all in one fell swoop. We had an agreement ... we counted on that budget ..."

"I know. That's one reason why I want you to write a book."

Diana forestalled Olaff's startled rejection.

"All you have to do is find out the publication date of *The Folly of Fashion* ... keep checking because publishers change these things, I've discovered, and make sure our book comes out on the same day exactly. It's to be written, illustrated, printed and bound in time. We shall give it away in supermarkets, greengrocers, book shops and libraries throughout the country. It's to be called *English Garden Treasures* and it's got to look as though it's worth paying for. I bet more people read it than read *The Folly of Fashion*. Try and ..."

"Diana, *Diana!*" Olaff was scrambling to keep up with her darting thought processes. "It will cost a fortune!"

"You tell me what kind of a fortune," she told him, "and I'll find it. You should make a nice profit."

"Agency contribution," Olaff amended dazedly. Only tradesmen talked about profit.

"We're not nearly grand enough to know about these subtleties, are we, Mr. Sedgely? You'll have to forgive our crude, rustic way of putting things, Merlin," Diana teased the sweating executive kindly.

With his face and shoulders hidden among the vine foliage, Sedgely emitted a chortle of derision. Olaff remembered his disparaging remarks about the first drafts of the recruitment advertising. The man was a menace.

The cell telephone which lay on the table buzzed politely.

"Ah! Bob says your best train back to London is due in three minutes' time." Diana smiled. "He can hold it for fifteen minutes if we're not quite finished. But we are, aren't we?"

Merlin Olaff was walked up the lane and loaded on to the train with still further ceremony. Settled into a corner seat with a wicker luncheon basket prepared by Mrs. Sedgely, he watched Bob execute some balletic stage business with whistles and red flags. Nidcaster had a very disarming way of making people feel important.

Epoch's new Public Relations Division was established within three weeks flat. What Diana Neville wanted today, Merlin Olaff urged, others would clamour for tomorrow. She was a weather vane.

❦ THAT WAS A very different thing from what Diana herself told the many gatherings in draughty village halls and parish rooms up and down the country. She called herself an "ordinary woman," but after a year's feverish activity, of lectures and interviews, the world was beginning to call her a prophetess. Diana thought that very silly. But in business circles, they said it wasn't far off the truth.

English Gardens expanded. Diana said it was a kind of commercial sub-culture. The trading figures said otherwise. It was the gardeners themselves, joining the organisation in their scores and hundreds, who made the company what it was. A network of friendship across county boundaries had evolved. Letters and telephone calls, even faxes, flew from cottage to castle, from industrial terrace to cathedral close. Expertise was shared, cuttings and seeds were exchanged. There was a lot of learned chat about plant physiology.

In the Welsh Marches they were having some success with medlars. A gourmet's treat, they said, but a retailer's nightmare. The things looked so awful when they were ready to eat. There was talk of marketing speciality preserves. The thing had a life of its own.

A new edition of *English Garden Treasures* was already in preparation. Free to "members," as Diana called her gardener producers, the new book would be sold at a market price to the public. The first edition had been an outstanding success. If it did not quite overshadow Michael's book, it adduced very appealing counter arguments. Paid for partly by donations and subscriptions from various horticultural and organic growing societies, the volumes already had a second-hand value. The author, Epoch's senior copy writer, ditched his job with the agency. He joined the company as Area Organiser for Cornwall, Devon and Somerset. It suited his ulcer better, he said.

The supermarket chain first mooted to Diana by Epoch and Cedric Lafontaine were keen to stock English Gardens' products. Diana said no. Not yet. She couldn't guarantee them a reliable supply without letting down the independent greengrocers and restaurants who had supported her in the beginning. The supermarket would have to wait until next year or the one after that. A queenly dismissal. The industry journals seethed with gossip. Was this company really going to change the face of the fruit and vegetable market? Nightmare or dream? It depended where you stood.

Philip Strang-Steele knew where he stood. He stood to lose if this nonsense got a grip. True, so far English Gardens had made only the most minuscule dint on his agricultural product sales figures. But it was perceptible. Just. On the other side of the books, Fernley was doing good business with English Gardens. Every account paid on the due date. And that was in spite of the tight credit policy they'd imposed on her company. But to Philip that was of small importance. Growing was his core business. Distribution was a sideline.

He contributed a few steadying articles to the trade journals. A passing fad, he said. English Gardens would either sink without trace in due course, or become an extension of the Women's Institute. A footling enterprise. It could never make any significant difference to the serious business of producing food for a nation of fifty-five million people. He referred readers to the excellent chapter in Michael Neville's book. The editor struck that line out. It was a little too near the knuckle. Strang-Steele didn't realise. Half the time, the man lived in a vacuum.

Philip, of course, knew that Diana Neville employed his son, and that English Gardens was, in a manner of speaking, his own customer. He did not know that the jailed author of *The Folly of Fashion* was married to Mrs. Neville, or that he had ever seen her before.

As a rule, Diana never read the trade journals. They were tedious beyond belief. What she did read were the cuttings forwarded to her by Epoch. The agency had briefed the cutting service to clip every reference to English Gardens without exception. Mostly what arrived on Diana's desk were articles prepared by Epoch themselves. But increasingly there was independent coverage of the company. Philip Strang-Steele's contemptuous words spurted up at her like sulphuric acid. How dare he? How *dare* he?

Her first impulse was to show the piece to Alisdair. Then she thought better of it. There was nothing he could do. She remembered, too, his forbearance in not speaking of Michael's literary handiwork. She owed Alisdair the same gentleness he had shown her. One could not be held responsible for one's relations.

Instead she wrote directly to Strang-Steele, care of the journal's editor. Naturally, she typed the letter on the English Gardens' letterhead.

Dear Sir,

With reference to your article which appeared on page 24 of the July issue of *Foods Industry*, in which you make some damaging remarks about my Company, I wish to register the strongest possible protest.

I expect you to make immediate arrangements with the editor to withdraw those remarks and publish an apology. If you do not, I shall place the matter in the hands of the company's solicitors.

You are, I suppose, unaware that as a customer of Fernley Distribution, a company incorporated by your Group, I am, in fact, a customer of *yours*. Had you known that English Gardens therefore contributes something to your own profits, I assume you would have avoided denigrating their source.

Yours faithfully,

Diana Neville.

Having studied the letter at odd intervals over the next two days, Diana decided to send it. And a copy to the editor. She had put pen to paper in anger but nothing altered the facts. Philip Strang-Steele had openly declared himself an enemy. A wanton destroyer.

The journal was a monthly. Except for a busy few days before publication, the editor worked from home. His secretary was on holiday. The letter rested in her "in-tray" for a week.

During the same week, Diana had a speaking appointment in a Lincolnshire village. Ashe Barkwith. It lay twenty-five miles to the east of the A1. In her new Peugeot, Diana calculated she could give her talk at seven o'clock as arranged and be on her way again by half past nine. There would be no need to find an hotel. She could get home before one in the morning.

❦ IN THE ADJOINING parish of North Barkwith, Philip Strang-Steele prepared to hear the famous Mrs. Neville's talk with a mixture of curiosity and boredom. He wouldn't have known about it if it weren't for his housekeeper, Mrs. Lightbody, happening to mention the matter. And then he'd spotted a scrappy-looking advertisement on the parish noticeboard last Sunday across at Ashe. He would have liked to remain aloof. But this was business. Up to a point. Complacency didn't pay.

The twin villages of Ashe and North Barkwith no longer boasted a vicar apiece. Along with other hamlets in the area, they shared a peripatetic clergyman who would read the Sunday services one week here, and another there. Under these sparse arrangements, Philip had become a church warden.

He had accepted the post not out of religious fervour but a drizzle grey sense of duty. He was, the vicar had reminded him, a resident of standing in the community. The vicar was not the sort of man who permitted old-fashioned words such as "Squire" to escape his lips. He called himself the "priest in charge," possessed a fast motorbike and a briefcase that looked like a handbag. Philip regarded him with simple incredulity.

Last Sunday, matins had been at the Ashe Barkwith church. Philip had read the lesson with dry efficiency and maximum audibility. He "read lovely," his housekeeper was kind enough to say, standing by the lych gate. It was there that he had read the English Gardens' advertisement, printed on cheap pink paper and bleached by a fortnight's exposure to the elements.

On this warm August evening he stood in the hall, debating whether to walk the two miles to Ashe Barkwith across his own fields or take a car. Mrs. Lightbody had set off in her Mini long since. She was having high tea with her sister first. Mrs. Lightbody was an English Gardens fan.

"Why don't you start here, sir?" she had asked when serving his supper the previous night. "Be an interest for you. There's that old walled garden going to rack and ruin . . . must be a good four acres there."

Philip had thought that a singularly inept suggestion. He had given Mrs. Lightbody what she called his "Grimsby Dock" look. Cold as sleet.

"Good thing he isn't married," Mrs. Lightbody told her sister over finnan haddock and fruit cake. "Be like going to bed with a sack full of ice cubes." She chuckled. That was a very forward thing to say about Mr. Strang-Steele. Not quite true, either. Handsome, he was. Such a waste of a man. "There's nobody but me would put up with him," she sighed. "Fair though, and generous. I'm to have one of them there new Metros. Not the basic model, either. What do you think about that?"

Mrs. Lightbody's sister murmured her envious approval. Working up at the Court was no pushover, she didn't doubt. But Strang-Steele knew how to look after people.

"I'll bet you he walks and brings a brolly, as like as not," Mrs. Lightbody grumbled as they did the dishes. "Pessimist, he is. Then he'll want a lift back with me. Mini wasn't built for a man his size."

Philip's housekeeper was correct in her surmise. Her employer's behaviour, like his views, was invariably predictable. Not that he didn't agonise.

He would walk, he decided. He always walked in the country. The sky had been cloudless for the past five days. That didn't mean it would stay that way. He selected a large multicoloured golfing umbrella from the ugly wrought iron stand near the door. He looked down at his well-polished brogues. They would get dusty . . . or wet. They were good shoes. Hand-made. Lobbs. He changed into Wellington boots, tucking his cord slacks into the tops. Would it look discourteously casual? No, he didn't think so. Not in the Parish Rooms. He was only a simple farmer, after all.

The hubbub in the Parish Rooms hushed a little as he entered. Mr. Strang-Steele wasn't noted for joining in village affairs. There was no side with him, though. It was just that he kept himself to himself. On the whole the Barkwiths were glad of that. He wasn't what you'd call a genial man.

There was a general pretence of not watching as Philip seated himself on the back row of stacking chairs. Aware that his presence was having a dampening effect, he endeavoured, unsuccessfully, to make as little of it as possible. He looked down at the splintered floorboards. Dangerous. The village schoolchildren did gym or something in here. They ought to be replaced. He made a mental note to do something about it. Alisdair had got a spell in his knee once and it had gone septic.

"This evening," the vicar broke in on these ruminations, "we are very fortunate to have Mrs. Diana Neville with us."

Philip looked up at the podium. He assumed Diana Neville was a woman. He could see no sign of one. There was only the vicar and a fellow church warden fussing with a baize tablecloth and carafe of water. The usual luxuries laid on for speakers.

There was a pause as the rest of the audience also reached the conclusion that Mrs. Neville was with them only in spirit.

"She's just arrived and is . . . er . . . changing her shoes," the vicar improvised. Actually, Diana was making use of the newly refurbished ladies' room. Another Strang-Steele benefaction.

When she walked on to the stage, Philip felt the world lurch. His mind heeled over like a yacht. He was touching the sea. Waves were coming up to engulf him. He forgot to breathe. To blink.

As if trying to escape the big thing, his brain took in the little things with ridiculous clarity. The ear-rings of the woman in front. Beaten copper discs. The rivets on the back of her chair. They all had rivets. Three on each side. Slowly, very slowly, the tilting room righted itself.

He had been mistaken. If he looked again, he would see it was not her. Not *her*. Only like her. Things like this did not happen. Not to him. Or anyone. His eyes went on lying. Patiently, Philip waited for them to stop. They would be truthful again in a moment.

Stubbornly, the apparition refused to disappear. She looked somehow different from the way Philip had remembered her. On that train and outside the Tsaritsa in Harrogate. Then she had been . . . smart . . . was that the word? Yes, fashionable. This lady in her starched muslin blouse and cotton print skirt was not the same. And yet there was a consciousness in it. Something knowingly pastoral. Inwardly, Philip rebelled at her masquerading as a peasant woman. Then he caught himself. She was nothing to him. Less than nothing. A nuisance. A person he did not know. Did not wish to know.

There was something in her manner, too, that was not familiar. The reserve had gone. Before, he remembered, her poise had consisted in an unbreachable privacy. Now she waited confidently, like a seasoned performer, while the enthusiastic clapping died away. The violet eyes which had blazed at him for a second only, and then been so determinedly lowered, were now wide open to all.

"I can't tell you how glad I am to be in Lincolnshire this evening, and how grateful I am to you all for your kind invitation and even kinder welcome."

Philip realised he had never heard her voice before. Its

notes were piping pure, a tuning fork rung against a glass, and it had a middle register to it. That was more like a harpischord, threaded and mellow. There was laughter behind the sound, banked up and contained. He wasn't listening to what she said. He had known her face, her hands, the texture of her hair ... but nothing of the person to whom they belonged. He had known her name ... he had known *a* name and everything that went with that name except its physical being. The separate realities, two beads of mercury, rolled together and became one indivisible whole. The same substance.

Diana saw nothing but a sea of pale, attentive faces. The lights were switched off and her projector switched on. Slide followed slide. Sedgely at Gilbert's Tower, an English Gardens' packing station, Major Garside digging his heavy clay soil, an English Gardens' van arriving at the Tsaritsa's kitchen door, Alisdair chatting to Gholam Khan. There were many others.

She spoke for forty minutes, vivid and assured. Her audience was still, enraptured by the new worlds she uncovered for them. By the time she had finished, almost everyone had a question to ask, an impetuous need to know more about the people she had introduced to them. She had woven a connection of roots, both human and vegetable, shrunk distances.

Philip just wanted to speak to her. About anything. As long as his voice touched her and hers touched him in return. He disliked her ... everything about her ... except herself. She was a dreamer ... impractical ... a beguiler. He wished she had not come ... that *he* had not come. The lights went back on.

The Barkwiths' people rustled and muttered shyly.

"I'm sure Mrs. Neville," the vicar encouraged fussily, "would welcome any questions we may have."

Of course, Diana knew, it takes a little time in circumstances like these for one person to pluck up the courage to be the first to speak. She chatted easily, re-arranging slides, threatening gently to go. But they wanted to keep her.

"This organic business," a ruddy faced young man lumbered to his feet, "I've been a bit interested. But what do you do for a winter wash for fruit trees? What is there that's strong enough?"

Diana was ready for this question. It was a familiar one, constantly raised.

"Mr. Sedgely, I know, though he would never tell me, thinks that a solution of urine, water and soap flakes does a splendid job on dormant trees." It raised a gust of shocked amusement, as it always did. The contrast between Diana in her snowy muslin and the very thought of something as coarse as urine was piquant. "However, what he actually uses, probably out of respect for what he imagines to be my delicacy, is a weak solution of Bordeaux mixture."

Philip was on his feet instantly. There would never be a better moment than this. "All right, Alec."

The original questioner's voice subsided. He sat down, collapsing into shrivelled smallness like a pricked balloon. Mr. Strang-Steele had taken charge, commandeered the question. He had automatic, unquestioned priority.

Isolated on the podium, Diana watched in dismay as the things and people around her started to recede and grow smaller. Everything was a long way away. Seen through the wrong end of a telescope. Specks of matter moving slowly. Disassociated from sound.

"Perhaps you could tell us," Philip challenged, "how it is that agricultural products, noticeably your extremely pricey peaches, can possibly be described as organic when you tell us yourself they are sprayed with a preparation containing copper. Bordeaux mixture. Copper is a dangerous substance." He went on and on whilst Diana's thoughts raced. Had he received her letter? How far had he come to torment her? "Cynical breach of the Trades Description Act . . ."

When he had finished, he remained standing. His hands were in his trouser pockets. His eyes held hers, daring her to flinch or flicker. He hated her. She hated him. The yards of space between them were empty. The other people in the room had diminished to nothing. Lifeless lumps of clothing stuffed with straw.

At first, Diana's mind would not obey her. Her tongue lay frozen in her mouth. He must think she was afraid. Suddenly, she didn't like her clothes. To meet this man, she should have worn something stricter, harder. Armour. And she was cold, clumsy with cold.

"Shall I re-phrase the question, Mrs. Neville?"

No! He should re-phrase nothing. Damn him.

"No, Mr. Strang-Steele. I understood your question perfectly."

She knew him then. Philip could have turned cartwheels.

Diana answered him. Taught by Alisdair, she knew every word of the complex scientific arguments. She could quote the authorities, admit each area of doubt before others picked on them . . . weigh the evidence. In spite of himself, Philip was impressed.

"And, as you may not know, there is no regulation yet in force which defines the requirements for produce described as organic. In this matter, growers and institutes are completely self regulating. We proceed cautiously, as our knowledge allows. Certainly, no English Gardens grower sprays his stock with Bordeaux mixture more than once a year and at a maximum solution of thirty per cent. Does that answer your question adequately, Mr. Strang-Steele?"

Philip liked the sound of his name on her lips. He wanted to hear it again. She was still talking.

"I hope it does because, I confess, I'm dependent for my own information on my Technical Director, Mr. Alisdair Strang-Steele."

Diana placed the dart adroitly. It brought the rest of her audience back to life. A morbid thrill stirred in the room. The Barkwiths were getting more than their penny's worth. Two and two were instantly totted up to make five. Squire'd taken against Mrs. Neville . . . and Mr. Alisdair, rarely seen in these parts now, he'd taken up with her. Well, fancy that.

They couldn't blame Mr. Alisdair, she was a lovely looking woman. Oh yes, pretty as a picture. But nearly twice his age, surely? Dear, oh dear! What a coil. No wonder Mr. Strang-Steele was so down in the dumps the whole time. Now they'd have made a pair.

The vicar, too, knew something had gone wrong.

"Well," he rose from the front row and turned to face into the body of the hall, rubbing his hands, "I'm sure we'd all wish to thank Mrs. Neville for coming so far and giving us her fascinating talk. Real food for thought, I'm sure."

It was the same weary pun made in every vote of thanks Diana had yet heard. Ballet school stage-craft lessons were a help. The twinkle of newborn merriment sprang into her eyes automatically. She didn't have to think about it. Her mind was still on Philip Strang-Steele, though she was refusing to look at him any more. He was still standing up. Why didn't he sit down?

"So, if nobody has any further questions . . ."

Philip did not have to say anything. The laser beam of his intent silenced the clergyman's routine babblings.

"Yes, I have. Just one more."

Diana turned composedly towards him, her head cocked a little on one side. The gesture, gracefully tolerant, infuriated Philip. Was she deliberately goading him? Wishful thinking, he mocked himself.

"Can you honestly tell me that the peaches, for example, marketed by your company at three times the price of French imports, are worth the money?"

"Why no, Mr. Strang-Steele," Diana replied lightly, "I cannot tell you that. You see, I have never had to buy one. So I'm afraid it is our customers you must ask. They buy them, you see."

Casting aside any pretense of minding their own business, the Barkwith villagers burst into noisy clapping. Good for Mrs. Neville. Squire had been worsted and no mistake. Ashe Barkwith had never seen the like. No, nor North Barkwith, either, Mrs. Lightbody discreetly assured her neighbours.

What happened then, nobody but Diana saw. Philip Strang-Steele, still standing, folded his arms and leaned back appraisingly. He looked at her without expression for a long moment. She was the only one then facing him. Everyone else was looking forward, at her. Eventually, he unlocked his arms, letting them hang loose at his sides. He raised the fingertips of his right hand and placed them against his mouth and then waved in negligent salute.

A kiss? An insolent, arrogant kiss. Diana looked away sharply, feeling the blood rise to her cheeks. The horrible, hateful man. When she looked back at the place where he stood, he had gone. There was a patch of staring emptiness in his place.

❧ FOR ONCE, DIANA did not partake of the usual coffee and buns. Nobody seemed to have much time for her. The villagers of Barkwith were caught up in the excitement of an intangible, cathartic event. They grouped and huddled, glancing sideways at her, excluding her. Diana felt that they wished her out of the way. Her purpose, whatever it had been, was served. Something of greater importance than herself preoccupied them.

"Well, I ask you? Going off like that . . . he never even asked me . . . I've never known him to be rude before . . ." The sharp fragments of conversation crackled around her. The village people were like a rookery, chattering after the passing of a summer storm.

She went, taking formal leave of the vicar. She had a long way to go. He understood. It had all been most stimulating. A memorable evening. Memorable indeed. Everyone was most grateful. He could hardly wait to be rid of her.

Driving out of the village, Diana saw a lone figure in the distance, walking through the stubble of a cornfield. It was him. She would have known it, even if it had not been for the golfing umbrella. He took long, powerful strides with his head bowed. What had he meant . . . waving a kiss at her? Or had he just waved? In the centre of her gut she felt a hard knot. It was a pain trembling on the edge between hunger and nausea.

Fat drops of rain began to fall, dropping with pebble heaviness on the roof of the car. In the cornfield, the golfing umbrella went up.

Swinging the Peugeot on to the long, straight road leading to the A1, Diana put her foot down and drove with concentrated fury. The evening was best left far behind. It had been a failure.

After the first fifty miles, she found herself forced violently and frighteningly on to the hard shoulder. A police car cut in, stopping inches from her bumper. Diana wound down her window in angry astonishment. There had very nearly been an accident.

"Didn't you see us flashing you?" The crag faced constable was aggrieved. The shoulders of his uniform were dark and steaming from the rain.

"You mean that blue light?"

"Yes, madam. That blue light." The man was almost shouting.

"Yes, I saw it, but I didn't think it had anything to do with me," Diana replied, innocent and wounded.

"She didn't think it had anything to do with her," the con-

stable mimicked sarcastically for the benefit of a younger policeman who approached the car, adjusting the fly zip of his
trousers. The older man leaned into the car and put his face
near Diana's.

"What speed do you think you were travelling at, madam?"

The younger man pushed him aside and looked into the car
before Diana could answer.

"Why, it's Mrs. Neville, isn't it? My Dad's in English Gardens. Nectarines and little spuds."

"I *know*, the size of marbles. So you must be . . . Ted
Beasley's son?"

A grin of delight spread over the young policeman's face.

"That's right. Um . . . touching a hundred, you were, Mrs.
Neville."

For the second time that day, Diana flushed. She really had
no idea how fast she'd been driving. Her mind had been on
Philip Strang-Steele. Now, her features registered an acute sorrow.

"That's all right, Mrs. Neville. I think we can let her off, this
time, don't you, Mike?"

Appealed to, the older man relented.

"Just take it steady, Mrs. Neville, please. You gave us a
scare."

Diana drove on with tears of humiliation and fatigue pricking at her eyes. Speeding! It really had been a very bad day.
Philip Strang-Steele seemed to have pulled her inside out.

She reached Nidcaster an hour earlier than she had expected.
It had been dark for a couple of hours and the night had the
perfumed, velvet quality of that very first night at Gilbert's
Tower. It was good to be back, even after a few hours' absence. The church clock struck midnight as Diana shut the garden door, inhaling the honeysuckle's breath. There had been
rain here, too. Good. It was needed.

A light from the drawing-room windows gilded the dark terrace. That was surprising. She would have thought Yolanda
would have gone to bed by now. Alisdair was going to take
her out to supper at the Tsaritsa. A terribly grown-up treat. It
was sweet and thoughtful of him because Diana hated leaving
Yolanda quite alone at night. But Alisdair wasn't one for late
hours. How very odd. Diana fervently hoped nothing was
wrong. She couldn't face one single other thing today.

The front door was flung open before she reached it, and Yolanda, vivacious and shining eyed, tumbled down the steps into Diana's arms. Alisdair was framed in the doorway, his tall figure silhouetted against the muted light in the hall.

"Mummy, oh Mummy! I couldn't wait for you to come! I couldn't possibly sleep and not have told you. Alisdair and I are going to get married. Isn't it wonderful? He's loved me all this time and never said a thing about it. Isn't he just incredibly devious?"

So fond of your daughter . . . Diana heard old Mme. Strang-Steele's words anew in her memory. It was a warning she had not heeded. Or had it been a statement?

Yolanda was a hot, bubbling spring of happiness. Nothing would stop her in the full flood of her triumph. Even while she embraced her daughter, Diana resented her action. Somehow or other, these Strang-Steeles were colonising her world, her possessions. She hated her face for smiling at their behest, hated standing outside her own front door whilst she was told what would happen. They had penetrated her territory and she was defenceless against the invasion.

"I tried to ring Daddy, but it was too late to get him. I'll speak to him tomorrow evening. Look, I've got a ring . . . only a temporary one till I can choose what I like, but I think I'll keep this one, it was *Grandmére*'s, grandmother's."

It was a pretty thing. Two intertwined hearts of rose cut diamonds with a lovers' knot.

Diana looked up at Alisdair. He stood, arms folded, leaning the point of his shoulder on the door pillar with his head tilted on one side. He smiled with his lips closed and his eyelids half lowered. He looked like his father. Why had she ever let these people into her life?

"Well, darlings," she said flatly, "may I please come into the house?"

CHAPTER
10

❦ "You wanted me?"

Yolanda pushed open the dining-room door and looked around as if she hardly knew the place. It was very rarely used and never had been in Diana's time. A parade of oil painted FitzGilbert ancestors, their satins dulled behind deposits of grime, lined the wall facing the shuttered windows. Two of the shutters had been prised open and shafts of dust laden sunshine penetrated the far end of the room where Diana was examining the contents of a sideboard. Yolanda shivered, drawing her cotton robe more tightly about her.

"Yes," Diana turned, pausing in her half hearted enumeration of Georgian spoons. "But first go up and get some clothes on. It's nearly ten o'clock. What will Mrs. Sedgely think?"

Yolanda shrugged, puzzled by her mother's clipped tone. "Why should she think anything in particular?"

"Look, Yolanda," Diana scooped up the spoons and returned them to their baize lined nest, "quite frankly, I have some things to say you may not like. I imagine you'll have things to say in return. You'll say them better with some clothes on. It's a question of fair play. Go on."

Yolanda withdrew, leaving the door swinging wide on its hinges.

Typical. Thoughtless and slap-dash. Yolanda was no more fit to be married than she was to be an astronaut, Diana thought. Certainly not to the painstakingly conscientious Alisdair. It had nothing whatever to do with his name being Strang-Steele. Nothing at all. An irritating coincidence. Prejudice did not enter into the matter.

Diana drew a line under her thoughts. She sat down in the elbow chair at the head of the long table and waited.

The previous night she had made only non-committal remarks concerning the supposed engagement between her daughter and Alisdair Strang-Steele. No, she had not suspected anything, she said. Yes, she certainly was surprised. It was very late and she would like to go to bed. She would see them both in the morning. A kiss on the cheek for Yolanda, a light pressure on the arm for Alisdair. More of a push, actually. She had walked up the stairs stiff backed, hoping they would understand. It would save so much trouble.

A few minutes later, in her bedroom, she had heard Alisdair, round voiced with merriment on the front door steps. Clearly, the message had not been received. Diana had switched out her light then and finished undressing in the dark. There were to be no bedtime confidences with Yolanda about young Strang-Steele. Neither he nor her daughter appeared to have any conception of how far they had overstepped the boundaries. They were about to find out. In turn. Yolanda first.

Yolanda returned to the dining-room within ten minutes, wearing jeans, a white Aertex shirt with a navy Guernsey slung negligently around her broad shoulders. Diana felt a pang of motherly pride. Yolanda had always been a beautiful child. Now, in the first magnificent flush of womanhood, she stopped the heart. Like a rose at the open bud stage, when the shape is tautly seductive, the colours intense and the potential still so great. No, Alisdair should not have her for the asking. The thing was impossible.

"You might have told me, Yolanda," Diana drew out the chair beside her.

"It's cold in here," Yolanda evaded. She looked down at the walnut chair as if it might be electrified.

"Yes, isn't it? Put your sweater on," Diana replied drily. The dining-room was the place to talk. Harsh words, once spoken, could be locked up and left behind to decompose. So much lumber. And there was no nagging telephone. Yolanda sat down reluctantly.

"You see, darling, I really cannot allow it. You and Alisdair . . ."

"We don't need your permission." Yolanda flared up instantly. "I'm of age. I'm eighteen."

"Exactly. Eighteen. You have no job and no money, and consequently, no choice. Don't you see, sweetheart, you're simply too young?"

"You were eighteen when *you* married Daddy."

The jaw clenched tension which Diana had dreaded to see on Yolanda's face since her babyhood settled like a black crow over her features.

"I was. And in those days, I needed my parents' permission to marry at that age. They gave it. I do not give you mine." Diana spotted the flaw in her argument before she finished speaking. "You may not, as you say, need it, but I do so hope you want it."

Yolanda shook her head, unimpressed. Under the table, Diana clasped her hands tightly. Why had she been left to cope with this alone?

"Your father," Diana went on, "would . . . will feel just the same. Believe me, we both want only the best possible . . ."

"It doesn't matter what you want," Yolanda stood up, knocking the chair back violently. "I don't need a job or any money. Alisdair has a job and a house. He earns . . ."

"Thirty-five thousand pounds a year before tax and very considerable fringe benefits. I know. I pay the money and provide the fringe benefits. I can take them away, too."

Diana hated the words as soon as she had said them. How could she have stooped to threats? But her blood, which normally ran so tranquilly in her veins, boiled. The Strang-Steele marriage was out of the question. From every standpoint, undesirable. The very suggestion was laughable. The memory of Louise Strang-Steele calmly appraising her house, her daughter, her possessions, now seemed grotesque. In retrospect, it was so obvious. Insolent. And Yolanda, she had her life before her . . . three splendid "A" levels . . . the chance to be qualified . . . independent. The chance Diana herself had so nearly missed.

"You talk about fair play!" Yolanda fired back. "You wouldn't . . . you couldn't . . . I never thought you were a blackmailer. You have changed." She eyed her mother open mouthed. The unconcealed shock on her face shocked Diana in her turn. When and how had she become a monster?

"How do I seem to you, Yolanda?"

The question, unexpected by either of them, received no immediate answer. Diana marvelled at her own sudden curiosity. She had always borne Yolanda's opinion like a pack animal does, unable to see its load. There could have been no point or dignity in knowing what it was. She had brought Yolanda into the world and must love her, whether or not she was loved in return. Protect her, whether the securing bonds chafed or not. Nature's own treadmill.

"You're my mother. How do I know how you *seem*?" Yolanda faltered at first.

It was one of those meaningless questions that older people asked you to make sure that whatever answer you gave, it was the wrong one. A stubborn, repudiating silence was the best defence. But Yolanda was tempted. The moment when those throbbing boils of resentment flirt with the scalpel of truth had arrived. Between mothers and daughters, there is always such a moment. There would be pain, short and sharp, followed by an explosion of evil puss and relief.

"I suppose, when I was little, I was fascinated by your ... squashiness. I mean, whatever I did or said, you never stopped being patient. I could go on and on. Sometimes I did whatever it was over and again and then just one more time, even when I was sick of it, just to see if I could crack that famous self-control of yours. You never yelled or smacked. It wasn't that I thought you were weak. Not at all. You were strong in a rather terrible, depressing way. Vulcanised rubber. Most of the time, I think I took it for granted that you might not be very happy ... not like I was happy, or Daddy. But I thought you were used to it. It was the way you were."

Yolanda picked up the toppled chair absently and stood looking down at the worn needlepoint seat. The arms of FitzGilbert of Leypole. Diana stared unseeingly at the heraldic blazon too, transfixed by the hideous, pitiable reflection of herself mirrored in her child's eyes. She grieved for both of them. Whatever made people think love was a joyful thing? Sometimes, perhaps mostly, it was a soul warping prison. Yolanda had said so.

"You were so dogged," Yolanda went on, "and I counted on that. Daddy was fun. He made everything fun. But you were ... Well, I suppose we used to gang up on you a bit."

"I see," Diana said. "You enjoyed that, did you? And now?"

"Oh, it all changed. I say, couldn't we have some coffee or something?"

"No. I don't think so." Diana's voice was ragged. "I think you'd better finish what you've begun."

"All right." Yolanda sat down heavily beside her mother. The twinned hearts of Alisdair's engagement ring shone on her interlaced fingers. Strong, capable hands. "If you want. But don't blame me for all of this. You began it. Not me. Yes. It all changed. When Daddy went to prison and you came down to see me at school. You were different."

Yolanda's blue eyes searched her mother's face questioningly. Did she really want to hear more?

"Go on."

"You were sort of excited. It was when you'd had the idea for English Gardens. You were happy. Indecently happy. Free."

Yolanda waited for her mother to sign her to continue.

"Didn't you like that? Didn't you like me being happy?"

Yolanda hesitated. It was very difficult to put these things into words.

"It sounds awful, but no. I didn't. I wasn't used to it. And with Daddy gone, it was as if you'd split off from both of us. Become unconnected. You were alone for the first time. But not lonely."

And I should have been. Diana nodded.

Perhaps there was no perfect way to be a single parent family. Not for the child. You took yourself back, repossessed your mind and body. But the indivisible substance was hacked apart at a cost. Sooner or later, the blood seeped through the bandages. The child bore the larger share of the wound. But Yolanda had never screamed till now. It was too late.

"Before, you'd had to be there for us, and then suddenly, there was this person who seemed to think she could do anything she wanted. Just like . . ."

"Daddy?"

"Yes. It didn't feel right. Not natural. I felt very unsafe." Yolanda turned her head away and looked upwards, waiting for the next words to come to her. "You see, I hadn't done anything to make you love me. I hadn't needed to because you just did. Once you could choose, I felt cheated somehow. And frightened.

"Oh, I know," Yolanda forestalled the beginnings of Diana's

protest. "You went on doing all the right things, however busy you were. You came to all the school plays I was in. You watched me in the Yorkshire Schools Tennis Tournament and I went on the school skiing trips even when you were skint. You were there to pick me up at the airport when I got back ... but you didn't look anxious any more. Not about me."

"And you felt I was out of reach of your hateful little torturings," Diana flung at her. "Was that the trouble?"

"Yes. No. Kind of. Most people can't wait to get their mothers off their backs. Mine just climbed down of her own accord. So I had to grow up whether I liked it or not. Alisdair noticed. You didn't. You were too busy getting famous and being happy. Oh well, earning a living too," Yolanda conceded hastily. "That's it, really."

"And Alisdair?" Diana returned to the real subject of the conversation. The catalyst which had caused this confrontation. "Where does he fit into this picture of callous maternal neglect?"

"Didn't you notice me falling in love with him?"

Diana had not noticed. She had seen only what she had expected to see. A cheerful, older brother—younger sister relationship, teasing and affectionate. She had been glad of it. A security that had been free of charge. Love, passion, sex —none of these things had entered her head in connection with the two of them. There was the age difference, for one thing. Ten years.

Now she saw it all. Accustomed to Yolanda's appearance, she had not calculated its impact on anybody else. In a little over two years, it had matured from a gawky, almost boyish handsomeness into a rounded splendour. And Yolanda, hungry for confirmation of her attractions, had turned to Alisdair. Was she pretty? Was she lovable? Would men ever want her? All those urgent questions which mere looking glasses throw back unanswered. Alisdair had filled the father's reassuring role, the one Michael would have played so well ... but Alisdair had not been her father. So instead of telling Yolanda that no man could ever be good enough for her, as Michael would have, Alisdair had pronounced her good enough for him. But not too good.

"Have you slept with him?" The vileness of the question

tasted unpleasantly on her tongue. Diana did not want to ask but she must know.

"No. I would have done, but he always steered clear. If ever I got a bit . . . ardent, I suppose you'd call it . . ." Yolanda sighed. How could her mother possibly have any idea? "Anyway, he just laughed and said I was overfed and underworked. I was terribly upset once. I thought he meant I was fat. He was very sweet about it. But no, no sex."

Diana's relief showed on her face. It would have been a distasteful complication. "Well, that's something. Very chivalrous of him, I must say. A knight in thornproof tweed."

Yolanda grinned but Diana refused to enjoy her own joke. She should not have made it. Inept. She got up and began to pace around the table.

"Darling . . . No! Please, you must allow me to finish. You've said a great deal and now it's my turn."

Yolanda subsided.

"Alisdair is the only remotely suitable man you've ever met. You must not resign yourself into his hands or anyone else's until you know a lot more about yourself and the world."

"You did."

"Yes, I did. And since this seems to be a day for home truths, let me tell you, I wish that I hadn't. It's something I didn't realise until quite recently. Now I do. You see, I never had a chance to become *me*. And then, because of your father's misfortunes, when it was almost too late, I had to . . ."

At that moment Mrs. Sedgely opened the door. "It's Centa Supermarkets on the telephone for you, Mrs. Neville."

Yolanda groaned and dropped her head into her hands. "Business, business, business!"

Diana was stung. Didn't Yolanda realise? Businesses were like babies. Once you had one, you had to take care of it round the clock or it died. Damn Centa Supermarkets.

"Tell them I'm tied up for the rest of the day, will you, Mrs. Sedgely? I'll speak to them later. Would you be very kind and bring us some coffee?"

"Thanks. It's nice to come first for once," Yolanda mumbled the words almost shyly as the door closed behind Mrs. Sedgely.

"That's all right, darling. You do come first, you know." Diana patted her daughter's shoulder. "You always have . . . it's just that . . . you see, your father . . ."

"Do you mean you were unhappy with Daddy?" Yolanda twisted round in her chair. The look of scandalised incredulity on her face made Diana smile. Daughters. They never judged their fathers, only their mothers.

"No. I was unhappy with myself. Thanks to your acute observations, darling, I realise that now. It wasn't your father's fault. It wasn't anybody's. When I married him I had limbs and feet as hard as iron. But inside, my emotional bones were soft. I had no shape. I simply flowed into every corner of the mould I found myself in. My marriage. Outside it, I had no existence. I was deformed. I can't let you make that mistake."

They argued all morning, back and forth.

"Will you really sack Alisdair if we get married? It won't really matter. His father's very rich, you know."

Diana's eyebrows rose. "Oh, he told you that, did he?"

"Not in so many words, but these things come out." Yolanda poured the second cup of coffee peaceably. The boil was lanced. Now she was one adult negotiating terms with another.

"No," Diana took the cup from her daughter's hand, "I shan't have to sack Alisdair. He likes his job too much to marry you against my express wishes. And, I must say, I like him, despite his impudence. But he has done wrong. Very wrong."

"Supposing," Yolanda lowered her cup carefully, "his father gives him a job?"

"Then," Diana spoke with deliberation, "it will all be rather sad. I shall not feel able to speak to either of the Strang-Steeles for a very long time, if ever. I dislike Mr. Strang-Steele senior and I think the feeling is mutual."

Yolanda's evident amazement gave Diana a moment's sour amusement.

"Oh yes, I know him. He is, as you say, very rich. And a complete lout. So I don't know where that would leave you and me."

"Well, I'm sorry, Mummy," Yolanda gathered the coffee things together and replaced them on the tray. "I know I've often been ghastly to you and I wish we'd talked like this a long time ago. But it's too late now. You'll be rid of me. I'm going to marry Alisdair whatever you say. You see, I'm not like you. I've always had one of those internal shapes. Just like my outside one. They match."

❦ THEY TOOK THEIR lunchtime snack to the rusty wrought iron bench beneath the book room window.

It was still warm enough to eat outside and the old espalier pear was in fruit. A *Bon Chrétien*, Aunt Thea's inventory had said. Grown from seed, it had flourished on the western wall of the Carolean house for a hundred years. Very soon its life must be over. Its quiet companionship would be missed. Sedgely had said not to worry. He had its descendants, in various stages of development, dotted about the orchard and in the glasshouses. But which of the seedlings would have proved true was difficult to say. One of them would be chosen to replace its great forebear. One day.

Diana reached up and pulled at one of the yellow fruits. It fell gratefully into her palm as the cell telephone buzzed beside her on the bench. Yolanda screwed up her face but without rancour.

"There is a person to person call from Mr. Strang-Steele for Mrs. Neville," the operator said. "From France."

"Please tell the caller he has rung at an inconvenient time. Mrs. Neville is busy."

Diana switched off the power and bit into the pear. She was pleased with herself. She hadn't hesitated. Decisiveness was something she had discovered in herself during the past two years. How good it was to know your own mind, to shape your life.

"How's that? Two business calls forcibly rejected in favour of quality time with my daughter. Isn't that what they call it now? I'm improving, don't you think?"

"Better and better. Who was it?" Yolanda asked, not caring.

"Nobody who can't wait. A supermarket buyer. Alisdair can deal with him."

After I have dealt with Alisdair, Diana added silently.

❦ CONVERSATION WITH ALISDAIR was unrewarding. He was not contrite.

They talked in the small office which led off the mainframe computer room at the industrial estate. Diana did not like the place. With its small, high windows cut into breeze block walls, it housed the necessary squalor of calculation which underpinned the magic. It was Alisdair who had refined and perfected its activities. She walked into his office without knocking.

"You should have asked me, Alisdair. Why didn't you?" Diana spoke without preamble.

"Because you would have said no." Alisdair swung round from where he had been inputting some figures on a terminal keyboard. "And then I should have had to propose to Yolanda, knowing you disapproved. You would have been cross with me twice instead of once."

The rabbit punch of Alisdair's logic winded her momentarily. She sat down on a typist's chair.

"And you thought if I had only one lot of anger to get over, the quicker I'd come round and agree. Is that it?"

In spite of herself, Diana had to strangle laughter. Alisdair wore a pair of horn-rimmed spectacles for his work at the central computer plant. He appeared to her now as a studiously megalomaniac schoolboy, marshalling his pet mice for an experiment of his own devising. For the purposes of the exercise, she realised, she was one of the mice. A mouse whose behaviour had been predicted to a nicety. Or so he imagined.

Unabashed at the charge, Alisdair smiled his slyly attractive smile. "Something like that. Yes. What have you got against me, Diana?"

"Nothing personally. But I think this is very ill-judged. Not like you. Well, perhaps it is. You prefer to keep things to yourself, don't you?"

Alisdair grimaced slightly and turned back to the keyboard. He tapped it thoughtfully and then cleared the screen.

Diana noticed the way his hair, a little long, curled round his ears. It wasn't very difficult to see what Yolanda had fallen for. He exuded a heath textured, leather smelling masculinity. He should have kept it to himself. Deodorised it. She would like to have pulled those crisp Strang-Steele curls out by the roots. Or stroked them. Once, she had wished for a son.

"Father, you mean?" Alisdair acknowledged the reference to his earlier, minor deception. "Yes. Well, that's another problem we have, I'm afraid. You see, he's found out about your husband."

Diana flinched. The cupboard door of her private life had always been open, the skeleton clearly visible. It was simply never alluded to.

"I see. Didn't he know before? Most people do."

"Ah. Well," Alisdair turned around to face her again, "Dad works on the ivory tower system of information retrieval. Underlings hoist it up to him when he sends down for it. Not unless. Consequently, an awful lot of life just passes him by at ground level. When I told him I was going to marry your daughter, he thought it was time to find out exactly who you were. Actually, of course, just about anyone could have told him. Apparently, the editor of *The Grower* put him broadly in the picture and then his stockbroker filled in the lurid details. I'm afraid he didn't like it. Pretty strait-laced."

Diana flushed with mortification. Had Michael thought of *this* when he started embezzling other people's money or whatever it was he was supposed to have done. Yolanda was not wanted because she was a criminal's daughter. For the first time she allowed herself to think of Michael as cruelly as that.

"And would you still marry Yolanda, knowing that your father was against her?"

"Of course. I have to do what I want. I always have."

Diana was taken aback. How exactly like Yolanda he sounded.

"And if she would still have me ..."

"You get a bronze medal for sensitivity ... but would you marry her knowing that I disapproved?"

"Don't rush me, Diana. I would have to think very hard about that."

She contemplated him speechlessly.

"Rush you? Isn't it you who's been rushing my daughter? What on earth makes you think you want to marry her? Forgive me for saying so, but this cradle snatching seems needless to me. You could have ..."

"Anyone?" Alisdair caught the stray, unintended compliment neatly. "Yes, I suppose I could. There are a lot of very greedy girls about. But Yolanda and I, we're a matched pair. We have so much in common, and now even our revered parents are in total agreement."

Diana left the industrial estate in a ferment of confused emotions. To have her lovely child rejected because of her father's crimes . . . to have her married at all . . . And Alisdair, coolly picking his way through the minefield as if the only thing that mattered was that he should have what he wanted. What he wanted was Yolanda. Was there any real reason why he should not have her? Diana batted the thought aside impatiently. Absurd. She must not be railroaded by Alisdair's arrogance. Or his father's. Only Yolanda mattered. What was best for her.

The thoughts whirled through her head as she nosed the Peugeot through the market day traffic. A few people waved to her. She waved back abstractedly. The day had turned cool and windy with a few drops of rain in the air. The stallholders were packing up early. Discarded cardboard outers and wisps of tissue tumbled sporadically in the breeze. Nidcaster was out of sorts. A holiday would have been nice. No chance of that.

At Gilbert's Tower, Dorothy, the local girl who acted as her secretary, had left for the day. She had written several memos and reminders as usual. Philip Strang-Steele had rung again. He would try later. Diana winced. What was he going to do? Lecture her about her leprous condition as a convict's wife? A thick skinned bully boy.

Michael wanted her to call him back this evening at the usual time. Yolanda had gone out to a film in Harrogate with a girlfriend. She would stay at the friend's flat for the night. Rather cool, that.

Feeling, all at once, threatened, nagged and deserted, Diana picked up the messages and dropped them disgustedly into the book room wastepaper basket. She went into the kitchen and made a cup of tea. The place smelled of newly baked bread. Mrs. Sedgely had left the loaves out on cooling wires. Diana picked one of them up, fondling its dry, fragrant warmth. Mrs. Sedgely liked her to see the bread before it was put away. Its usually reassuring properties had no effect today.

In the vine conservatory, Sedgely was adjusting the ventilation, his customary last job before going home.

"What do you do, Mr. Sedgely, when you're totally and utterly confused by life?" Diana dropped disconsolately into a basket chair.

"I wait for it to sort itself out, Mrs. Neville, love," Sedgely replied in the tone of one accustomed to deal leniently with the errors of fate. "And like as not," he went on, removing the china mug from Diana's hand, "I drink a bottle of parsnip wine while I waits. I'll go fetch you one up."

Sedgely had an inkling of what troubled Diana. There was a ring on Miss Landa's finger, Mrs. Sedgely said, and not much doubt where it came from. It matched the heart t'bairn wore on her sleeve. Been quite a carry on in t'ouse that morning, by all accounts. Young Mr. Alisdair'd overstepped t'mark if Mrs. Sedgely's assessment o' t'situation were owt to go by.

"No, Albert, don't," Diana resisted his offer gently. "I'll get it myself, later. Just tell me one thing. I heard you telling Alisdair you worked for his father once."

"Well, it were a ganger I worked for," Sedgely interrupted.

"Yes, but you knew him—Mr. Strang-Steele, I mean."

"To nod to, aye, but . . ." Sedgely conceded reluctantly.

"What did you think of him?"

"He were a toff. A proper gent. No side, like. And he made sure we got us proper wages with no nonsense from t'gangers."

The six o'clock bells signalled the hour sacred to Sedgely's tea, putting a stop to further conversation. After Sedgely had gone, Diana meditated his words whilst contemplating his red cabbages, swelling in their regimented dozens. Sixty of them this year. What did Sedgely do with so many?

It was too late to ring Michael back, now. Perhaps if she rang the staff in the duty room they'd give him a message that she'd tried and would try again tomorrow. Then he wouldn't be quite as savage when they did speak. These manoeuvres were always the same. Damage limitation.

When Philip Strang-Steele rang again, she decided, she would speak to him. As Alisdair said, they now had something in common. An overwhelming desire to remain unrelated by marriage.

❦ PHILIP STRANG-STEELE DID not ring again. Instead, he sent a fax. It chattered out of the book room machine the following morning before Dorothy arrived for work. It was written in manuscript, a thick italic hand with firm, straight lines.

Attention: Mrs. Neville.
Failed contact yesterday but believe we should talk over family matters. Know you are busy but suggest meeting at

my mother's home, *Manoir des Evêques*, near Rouen. Two best routes via Leeds/Bradford airport to Charles de Gaulle (will send car to collect) or night ferry from Hull to Zeebrugge (will also send car there). Please signify preference and my secretary will make bookings and arrange tickets.

Very glad if you will come. My mother tells me she owes you hospitality. Delighted to return this. Watched your career with interest lately. Guess change of scene not unwelcome. Suggest say nothing to children.

Regards: Strang-Steele.

Diana read it and re-read it with stupefaction. As she did so, something twitched at the corners of her mouth. However much she tried to discipline the tick, it kept coming back. There was another feeling. A lark soaring effervescence inside. She felt restless. A cup of coffee? A walk? A cigarette? Ridiculous, she didn't smoke. Never had.

The telegrammatic style was barbarous. Compelling, though. The "i" dots were all open circles. Artistic? Her mother had once said it was a sign. And the content. Well, nobody said "masterful" any more. It was a word that belonged in romantic novels that were old-fashioned when *she* was young. Direct, then. It was conspiratorial ... almost intimate. And generous, too.

Diana made up her mind quickly. She would go. What had she to lose? She could turn round and come home the same day if she wanted. An adventure. Though, of course, nothing had really changed. The sea. She would go by boat. It would be more ... fun. Yes. Why not? More time to think that way. Clothes. How many? What kind?

A little ashamed of her own skittishness, Diana repeated the list of things which should re-attach her feet to the ground. She was a middle aged married woman with a nearly grown up daughter. And a husband in prison. She was going to France to tell a man she had no reason to like that she no more wanted Alisdair for a son-in-law than he wanted Yolanda for a daughter-in-law. Their personal relationship, such as it was, would end there. The business contact was unavoidable. Fortunately, it was remote. A cryptic reply was returned.

Agree suggestion. Grateful invitation. Prefer sea route. Can leave soonest passage available. Regards. D. Neville.

His style was catching.

Someone would have to know, of course. Sedgely. She would give the contact details to him. He could be trusted. She would say nothing to Michael, she decided. He would be bound to interpret her trip as a taunt. In the end, Diana did tell Michael. She had not really intended to but one thing led to another. He was grudging and monosyllabic when she rang him, punishing her for the previous day's forgetfulness.

"I'm sorry, didn't you get my message? I had so much on yesterday, it slipped my mind."

"Can't be many wives whose husbands slip their minds. Not faithful wives."

There had been a quarrel then. One of those choreographed arguments in which Michael proposed the hundred and one things she might have done but knew she had not. It was the same weary, worn out scenario. Diana defended herself against the empty accusations. Greville Goodwynne's name came up. Who else was there? Michael pretended to be persuaded of her innocence, very, very slowly. Somehow or other, Diana ended up pleading to be forgiven for allowing Michael to think she had done the things she had not done. The moves were well charted, the end always the same. It was made clear that Diana was guilty of some unnamed offence. Otherwise there could have been no quarrel. Michael was placated. Diana was exhausted.

"Let's just leave it, shall we?" Michael said finally. Did he know that he said that every time? Diana wondered.

"I'm going to France tomorrow. Just for a day or two," Diana said with vengeful *insouciance*. "Some business but . . ."

Michael slammed the telephone down immediately. The hollow rattle was the sound of Diana's own heart plummeting. The pleasure of revenge was all in anticipation. The dish which looked so appetising tasted of nothing and was paid for in despair.

Attempting an inner resolution, Diana walked upstairs to start packing. No, she would not ring Michael back. The price of harmony between them was reaching a level she could no longer bear alone. His jealousy was a morbid appetite. To indulge it was like pushing dope to an addict. She would not do it again.

A door slammed above on the attic floor and a jangle of pop music started. Yolanda. There were no carpets in the rooms up there. Something would have to be done about sound insulation. Michael would need a study of his own when he came home. Somewhere to write his articles. She would spend some money on decorating and furnishing it for him. A welcome home present. He would need a dressing-room, too. The private places that a man like Michael must have.

Diana went on selecting the best and newest of her undergarments for the Strang-Steele visit. The drawers stuck in the chests, and she jiggled them free with patient, affectionate skill. The humidity in the house fluctuated so frequently that furniture, doors, even panelling and skirting boards changed their dimensions and shape like living things. A single, long-noted whistle in the chimney was a message from autumn. It would come early this year. The dried honesty in the hearth rustled its papery coins in reply. Diana enjoyed the perpetual dialogue between the house and the weather. Michael would want to block the flues, still the draughts and silence the window panes. She would not worry about it now.

There were other things. Sea sickness pills. The crossing might be rough at this season. She found an old packet at the bottom of her dressing case. Were they any good or not? She couldn't remember when she had bought them or why.

She had drawn the curtains and was trying on half forgotten evening gowns when Michael rang again.

"I forgot to say," he sounded gruff, "there's an open day in a couple of weeks' time. You might be interested and I'd like to see Yolanda. My parole board comes up soon. Looks good if the family's seen to be the right stuff. Will you be back in time?"

Diana assured him warmly that she would. She was distressed. Now *he* was the suppliant. That was not what she wanted, either. This endless cycle of brow-beating and servility must stop.

"Yes. And I think we should all talk about what Yolanda's going to do with her life. I'll look forward to it, darling. Goodnight."

He doesn't even want to know why I'm going to France, Di-

ana muttered to herself as she fanned the shell pink chiffon
skirts of an old Lanvin gown. It was very simple. Cut like a
doric *chiton*, the hems of its many layered skirts were each
edged with a narrow binding of silver. There was a cropped,
long sleeved jacket encrusted with bugle beads and opalescent
sequins. She might not get a chance to wear it. But she would
take it. She had always loved it.

Yolanda tapped at the door and came in.

Diana started. She felt vaguely foolish. Surprised in an act
of self-love. "Oh, supper time, is it? You've caught me out,
darling. Miss Faversham amid her ancient finery. Past glories.
Day dreams . . . one has them, you know," she started to excuse herself.

"Fantastic! You've no idea how good you look in that dress,
Mummy."

Oh, but I have, my dearest daughter. Oh, but I have!

 PHILIP CAME TO meet her himself. Recognising his tall figure
on the quayside, Diana was unnerved. The long drive she had
expected behind a silent chauffeur had been earmarked for
planning. She would decide on the journey what she should
say . . . what she wanted to achieve. In the last twenty-four
hours these things had become less distinct. But now the time
had run out. She would have to play it by ear.

His eyes scanned the decks. He wore grey flannels and what
Yolanda would have called a "sweatshirt." It was white and
suited him. His hands and face were tanned. He looked youthful
and relaxed. Diana waved tentatively. The movement caught his
eye and he smiled, showing a row of even white teeth. He held
up his hand like a traffic policeman, commanding her to stay
where she was. Then he ran back to the terminal building with
long, loping strides. What did he mean?

The ferry was unloading the car passengers first but a companionway was being wheeled to the side of the vessel. In a
moment they would make her disembark. The staccato shouts
of foreign officialdom stabbed through the screams of wheel-
ing gulls. Foot passengers still aboard bent to struggle with
hold-alls and plastic bags bulging with bottles and cigarettes.
Duty free. Uncertainly, Diana hung back. This did not look
like a good place to get lost. What should she do?

Some iron gates opened to one side of the dock and a silver-grey Bentley passed through them to draw alongside the companionway. It was him. He got out of the driver's seat and started threading his way upwards through the descending throng until he reached her.

"There. I can arrange most things but not porters. Will you make do with me? What have you got?"

Close to her, he felt ... large. Everything about him was large.

Diana indicated her suitcase and dressing case rather limply. Her arrival speech died on her lips. It wasn't designed for delivery on a dockside, anyway. She hoped her suitcase didn't look too big. It had been difficult to know what to bring.

"I'm so very ..."

He picked up her cases and nudged her arm very gently with his own.

"Let's clear out of here first. Then we can talk. Come on."

He installed her in the front seat of the Bentley, put her luggage in the boot and asked for her passport. After a few moments' rapid, cordial conversation with a man in a *kepi* with gold rings round his arm, the Bentley slid away from the quay.

"One of the advantages of being a regular exporter," he looked sideways at her. "You don't have to mess around. I send a lot of stuff for canning from here. It's little green apples one day and by nightfall a day later, it's apple sauce, somewhere in Hull." There was a faint glimmer in his eye.

Diana did not rise to the bait he dangled. He would have to do better than that.

"But you don't send cargo on the ferry, surely?"

They talked about transport. The best way to travel from Yorkshire and Lincolnshire to France. Leeds and Bradford ... often fogbound. Teeside Airport ... not bad. East Midlands a possibility. Hull good but a longish haul. Not crowded, though. Not like the Channel port approaches. Goole no use except for Scandinavia. Fine if you were buying bacon or timber. Crossing continental borders was no problem now. The Humber Bridge ... a commercial disaster. Except for Strang-Steele. Yorkshire and Lincolnshire ... worlds apart.

Diana could contribute little. She had never been anywhere outside the United Kingdom since she left London. "Oh's" and "Really's" filled the spaces.

They were both nervous. Wanting to say they were grateful

for the truce, they confined themselves to the banal and probed the outer surfaces gingerly. Where were the safe areas? When would they have to talk about the things which both united and divided them? Not yet. A blind date.

"By the way," he changed the subject without warning. "I've arranged to withdraw my remarks about your company. An abject apology in ten point type. Bold. Right hand page, centre fold. The editor's doing my humiliation proud. I'm afraid I've got a lot of ground to make up with . . ."

"Don't," Diana cut him short. "Not now. It's not what I came for."

"No," Philip agreed sombrely. "No business talk . . . unless you want."

They were travelling through the flat Flemish countryside. The morning was fresh with white cumulus clouds sailing high in the sky. The poplar trees shivered, their silver backed leaves reflecting in mirror bright canals and ponds. The rush of fast German cars passing them on the road. Bicycles, ducks and windmills in the middle distance. The very last days of summer.

"You mustn't mind me, you know," Philip said suddenly. They had been quiet for a mile or two. "You just nod off if you want. No need to make polite conversation."

He thought she was tired. But the crossing had been calm, the ferry half empty. She had had an outside cabin to herself with a shower room. But although she had slept very little, she couldn't possibly lose consciousness now in the presence of this nerve wracking stranger.

"Are you quite comfortable? Not too warm? Or is it too cold?" He started to show her the workings of the car's heating system. She sensed he was proud of it.

"This is an old car, isn't it?" she asked with well-meaning, feminine tactlessness. He kept his eyes on the road, the corner of his mouth curling downwards in wry deprecation.

"*Vintage* is the word I'd have chosen myself," he reproved. "But yes, it's old. Nineteen sixty-two. It's my 'off duty' car. I think it belonged to one of the Beatles once. Do you remember them? No, of course you don't. You were only a baby."

A pleasing miscalculation. Diana had been twelve in 1962 and an ardent fan. But the flattery, intended or not, was emollient. Like expensive bath oil. Soothing. She fell asleep.

They arrived at the Manoir Des Evêques in time for a late lunch. Diana woke up just as they turned off the main road into the village.

"Oh! I'm so sorry! How perfectly dreadful of me."

"Not a bit. You have been the most peaceful companion. And missed some very tedious scenery. I thought of stopping at Amiens for lunch but I couldn't bring myself to wake you."

Diana noticed the travel rug spread over her knees. How had he done it without waking her?

"At the frontier. You had gone a shade paler, like a very tired child does. How do you feel now?"

It felt oddly agreeable to have this big man clucking over her. Cherishing her.

"Where are we?"

"Home. Look."

The Manoir was framed by a crescent of sweet chestnut trees. It was like a grown up version of Hansel and Gretel's cottage. The steeply pitched roof was thatched, randomly pierced by twinkling dormers each with its own miniature thatch. Peeping eyes. Beneath the broad eaves, the remaining two stories were richly timbered and ornamented. A tiny figure standing in what looked like the main doorway made her realise the scale of the house. The place was huge. The car ran under a kind of gatehouse in a similar style.

"I don't know what to say. I'd no idea there were places like this. Thatched palaces."

"It's fifteenth century, basically. It belonged to the Bishops of Rouen. A kind of country retreat and a source of income, too. My father bought it for a song just after the war. The house was falling down then. Half the roof was off and there were pigs living in it. Restoring the place took him the rest of his life. Fortunately he got the main things done before the cost of labour became ruinous. An academic's salary wouldn't get you very far with a reconstruction task like that these days."

There was so much to know about him. Diana learned some of it over the next twenty-four hours.

Louise professed herself quite overcome with the pleasure of welcoming her dear, dear friend to her house. Sincere? Maybe not. But irresistibly charming. What could Diana do but tell her that she was glad to be her guest? She had accepted a part in the charade and must play it.

Lunch, a luscious, butter and cream smothered succession of dishes, was eaten in the great hall, beneath a hammer beamed ceiling so intricate it looked like wooden lace. They were served by a muscular looking girl in a very smart lilac uniform. The conversation was in English, to Diana's relief. Her French was barely adequate and rusty at that. At a loss to know what to admire when everything was so much beyond praise, Diana mentioned the *quenelles de brochet* and salad of mussels with rice.

A few *nit wits*, Louise acknowledged modestly. Diana was mystified.

"My mother means *tit bits*," Philip translated helpfully. "She is reserving her big guns for this evening. She thinks you need building up."

"But of course! And when we heard of this tragic affair of your husband . . . Well, one is not astounded, madame, that you are so . . . meagre. That is the word, no?" Neither Diana herself or Philip were given the chance to substitute a kinder one. Louise rattled on without pause. "So I thought we must all meet to consider the position. With our young people on the threshold of what we all hope will be a blissfully happy . . ."

Philip's glance stopped his mother in her tracks. That was not, it turned out, quite what she had said at all. The slant of her remarks had been entirely opposite. He did not give her away just then, but after lunch was over and Louise had retired for her nap, Philip took Diana for a stroll out of doors into the apple orchards.

"I seem, after all, to have brought you here under false pretences. You see, my mother gave me to understand, in a rather alarming display of hysterics . . . not easy to ignore at her time of life . . . that in no circumstances would she countenance the marriage of my son to your daughter in view of your husband's unfortunate position."

Diana was silent, not quite understanding the drift of what he was saying. The objection had been his own, surely? They walked between evenly spaced rows of trees. Most of them were bare of fruit now. Just ahead, a sort of mobile crane was working its way along, stripping the apples with ruthless efficiency. Apples, as far as the eye could see. Golden Delicious. Only they were green. Unripe.

Intercepting her glance, Philip placed a hand beneath her elbow and steered her towards a meadow. Apples would be a distraction. But Diana was not thinking about them.

"You mean, you don't mind?"

"Don't misunderstand me. I'm concerned, of course. But I'm not in a position to dictate to my son. Apart from the cost of his education, he's never taken a penny from me. In the latter stages, his research work was funded partly by industry institutions and partly by commissions he found for himself. So you see, he owes me nothing. I wish he did."

"Mr. Strang-Steele . . ."

"I wish you'd call me Philip."

Diana looked up at him. He was walking with his hands in his pockets, his face slightly averted as if he feared a rebuff.

"I should like that. My name's Diana, you know." The reply was drawn from her before she had time to consider it. She wanted them to be comfortable together.

"I should think everybody knows that. In Britain, at least. Strange to think I met you before you became a household name . . . on that train. Do you remember? No, why should you? I don't talk to people on trains, as a rule. You were very determined not to be the exception. I had no idea who you were, then. And no idea who you were going to become."

It all came out. The discovery of Yolanda's father's identity had disturbed Philip. He had told Louise, who had declared the marriage of her grandson to such a person would kill her. Diana greeted the news woodenly.

"Indeed?"

"A trifle overstated, I know. But I'm very attached to my mother. I suppose I give in to her far too much. She probably won't last much longer, either. But I depend on her company. By the way, I'm sorry she made a nuisance of herself in Yorkshire. Yes, she told me about that. Most reprehensible. She really is quite uncontrollable. My father spoiled her, you see, and I spoil her too. It's too late to change anything."

"Yes, but I still don't see . . ." Diana found she had fallen behind him on the narrow path which led through the meadow. She stumbled over an exposed root. He turned and held his hand out to her as if to a child, squeezing her fingers lightly before releasing them.

"Sorry. Wandering off the point. Yes, well, I rang Alisdair and said couldn't he at least wait a little. *Grandmère* hasn't very long to live . . . she has angina, you know . . . and your daughter is very young. Alisdair said he'd waited already and would wait no longer. *Grandmère* was a manipulating old bully. Which, I'm afraid, she is."

Philip paused, waiting to see if Diana would add anything. She did not, sensing a test. The privilege of criticising Louise was reserved exclusively for her son.

"I asked Alisdair what view you took of the engagement. You were not, apparently, in favour of it but could do nothing to stop it. By this time, I was furious with both of them. My son and my mother. I dislike ultimatums. And disorder. I told my mother that the very least we could do was to talk to you. Funnily enough, she agreed to that immediately . . . suggested we invite you here."

"Really?" Diana drew a blade of long grass from its sheath and started pushing the seeds off the end. "So it wasn't your own idea?"

"No," he looked over his shoulder at her in surprise. "It's my mother's house, you see. I would have gone to see you somewhere else . . . wherever suited you."

"And you didn't think it's in the least bit odd that your mother should offer to receive the mother of the very person to whom she strongly objects as a wife for your son . . . ?" Diana's voice trailed away. For a few moments there was nothing but the soft thud of Philip's feet on the path.

"Well," he answered her finally, "I suppose I thought she'd rather I didn't go off and leave her just now. The apple harvest is one of the times we always spend together." He had said that before and it was Philip's turn to fall silent.

"Even odder that she should have appeared to have changed her mind about Yolanda, after all, wouldn't you say?"

"I must say," Philip did not address her point immediately, "I haven't seen her quite so excited at the prospect of a visit from anyone since my father died. Fairly started cracking the whip in the kitchen." He turned and Diana saw him smile broadly. "There was uproar in the linen room. Where was this and what had happened to that? Yes, I suppose you're right. A bit odd, as you say."

"Hm," Diana underscored the point. "And all of this for a casual acquaintance ... the wife of a person in an *unfortunate* position ... as you so kindly express it."

Hunching his shoulders, Philip made no comment. Diana's summary of his mother's behaviour was valid. There was none of Louise's consistent, if eccentric, logic here. He was puzzled.

To Diana, the convolutions of Louise's actions made a pattern only partially visible. She viewed the maze at an angle. Not every blind alley, twist and turn was revealed. However, the old lady's violent rejection, followed by a warm invitation and complete capitulation over the proposed engagement had secured a certain compression of events.

Diana had indeed come to the Manoir des Evêques, been feted, and was now walking ... in every sense but the physical, hand in hand with Philip Strang-Steele. A gunpowder trail leading to a cleverly deployed stick of gelignite. The arrangements, Diana did not doubt, were aimed at exploding her own refusal to countenance the marriage. She was to be dislodged from her position like a stubborn boulder from a quarry. Like grandmother, like grandson. Corner cutting exercises. Shock tactics with charm. Perhaps they had colluded.

"So it looks," Diana said pointedly, "in the final analysis, as if I am the only one who still objects to the marriage of my daughter with your son. Why do I end up feeling such a boor about it all?"

"Please don't feel that," Philip said quickly. "You've been messed about and misled. Tell me what, if anything, I can do to help."

Diana had no difficulty in conveying her own apprehensions to Philip. Eighteen was too young to decide on anything so momentous as a marriage partner. He agreed. The quickest way to separate Alisdair from Yolanda was for Diana to dispense with Alisdair's services. It was Philip's suggestion. Diana had thought of it. She was loath to do it. Send Yolanda abroad for a while. Would she go? Would Philip support them financially if Alisdair did leave English Gardens? Certainly not. Not without Diana's knowledge and approval. He would not be an accomplice in what would amount to abduction. And

Louise's objection. Was it real? Had it ever been? Should it be considered at all? No.

"About my husband. I'm sorry to have brought all this trouble into your family. You must feel it a contamination of some kind." Diana was torn between the demands of honesty with her host and loyalty to her husband.

Philip would not allow her to go further. "I would prefer it otherwise but I don't know your husband. I can't judge him. And as for your daughter . . . people might inherit a tendency to house breaking or robbery with violence," his mouth curled in what might have been a quirk of humour, "but not, I think, to financial chicanery on the scale of your husband's. You would need a doctorate in pure mathematics to begin. Or so I hear. Is Yolanda mathematically gifted?"

A joke? Diana did not dare laugh. Philip sounded so perfectly serious, as he had a right to be. His son's happiness was also at stake. She had not thought of it quite like that before. She should not even *feel* like laughing.

"Wouldn't you mind being related, even by marriage, to . . ."

"An exceptionally brilliant man who is also a thief?" Philip lifted one eyebrow quizzically and smiled grimly at her. "Yes. I will mind. But we can't choose our relations, can we? In-laws are in the high-risk area. Our children choose them for us. Ultimately, we're helpless . . . stuck with people we neither like nor love nor respect."

He walked on for a moment, saying nothing.

Diana considered the outer darkness where dwelt the people whom Philip Strang-Steele neither loved nor liked nor respected. She found she did not really wish to share their exile. Then she pulled herself together. This diffuse wool gathering would not do. Philip was talking again.

"It's too late, Diana," he went on at length, "for anyone to do *me* harm. Not commercially. And I've no escutcheon to worry about. My grandfather was the sixth son of a prolific but impecunious laird. He got a small farm out of it . . . not much more than a croft. As for my father . . ." He nodded, seeing Diana's surprise. "Yes. And up in the wilds of Fifeshire there wasn't much to do but get educated. My father walked to school and back five miles through the glen every day till he was sixteen. Bare foot, too, if I believed him. Scots get a trifle romantic about their early privations, you know. Anyway, he ended up Professor of Music at Edinburgh University after a stint or two in Glasgow and Vienna. He met my mother there. She's the one with the social pretensions. How about you?"

Diana found herself telling him all about her own musical father. Her girlhood home in Kensington. Her life at the Royal Ballet School, her marriage to Michael and finally, about the FitzGilbert connection and Aunt Thea.

"Michael's father was some sort of engineer in Birmingham. They didn't have any money to speak of. Anything Michael had, he got for himself. Another self-made man."

"And a thin trickle of blueish blood on one side in both cases," Philip tied off the loose ends.

There was nothing more to be said.

"When will your husband be released?"

"In a year, officially. But it might be as soon as next March."

"What will you do then?" He stood still, halting abruptly on the path and turning to face her, blocking any escape.

"I will carry on." Diana looked straight up into his eyes, the violet deepening in her own as she spoke. "Michael is my husband. For better or worse . . . all those things. He is the father of my child. He will need me."

Philip kissed her then. It happened quite suddenly, with no preliminary, full on the mouth. She held her hands stiffly at her sides, not resisting him but not encouraging. Eventually, her arms slid round his waist and he moved his face till his cheek lay against hers. He had to stoop to her somewhat.

"I'm sure you must be getting cramp," Diana offered a way out in a small, polite voice. They could not stand there like that for much longer. He let go of her at once.

"I'm sorry. I should not have done that."

The gravity of his outward demeanour was total. His eyelids drooped apologetically, veiling a flash of triumph. He had waited a long time for that. The chance might never come again.

Diana checked an impulse to tell him he need not look *quite* as sorry as all that. No harm had been done. A stolen kiss, late in the day, late in the summer . . . at the very end of youth. Everyone should do it once. And then forget it. She dared not think how much she had liked the embrace. How strong and warm his arms had felt.

"I rather wish you hadn't done it," was all she said.

A ridiculous tear formed in the corner of her eye and rolled down her cheek. Philip caught it on his fingertip. He examined it as if, like a crystal ball, it could reveal secrets. Uneasy, Diana put her hand over the finger and wiped the droplet of moisture away. It must all end now.

"You've been through a lot." He put a hand on the back of her neck briefly and then let it fall. "We'd better go in."

They made their way back across the meadows towards the Manoir, walking self-consciously apart. A distance tacitly agreed to denote friendship but not intimacy. They talked about Alisdair and Yolanda. A reasonable compromise could be reached. Philip would sleep on it, he said, and come up with a workable formula.

By silence, each convinced the other that the incident in the meadow was of no importance. The sort of accident from which adults recover quickly.

❧ DIANA'S ROOM, WITH its miniature pepperpot turret and odd angles, must have been one of the finest in the house. It was lined like a jewel box in silk damask and lavished with a profusion of flowers. Not shop bought flowers, either. They were roses from the Manoir's own garden. Someone had spent time cutting and arranging them. Somebody with taste and a practised hand. There were English pillows on the bed, too. Not the square, French kind. Thoughtful. English books on the bedside table. New ones. Gossipy biographies and thick, escapist novels. Bought specially, Diana could not doubt. The linen was fragile with age and very precious.

It added up to the subtle message of one sophisticated woman to another. This is the best I have. The work of my hands. You are among the few who will know how to value it. You are more welcome than any words can say. On all this the mistress's signature was unmistakably etched. Diana knew. It could not be counterfeited. *Louise*.

"No, *chère Madame*," Diana murmured to herself as she gathered together things for the bathroom that evening. "I shan't be seduced or charmed. You have done your best for your grandson . . . but my answer is still no. No Yolanda."

Satisfied that she had evaded the only snare she saw, Diana gave herself up to creating a dense froth of extremely costly bubbles, all vigilance relaxed.

But Diana had missed the point. Louise had more than one object in view. More than one hook on her line.

When she returned from her bath, Diana saw that Marie, who had unpacked her suitcase for her earlier, had laid out the shell pink gown. On the dressing table there was a collar of blush coloured pearls with a diamond clasp in the shape of a bow. Five evenly matched strands. The collar lay on a note from Louise. "Do give me the pleasure of letting me see this worn again. It is a bridal piece, fit only for a lovely young throat. Please, don't disappoint me."

Diana havered. She was tempted to refuse. But the necklace was offered to her, not Yolanda. What harm could it do now, to indulge the old lady's whim? She tried it on. Captivating. Rejection would be . . . boorish.

❦ PHILIP GREETED DIANA'S initial appearance at the foot of the staircase with a politely appreciative murmur. Then, looking hard at her and appearing to lose interest, he turned away. Staring at the broad, blank expanse of white dinner jacket, Diana knew a moment of feminine pique. She could not, she told herself crossly, look much better than this. What had she done wrong to make him so suddenly busy with bottle openers and ice buckets?

Louise, sprightly in black lace, with a lorgnette suspended around her neck on a ribbon, brushed the moment's awkwardness aside. She insisted on conducting the most thorough examination of Diana's *grande toilette*, as she called it.

"Hm. *Exquise, ma chère*. Lanvin . . . she is unbeatable for *les robes du soir* . . . no? Marie, she tell me you have this gown. That is why . . ." Louise tapped the pearl collar with her forefinger and smiled. "It is quite perfect, no? Philip," she demanded peremptorily, "bring Diana some champagne."

He did so, handing her the flute, straight faced. His eyes were flat and grey, the summer's day warmth all gone. Diana made nothing of it, other than that he was uneasy with her now, after what had passed between them. Not, she concluded pettishly, quite as sophisticated as he looked.

During dinner, it was Louise who was left to make all the conversational running.

"What do you think of my dessert service, Diana? I may call you that, may I not?" She waved her lorgnette in the general direction of the tiered yellow comport, chipping the gilded edge. Philip shrugged tolerantly.

"It is Limoges. Fifty pieces. Hard paste porcelain. Quite a different thing from your English soft paste. It is very special with these portrait cartouches. Philip, he knows nothing about such things."

"I know enough to know there's about nine pieces left that aren't damaged," he sighed.

"Stupid boy!" Louise countered genially. "Count your money and allow me to know the contents of my own china cupboards. Pah! Always, my Philip, he know everyone else's business. As a child in Edinburgh, he wished to check my housekeeping accounts. I was being swindled because I was a foreigner! Imagine!"

She was full of anecdotes concerning Alisdair's and Philip's respective boyhoods. So alike, they had been. *"Chips off the old rock."*

In the strained atmosphere, neither Philip nor Diana had the heart to correct the small mistake. It was better than the original cliché anyway. The lightning crackle of communication that had existed between them that afternoon was extinguished.

Later, Diana was shown a collection of antique musical instruments. They were displayed in a small room papered with a patchwork of yellowed score sheets stuck down with glue and thickly varnished. On the floor, a chequerboard of black and white tiles was littered with piles of old books and dog-eared manuscripts. Some had clearly been cannibalised to adorn the uneven walls. Of these, one was entirely covered in flat, bright, mirror glass, doubling the size of the room and affording alternative views of the things within it.

"My little museum," Louise announced as she opened the door. "Do you not find the *décor* amusing? When my son has an idea, it is always what he calls 'cost efficient.'"

Philip prevented his mother from dilating further on his character. There had been quite enough of that already. "Would you care for Cognac? Or will you have Calvados?" He had not used her name since the afternoon. Chilled, Diana declined. Coffee would be enough.

"Ah, but no! You must have Calvados, *ma chère*. It is the *digestif* of the region. A distillation of cider. We have our own, too, do we not, Philip? There is still some left that was made before the old trees were cut down. Funny old things with the names of queens." Louise tapped Diana on the wrist and pouted comically. "Now we have Golden Delicious. They are cost efficient, you see. Get the Calvados, Philip. Diana is a judge of these things."

In his absence, Diana endeavoured to ply Louise with intelligent questions about the exhibits. Spindly, elegant keyed instruments were disposed about the floor whilst wind instruments with lutes and mandolins lay on the shelves with faded ribbons trailing.

"My husband collected them," Louise told her as her son re-entered the room. "And when Philip was in his twenties, he used to say that the sight of any musical instrument affected him like a beautiful woman before she first speaks."

"But what a clever thing to say," Diana looked wonderingly at him. "And how very romantic."

Philip's answering smile was wintry.

"He used to say," Louise amplified, pleased with her guest's reaction, "that they were more mysterious and stirring to the heart by far than that fat Italian woman with diseased gums . . ."

"The Mona Lisa!" Diana produced a spurt of laughter. "Is that what she has, gum disease?"

"Or neuralgia. That's what my father believed," Philip replied, grateful for the line she had thrown him. There were times when Philip wished he could call back all the words he had ever spoken. Some for revision and most for suppression. On the whole these days, he stuck to what his father had termed his "turnip talk." Louise was never tempted to quote that.

"I wonder if your father ever met mine," Diana said. "Did he ever conduct? Yours, I mean."

With the spotlight deflected from himself, Philip was soon coaxed into better spirits.

"You play, don't you?" he addressed Diana. "Have a shot on that clavichord. It's like a batsqueak compared with a piano."

He opened the lacquered case for her, revealing the tiny ivory keys. Saffron with the touch of generations.

"Like the flirtatious smile of a derelict beauty?" Diana hazarded her thought, forgetting Louise's presence. Louise, however, did not connect herself with dereliction.

"Now you can laugh at *me*," Diana added quietly. "How's that for a spot of callow lyricism?"

"The voice quavers too," Philip emitted a short bark of amusement. "But you can get an idea of what it was."

"Greensleeves?" Diana proposed while he adjusted the stool for her. "I'm afraid it's all I can remember."

"Perfect. Go ahead and try it."

She made a poor fist of it. She hadn't practised for years. No more had he, Philip said. He put down his brandy glass and cigar on the painted case and leaned over her to try the piece himself, with infinitely better results. He really *was* musical. Diana sat perfectly still. Imprisoned between his arms but not touched by them, she felt a delightful, culpable tremor of anticipation.

Glancing up from the keyboard, she saw herself reflected with Philip's head, so close to her own, bent in concentration. Behind them, Louise tapped her satin shod foot softly on the tiles and watched them. Every detail precise and crisp. It was like living in a painting. And almost all, but for herself, in black and white. A composition executed by Louise? The thought flashed by before Diana could catch it. Philip straightened as the last tinkling note died away.

Louise chose that moment to ring for Marie. She was going to bed. Philip and Diana must not think of disturbing themselves. They made such a charming picture together. And out of doors ... such a moon. Why did they not go for a little *promenade*? It was cool, but Marie would bring Diana a wrap.

"That necklace," Philip demanded brusquely as soon as the sound of Louise's heels had clicked away into the distance. "Where did you get it?"

Diana's hand flew to where the diamond clasp nestled above her collar bones. Her face flamed. Was he accusing *her* of being a thief now?

The word he had used of Michael slashed at her memory of the afternoon. To Philip, she and Michael were one and the same, after all. Tarred with the same shameful brush.

"It was left in my room . . . Your mother . . ." It did not take long to explain. "Your possessions are safe with *me*, Mr. Strang-Steele. So be easy in your mind. I shall leave them all behind."

"I'm sorry. I have upset you. It's a long time since I saw those pearls. My wife was the last person to wear them. They suit you."

Diana shook with anger and misery. Why had she not guessed? Obeyed her first, wiser impulse? Found some excuse, some imaginary fault with the clasp? She struggled to undo it now, her fingers clumsy.

"No. Please. It was a shock, that's all. I'm afraid a trick of some sort has been played on both of us. Just for a moment, when I saw you, I . . . and with your hair like that . . ." He took a step towards her.

"It's my fault. I should never have worn it." Diana succeeded in divesting herself of the jewel. She held it out to him and he retreated from her, refusing to touch it.

"Look, it's my place to apologise, not yours. At least forgive my mother . . ."

"Don't, please, say anything more," Diana put the pearls down on the clavichord. "I'm sure your mother meant only to please me and never thought of distressing you. I wish she had given more mature thought to *my* situation."

"What *can* you mean?" Philip asked coldly.

"A thief's family are always vulnerable to misunderstandings."

Philip went white. He started to protest but Diana silenced him. "I'm so sorry. It has been a mistake. Good night."

He could do nothing to keep her.

Reaching her room, Diana found a note from Louise. It implored her not to rise early. Coffee would be brought to her at 9 am. Diana screwed the note into a tight ball and hurled it into the wastepaper basket. Mad, senile, vicious. What did Louise want of her? It was interesting, Diana thought, that the old woman was not too blind to write notes.

Diana lay awake most of the night, wishing she had not come.

IN THE MORNING, after breakfasting in her room, she was directed to the stiffly disciplined rose garden which lay behind the house. *Monsieur*, she was assured by the maid she had seen yesterday, awaited her there. Diana went to join him, expecting only to say goodbye and ask how she might obtain a taxi or hire a car. Her presence here, she felt, must be an embarrassment since yesterday evening's fracas.

Philip was feeding fish in the formal tank when he heard her step on the gravel and turned to greet her.

"Ah, good," he said briskly, "I hope you slept better than I did, but at any rate, I have had time to consider our problem. Alisdair and your daughter."

His solution involved draconian measures. Alisdair was to be told that his engagement must last two years. He knew, he said, that a longer moratorium of three years would suit Diana better. Until Yolanda was twenty-one. But that, Philip said, was unreasonable in Alisdair's case. He was already twenty-eight. Two years was the compromise on offer.

"If he defies me and marries within that period, I shall disinherit him."

Diana was appalled. It was too much. "I have no right to ask you to risk such a thing within your own family. You have no other children and . . ."

"Believe me, the risk is infinitesimal." He allowed himself a bleak chuckle. "I know my own son to some extent. A determined man, yes. But not a reckless one. And a Scot. He will think it worth a wait of two years to protect his future—and that of his fiancée. I imagine that will fix it for him."

"It sounds awfully like blackmail, or bullying," Diana objected weakly. She had tried something of the sort herself, without success.

"It's a bit of both," Philip confirmed cheerfully. "It's the only effective response to the kind of chicanery my family go in for." He gave an upward, unconscious glance towards a first-floor window of the house. Louise's bedroom, Diana was sure. "We're entitled to defend ourselves with any weapons that come to hand. With a sledgehammer, you don't have to wonder about the outcome. You can depend upon it."

Diana was speechless. He had allied himself with her cause so completely, as if the previous night's coolness had never been. There was a certain gleeful savagery about him this morning that made her glad he was on her side. He would make a bad enemy. She prayed Alisdair would not cross him, for his own sake. And yet he was the only man Diana could think of who would dare.

The necklace affair had been largely her own fault, she thought now. She had over reacted, shown a sensitivity out of proportion to what was required. But she could not bring herself to speak of it. Surprisingly, Philip did.

"I would like you to know how sorry I am that business with my wife's pearls spoiled your visit. I expressed myself very badly and . . ."

"Not at all. I hope that's not why you . . ."

"Absolutely not. I never do anything unless it pleases me to do it."

Diana heard the echo of Alisdair's voice in his father's words. An authentic Strang-Steele utterance. Honest, arrogant, infuriating and, somehow, totally admirable.

"I shall write to Alisdair today and make my intentions known to him. In two years' time, your daughter will have forgotten my son, or both will have demonstrated a steadiness of purpose which must inevitably be rewarded. That's the best I can do. Trust me, it will be sufficient."

Curtly waving Diana's further expressions of gratitude aside, he tugged the stem of one of the lilies to make the water move.

"There are some pretty venerable mirror carp in here. It's the site of the original stewpond, you see."

A craggy snout broke the surface and Diana watched as Philip lobbed fragments of biscuit accurately into the creature's open maw.

"That's Hercule," he said, brushing off his hands. "He really prefers brioche."

"Maybe his gums aren't as good as they were," Diana suggested hopefully. She wanted to make him laugh. Philip regarded her unsmilingly. Evidently, he reserved his smiles for moments of his own choosing.

It was almost time to go.

"I don't know," he said, "when we may meet again, if ever. It has been more than pleasant to have you here and I wish . . ."

"I can only thank you for your generosity and understanding," Diana broke in swiftly. Her heart lurched idiotically. It was better not to know what his unspoken wishes were. Unless it had been his intention to refer to the wretched pearls again, those wishes of his could only fall short of her hopes or exceed what it would be safe to hear. "And your mother, of course, for her wonderful hospitality."

Philip said nothing immediately but glanced up again to the window with its long, arching eyebrow of thatch. Louise was up there, rebuked and licking her wounds. Diana hoped so. Poor old lady.

"Hm. I'm afraid it has been somewhat maladroit," Philip said shortly. "I have dealt with the matter."

Diana found herself feeling very sorry for Louise, whatever her extraordinary actions had signified. "Give her my love, won't you? And tell her I shall write."

Philip's eyes warmed fleetingly.

"That is gracious of you. At the moment, she is resting. Too much excitement is bad for old ladies of my mother's disposition."

The remark seemed to call for some kind of pleasantry but Diana refrained from making it. Philip's sense of humour was unpredictable.

She departed from the Manoir in a chauffeur driven car. Philip was disappointed, he said, that some local business prevented him from accompanying her to the port. Finding herself surprised and regretful at the abruptness of the parting, Diana did not entirely believe him.

Before handing her into the car, he kissed her formally on both cheeks in the French fashion. Only the barest contact and a symbolic explosion of the lips. But he held her hand longer than he need and watched the car out of sight.

The meeting had been shot through with conflicting signals.

Philip Strang-Steele was not one man but two. He showed the contrasting sides of himself in brief, alternate glimpses. Like the figures on a Swiss barometer. In and out. Rain and shine.

Rocking on the North Sea swell that night, Diana abandoned her attempts to read the crime novel she had brought. The marionette characters and Cluedo game setting failed to drown the clamour of recent memory. The interior landscape of her life had changed. Switching off the bulkhead reading light, she resigned herself to exploring its contours.

It occurred to her briefly that the pearl collar might have been Louise's way of giving her unspoken support to a liaison between herself and Philip. The notion was as preposterous as it was ugly. One did not present a mistress with the jewels of a deceased wife . . . or act the part of procuress for a middle aged son. Or dangle bribes in a married woman's face. Louise was capable of many things, but not, Diana suspected, bad taste.

And now, she was very much in Philip Strang-Steele's debt. It was not a thing she had wished for and her gratitude to him was real, if subdued.

Two years was a long time. She was sorry now, in a way, that they would, as he had himself warned, almost certainly never meet again. It would not be necessary. And if it ever was, Michael would be with her then. Home again. She missed him. Philip had called forth that need in her.

Diana tossed and turned in the narrow berth whilst a party of drunken Dutchmen roamed the cabin decks all night.

CHAPTER
11

❧ "A COMPLETE WASHOUT," Alisdair removed his dripping cap and kissed Yolanda on the cheek. He panted slightly with the effort of running down the rainy street. "We blew it."

They met just inside the foyer of the Franz Josef Theatre in Harrogate.

"Are we late, or do we have time for a drink?"

"Far too late," Yolanda reproved. "I've arranged things for the interval, though. Leave that mac with the coat woman. What was a washout? Where have you been?"

"I've been getting my ear chewed off by my father." He took Yolanda's arm and shepherded her up the stairs.

"You might have changed your boots."

"Didn't have time. He was in full cry ... on and *on*. I'm sorry, it's no go. *Grandmère* let us down."

"Oh, no!" Yolanda's hand fell from the stage box doorknob. "What happened?"

"You might well ask," Alisdair snorted, hustling her inside. "It'll have to wait till the interval."

"No, it jolly well won't. Tell me what went wrong. I thought *Grandmère* was infallible. That's what you said ..."

The house lights were already dark and the curtain up. The stage was empty but in the stalls, irritated patrons were glancing up towards the source of muffled commotion.

"I can't think why you like it in here, Landa," Alisdair hissed. "It's the worst view in the house."

"It has the best view of the audience which is what counts," Yolanda snapped back. "Also I can tuck my feet up your trouser legs in comfort. Now tell me ..."

"Sssh!"

Yolanda was obliged to sit through the first two acts in a fever of impatience. The progress of the action unfolding before her scarcely impinged on her consciousness as she mentally reviewed the scenes to which she had not been a witness. They should have gone like clockwork. *Grandmère* had virtually guaranteed positive results. She was an expert.

In the circle bar later, she received Alisdair's comprehensive report.

"Which do you want first?" Alisdair asked her glumly. "The good news or the bad? This yours? *Whaite waine*," he pronounced the words with comic refinement.

"The good news, please," Yolanda took the drink from his hand. "It can't be that bad."

"No, it isn't. Dad gives us his blessing."

"What's that got to do with it? We knew that would probably be OK. It's Mummy ..."

"Exactly. Well, your mother hasn't changed her mind."

"But that was the whole point."

"Yes, I know. Well, I'm afraid *Grandmère* muffed her lines for once. Not a success, I gather." Alisdair repressed a temptation to describe the size of the *débâcle* all at once. The patient should always be left to ask for the next, measured dose herself. That worked best with Yolanda, he found.

"Oh. So what's the bad news, then?" Yolanda abandoned her glass of lukewarm acid with a grimace.

"My father has decided to back your Ma up by threatening to cut me off without a shilling if we go ahead before two years are up."

"But that's blackmail," Yolanda said primly. "He can't get away with that. I scotched that one with Mummy."

"He can and he has."

Thunder clouds gathered over Yolanda's broad, beautiful brow. "What the hell do you mean? You aren't going to give in, are you?"

"Don't swear," Alisdair chided automatically. "Of course I am. What genuine choice do I have?"

Alisdair was still putting his case long after the second bell had gone and the bar was deserted.

"You must see," he urged, "it isn't the money itself I care about. It's my father who cares about it. It's his ... er ... I don't know, creation. If I throw it over, he'll think I'm throwing him over. Darling, apart from you and your mother, and *Grandmère*, of course, he's all I've got. I want you all together and happy with each other. I don't want to start with a rift. Honestly, do you?"

Alisdair knew how to spirit the answers he wanted from most people. And although Yolanda was more challenging than the majority, he managed.

"And let me tell you, Dad's little scheme wouldn't come off at all if I wasn't determined not to deprive you of the future security you should have. That's what he's been playing on. A wily old pike, my father."

"Huh. And you're the pikelet, I suppose," Yolanda jibed grumpily.

"That's a kind of crumpet, darling," Alisdair pointed out smoothly. "So it's not a wholly inaccurate description."

"You smug, self-satisfied . . ."

"As you say, dearest one. But I'll wait if you will."

"What choice do I have?"

"Roughly six million other blokes . . . that's a seat of pants estimate."

"Don't be stupid," Yolanda snarled harmlessly. "Come on. Let's go."

On the way back to Gilbert's Tower, Alisdair amused Yolanda with some choice extracts from his father's letter, the precursor to the telephone call which had delayed him at the start of the evening.

"You do understand, darling, don't you, that my father will come after me with a shot gun if I . . . and here I quote, 'force attentions on you that no gentleman would contemplate in connection with a girl still under her parents' protection . . . let alone one whom he intended to introduce as his future wife'?"

"Is that what he said?" Yolanda laughed in spite of herself. "Really?"

"Every golden syllable. Oh yes . . . and he 'reprobates the lack of moral fibre that induced me to have recourse to *Grandmère's* dubious strategies' . . ."

"But it was her idea, basically."

Alisdair waived that objection aside testily. To have said it would merely have brought down another lecture on his head about never shifting responsibilities on to shoulders too frail to bear them.

" 'No gentleman,' " he quoted again, " 'would have allowed an old lady to take steps on his behalf which could only expose her to censure.' "

"Whew!" Yolanda blushed in the darkness. She felt the reproach as keenly as if it had been directed at herself.

"Now you know the kind of letters I got at school."

"I feel I ought to own up."

"Darling, you did nothing."

"I agreed."

"My little love, you are easily led. Below the age of, er, strategic consent. You are discharged from the dock with an order for care. Mine, I hope."

For once, Yolanda was grateful to be supposed feeble.

"He must love you very much," she said with a sudden insight into her prospective father-in-law's craggy, paternal emotions.

It was Alisdair's ears that turned vermilion this time. He said nothing. It was not the sort of thing chaps talked about.

"How did *Grandmère* come to louse up so badly?" Yolanda asked quietly after a moment.

"Well, from the little Dad said," he pulled the handbrake on sharply outside the garden door at Gilbert's Tower, "she went in for some unscripted stage business with an old necklace of my mother's. He wouldn't say any more about it except that it had upset him, embarrassed your mother quite terribly and, ultimately, got poor *Grandmère* into an awful lot of hot water with him. If you ask me, I think she was trying to do a little extra-curricular matchmaking. Kill two birds with one stone."

"But Mummy's married."

"Quite so. Sorry. Anyway, that's what made him smell a rat. A put-up job, he said. The scenery wobbled."

"Oh, dear."

"Yes, it was all pretty oh dearish. Poor *Grandmère*. I'm afraid she took the rap for us."

"We'll have to do our own dirty work in future. Let *Grandmère* retire."

"Oh no, I've learned my lesson," Alisdair leaned across her to open the passenger door. "I won't come in Landa."

"Like hell!" Yolanda slammed the car door behind her emphatically. "You'll never be able to resist giving things a tweak."

"Yolanda, darling, please don't swear," Alisdair climbed out of the driver's seat. "And don't beat up my car like that. Kiss?"

"Don't you mind, Alisdair?"

"Of course I mind. Two years is two years. But we've been nabbed. And darling, I know this is a very wrinkly thing to say, but I think my father really does have your welfare at heart."

Obliquely, Yolanda had the same impression.

"So do we have a deal, Landa?"

"What we have is your father's unrefusable offer. If you want to call it a deal, I will too. Do you think he took a fancy to Mummy? Mr. *I'll do you a deal* Strang-Steele?"

"Everyone does, darling," Alisdair stroked her hair, "but my father just isn't the kind of man who goes around making passes at married ladies. He's a stuffed shirt. Good night, seraph features. Your cat's come to fetch you, look."

The orange cat was glaring down from the arched door lintel, kneading the honeysuckle vine with ermine tipped paws.

Alisdair drove home thinking how best to express himself to Diana the following day. Luckily, his father hadn't shopped him to Landa's mother. Decent of him in the circumstances. Diana need not know quite everything. It would not be good for her. Or him. His father had once told him that success largely consisted in the correct management of failure. Thirty was a perfectly good age to get married.

There would, of course, be a need for some alternative creative outlets. No doubt they would present themselves in due course. Alisdair was never at a loss.

❦ DIANA HEARD ALISDAIR'S edited version of what had passed between himself and Yolanda with every appearance of surprise, sympathy and reserved approval. Philip's proposals, as he termed his coercive arrangements, were to be laid at his door entirely.

"The fact that I make advance mention of them to you," he had said gallantly, "need in no way implicate you. What I do, I do on my own initiative."

"This wasn't a plot, by any chance, was it?" Alisdair concluded his narrative whilst indulging the orange cat's new found taste for chin scratching.

"Good heavens, no," Diana exclaimed on her cue. "I couldn't rig up so much as an after dinner charade. I'm sure you know that."

"No, I didn't think so," Alisdair agreed rather smugly. The pet mice were all back in their cages now, more or less.

Diana dismissed him with something between a handshake and hug, as much to hide her own smiles as anything. She toyed with the idea of writing to Philip with a description of the interview. Perhaps he would not be amused. And in any case, there was no time for frivolous, personal correspondence. A build-up of documents to sign, queries and messages occupied her time fully for the next three days. Diana's "holiday" had not been restful and she was too tired at night to do anything more than fall into bed. It couldn't go on like this. Soon she would need somebody else on the administration side. A top-notch executive, not an amateur like herself. But how could she afford it? And Mrs. Sedgely was already down for a hip operation. What then?

Michael's release, when it came, would more than double the quantity of laundry, cooking and cleaning to be done. Would Michael himself be able to help with the business? Would he want to? Would it work?

The Strang-Steele imbroglio faded into the background.

❦ "SHIT!"

Michael pressed his finger to the place where a minute bead of blood oozed from his razor nicked chin.

The accommodation block was deserted now. The other men had gone to greet their families arriving in the main foyer. Peering into the shaving mirror, Michael rehearsed the schedule of events. 9.45 am, families arrive. His watch showed 9.55. Diana would be there by now with Yolanda. She was always prompt. Never kept anybody waiting. 10 am, informal reception with representatives of the legal profession, Home Office, financial institutions and selected academic specialists. In other words, a cosy get-together for sinners, judges, gaolers, victims and busybodies. A crowd of wallies, most of them, Michael sneered inwardly. The slug-soft underbelly of a liberal society. Compassion was another fucking fashion. The taxpayer footed the bill for that particular set of Emperor's new clothes. Pity he hadn't thought of it when he was writing his book. Michael reached for the caustic stick with his left hand. His eye caught the cuff flapping on his only civilian shirt. It was the one he'd been carted off to Brixton in. Should have told Diana to bring some cuff-links down with her. Only losers wore buttons.

Ten o'clock. They'd be pitching into the coffee and biscuits now. A load of boring old farts patting the kids on the head and trying not to patronise the wives. Michael had timed his appearance in the foyer for ten minutes past the hour, just five minutes before the Governor's inaugural address. Any later and the screws would come looking for him. Show up earlier and his absence wouldn't provoke any discussion of his achievements. By the time he got there, Michael calculated, attention should be pretty well focused on Programme Participant Neville.

With any luck, the Governor would have got around to dropping the words "early release" into the right ears. Parole boards were dodgy. The decision needed making before those fat, self-righteous asses ever hit the moulded plastic.

Michael gave himself a final glance in the mirror above the hand basin in Room 91. A couple of years in the slammer hadn't done his looks any harm, he reckoned. The whites of his eyes were clearer than they'd been for years. No booze, or precious little, accounted for that. And his body, toned by daily workouts in the unit gymnasium, was in shit hot shape. If anything, the Armani blazer fitted him better now than it had on the last day of the trial. A fucking farce, that had been.

He parted his lips and grinned widely. Not bad. When he got out he'd have the gold filling on that molar replaced. Gold was naff. He ran his fingers through the waving, corn coloured hair. Great. He was ready for anything. For choice, a good shag would come top of the list. No chance of that.

In the foyer, Michael's appearance caused the expected rustle of relief amongst the staff, and recognition amongst the invited officials. There was a momentary hush before the hubbub resumed. Michael Neville was a bit of a phenomenon. He had his own weekly column in the financial section of one of the big Sundays now. Racy stuff it was, too.

As far as the Governor was concerned, he was the living

justification for the Programme and the best hope of keeping the unit open in the face of swingeing budget cuts. Michael was well aware of it.

"Oh, here you are, Neville," the Governor turned back immediately to the Home Office grandee with whom he had been speaking. "I'm a big believer in setting goals and letting go when they're achieved. Over cook it and you're going to have a mess on your hands and a lot of wasted funds. Funds, I need hardly remind you, that are badly needed for new offenders."

Michael smiled. He couldn't have put it better himself. His name, he was sure, had already cropped up in that little confabulation, and would do so again. Individual attention to individual cases . . . or unique advantages for unique individuals. It all depended who you were and how you looked at your surroundings.

Michael Neville was never vague about identity or environment. What kind of animal in what kind of terrain? He knew what he was. A predator in open savannah. The pickings were easy, but it was necessary to tread softly. There was little cover.

A uniformed officer pushed his way through the tightly packed crowd.

"For God's sake get a move on, Mike. What do you think this is? A film premiere? Your wife's waiting."

He saw her then, standing in front of a portrait of the Queen with Yolanda beside her. She was talking to a sweaty little jewellery shop manager. Got caught with his fingers in the till. His wife had left him. Prick. Landa looked bored out of her beautiful skull. Diana had always spent too much time on lame ducks.

Diana. Michael had almost forgotten what she looked like. He could remember the colour of her hair and eyes but not the subtle things, like the tone of her skin and the way her eyelashes swept downwards before she smiled. She'd changed her hairstyle. It had grown longer and she wore it in a smooth chignon at the nape of her neck. It sprang thick and luxuriant as ever from her hairline with its widow's peak. She looked good. Too good. She looked ten years younger.

Michael felt the stirrings of an obscure resentment. The forties. It was a good age for a man. The best. But Diana? Something was not quite right.

"Daddy!"

Yolanda broke away from the group and waded through the intervening, chattering knots of people. To Michael's eye, his child was another surprise. Grown up. Viewed dispassionately, a bit of all right. She would be, of course. A Neville, through and through. Looks that lasted. Like his.

The anomaly in his attitude did not strike Michael. Wife and child. He expected different things from them.

"Hello, darling. How's my big, beautiful girl? Hey, what's this?" Michael caught Yolanda's wrist as he hugged her tightly. "A ring? What the . . . ?"

"It's one of the things we have to talk about today, darling." Diana came up to them and opened her palm. On it lay the gold and lapis lazuli cuff-links he had urged her to sell on the day of the verdict which had separated them.

"I said you would need these again, didn't I?" She offered him her cheek. Michael had never liked warmer displays of affection in public.

He kissed her swiftly, as a cockerel pecks a hen.

"Hey, thanks. At least you didn't sell these." He tossed the links in his hand coolly. He kissed her again, awkwardly.

He smelled something on her that could not be named with one of those barmy titles marketing chaps put on perfume bottles. No chemist could ever come up with an approximation to that whiff. No way. He identified the odour of his wife's skin in a single reflex of animal recognition. Success.

Women had always smelled it on him. He'd smelled it on other men. Now and again. Nature's own designer label. An hormonal signature that no perfumier could forge. It was both warning and enticement. An invitation to moths to burn themselves. *Diana?* At a level well below the mental, Michael felt threatened.

"Ladies and Gentlemen," an officer's voice rose above the noise, "please take your seats in the gymnasium for the Governor's address."

"It's like Speech Day, isn't it?" Yolanda muttered. "With me and Mummy as the parents. Are you getting any prizes, Daddy?"

He hugged her again, spontaneously.

"Sure. You're my prize, smart ass."

* * *

GENEROUS MENTION WAS made of Michael's new found direction. He would, the Governor said, be signing copies of his book, now out in paperback, in the unit library between the hours of 2.00 and 3.30 in the afternoon. The vibration of pride which emanated from Diana was almost tangible. A book was a book. A tremendous achievement, whatever it said. And in the end, Michael's hadn't damaged her much. She had swung away from the body blows. Forgiven and almost forgotten. Michael felt her hand creep into his.

"Hope to have a word with you later, Mrs. Neville," the Governor said to Diana as his audience spilled out of the gymnasium into the corridor. "My, how this young lady's grown up." He pressed Yolanda's hand warmly. "So what's next for you . . . ?" Smiling apologetically, the Governor was borne away on a tide of questions from men in suits with plastic name tags.

The rest of the time before lunch was devoted to a tour of the prison. The programme participants took it in turns to man the various production units.

Not required for any of this, Michael sauntered from the machine components shop to the pig rearing unit, kitchens, laundry and joinery shed between Diana and Yolanda. With his left hand on Diana's back and his right arm around his daughter's shoulder, he was conscious of cutting a dash. They looked the goods, the three of them. Michael congratulated himself.

In narrow spaces and doorways, a hint of deference made itself felt. Guiding his family from place to place, Michael assumed the manner of a detached visitor, emanating authority from every pore. Instinctively, uniformed officers, officials and fellow prisoners with their own families stepped back to allow the Nevilles to pass. There was an implied assumption that they were a special case. Michael's talent for maintaining an uncomfortable level of tension around him ensured that nobody confronted him, found the specialness at all spurious. Not until the movement had passed and it was too late.

"Bloody nerve, has Neville," an officer complained to another once they were out of earshot. "Who does the fucker think he is? The Duke of Plaza Toro?" He ran the Gilbert and Sullivan Society.

"Makes my boot itch," his companion agreed dolefully.

"Can't touch the sod. Governor's pet. A perfect programme result. That's what he is. Arrogant bastard."

"Hi, Mike!"

A thin, intelligent looking man bending over the computer lathe Michael had once used himself greeted him submissively. The man glanced at Diana and then dropped his eyes. He did not, Michael noted with satisfaction, ask to be introduced to his wife. That was as it should be. Middle management types should know their place. Even in here. Particularly in here.

Not liking the unspoken prohibition, either for herself or the man at the lathe, Diana spoke to him. Unfriendliness in such a situation as this would be doubly mean. One way and another, they were all in it together. Her query was footling enough but the man looked up gratefully and, glancing at Michael, silently asked his permission to respond. Michael turned his back and, pulling Diana away by the arm, replied to her question himself.

"Don't get too involved with these people, Diana," he finished. "They're not your kind."

"Oh, I think they are, darling," she picked a thread from his sleeve. "Some of them, anyway. You, for instance."

He caught her hand and thrust it back at her, searching her expression. Just what the hell did she mean by that? "Don't paw me in public," was all he said. "You know I don't like it."

"Sorry," she replied simply. "It's hard to be so near you and . . ."

"Yes. Well, it'll soon be over. What do you think it's been like for me?"

Michael had certain convictions about sex. To a man like himself it was meat and drink. He could get it anywhere though the quality varied. He could even get his rocks off on a girlie magazine as he'd discovered in the past couple of years. Sexual slumming. With women it was different. For a woman like Diana sex verged on the sacramental. Locked up and private. Exclusive. That was fine by Michael. Her function in his life was to look both desirable and unavailable to other men whether he wanted her or not. That's what you got married for. Not sex. Not in the long term. Just now, he wouldn't have minded screwing her. Knock some of the shine off her.

"Where's Landa got to?" Michael looked at his watch. "Lunch next. Some of the kitchen blokes are holding on to a good table for us. We want one to ourselves, don't we? No frigging small talk. What's this ring she's wearing?"

Diana was keen to explain. It had to wait until Yolanda was found by an officer in the pig unit and brought to them.

The mystery of how Michael could possibly reserve a table at a function where it must be at least tacitly understood that, as an offender, he ranked far below the Governor's invited guests, was soon revealed.

The unit dining hall was crowded with people sitting at small tables covered with disposable paper cloths. In the high ceilinged space, the clash of dishes with voices rose in the air and thudded back, strafing the air with a hailstorm of sound. There was a long queue for the buffet. Those who had made their selection from a variety of hot and cold dishes stood desperately quartering the room with their eyes for any sign of a vacant table. There was only one and that was ignored. Following Michael towards it, Diana saw why.

Piled high with dirty dishes and overflowing ashtrays on a cloth sodden with spilled soup, the table was clearly not for use. A staging post for the staff.

"Shouldn't we join the queue, darling?" Diana suggested. "We'll just have to wait our turn for a table."

"Watch this, Landa," Michael held a chair out for his wife.

She looked at him uncertainly and sat down, squirming inside. This couldn't be right. The table was out of service.

In a trice, men in white overalls appeared as if from nowhere and whipped the soiled things away. A fresh cloth and clean cutlery materialised in their place. It took seconds to do. Michael leaned back in his seat with an air of controlled disgust as if he were a customer in a restaurant.

Yolanda laughed, delighting in her father's cleverness. Diana flinched. This was so dangerous. Michael couldn't get away with behaving here as he had always done in the past. And it wasn't like him to misread a situation. To oppose him openly would draw attention to what they had done. What would the people around them think? She found her mind busy with the excuses she would make for all of them.

"Rack of lamb all round, wasn't it, Mike?" A white overalled man with a paper cap on his head mumbled from the side of his mouth. "We've kept some back for you."

Michael grunted. In a moment, plates were brought and palmed on to the table with a conjuror's sleight of hand.

"Tuck in," Michael urged. "Got a fellow in here now who used to be a big time chef. Started fixing the menu in some up-market eatery in London. You know, cod instead of halibut and a nice little margin for him. He started the catering programme in this place. This is today's star dish."

Diana ate mechanically, swallowing with difficulty. Good though it was, the food might as well have been hay. While Yolanda explained the ring on her finger to Michael, Diana struggled to make sense of her conscience.

It was nothing, surely, but a violation of the queue taboo? She was a fool and a coward to recoil so from her husband's act. In this enclosed world, her husband's world, only he could know the codes. And wasn't it stupid to confuse mere brashness with sin? What a dire word that was. Why should she think of it? Madness.

Michael could not take them out today and buy them a meal. He had not seen either of them for a long time. It might be many months before he saw them again. He loved them. And in this place, for all its unusual forbearance, his manhood was humbled. The large gestures by which Michael expressed his virility were impossible here. To let herself and Yolanda know how dear they were to him, he had done this thing. Used the little leverage he had. Obtained an advantage for them by unfair means since fair ones were denied him. She ought to be glad that Michael still had the ingenuity to discover and use power. This demonstration of it was a gift. Flawed perhaps, but offered with love. It should be received gladly.

"Say, Diana," Michael's voice broke in on her thoughts, "do you have any idea who this bloke of Landa's is?"

Michael's plate was empty, only cleanly picked bones remained. He used to leave so much food, Diana remembered. All of this had been good for him, in a way. He looked so handsome and healthy.

"Yes, of course I do."

"No, no. I mean do you know who he really is?" Michael's fist was bunched on the table in front of him. "Strang-Steele's fortune is generally estimated at . . ."

"Yes, I know he's a rich man, certainly." She could not bear him to go on and name figures. Too graceless. It was no longer as a rich man that she thought of Philip Strang-Steele. He was a quiet, domestic man. Impulsive one moment, despondent the next. "It really doesn't affect the matter."

"No, Daddy, it really doesn't," Yolanda began, alarmed by the familiar battle light in her father's eyes. It would be awful if her parents quarrelled in front of her. In front of other people. For the first time, it seemed like a possibility. They had no right to quarrel. They were too old.

"Ssh." Michael took his daughter's hand and held it tightly. "You leave this to your Daddy. I think we'd better be pushing off to the library. We can talk there until the punters start arriving." He cocked his head in the direction of the exit and rose.

The family conference in the library never took place. Diana barely had time to say that she thought Yolanda ought to embark on some further course of study, or perhaps vocational training, when the Governor came bringing half a dozen visitors with him.

"Bollocks." Michael mouthed his comment on Diana's opinion, converting the silent shape of the obscenity to a devastating smile.

"And here's Mrs. Neville, too," the Governor informed his party. "Quite a celebrity in her own right, nowadays. Some of you may know ..."

They did all know. There were handshakes and smiles.

Diana was sorry. It was Michael's day, not hers, and she saw the edges of his smile decay. When *would* they get some privacy?

"Now do be a sport, Mrs. Neville," the Governor appealed to her. "We'd like you on the panel of the Wives' Forum in the Common Room. It won't take long."

Diana had no serious option but to fall in with the Governor's plans. He wanted her to get the discussion on the problems of separation going. She was a public figure, accustomed to public speaking, he said. She did not want to do it. But public service ... it was part of the job. And part of helping Michael. Being the *right stuff*.

Yolanda elected to stay with her father. Over the course of the afternoon Michael signed a lot of books. It was Yolanda who handed them back to their purchasers and said the insincere, uninteresting things that the occasion called for. "A lot of hard work . . . Family knew nothing about it . . . Complete surprise . . . Oh no, not surprised he could do it . . . Carry on, obviously . . ."

She was managing very well, Michael noticed on the periphery of his mind. Just the ticket. Yolanda would never need to do or be anything more. Why should she? She was made. A heartbeat away from one of the country's greatest fortunes. She shouldn't miss it because of some numbskull, born-again feminist prejudice of her mother's. Or jealousy. That happened with women. Maybe it was keeping up with Yolanda that had made the change in Diana's looks. Trying harder. It wouldn't last.

Toiling over the books . . . *Best Wishes, Michael Neville* . . . until his hand ached and his eyes began to find the sight of his own name absurd, Michael wore a pre-formed rictus of affability. Largely oblivious to the murmurs of thanks and congratulation around him, mentally he structured one of those single sheet reports on which his life had been based. Position, objective, obstacles, strategy.

The Farm Boy, as the City nicknamed Strang-Steele, was a far richer man than Michael Neville had ever been. He just went on piling one currency note on top of another, joining one hectare to the next. Never sold anything. And the supercilious swine never borrowed, either. He only lent. He held a lot of other people's paper. It was rumoured he had possessions he knew nothing of. That he lived like some sort of down at heel squire over the shop. A tight wad who didn't know or care how much he owned. His money had a life of its own.

Feverishly, Michael contemplated the Strang-Steele fortune. He was not motivated by ordinary, everyday greed. He was romantic about money. When the sums were large enough, it ceased to be a mundane means of exchange. It became an idea, a system of metaphysical belief. A centrifugal force which kept the planet spinning and permeated every cell of the living world. To live near it was to be an Olympian, to ascend the high places of the spirit. Through his daughter, Michael saw the means of pitching his tent near the mountain. There should be no cock-ups.

When the books were finished, Michael took Yolanda aside into a small room adjoining the library. It was equipped with a word processor, photocopier and racks of stationery and reference books. It was where he worked.

"Do you want to marry young Strang-Steele, Landa?" Michael put both his hands on Yolanda's shoulders, pushing his face close to hers. "Look at me."

Yolanda was confused and uncomfortable. This was not the kind of relationship she had with her father. Not this intensity.

"Yes, of course I do. And when . . ."

"No. That's not good enough. Never hesitate," he shook her hard, "not for a moment. Right or wrong, go for what you want. Don't dither. If you screw up, well, OK. Try again. But if you fart about, you'll never get anything."

Yolanda disengaged herself as tactfully as she could. The room was very small. She felt rather peculiar. Proud as any girl who is loved, she had wanted to talk about Alisdair. Alisdair the man, the person. What he did, what he said and how he *was*. Somehow he'd got lost, blurred and out of focus. Of course, although her father had seen him once, he didn't know Alisdair.

"Do you think Mummy will have finished doing her stuff?"

"No. I don't know. This has nothing to do with your mother. It's you and me, Landa. You're grown up now and we're one of a kind. Listen to me and you'll get what you want."

Her father's words struck Yolanda's ears like brick bats. Flat and hard. It was not some inanimate *what* that she wished for. It was who, surely? It made a difference. Her doubts were cringing newcomers, outfaced by her father's brutal rationality.

"If you wait two years you'll lose the initiative and Strang-Steele with it. The ball's in your court. If you want him, you'll bash it back so fast he won't know what's hit him. Bugger his father and frankly, darling, bugger your mother. Tell Strang-Steele he marries you now or you forget the whole thing. There's a straight million pounds to go with you, fair and square, and if he can't make himself independent on that . . ."

Yolanda stopped him with an inarticulate noise in the throat.

"Sure. Don't think I'd leave us destitute, did you? I always kept something for a rainy day holed up in a numbered Swiss bank account. Right from before you were born. I added to it over the years . . . a bit here and a bit there. It was one thing those cock suckers couldn't get their hands on . . ."

"But Daddy, a million pounds . . ." Yolanda thought of her

mother. She had worked so hard, become so different and all the time . . .

"Don't kid yourself. It's not nearly as much money as it used to be. Price of a couple of houses, basically. And not such big ones at that. But I started with less, a lot less. Sweet bugger all, in fact. You can have it. Marriage settlement. I've earned a bit lately and there'll be something left over in that account."

Michael sat perched on the edge of his desk, arms folded surveying his daughter. He saw her as an extension of his own arm. It infuriated him, too, that Diana should wield such control over Yolanda. She was *his* child. Always had been.

"Daddy, you don't understand. Alisdair's father . . ."

"Not concerned with him, are you? You tell that son of his to get off his backside and marry you. Bloke who knuckles under to his father at that age isn't worth bothering about. He'll come round, anyway. Not a lot of choice, has he? Men like Strang-Steele don't leave their money to donkey sanctuaries."

Caught in the headlights of her father's personality, Yolanda was dazzled. And frightened. What if he was right about losing Alisdair? There was peculiar contrast, too, between the style and content of the advice with which Michael was bombarding her and that which Alisdair had received from *his* father. Who was right about what? She was confused.

"Supposing Mummy . . . ?"

"I'll bet you a pound to a pinch of shit your mother cooked this up with Strang-Steele herself."

It was the purest guesswork, the inspiration of the moment. All Michael knew was that his wife had recently gone to France. City gossip had long made it known that the Farm Boy spent up to half the year there. Why else would Diana go? Uglier thoughts darkened Michael's face for an instant and were dismissed. Not Diana. No.

It worked. Michael had always known how to set Yolanda against Diana. He did it without thinking. An automatic exercise. Creative control.

"All right, Daddy, you're on." It was the easiest thing to say. Anything, now, to get away from the subject of Alisdair.

Michael grinned. "That's my kid talking. Can't have people

running your life for you at your age. I was younger than you when I bought my first Jag."

Yolanda could not miss the link between Alisdair and a motor car as objects to be bought. It was accidental and fell quickly from her mind. A faulty connection.

"How did the books go?" Diana asked when she joined them for tea.

"Like hot cakes, didn't they, Landa?"

The stagnant atmosphere of the prison sparkled in Michael's nostrils like fresh, Alpine air.

PART THREE

CHAPTER
12

YOLANDA SAID NOTHING to Alisdair regarding her father's startling reaction to the news of her unofficial engagement. Firmly as she tried to set it aside as an aberration of no great significance, fragments of her conversation with Michael, closeted in his small, clinically neat workroom at the prison, kept exploding in her memory like hot chestnuts. The kernels were not sweet.

She had looked forward to introducing Alisdair to her father, but now the pleasure of anticipation had turned to dread. During the weeks that elapsed before Michael's parole board, the days peeled from the calendar with frightening speed.

Yolanda began to hatch unrealistic schemes to keep the two men apart. But Alisdair was not a school essay that could be "lost" on the day the assignment was due. There would be a confrontation. Her father, she knew, would speak his mind and Alisdair, who had never once spoken harshly to her would, Yolanda was miserably certain, unleash a controlled fury on the only other man she loved. Mediation would be impossible.

When news of Michael's parole came, Yolanda's joy was curdled with fear of what he would do to her life.

"How is your father, then?" Alisdair noted the letter in Yolanda's hand as he bounded up the attic staircase at Gilbert's Tower to meet her at the top. "Did you see his article about bank advertising in the *Telegraph* this morning? Hard hitting stuff. It seems your Dad's on the side of the angels. Got his parole too, your mother says. Home by Christmas."

"Are you staying for supper?" Yolanda asked him wanly, folding the letter quickly.

"Mm. Yes, please." Alisdair cupped Yolanda's face with his hands and kissed her firmly. "I must say, I'm looking forward to meeting him. Sounds quite a guy. What's up with you? You look as though you've lost a quid and found sixpence."

Only half aware of what she had been doing, Yolanda had already told Alisdair stories about her father which served to illustrate the cast of his mind. There had been no childish problem of hers, real or imagined, large or small that Michael had not solved with money.

There was, Yolanda recalled painfully, the pony that did not win in gymkhana events. Sooty, a New Forest cross. A long suffering little beast, he had disappeared from the Brereton stables overnight. His replacement, a slick, slender Welsh Mountain mare, carried all before her. For a couple of years there had been red rosettes all the way. That was what Michael expected and at twelve years old, Yolanda had been happy that her father was proud of her equestrian triumphs. But she had missed Sooty. It had taken until now to mourn him without reserve. Describing it all to Alisdair, Yolanda had wept like a child.

"Landa, your Sooty sounds as if he was an ideal second pony type to me," Alisdair had comforted her. "He's sure to have gone to a good home. Animals like that are always in demand. How old was he?"

"Ten."

"There you are, then. No nonsense but plenty of work left in him. Don't be afraid, darling. He almost certainly died peacefully in a bed of clean barley straw. Good God, he might still be going strong. Plenty of native pony breeds live to be over twenty.

"Your father probably got the chance of a good home for him and didn't want to miss it. Don't worry about it any more. Whatever's brought all this on?"

Yolanda could not bring herself to say.

There had been the tale about Tiverton Abbey's wretched tradition that every girl in the school should knit a pair of socks by the time she was fourteen. Four needles and fine yarn had been too much for Yolanda, who had never knitted anything before but a wavy edged scarf. A tear stained letter, threatening violence if she were not excused the socks, brought a postal order by return.

"Silly kid," read her father's accompanying note. "Always buy in the services you can't perform yourself or don't want to. Here's a few quid to give any girl who'll finish the stupid socks. If the rate for contract knitting has gone up, let me know."

Alisdair had doubled up with laughter about that. Had it worked?

"Like a charm," Yolanda told him, smiling herself at the memory. "Amanda Pringle did it and Miss Mackie, our home economics mistress, never knew the difference. But it was cheating, wasn't it?"

"Oh come on, darling. It was pretty harmless. Keep a sense of proportion. If my Dad had come up with a way of getting me out of Corps, I'd have grabbed it with both hands. I hated playing toy soldiers."

"But he didn't, did he? And you didn't think of asking him, did you?"

"Only because I knew it wouldn't wash."

"But don't you think there's a limit to what you can buy . . . things you really shouldn't even try to buy?"

"What? Like my father and his two years . . . ?"

"But that's different," Yolanda protested. "He's buying *me* time, even though I don't want it. He's being generous, in a way."

"Don't ask me, Landa," Alisdair said, "I'm just a horny handed son of the soil. Moral philosophy isn't my drop. Your Dad sounds OK to me. I bet he gets on with mine like a house on fire in the end."

Alisdair sensed no warning and Yolanda fell back on hoping for the best.

At least Alisdair was going away for Christmas. She would have a few days, a week or more, in which to talk to her father. When he understood everything properly, perhaps when he had met Alisdair, he would leave everything as it had been arranged. She would tell him that was what she really did want. Two years to complete her newly undertaken business course. If she convinced him of that, then he surely wouldn't do or say anything to frustrate her. He never had before. Yolanda wondered why she had not thought of this simple fact at once. She had been an idiot not to see it.

The mountain shrivelled to a molehill and Yolanda could

laugh at herself. It was going to be the most perfect Christmas ever, the third at Gilbert's Tower.

❦ No such clouds darkened Diana's preparations for her husband's homecoming.

The room in her heart that had been kept for him was swept and enlarged. He was to occupy it once more. Resentments, misunderstandings, quarrels brought on by separation . . . they were there like woodlice lurking in the corners. Consciously and systematically, Diana cleared them out of the way to make clean space for what she believed would be the best years of their lives together.

Outward rehabilitation was unnecessary. He had done that himself. Michael was not coming back to a world that was cold against him, but one which had learned to appreciate him in a new role. Diana longed for that smaller, more critical world of Nidcaster and English Gardens to welcome him, too.

Christmas would be felicitous timing. Michael could meet everyone in the safety of the home she had prepared for him. The hospitality that Gilbert's Tower normally extended at Christmas to neighbours, business associates and, on the night of the traditional Mummers' Play, the townspeople too, would afford a marvellous opportunity for her husband to appear at her side as host. Michael would be seen to advantage at the head of his own table. To have him take his place there would crown three years of waiting and effort.

Long before the parole board had sat, Diana had planned the programme of Christmas events, drawn up menus and sent out invitations. With only the smallest amount of luck, there would be a great deal to celebrate.

Waiting and hoping is exhausting work. Diana filled the time with practical activity which was the expression of those hopes. And although she said nothing, Nidcaster knew how to interpret the succession of tradesmen and craftsmen's vans drawn up outside Gilbert's Tower.

"Reckon they're expecting him 'ome any minute," it was muttered in the Rose and Crown.

In his corner by the bar, Sedgely would neither confirm nor deny the rumour. Privately, he viewed Michael Neville's advent with disfavour. His own pre-eminence at Gilbert's Tower was threatened.

"I 'ope he's worth all t'trouble," Nidcaster's leading plumber groused over his pint of mild and bitter. "Three baths I ordered for that bloke before Madam said one on 'em would suit His Majesty. Five foot bleeding nine an' he wants summut long enough to lie down in. I were that brassed off, he looked like getting a lead lined coffin at one point."

In the Liberal Association rooms, the editor of Nidcaster's tiny but envenomed weekly, the *Bystander*, listened with interest while Willy Waterhouse (pronounced "Wattras," as in mattress) described the curl mahogany wonders of the room his general cabinet making and joinery firm had been fitting at Gilbert's Tower. A worthwhile contract.

"Them cupboard doors slide like silk . . ."

A dressing-room, the editor concluded. For a gentleman. A few further questions regarding the room's position and other fitments and he was sure. So the unknown quantity was about to hit town. Bit of a scoop. News was short. The editor's mind flirted with a piece about Nidcaster's newest and most notorious resident. Jailbird in clover . . . that kind of thing. No, he admonished himself with a sigh. It would never do to tread on Mrs. Neville's toes. Too much useful copy came out of Gilbert's Tower as it was. No doubt she'd give the *Bystander* a statement when she was ready.

Ten days before Christmas Diana did just that. The prison Governor rang her at Gilbert's Tower to tell her of the parole board's favourable decision.

"Nobody is more pleased for you, Mrs. Neville, than I am myself. Now give my regards to that lovely daughter of yours and a very happy Christmas to you all. You'll have Mike with you in thirty-six hours. Don't drive down, we'll pop him on the train. Give him a bit of time to adjust."

At Epoch, they had some trouble adjusting to the news. Diana instructed them to send a press release to every national newspaper. She would attend to the local ones.

"I want you to make sure Michael gets a fanfare this time . . . not the mud slinging he got three years ago. It's all over, Merlin, and I want him to know it."

Merlin Olaff's suggestion that this was a personal matter, outside the scope of the English Gardens' public relations campaign, fell on stony ground.

"I thought you said everything to do with me was also to do

with English Gardens? Anyway, Merlin, just do it, please. It's important to me."

Olaff prepared to fulfill his orders with many misgivings. It was more than probable that the press would cover Michael Neville's release in any case. It was news. Nor was it likely that any journalist would need to rely on an agency tip for an angle. They'd have one of their own. Sending out premasticated, slanted material might stimulate negative comment. There was just no tactful way of getting that over to Diana at the moment. Her voice on the telephone had been a cadenza of exaltation.

It was generally held at Epoch that English Gardens was less of a business and more of a self-funding movement. The style and stability of Diana's leadership kept it in being, nothing else. As for her husband, he was not an asset.

Epoch had hoped to keep Michael Neville right out of the picture. From an image point of view, everything about him was wrong. Whichever way you looked at him—clever guy, survivor, sophisticated villain—the public would see him as an inappropriate feature in a smiling landscape. In plain terms, a blot. Olaff feared the tabloids might see it the same way. Scandal was in short supply at the moment. Still, it *was* Christmas.

Merlin's face brightened at the thought. Yes. The season of goodwill and "coochy coo" stories. That was the way to handle it. And a picture was worth a thousand words. In this case, much better. He began to dial the picture editors of all the nationals.

LEAVING HER CAR in the station yard, Diana was displeased to see a knot of photographers on the platform. This was a private occasion. Even Yolanda had elected to go to her lectures as usual that morning to give her parents time alone. She would join them at lunchtime. Spotting her, the men rushed forward, flashing bulbs in her face.

"Give us a big smile, love. That's it . . . a big smile for the big day . . ."

"If I'd known, we could've turned t'brass band out for 'im, Mrs. Neville," Bob remarked laconically as he passed her with his block of dismounting steps. "Thought you'd want it quiet, like."

"I do, Bob. This wasn't my idea. I'm afraid my husband won't like it at all."

"Get away with you," Bob consoled her. "He'll notice nowt except thysen. Mark my words. Just you catch hold of his nibs, gerr'im off to t'car. I'll head yon nosey buggers off. Steady on now, he's 'ere."

Michael's face flashed into view as the train's brakes squealed. His features were flat, like a photograph. He was standing ready at a door and leaped down athletically before Bob could thrust his way through the pushing newspaper men to carry out the ceremony of the steps.

"This way, Mike ... How does it feel? Give the wife a smackeroo ... Where is she?"

Diana winced. This was awful. Perhaps she should have waited in the car park or sent a taxi. She found herself hanging around on the fringes of the crowd with Bob until somebody snatched at her sleeve.

"Here she is! The little woman ... give her a kiss, Mike." She was thrust into Michael's arms like a parcel.

Michael encircled her shoulders with his right arm casually while he talked to the men. He parried their questions easily, laughing and enjoying the attention. But this was a photo call and they all wanted him to kiss Diana.

"OK, OK, fellers. Here goes."

He leaned down to cover Diana's mouth with his own. It was not a thing he would normally have done in public and the touch of his lips on hers felt as inert and impersonal as glove leather.

"How's that?" Michael demanded, straightening.

"One more ... Di looks as though she's gonna cry."

"*No* more," Diana snapped. "I'm sorry but my husband's had a long journey. I'm sure you understand we want to be alone. Please excuse us now."

"What the hell's eating you?" Michael asked her as she turned the car in the yard.

"What do you mean? Haven't you any luggage?"

"No. Some files and things. They'll come on later. What's with the Greta Garbo stuff ... I want to be alone? *I've* had three years of that."

"Michael, darling, so have I. I only wanted to be alone with you."

"Plenty of time for that," Michael remarked. "We're not going into purdah for Christmas, are we?"

Diana had told him all about her plans for Christmas by the time they reached the garden door.

"The big night, as far as our friends are concerned, is the Mummers' Play night, the day before Christmas Eve. You remember, I've told you all about it before. Well, we're giving a large dinner party to introduce you to everyone and then loads of people from the town will come on after dinner to see the play. It will be packed. Frankly, everybody's bound to be curious about you, so I thought . . ."

"Sounds like another public relations stunt to me," Michael was hardly listening. He was looking at the impressive height of the Tower's boundary wall. It was in pretty good nick, too. Repointed. Diana had been making some money.

"Darling, it is in a way," Diana replied to his comment. "I'm so very proud of you. I want to show you off. Come and see everything I've done inside to make you comfortable. I bought a picture for your study yesterday. It's your sort of thing. I think it's awful . . . it can go back if you don't like it."

Disappointingly, Michael made no favourable comment on the painting or anything else.

"Thanks," he said briefly, in response to Diana's guided tour of the arrangements made for his comfort and convenience. "I'll need a secretary but it's better I find my own. Get on to an agency tomorrow morning, will you, sweetheart, and tell them to send some girls round to see me. A temp will do."

He threw the words over his shoulder as he stood at the dormer window of his study, looking down into the garden. Diana swallowed. She had become unaccustomed to taking orders.

"Come here," Michael swung round from the window. His light eyes sparkled. Diana hesitated. "Come here," Michael repeated. "You're very uppity all of a sudden. Aren't you going to give your husband a kiss? I walk into the house and what do I get? A lot of stuff about sock drawers, water pressure and photocopiers. What I want is nookie."

"I'm sorry, darling," Diana apologised, laughing at herself, "I must sound like a cross between a gentleman's gentleman and top girl in a typing pool. What I'm trying to say is . . . It's just that I'm nervous, you see. That nonsense at the station threw me rather. I wanted it to be quite different . . ."

She was engulfed in an asphyxiating embrace. Michael's arms were like steel hawsers. "Let's see how different *this* is," he muttered hoarsely, covering her throat and face with hot, rough kisses.

At first, her body responded to his as it always had in the past. It began to open to him, weakening her muscles and numbing her brain.

"Not here, darling. Anyone might come up . . . my secretary. Let's go downstairs to my bedroom . . ."

Michael wasn't listening. With one hand he loosened his fly, restraining Diana's mild, protesting struggles effortlessly with the other. He pushed her to the ground, holding her wrists above her head, hard against the floor. He had often done something like it before, in fun and in bed. Diana knew she was a prude, but she feared interruption. The arch of her welcome for him, widening within her, narrowed and closed. She could not do it. Not here.

"Please, Michael, no. Really, I can't." He released one of her wrists to search beneath her skirt. She hated making love in clothing. Unbathed. And she hated doing anything at the wrong time in the wrong place. This was not as she had planned it. Grabbing his hand, she tried to sit up, but he dropped the weight of his chest on to her, expelling the breath from her lungs.

"No! I'm not ready. I don't want . . . Couldn't we wait? Yolanda will be home soon."

"Why do you bloody women insist on wearing these passion killers?" Michael grunted, tearing at her tights.

He took her, driving himself forward, blunt and rigid. Diana cried out in pain. She drummed her fists on his back, shrinking away. Michael grasped her hips and pulled her on to him. She sheathed him, too dry and too small, against her will.

"Stop! I can't bear it. Please! It hurts."

He climaxed rapidly, pulling himself from her and spurting semen on to her clothes. There was an odour, sharp and acrid. Diana was aware of tears on her cheeks. Pain, anger, disgust. No. She wiped the slate of her mind clean and wrote surprise there instead. Sometimes, she had found in the past, it helped to rechristen her emotions. It helped to control them.

He rolled off her and lay on his back.

"Something to be said for wanking, you know. Sharpens

your appetite for the real thing. Good, that. Got anything to drink in this dump?"

Diana twitched at her skirt, trying to recover the seemliness which had been snatched from her. Her fingers encountered slime and she felt her stomach heave. She lay back again, willing her equilibrium to return. Perhaps she had been childish to expect Michael to wait until the household was quiet, the lights low and supper cleared away. Their physical reunion should have ended a perfect day. Sealed new commitments, new bargains.

Far below, the familiar clang of the garden door sneck announced Yolanda's arrival. There was to be a late, celebratory lunch.

"Is he back?" Her voice carried strongly on the clear wintry air. Sedgely, who was sweeping up the last of the fallen leaves, answered her, his words indistinct.

Down there, outside, it was a different, innocent world, one from which, for a few incomprehensible minutes, Diana had felt herself exiled. Carried away in a sealed, soundproof capsule. Incapable of rescue. She got up, smoothing her hair behind her ears. How must she look? She must pull herself together. Adjust. This was a happy day. There was so much to be done, to show and to explain. Things she had longed to share.

"I said is there anything to drink?" Michael sprang to his feet. He straightened his own clothing, relaxed and debonair.

"Of course there is, darling. Champagne. Lots of it. Why don't you go down to Yolanda while I go and tidy myself?"

Diana dropped every one of the garments she had been wearing into the bottom of the linen basket. They were there for weeks before she burned them in Sedgely's large new garden incinerator.

❧ "NOT MARRIED YET, Landa?"

Michael's eyes swept round the dining-room, taking in the portraits and the silver. He helped himself to gravy from a sauceboat with the capacity of a bucket. It, like everything else here, looked as though it might have some kind of value. He didn't go for antique stuff. All right if you wanted to live in a mausoleum.

"Well, when's the wedding?" he insisted. Diana had left the

room momentarily to fetch something from the kitchen. It was the first meal they had eaten in the dining-room. The effort, which was considerable, had been made in honour of Michael's first day at Gilbert's Tower.

Yolanda, with her mouth full of Mrs. Sedgely's sage and onion Yorkshire pudding, shook her head. "Oh, Daddy, that was a joke. Alisdair'd run a mile if you offered him a brass farthing, anyway. I've got to finish this course I'm on first. I'm pretty good, you know. We had to do an exercise last week . . ."

Throughout her explanation, Michael stared at his daughter with eyes like tiles, taking nothing in.

"It's very practical," Yolanda emphasised. "Everything from loan servicing to promotional budgets and nitty gritty about VAT . . . the sort of thing Mummy had to learn by trial and error . . . Well, she always said you taught her a lot without her realising it."

"Sounds a barrel of laughs." Michael turned his head and begun to drum his fingers on the table rhythmically. "Fancy Gstaad for Christmas . . . or does your boyfriend want you?"

"We thought you might want me," Yolanda replied, taken aback. "I'm going to join the Strang-Steeles for New Year. They're Scottish so that means more to them than to us. We'll have Christmas here, just the three of us. Well, Mummy has to do a bit of semi-business entertaining . . . they're all friends, really . . . You've really no idea how pretty it all is here at Christmas . . . Did you know Mummy's the hereditary Lord of the Manor of Leypole? Not as grand as it sounds but . . ."

"OK, OK," Michael hushed her. He groped in his blazer pocket for a cigarette and lit one, blowing the first plume of smoke into her face. "No need to get your knickers in a twist, Landa. I shan't come between your sainted mother and her business . . . just thought you and I might take off for the bright lights . . . have you back in time for New Year . . ."

Yolanda's expression was stony. Michael was doing no more than he had always done. Dangling a jewelled bauble just out of reach of his infant daughter's fingers. One she could grasp if she were willing to desert her mother. A child no longer, Yolanda rejected the pitiably tawdry bribe. A bargain had been struck between herself, her mother, Alisdair and Alisdair's father. A pact which could not be broken without damage to all.

The time for those childish, destructive trials of strength had gone by. Who loves who the most? Who rules the roost? Who is master here? Dangerous toys that had been put away.

"Daddy, Mummy will need you here. There are people you should meet. It would be awful for her if you went away now. She's got everything planned."

"Looks like it. I prefer to do my own planning. Where I live, how I spend my time, for a start . . ." Michael tipped the silvered almonds from a bon bon dish and crushed out his cigarette messily. "I thought you would too, Landa. When do I get to meet Strang-Steele . . . or has he gone running home to his filthy rich Daddy already? Pity you didn't test his mettle the way I told you."

"Daddy, please. I really *do* want to finish the course before . . . For pity's sake don't say anything to Alisdair. Everything's all right as it is . . ."

This painful conversation was cut short by Diana's reappearance carrying a roast sirloin of beef. Handling the dish and the door was awkward for her. Yolanda leaped to her feet, going to her mother's aid.

"Oh no!" Diana sighed, "I've left the claret in the kitchen . . . it's open, standing by the stove. Darling, I wonder, could you just . . . ?"

"I'll go," Yolanda volunteered quickly.

She found she didn't want to be left alone with her father again. Not even for a few moments. He seemed so tense and restless. The planes of her mother's face were tight as if something definite had already gone wrong.

"I'm just off, love," Mrs. Sedgely was shrugging herself into her coat as Yolanda reached the kitchen. "There's my Summer in Winter pudding in the fridge for afters and a pint of thick cream. See to it your father gets plenty and let me know what he thinks to it . . . 'ere, Miss Landa love, what's up with you? You've a face as long as a wet week."

Yolanda said it was nothing and forced a smile as she bent down to pick up the bottle of wine. Mrs. Sedgely was not fooled.

He'd a way with him, Mr. Neville. There was no denying that. But he'd a lot too much off as well to say this was his wife's house, not his. He'd not been in her kitchen two minutes before he was mocking the old stove. A museum piece, he'd called it. Said she'd have a brand new Aga before the week was out. And who was to pay for it? Mrs. Sedgely had asked herself indignantly. Telling her to call him Michael and asking her Christian name. They might carry on like that in London but it wouldn't do in Nidcaster. Sedgely'd have a mortal fit if he tried calling *him* Albert.

Yolanda's grasp on the bottle was loose. It slipped through her fingers, breaking on the tiles. The red fluid spilled, soaking the rag rug. She found herself convulsed and in tears.

"Nay, Miss Landa, love." Mrs. Sedgely stooped painfully to pick up the fragments of broken glass and suddenly found Yolanda's arms around her. She was sobbing hysterically. Been very out o' sorts lately, had t'bairn, Mrs. Sedgely thought. Anyone would have thought she were worried about summut.

"If you ask me," the older woman said grimly, "a lot too much 'as been built on this. It was bound to come as a bit of an anti-climax, like."

"It's Daddy," Yolanda choked out unnecessarily. "I don't think he likes it here."

"What makes you say that, love?" Mrs. Sedgely soothed tactfully, though she herself had sensed the unease in the house, the dislocation. For a start, the orange cat had stalked out of the kitchen door the very moment Mr. Neville had walked in the front.

"He's not been here above a couple of hours. It'll feel strange to 'im. Take him a while to shake down. You weren't that suited yourself when you came. Proper little madam, you were."

Yolanda regained command of herself quickly, stiffened by the elderly Yorkshirewoman's brisk sympathy.

"I think he's going to make us leave Gilbert's Tower." She had been about to say something about Alisdair but an ingrained loyalty gagged her in time.

Mrs. Sedgely drew herself up. "Now listen to me, Miss Landa. This is your mother's house and if I know owt about her, she'll not be leaving it. Now I've to get on home. Dorothy's having her bit of dinner with us today to leave the three of you time to talk. There's another bottle like this on t'larder shelf, though it'll be a bit cold. You'll have to draw t'cork, mind. Well, give it to yer Dad to do, eh? Make him feel useful."

But with his customary energy, Michael had already found a use for himself.

"What have you been doing, Landa?" he asked her jovially when she returned to the dining-room. "Treading the grapes? I've just been telling your mother she should float her company on the stock market. Only way to begin getting seriously rich. I'll start sounding out some likely stockbrokers tomorrow."

Yolanda grinned. The temperature in the dining-room had gone up a degree or two. Her parents were smiling at each other.

"Can I look over your shoulder, Daddy? We're doing flotations at college next term."

"No, you can't. You can mop my fevered brow at frequent intervals and bring me cups of coffee. That goes for both of you."

Diana and Yolanda exchanged a relieved glance. Things were back to normal. A discarded normality, it was true. But Michael had to begin somewhere. He had a lot of catching up to do.

As Diana lay wakeful beside him that night in Aunt Thea's old bed, she listened to his deep, even breathing. Michael could always sleep. It was one of his great, inimitable talents. And somehow or other, he always occupied the middle of the bed.

❦ DURING THE NEXT three days, Michael was left largely to his own devices. He had, he said, plenty to do to get the company's ducks in a row, ready for flotation in the New Year.

Glad to see him busy and content, Diana raised no immediate objection when he took over the book room temporarily. That was where all the company books were, after all. At least, there was no more talk of going abroad for Christmas or, worse still, shutting up the house and taking a flat in London. Neither was remotely possible, anyway. As for the idea of letting the company go public . . . well, there was no harm in considering the options.

English Gardens was balanced on a knife edge. The debt to Lafontaine Frères had been serviced unfalteringly and the capital sum very nearly paid off. But the profits from such a many tiered operation were slim. Insufficient to justify a further advance. And yet there were countless enquiries from both gardeners and retailers in Scotland and Ulster. Why, they wanted to know, should their countries not be included in the scheme? There were willing suppliers and eager customers for the asking. It was only the costly infrastructure of print shops and packing stations which held further expansion back.

Privately, Diana was forced to acknowledge the near truth of what Philip Strang-Steele had predicted. She could see a time coming when, despite the pleasure English Gardens gave to producers and customers alike, the gross profits would be insufficient to effect repairs to equipment or pay the salaries of people like Alisdair. It would not matter, Diana had argued with Cedric Lafontaine, if the company never made a great fortune for her, as long as it remained healthily in being. It had a value, Diana had urged, that was beyond price.

"But the price must be paid," Cedric demurred, "and not, alas, by us, Mrs. Neville. We *are* in business to make money. Have you ever considered charitable status for English Gardens?"

Diana had and rejected the notion. She wanted a real company competing in the real marketplace. Not a worthy cause hung about with the trappings of tax advantages, begging bowls and excuses. Michael, in a chance remark, had given a clue to the solution. If he was happy to pursue it, she was happy too. He was settling down, finding his feet.

Ignoring the girl's mutinous expression, she instructed Dorothy to give Mr. Neville all the help he needed. Dorothy was soon won over. By an initial show of indifference, Michael lost no time in goading her to coquetry. Rationed pats on the rump blended with macho declarations that the place of women, particularly pretty ones, was to be tied barefoot to the kitchen sink, had Dorothy quivering with simulated feminist outrage in no time. She was for ever in the kitchen, getting under Mrs. Sedgely's feet, making pots of *real* coffee for Michael, as she had quickly learned to call him.

"That one," Mrs. Sedgely muttered under her breath as she watched Dorothy's smugly swaying hips disappear from view, "had better watch her step." She beat the brandy butter into creamy smooth submission in record time.

Certainly, Diana had no time for watching developments in the book room. The preparations for the Mummers' Play, the first event on the Christmas programme and the stage upon which Michael was to make his first social entrance, claimed her full attention.

There were still some people in the town who attributed magical properties to the performance. Aunt Thea certainly had. Diana was unable to share her great-aunt's whimsical view of the thing, but recognised its ornamental character. As a finale to the dinner party she was giving for Michael, nothing could be more attractive . . . or more appropriate for a group whose interests were focused on the soil. It solved the problem of after dinner entertainment for a large party at a stroke. No need for card tables, or a questionable, hired cabaret. As so often before, Gilbert's Tower could supply the want from its own resources.

The play had its drawbacks. Security risks.

"Not a safe undertaking, these days," Aunt Thea had commented in one of the many appendices to her letter. "But you'll find the Nidcaster people will always identify a stranger to you. It's the mummers themselves who're the problem. They are literally in disguise and mustn't be recognised or it breaks the luck. So you have six unidentified men in the house. I lost a silver snuff box one Christmas but never mentioned it to the police as that seemed too much like luck breaking.

"The whole thing's an impenetrable fertility ritual and I'm quite sure it's good for our peaches, not to mention Father Murphy's damsons. Success," the note ended cryptically, "depends on careful attention to detail."

The so-called details were large in scale. As in the two previous years, Sedgely and Yolanda, with Ned Garvey and other volunteers, garnered fir fronds, ivy and prickly leaved holly from the forest across the river. With or without berries, Sedgely would only have prickly leaved holly for Gilbert's Tower. When Ned's biggest punt was piled high with the greenery, and he was about to pole it away, Sedgely stopped him. He went back among the trees and emerged bearing a bough of the forbidden smooth edged holly, though it had no berries.

"I thought . . ." Yolanda began, mystified. She had been told that the thornless leaves withered too quickly to make them suitable for decorating the house.

"Aye, well," Sedgely cut short the explanations, "situation's altered now."

Any fool knew that smooth holly was a wand of power to a woman. And them as didn't were better off not meddling. Mrs. Neville would need all the help she could get, lest her man get overmighty. Michael's occupancy of the book room had not escaped Sedgely's notice. He'd be hard to shift.

The little man snorted quietly as he threw the green talisman on top of the pile. It was bound to bring about a dilution of his own influence.

Ned, who, whilst scarcely conscious of it, had lived all his life amongst everyday magic, made no comment. Nor did he think in words. Dimly, his brain registered the fact that Albert Sedgely was responding to changed conditions.

At the Garveys' landing stage a hummock of mistletoe, pulled from the gnarled branches of Mrs. Garvey's Golden Pippin, lay waiting. The annual tribute to Gilbert's Tower, it was also a guarantee of safety in a season sensitive to spite.

❦ THE EVENING OF the Mummers' Play had always begun with a dinner party.

In Aunt Thea's time it was reduced to no more than a neighbourly supper in the panelled parlour where a handful of frail representatives of the local squirearchy had come to dine with their old friend. The two years since her death had seen the assembly shrink still further to a family party composed the first year of Diana and Yolanda alone, and last year Alisdair with Father Murphy. This Christmas marked a return to former glories. The dining-room was opened again and, with two leaves put into the table, twenty-four were to sit down.

Almost forcibly deprived of her wooden spoons, Mrs. Sedgely was more or less ordered to take her place as the wife of a director. Caterers would cook and serve the meal she had prepared. With a suitable show of ingratitude for the respite, she climbed into her brown taffeta that she'd had twenty years and wore her great-grandmother's topaz brooch. Sedgely was pleased with her.

"You look a bobby dazzler, lass," he enthused.

"None so bad y'sen," she remarked severely.

Sedgely had invested in a dinner jacket for the great occasion, the cause of some envious ribaldry in the town. But

Sedgely had had greatness thrust upon him and felt only a sense of righteous martyrdom in having risen to meet it. "It were only fitting."

Diana's other guests did not, mysteriously, include Alisdair. He had declined her written invitation formally at the last moment, pleading a prior engagement. Yolanda, who had intended to introduce her fiancé to her father on the Mummers' night, seemed cheerfully impervious to the snub. He had gone a day early to Lincolnshire, she told her mother blandly. Something to do with *Grandmère*.

Diana wondered if they had quarrelled. She hoped not. Christmas was a bad time to air differences. But it was too late to go into it now. It really was very bad of Alisdair to let them down like this.

"He could have told me earlier. Or you could. I was rather counting on him to take Mrs. Gholam Khan into dinner. I shouldn't have pressed her husband to bring her otherwise. Now what am I going to do? She hardly speaks a word of English."

"Father Murphy?" Yolanda suggested hopefully, as she helped her mother rearrange the place cards. "Clergymen don't mind helping with . . ."

"Out of the question," Diana despaired. "Father Murphy's a man who expects to be amused."

"In return for damsons."

"Quite."

Diana went upstairs to dress and apprised Michael of the difficulty. "I don't suppose you'd . . . ?"

"No, I bloody well won't. You're not lumbering me with some Kashmiri peasant woman. What's more to the point, why has Strang-Steele dropped you in it? He's made Landa look a fool into the bargain."

Diana knew that. The engagement between her daughter and English Gardens' Technical Director was widely known. But Yolanda was comporting herself with dignity and they owed it to her not to increase her troubles by pointing out the obvious.

Personal feelings and post-mortems must wait. It was Michael's evening, principally. His touchiness, Diana was sure, was evidence of nerves . . . of stage fright to which he could never admit.

There was a telephone message. Gholam Khan's wife had a

sick headache and could not come, by which Diana understood the poor Begum had suffered a last minute failure of nerve. Gholam would come alone. At least the numbers were even again. The perplexing matter of Alisdair's desertion was dropped.

Helping to zip up her white velvet gown, Michael deposited an unexpected kiss on his wife's naked shoulder.

"You know," he said, "If there's a woman coming here tonight who I prefer to you, I'll be surprised. I really will."

It was, by Michael's standards, a serious compliment. Diana remembered a time when it would have made her heart thrill with gratitude and fear. This time, she felt deflated. Short changed. Why could he *never* give with both hands?

Within half an hour the invited company was beginning to arrive.

The hall, where the play was to take place, had been transformed into a green forest clearing. There were chairs set around the walls and great logs blazed on the stone hearth. The main staircase and landing gallery would serve as seating for the townspeople when they came after dinner.

Lit only by candle sconces and oil lamps, the house was spattered with starry points of light in shifting expanses of shadow. By counterpointing gaiety with menace, the scene was set for pagan rituals of death and rebirth. Sedgely and his helpers had surpassed themselves this year. A faint, agreeable shiver went through Diana as she began to enjoy her own party.

"How nice to see you . . . You won't have met my husband . . ." Diana said it a score of times. "Yes, isn't it fun?" she replied to questions about the decorations. "No, I haven't a clue how long it's been going on. I think I might get quite scared if I did! Don't let the Nidcasterites frighten you. Some of them take it terribly seriously. No, of course not. It's just a terrifically good excuse for a party."

" 'Tis devil worship, no less," Father Murphy contradicted her to a startled supermarket owner's wife as he helped himself from a passing tray of cocktails. "I pins a battery of holy medals to me vest each year and survive the incident unscathed. 'Tis the dinner makes it worth the risk to me soul."

The dinner itself went well. Michael sat at one end of the table opposite his wife. Through the parade of candelabra, epergnes and flowers, he was virtually invisible to her. Diana hoped his companions suited him. They had been chosen more on the basis of precedence than congeniality. The newest important retailer and the wife of the oldest important supplier. She need not have worried. Michael kept Major Dick Garside's wife agog with richly embroidered tales of prison life, and the bluff, successful Yorkshireman on his left with speculations as to what improved manoeuvres would have prevented his arrest in the first place.

At Michael's end of the table, embarrassed titters advanced rapidly to roars of laughter. The appearance of the roast goose saw him complete master of a rapt audience. A likeable rogue.

Yolanda, seated in the middle of the table, had Father Murphy and Gholam Khan for neighbours. They leaned across her and behind her, sometimes craning above her head to exchange extreme and opposing views on religion. With admirable patience, Yolanda caught at mouthfuls where she could, ducking the impassioned gestures of the two men. Opposite, Mrs. Meers, the solicitor's wife, grimaced at her. Men were such boors. Yolanda smiled. They were enjoying themselves, that was the main thing.

So did everybody else. By the time the company rose to take coffee and brandy in the hall, it was eleven o'clock and time for the Mummers' Play. Many Nidcaster people had already taken up their positions on the staircase and in the opened doorways of adjoining rooms. As Diana had predicted, they were more numerous than in the previous two years. Human nature. They had tumblers of hot punch in their hands and the caterers' waiters were passing to and fro bearing salvers laden with mince pies and wedges of blue Wensleydale cheese.

There was a fusillade of hand clapping as Diana passed first into the hall, ahead of the guests. She stood framed by the arch of the short dining-room corridor to acknowledge the greeting with Michael beside her.

"Merry Christmas, Mrs. Neville! Aye, Merry Christmas, Mrs. Neville, love . . . and many more to come! Eee," one old lady quavered, "looks a queen in that there frock!"

Diana was glad when the barrage of goodwill died down. She wanted to avoid too much emphasis on herself. She had toyed with the idea of introducing Michael verbally at this point in the proceedings but dismissed it. It could go wrong.

The Nidcaster people gave a welcome when they were ready, not before. It was enough that he was with her now. Her partner.

The point had been made by the positioning of two identical elbow chairs in the traditional place of honour, at right angles to the hearth on the left hand side. Michael and Diana seated themselves there while Sedgely, always impressario at the Mummers' Play, lit the candles in the crude iron chandelier which would illuminate the action. It was hauled up to the ceiling by means of a rickety pulley system with much unwanted advice from the audience.

"Nay, lad, you'll brain t'lot of us if you do it like that . . ." chorused the staircase spectators.

"Can I give you a hand, Mr. Sedgely?" a young Fernley executive offered anxiously.

"Me bishop would take a dim view of me death," Father Murphy observed cosily, "were it to occur in this snake pit of sin."

After a few false starts it was done and Sedgely stepped up to the closed drawing-room door behind which the actors hid.

"Are you ready, Mrs. Neville?"

Looking round to see that all her guests were supplied with the elements of good cheer, Diana gave the signal.

Sedgely clenched his fist and thumped three times on the drawing-room door.

"Come out. Come out. T'Lady and 'er Lord will hear the play!"

Diana blessed him for that. For many a long year there had been only a "Lady" to witness the play. It was good that Sedgely had remembered that this Mummers' Night was different. She slipped her hand into Michael's, not caring who saw.

A succession of weirdly attired men burst rowdily into the hall. Their features were obscured by grotesque masks, and even their hands were gloved. Not so much as a familiar signet ring was allowed to give the identity game away. They spoke in stentorian bellows or high, falsetto squeaks. The disguise was complete.

Diana whispered hurried interpretations into Michael's ear of the puerile rhymes with which each mummer introduced his character.

"That's Father Christmas."

"Then why's he swinging that ruddy great club?"

"The Lord only knows. That's King George, only he's really *Saint* George . . . he represents England as a sort of cross between a Crusader and a corn god. He get's killed by the Turkish Knight, who is also Winter. And then the Doctor makes him better again because he's really Spring, you see."

"Clear as mud," Michael muttered. And indeed, apart from a scholar from the University of York who had, at his own request, been invited to scrutinise this living curio, nobody really understood it at all. That was the point, Sedgely had said darkly on Diana's first Mummers' Night. It didn't do to dig too deep. He had frowned rather severely, she remembered, at her answering giggle. Sedgely was a believer.

King George was killed twice to cheers from the audience. Then there was a quarrel between two of the characters over pulling his teeth. It was prolonged and dull, providing an opportunity for waiters to circulate stealthily, refilling glasses. The King was cured for the last time with an elephant's tusk. More cheers. Another row concerning the doctor's fee followed while the revived king was belaboured with a pig's bladder. Finally, the last character to appear, Helseybub, added to the mayhem by bashing all the other characters over the head with a frying pan.

"Am I not a jolly old man?" he enquired senselessly.

A storm of applause greeted the question. Helseybub, dressed in the parti-coloured hose of a medieval jester with a horned cap, jumped eight times in the air. It was the invariable finale.

"One . . . two . . . three . . ." the experienced part of the audience chanted loudly. On landing for the eighth time, Helseybub spun round and dropped gracefully to one knee before Yolanda. Unmasking himself, he carried her hand to his lips.

It was Alisdair.

Around him, the invited guests applauded the picturesque chivalry of the gesture. They knew no better. Diana half raised her hands and dropped them on the chair arms in chagrin. An annoying departure from tradition. People would make a fuss. Beside her, Michael continued to clap lazily. A subdued moan came from the staircase and landing. In the doorways, there were no smiles. Yolanda pulled Alisdair to his feet as if gathering him from a fall.

Alisdair guided her across the empty space in the centre of the hall to where her parents were.

"Good evening, sir," Alisdair nodded courteously in Michael's direction. "Alisdair Strang-Steele. Believe me, I didn't intend to present myself as a surprise package . . ."

"Nay, lad, nay!" It was Mrs. Sedgely who spoke. "You've taken all t'luck."

Alisdair swung round to look into her face. She was very angry.

" 'T is the devil's part you played, lad," Father Murphy sidled up, "and the devil's work you've done."

"Please don't be so silly, Father Murphy," Yolanda took her shocked fiancé's arm defensively. "You of all people ought to know it's just a bit of fun . . . like a pantomime."

Dazed, Alisdair turned away and began to explain to Diana why he had opted out of her dinner with so little notice.

Only half listening, Diana saw Sedgely over by the front door. Ashen faced, he was seeing the departing mummers off the premises. They went, still masked and known only to each other, their wives and sweethearts, to get into their cars and go home. It was that taboo that Alisdair had unwittingly broken. When that year's Helseybub had broken his leg only two days before, Alisdair had been approached as substitute. Nobody thought to explain to him that the ban on self-discovery was absolute and binding for all time. Not just till the end of the play.

"But it's impossible really," Yolanda pointed out to the group standing round Alisdair. "Everybody knows that the Vicar always plays Father Christmas. Why would he refuse Mummy's invitation three years running, otherwise?"

"Nobody knows for sure, I suppose. That's why his wife doesn't come," somebody said.

"Me brother in Christ is headed for the jaws of hell," Father Murphy sighed unwisely. He never knew when to stop.

The party broke up around them. The townspeople began to straggle out of the door, uttering their thanks quietly as they went. Some, in wordless distress, pressed Diana's hand. Mr. and Mrs. Sedgely were the first of the dinner guests to take their leave soon afterwards. The others followed. It had been a wonderful evening, they said. The play ... so odd. Had there been some problem about the ending? It was late, anyway.

"I'm dreadfully sorry," Alisdair dropped into a chair miserably. "I seem to have made a mess of it. I even left a dinner jacket here with Yolanda. You see ... I thought that after ..."

"Oh, shut up, all of you," Michael shouted, his face suffused with blood. "I've heard enough about it. A clumsy parlour game like that and you go on and on about it like a lot of old women." He broke off and stared round at the disbelieving faces of his wife and daughter. Alisdair's was impassive.

"You and me, mister. We've got plenty to talk about. Come into my study. There's some whisky in there."

"Michael, don't you think ... ?" It occurred to Diana that her husband was quite possibly drunk.

"Daddy, I told you not to ..."

Yolanda's attempted intervention was shouted down. "You two get to bed. You can clear up in the morning. Mr. Strang-Steele and I have some business."

Michael got up and went into the book room, slamming the door.

There was a moment's complete silence before Diana said carefully, "My husband is overwrought. This evening has been a great strain for him, Alisdair. I blame myself. After three years ... a large party ... too much excitement, too soon. I hope you understand."

"Shall I go and see what he wants?"

"No!" Yolanda clutched Alisdair by the arm. "Leave him alone! He's not fit ..."

"Maybe just some sensible masculine company and a mug of black coffee ... I would be grateful, yes," Diana said.

Yolanda fled up the main staircase in tears. Dumfounded, Diana watched her go. Surely Yolanda didn't believe the silly superstition?

The house suddenly felt cold. Nothing to do with hobgoblins, Diana pulled herself up sharply. Just the boiler thermostat. And the fires had died down.

"I have been trying too hard," Diana thought to herself sadly as she climbed the stairs. "Expecting too much, too soon."

CHAPTER
13

 THE NEXT DAY was Christmas Eve.

Alisdair telephoned early from Broughton and asked if he might see Diana alone before departing for Lincolnshire. There was fog on the roads. Woken by the call, Diana looked first at her watch and then at the empty space beside her. Ten minutes to seven. Evidently, Michael was sleeping in his dressing-room. Remorseful and afraid to disturb her? He and Alisdair must have sat up talking late. Poor Alisdair. Michael's state of mind was not his burden to bear.

Diana regretted, now, shuffling off her responsibilities on to Alisdair. A moment of unpardonable weakness. Still groggy from a brief, troubled sleep, she leaped to the obvious conclusion. Characteristically thorough, the young Scotsman felt he could not leave to begin his own Christmas holiday until he had reassured her. Alisdair always reported. More and more often, Diana found herself thinking her daughter a fortunate young woman.

"Yes, Alisdair," she agreed, fully awake now. "Of course. Do come. It *is* good of you. I'm so sorry I left you to cope. I'll get Yolanda up and we can have breakfast together."

"Thank you, Diana, but I'd far rather not," Alisdair replied tautly. "What I have to say won't take long. It's confidential and I'd prefer Landa to know as little as possible about it. I'll see her at New Year. If she's asleep, it's better to leave her. I'll be with you in twenty minutes."

Diana rose and dressed with her heart thudding. What appalling revelation had Michael made to Alisdair? Perhaps it was nothing to do with that. The business . . . She searched her mind and memory for anything concerning English Gardens that might warrant such an early meeting on Christmas Eve. There was nothing. What could Michael have *said*?

Downstairs in the kitchen she wrestled with the old iron stove. It was very nearly out. The caterers had left the flue wide open. They would, of course. By the time Alisdair stepped through the garden door, Diana's face was streaked with coal dust and her eyes pricking with tears of frustration.

"It's that damn thing," she said to Alisdair as she opened the door to him. A faint frown of distaste crossed his features. No matter what the provocation, he had never heard Diana swear before. It did not suit her.

"I'm sorry," she said, seeing the look on his face. "Why am I snarling at you of all people? It's Christmas Eve as well. Come into the book room. Wouldn't you like a cup of coffee at least?"

"No, really. Nothing thank you. I want to get on the road before there's too much heavy traffic on the A1."

Diana's acute ear detected the peculiarly detached, formal note in his tone. She noticed her own hand tremble on the book room's doorknob and her mouth was dry. Something unpleasant was about to happen. She pushed open the door and shut it again quickly. Michael was sprawled on the sofa there, half lying, half propped, his chin sunk on his chest. The room smelled. There was a bottle of whisky on the floor beside him. Empty.

"We'll have to use the drawing-room. It will be cold in there, I'm afraid . . ."

"The kitchen will do, Diana."

Hating the morning after the night before look of the house, she followed Alisdair back across the hall. She would never normally have left it like that. Michael, she remembered . . . how could she forget? . . . had actually ordered her to bed in her own house. At the age of forty plus. Some sort of nervous crisis. He should see a doctor. They would discuss it after Christmas.

"You must know, Diana," Alisdair drew one of the kitchen chairs away from the table for her, "how personally devoted I am to you . . . won't you sit down? I think you should."

Diana sat slowly. *Personally devoted* . . . words from a funeral oration. Time decelerated sharply. Seconds slid like tar from the clock.

"As an employer, a friend, the inspiration of English Gardens ... and, absurd as it may seem, a future mother-in-law. I ..."

"Please, Alisdair ... There's no need to ..."

But Alisdair would not allow his speech to be checked. He started to pace up and down the kitchen floor, his head bent and hands thrust deep into his trouser pockets.

"These past three years have been, I can honestly say, the happiest of my life. My adult life, anyway. The most creative, the most fulfilling. Well, you know all that. And Yolanda. The one person in the world I had begun to think I'd never find. I never once imagined I should leave here without her. If ever. But I do think now ..."

Diana got up abruptly, reeling with anger and confusion. Which was he doing? Resigning his job or breaking his engagement? She choked on her own saliva.

"Do let me finish, Diana. I've been up most of the night, trying to work out what on earth to tell you."

"Yes. Perhaps you'd better. This doesn't make a lot of sense." Diana controlled her coughing fit with difficulty.

"You may be aware," Alisdair went on, "that for some time now, my father has been wanting me to join his group. I have always resisted it. That kind of activity has never interested me but in all honesty, perhaps it's time ..."

"What is it? This just doesn't add up. Have you and Yolanda fallen out with each other? Tell me!"

Alisdair ceased his perambulation and turned to face her.

"No. Absolutely not. This has nothing whatever to do with Yolanda ... except as it may affect her as my future wife ..."

"Alisdair," Diana rose from her chair, keeping her voice low with an effort. Yolanda's bedroom was one of those above the kitchen wing. "Directors of companies with three month notice clauses in their service contracts don't resign before breakfast on Christmas Eve. Not because they suddenly fancy a change of career direction. What do you take me for? Now I think you'd better tell me exactly what all this is about while we're alone."

Alisdair sat down in the chair opposite the one she had just vacated. He bit his lower lip before answering.

"Well?"

"There is simply no proper way to say this," Alisdair glanced up at her before lowering his gaze. "But I cannot visit this house on a daily basis with your husband here. Nor, since it seems that he is, or will be, involved with the business, can I see any possibility of our cooperating effectively for the good of English Gardens. There. I'm sorry. It was never my intention ... I didn't want to ..."

Diana fell back into the chair, her face draining of colour. Her world was disintegrating. The world she had invented.

"What did he say?"

"Oh, really! No, Diana. You don't want to know all that." Alisdair tugged at the ragged end of his watch strap. "It's a personality clash, if you like."

"I don't like it. And I don't believe it. What happened? You owe me that, at least."

"All right, Diana ..."

"Ssh. Keep your voice down if you don't want to waken Yolanda."

Alisdair bit his lip again and passed a hand over his hair in a quick, unconscious gesture of defence. He was not afraid for himself. But every word that was dragged from him by Diana's determination was adding to a mounting scrap heap of destruction. He wanted to spare her. He wanted to save them all, if he could. Even Neville. Yolanda loved him.

"Listen, Diana. Your husband, without any provocation from me last night, used some words ... called me some names that no man with a shred of normal self-respect could forgive. He was probably drunk but ..."

"What names, Alisdair?"

Tired of beating so fruitlessly round the bush, Alisdair listed them. They were not edifying. "Sub-virile, mother-fucker, eunuch ... Do you want to hear any more?"

Diana shook her head and put her hand over her mouth. She was ashamed to have forced Alisdair to utter such words to her. He looked away.

"But why, Alisdair? Even if he was drunk and I think ..."

"Because he offered me money to marry Yolanda immediately and I refused it."

The statement floated away from him, crazy and insubstantial as a helium filled balloon at a fairground. It was ungraspable.

Diana sat silent and uncomprehending. One of them was mad. Or Michael was.

"This is very serious," she said eventually. "My husband has no money. Or very little . . ."

"According to him, he has somewhat over a million pounds in a Swiss bank account. Which is," Alisdair elaborated rather too primly, "in itself, illegal."

"Imaginary." Diana snapped. "If that money had existed, do you suppose my husband would have allowed me to leave London, alone . . . as far as he knew with nowhere to go . . . and not let me have *something*?"

She no longer knew what or whom she was defending. Somewhere in the background, a door opened. The book room. Alisdair began to rise.

"Ah!" Michael lurched into the kitchen. His evening clothes were in disarray, his face furred with grey blond stubble. He held the empty whisky bottle in his hand, swinging it like an Indian club. "The reluctant bridegroom . . ." He belched offensively.

"Well, Diana. I'll be off now," Alisdair said quietly. "Tell Landa I'll ring her tomorrow. We'll expect her on the thirty-first. I'm sorry you won't come too but . . ."

"A sparrow-fart tryst with my wife, I see," Michael blundered on. He was opening and closing cupboards in the dresser. "What do the pair of you get up to, eh? Holding hands? Or has she been coaching you in the basic duties of a husband all this time?"

Diana saw Yolanda poised on the threshold of the kitchen. She was wearing a blue dressing gown. Her face wore the expressionless mask of deep shock. How much had she heard? Between mother and daughter the indecency lay like a withered whore with thighs obscenely spread.

Diana opened her mouth, expecting sound. The muscles of her throat constricted. Her hands lay in her lap like lead. Her eyelids, too, were jammed open on rusted hinges.

"She's adequate in the sack . . . my wife," Michael prattled, "but definitely a beginner's ride . . . I say, what's this?" He stopped speaking momentarily to examine a half bottle of spirits discovered in a cupboard. "Feel like a heart starter, old boy?" But Alisdair had slipped noiselessly away, leaving a cream envelope on the table. The printed address on the flap was his own. His resignation.

"Pissed off, has he?" Michael looked round from the sink as the garden door clanged shut outside. "Shame. I was just getting to like him. Bit of a prick . . . but enough of a prick to stuff you with . . ."

Diana's eyes photographed the vacant space where Yolanda had stood.

Mechanically, she got up from her chair. She unhooked the frying pan from its place on the wall above the stove and brought it down on Michael's head. He turned to her slowly with astonished eyes and crumpled slowly to the ground. Diana covered her face. At least there was silence.

❧ THE RESULTS OF Diana's action were not as she feared. Michael was mildly concussed, no more.

"If he hadn't been half cut at the time, he'd probably never have lost consciousness," the doctor consoled her. "I'm more concerned about you, to be frank," he added, studying Diana's chalk white face. "Is there anybody who can come and stay with you . . . somebody you can talk to?"

The doctor was a locum. He knew nothing of Nidcaster and not much about Diana. Only that she was something of a personality and that her husband had recently been released from prison.

"That's a big strain for any family. Add it to the expectations people have of themselves and each other at Christmas . . . Don't blame yourself too much, that's all. Are you and your husband alone in the house?"

"No, there's my daughter."

"Was she involved in the, er, upset?"

"Yes. No. Look, what happened involved . . ."

The doctor brushed these attempted explanations aside skilfully. Diana did not press them upon him. He was a passer-by, not a physician who could heal the sickness at the heart of her family. It was Yolanda, she said, about whom she was most worried.

"I'd better take a look at her and then perhaps give both of you a mild sedative."

Yolanda's bedroom was empty. So also was the room upstairs in the attic where she kept her music making equipment, did her homework assignments and entertained her friends. A few gaily wrapped packages lay on her desk. Christmas presents. Ready to put under the tree.

The doctor left with a promise to call later in the day. Just now, he suspected, he was overstaying his welcome on ground where angels feared to tread. He recommended Diana take things easy, and not to worry. Michael was to have no alcohol. As for Miss Neville, she had probably taken herself for a long walk. The best thing for her. She would turn up when she was hungry. Youngsters always did. Kiss and make up, all round. That was the best prescription.

Showing him to the front door, Diana acknowledged the protective screen of platitudes with rueful, interlocking clichés. Amazingly understanding . . . Felt a complete fool . . . Grateful for his advice. The doctor did not want to be involved. There was nothing he could do, anyway. She closed the door on him, ready to begin searching through the rubble of her life. She must pick up all the pieces. Every one.

At first, Diana did not panic.

Wandering through the untidy house, she called Yolanda's name softly. There were half a dozen places she might be. She shouted louder. Nothing.

Outside, the garden was shrouded in mist. The stark, leafless arms of the fruit trees beyond the orchard wall seemed to wave as drifting vapour thinned and thickened about them. The silence in the house was profound. There was neither creak nor clatter . . . no wind-whistled tune. For the first time, it felt eerie. Out there, over the garden walls, it was Christmas. Within, time itself had been assassinated.

Diana stepped back from the brink of self-pity. There were things to be done and many more to be undone.

She went into Michael's dressing-room. He lay sleeping on the bed on to which she and the doctor between them had managed to move him. His dinner jacket and trousers had been flung on a chair. Diana folded the trousers and placed them in the electric press. Where were his shoes? She drew up the counterpane to cover the point of his shoulder. Michael flicked open his eyes and looked at her. Diana spoke to him. He did not answer, but closed his eyes again without any sign of recognition.

Seeing him there, it was difficult to believe what had happened. A lie had blotted out their lives. Shot from Michael's mouth at close range, his targets had fallen without a squeak of pain or gesture of self-defence. Alisdair, first accused of impotence, was cleared. There was an explanation. He refused to marry Yolanda because he was sleeping with her mother. Simple, really. Innocence made no difference.

Diana remained in Michael's room a while. She was half afraid to leave him. If she did, she thought witlessly, she might never come back.

The insane, contradictory things he had said were conclusive proof in Diana's mind that her husband had sustained a nervous breakdown. He had exploded like a mine, maiming everyone near to him with splinters of mindless malice. It was not his fault. It was hers. She should have been prepared. If only she had been able to leave Gilbert's Tower and take him away, somewhere quiet for Christmas, this would not have happened. And now, since nobody could help, nobody should know. Not for the moment.

Yolanda must be told to be discreet. She could not possibly believe what she had overheard in the kitchen. Any of it. Diana hoped very much that she would not repeat it. Even to the Sedgelys. They must manage everything together until the right sort of medical help could be found. A couple of days, that was all.

A number of possibilities passed through Diana's mind as she began to clear the previous night's debris from the shipwrecked rooms. Dirty glasses, cigar ash on the carpets, a lost ear-ring . . . a gold cigar cutter dropped in the hall. To restore order, that was the thing.

The Boxing Day lunch might still be possible. If not, she must cancel it today. She couldn't make up her mind. Christmas dinner? That only involved the three of them. It would help if she could talk to Yolanda. Where on earth *was* she? Perhaps Yolanda should go to the Strang-Steeles' early. What excuse could she make? Well, Alisdair would know everything, anyway. Would he tell his father? The idea was horrible. Merlin Olaff rang to wish her a Merry Christmas from all at Epoch. In the background, she could hear the sounds of a riotous office party. The agency's usual Christmas Eve thrash. They would shut up shop at lunchtime. The distant noise mocked the mourning in the house.

"What's the matter? You sound a bit down."

"Oh, nothing. We had a big party here ourselves last night. I'm clearing up."

Later in the morning, Sedgely paid his annual call of ceremony. No work today. He came alone, bringing the predictable Christmas gifts from himself and his wife. Liqueur soaked chocolate truffles and crystallised fruits. Edible jewels in paper lace nests. Mrs. Sedgely made them every year. She had not come herself. Bad with her hip. They'd moved her up the operation list at the hospital. Wouldn't be fit for cooking and such after that. Not for a longish while. They were deserting her, one by one.

"Where's Miss Landa, then?" Sedgely asked.

"I thought she might be with you," Diana replied, as that hope died.

"Nay, we've not seen her. 'Appen she's in t'town, like, doing some shopping. Will you want t'stove riddling while I'm here?"

"No, it's all right. I don't mind doing it. Will you have a glass of something, Mr. Sedgely?"

The offer was made in a tone that invites refusal. Sedgely was hurt but not surprised. Gilbert's Tower had fallen to the enemy. The place had new secrets now, ones that were hidden from him.

Diana gave him the large package of pipe tobacco and the pair of good leather gloves for Mrs. Sedgely. They were done up in foil paper with ribbons. "From Diana, Yolanda and Michael, with love," the tags read. It was the only time Christian names were used without reserve between the two households. In writing and at Christmas only. The etiquette was strict.

"Will we be seeing you at t'watch night service, then?" Sedgely enquired as he took his leave.

"I'm not sure yet. It depends a bit on my husband," Diana hedged. "He's resting this morning."

Sedgely walked back up the foggy lane to the muffled sound of the midday carillon. His teeth were gritted.

"A right carry-on last night," more than one acquaintance greeted him. Most were coming from the marketplace, where they were selling off turkeys cheaply at the last minute. "The lad was bound to make an 'ash of it. Him being a foreigner, like."

The prestige of Albert Sedgely was severely compromised. He was in charge of the Mummers' Play and he had let it happen. Catastrophic events were bound to follow. It stood to reason.

"Tell Mrs. Neville there's nowt in it," said the well-intentioned insincerely. "Nowt but superstition. How is she, any road?"

"She's reet," was all Sedgely would say. Few believed him.

YOLANDA GOT OFF the train at Retford.

It was a curious impulse. Retford was just a place on the way to London. She knew nothing about it. It seemed as good a place as anywhere else to exist. She stepped down on to the platform and looked around with unfocused eyes.

The expanse of redbrick terrace houses visible from the platform promised nothing. Their weary neatness and cramped uniformity inspired neither hope nor curiosity. Yolanda was drawn to their nullity. She walked to the barrier and gave up her ticket.

A few people stared at the striking blond girl. It wasn't so much her beauty that drew attention but her air of powerful detachment. She was a sleepwalker. Somebody who moved without the normal co-operation of brain and muscle. Her purposefulness, that of somebody who walks bravely towards the gallows. A firm, blind step into the void.

"Taxi, my love?"

Yolanda had not noticed that she was standing at the taxi rank but she handed over her small hold-all obediently. It didn't matter what she did or where she went. She was nobody, anyway. A person of no intelligence. A small island of rubbish bobbing helplessly on a turning tide. She would sink soon. The sooner the better.

"Where to, lovely?" The taxi driver turned to her, grinning.

"A guest house. One near the hospital. I have an interview in the morning."

The words came out of their own accord. There had been no planning.

"It's Christmas day tomorrow, love."

"Yes," Yolanda interrupted, unaware of the oddity of what she had said. She simply wanted the man to stop talking. "I'm a nurse."

The taxi man drove her without further comment to a brick built terrace house of some four stories with a card displayed in the window. "Vacancies."

"This do?" The taxi driver asked shortly. He was suddenly anxious to have this expensively dressed lunatic out of his vehicle. Yolanda assented and paid him. She had plenty of money. She could have gone to an hotel. But her brain was functioning on a single emergency engine only. Enough power for a crash landing.

The landlady wasn't sure. She hadn't meant to leave the vacancy card in the window. Not over Christmas. Still, she did just happen to have a very large room on the first floor with its own bathroom and a sitting area with coffee making facilities and TV. Of course, it was fifty pounds a week, the landlady hazarded a guess based on Yolanda's calf shoulder-bag and soft Loden coat.

Yolanda took the room. Payment in advance. A month. That was what the landlady suggested. Yolanda wrote the cheque passively. It didn't matter. An hour, a day, a week. Meaningless concepts. Every consecutive moment occurred to her like a new dawn. One image superimposed on the next like a flickering silent film. The film kept on running. That was the only surprising thing.

She waited in a dark parlour papered with huge, garish poppies while the landlady moved herself and her protesting husband out of their own living quarters. Times were hard.

Unpacking, Yolanda marvelled at the impracticality of the few items in the hold-all. Evening shoes. A bottle of sun tan lotion. Photographs of her mother, Alisdair and her father. She set them in a row on the cheap white laminate chest of drawers. Yes, she must look at them. She must look at them until she understood who they really were. And then she herself would evaporate. Become somebody else. Somebody real. It was a terrifying prospect.

For close on a week Yolanda slept and ate sparingly from the unappetising trays brought to her room. Meals were extra. They hardly seemed necessary but the effort of discussing anything was too great. In her own eyes, her wishes seemed of no importance. They were left-over twinges from the days when she had believed in her own substance. Like the pain in an amputated limb. Too silly to talk about. It was easier just to accept anything and everything that was laid upon her.

The day after Boxing Day she went out to buy some toothpaste. The little parade of shops near the boarding house bustled with the fever of provisioning that follows an enforced rest from shopping. Christmas was over. The newsagent was selling gift wrapping paper off cheap. In the chemist, the special boxes of talcum powder and bathsalts with church bells swinging joyously on the see-thru lids were half price. People were asking each other if they'd had a nice Christmas. They all had, Yolanda noticed. They wished each other a happy New Year. She was standing in front of a cut-price display of hot water bottles with Santa Claus packaging when tears began to slide down her face, heavy and slow like drops of hot glycerine. She did not even feel sad. Just numb.

Walking back to the boarding house in the raw damp air, Yolanda's mind uncurled from its hibernation.

Daddy had been right from the very beginning. That time in the hamburger place in Salisbury when she'd gone to see him, he'd asked who Alisdair was. Asked if he was her mother's boyfriend. Tried to warn her, even then. And his idea of getting Alisdair to marry her quickly. He'd known all along. His strange, erratic behaviour during the few days at Gilbert's Tower now made perfect sense. He was angry for *her*. Oh, why hadn't he told her straight out? It would have been easier to bear. Perhaps that was why he had wanted to take her to Gstaad for Christmas by herself. To break it all to her gently. And she had thought some terrible things about him. Misjudged him utterly.

The meaning of everything in her life was turned upside down. Alisdair and her mother. The way they kept praising each other to her. They were lovers, unable to stop themselves. Alisdair's engagement to her was a smoke screen. An excuse to stay close. He had never wanted to marry her. There was no way she could have known. She had never been in love before. Like a small child poking its fingers into an electric socket, she had been fearless. They must have laughed at her, the two of them.

Deliberately, Yolanda tried to imagine the way it must have been. Of course Alisdair had not wanted to sleep with her. He preferred her mother. She hurled a glass into the wash basin to shatter the revolting images. The basin cracked from side to side.

"It'll cost three hundred pounds to replace," the landlady said, pursing her thin, avaricious lips. "What with the cost of a good basin like that was . . . and the labour."

"I doubt that," Yolanda said calmly. "If you give me the name of your plumber I'll arrange for it to be done myself and pay him direct."

Scenting rebellion, the landlady retreated. She was beginning to find Miss High and Mighty Yolanda Neville a thorn in her side. Hadn't so much as the time of day for anyone. Thought a lot of herself. If it weren't for the rent, she'd give her notice. Stuck in her room all day. Sending her food back as if it were dirt. Where did she think she was? The Ritz?

Yolanda didn't know where she was. She was in limbo. At nights she slept with Alisdair's ring clenched in her fist. The feel and smell of his skin haunted her memory, tormenting her with absolute loss. He had never been hers at all.

Once or twice she dreamed about Gilbert's Tower. Reluctant to wake, she would try to hold fast to that falsely smiling enclave. Daylight stole it away from her with the strength of adult fingers removing a child's toy. At other times, her mother's face, kept at bay during the day, would hover over her bed. Shrieking in her sleep, Yolanda begged her mother to go away.

ALISDAIR RANG ON Christmas Day, as he had promised.

"Oh, thank heavens, you rang," Diana's relief overflowed. "I've been out of my mind with worry. Can I speak to Yolanda?"

"What do you mean? I've rung you to speak to Landa."

Diana had convinced herself that Yolanda had fled to her fiancé's father's house. In all the surrounding circumstances nothing could have been more natural. The words she had heard her own father speak would have been meaningless . . . self-evidently untrue. Alisdair had no idea that Yolanda had heard anything.

"Oh, Christ!" he said. "Poor, poor little Landa."

"But she couldn't possibly have thought there was any truth in it." Diana clung obstinately to that belief. "I'm old enough to be your mother, after all."

"Just. You'd have been fourteen," Alisdair calculated dourly. "Look, what are we going to do about this? We've got to find her. Are you all right, Diana? Do you want us to come up? We will, you know. Father and me, or just me. Whichever you prefer."

Hurriedly, Diana rejected these suggestions. She was no longer in a position to guarantee the welcome offered at Gilbert's Tower. Michael's behaviour could not be trusted. He must be kept quiet. The presence of another man in the house would drive him to a frenzy.

No attempt was made at Gilbert's Tower at even the most curtailed festivity. Michael mooched around the house, drinking canned lager in defiance of medical authority.

"Take more than a crack on the bonce with a frying pan to put me out of action," he said, pulling a Christmas cracker apart and placing the paper hat jauntily on his head. "I can think myself lucky it wasn't a meat clever, I suppose. I'd no idea you were such a tempestuous woman, Diana. Where's Landa?"

Diana moved to the other end of the drawing-room before answering him. She wondered if psychiatric hospitals had casualty departments. If only her own doctor would come back. He had gone skiing. Now it was just a matter of hanging on.

"Michael," she said gently. "Don't you remember what you said?"

Michael shrugged and tossed an empty can of Heineken into the log basket. "So, what did I say?"

"You said," Diana licked her lips, "that I was sleeping with Alisdair Strang-Steele ... my own daughter's fiancé ..."

"Oh, that! That was just a joke. Lighten up, for God's sake, Diana. No sense of humour, that's your trouble. Always has been. Want a beer?"

Diana shook her head. It wasn't really as mad as it sounded. Many a time in the past, Michael had excused his behaviour on the grounds of humorous intent. Protesters were always shouted down as Calvinist cunts. In those days, people would take almost anything from Michael.

"So where's Landa?" he asked again.

"She's gone, Michael. She heard what you said and she's gone. I don't know where."

Just for a moment, the swagger dropped from Michael's

shoulders. "Oh, fucking hell!" He threw himself down in a chair petulantly. "What a balls up."

It was the old trick. The disasters that Michael had accomplished were instantly assigned to some mysterious inefficiency of the cosmos. Something that Michael Neville, in his strength and wisdom, would have to sort out. Those who stood by and shuddered in the vibrations of his wrath were soaked in a backwash of guilt. Michael himself stood high and dry.

The familiar feeling of muddled helplessness settled over Diana like a cloak. She pushed it from her with an effort. Her home, her child, her business ... Michael alone had damaged them. He couldn't help it, of course.

"Why did you offer Alisdair money to break his agreement and marry Yolanda before she's finished her course?"

There was no single answer to that. Michael, irritated by his wife's acuity, got up and began to examine the forest of Christmas cards on the chimney piece. All Diana's friends. People he'd never heard of.

"Well why, Michael?"

"Seemed like a good idea at the time. Didn't want my Landa marrying some spineless little rich boy. You've got to wonder about a bloke who'd work for a woman. It was a way to see what he was made of. Yeah ... and you were being such a bore. A bread first, cake afterwards killjoy. So what's new?"

Michael did not mention his interest in the Strang-Steele fortune. Trying to force the Farm Boy's hand like that hadn't been so cool. Must be losing his touch.

"Tell me, Michael, just how much money *do* you have in Switzerland?" To Diana the question was academic, a mere expression of forensic curiosity.

Michael shrugged indifferently.

"Don't know. A thousand pounds, ten thousand pounds ... ten pounds. If you've got a nought on the end of it, you've got lift off. What the hell does it matter? Money. You can always get it."

It was useless to pursue the matter. Michael was habitually vague about money. Particularly his own.

"Don't you think there was something rather pathetic about offering Alisdair Strang-Steele what to him must have seemed a very small bribe to break faith with me and his father?"

It was a dangerous thing to say and Diana found herself poised on the balls of her feet. Michael had never hit her, but then, she had never pushed him this far.

"Yeah. Pathetic. Happy bloody Christmas, Diana."

He tore the seal from a new can of beer and, drinking from it, toasted her. Then he swept all the Christmas cards on to the floor.

❧ DIANA TRIED EVERYTHING.

The police were sympathetic but unhelpful. Was there any reason to think Miss Neville had been kidnapped? No. Later Diana realized she should have said yes. Had she taken much in the way of clothes with her? No. Well then, she was coming back, wasn't she? Did Miss Neville have a car? Yes, a Volkswagen Beetle, but she hadn't taken it. That made a kidnap more likely, Nidcaster's detective sergeant said, stroking his chin. He would bear it in mind. Had there been a family row of any kind?

"A grave misunderstanding, certainly," Diana replied diplomatically. Her daughter could well have walked out as a result of that.

"I can't help you then, Mrs. Neville, I'm afraid. People have a right to come and go. Tell you what, though. If Miss Neville didn't take 'er car, 'appen she scarpered on t'train. Might be worth having a word with Bob at the station. He doesn't miss much. Nosey bastard, like me. Savin' your presence, like."

Bob's omniscience in the matter of Nidcaster travel was of some use but not much.

"Ee, Mrs. Neville," Bob scratched his head under the signalman's cap. "I'm right sorry to hear that. Miss Landa got on t'stopping train to Leeds on Christmas Eve morning, right enough. Had a sort of bag with her. 'T weren't large, like. I took it for granted she were going into Harrogate. Christmas Eve . . . bad day to be in Harrogate with a car."

"How did she look, Bob? Do you remember?"

Bob was not used to being asked questions which involved subtle observation. The uncertainties of the British Rail timetable satisfied his intellectual needs.

"Well, she 'ad a green coat on," he replied doubtfully to Diana's agonised question. "And one of them head band things. Black it were."

"No Bob. I mean could you tell from looking at her how she might have been feeling?"

"Oh, aye. She'd summut on her mind, all right."

The Salvation Army had a missing persons service, Diana remembered. Directory enquiries told her the number. Shipley, in the West Riding. The number rang and rang. There was no reply.

It was hopeless. Yolanda might be anywhere at all. Sleeping rough in London, in a squat, in a shelter . . . at least she had some money. It would not last long. The Hermès handbag she had taken with her contained her cheque book. The day after Boxing Day was a Thursday. Diana rang the local bank manager and arranged an immediate transfer of funds to Yolanda's current account. If the bag were stolen from her, she would be destitute.

Alisdair rang every day. She could give him no news. There was still the slender hope that she might arrive at the house in North Barkwith on New Year's Eve. It was clutching at straws.

"My dear, my dear," Louise quavered on the telephone as that day came and went, "what can I say? I shall pray." A sure sign of desperation in that redoubtable lady, Diana thought wryly. She couldn't imagine Louise having much faith in the administrative powers of God. If only she had herself. More straws.

From Philip, there was nothing. Diana was relieved. She didn't know how much of the story he or Louise had been told. She hardly dared think. The trouble that had fallen on her house was a disfigurement. A new disgrace that enveloped them all. In the opinion of a man like Philip Strang-Steele, they would never recover.

But Diana was in Philip's thoughts. Warned to stay out of it, he chafed with frustration. He wanted resolute action. As the church bells rang out across his brown Lincolnshire fields on the morning of New Year's Day, he made up his mind. Better split the available forces. Alisdair could host the tenant farmers' rough shoot on his own.

"She may not want any help but she's going to get it," he shot at Alisdair over the breakfast table. Devilled kidneys and kedgeree. Mrs. Lightbody's special for shooting mornings. He pushed his plate away sharply. "Time's going by. We can't wait any longer. I hope to God it's not too late already. You stay here in case she turns up."

🎣 THE IRON DOLPHIN knocker thundered through Gilbert's Tower less than two hours away. It was Michael who opened the front door.

"Aha! Strang-Steele, I presume," Michael smirked confidently, extending his hand. "Michael Neville. Got a line on my daughter, I expect. Nick of time, my dear fellow. Wife's coming unravelled." He tapped his nose with repellent roguishness. "Have a drink?"

"I don't believe we've met," Philip eyed Neville with stone cold contempt. Ignoring his hand, he walked straight past him into the house.

"Get your wife."

CHAPTER
14

❧ NOTHING BECOMES A man like righteous indignation.

On Philip's handsome features outrage was nobly marked, deepening the channels that ran from his nostrils to the corners of his mouth and seating judgment on his brow. His winter grey eyes were hardened to a sword blade blue.

"This is a sorry state of affairs, Diana," he stated, investing the common phrase with majesty. "Highly unsatisfactory."

"I couldn't agree with you more." Diana greeted his tightly buttoned understatement wanly. She walked down the main staircase, offended pride warring with gladness at seeing him. But she wished most fervently that he could not see *her*.

A week of highly coloured imaginings about Yolanda, the strain of incarceration with Michael and the overwhelming difficulties associated with Alisdair's resignation had taken their toll. Diana had lost five pounds in weight which she could ill afford to do. The day before yesterday, she would normally have washed her hair. Just now, at the news of Philip's arrival, she had made up her face with the hurried, over liberal hand of those who must make a public appearance in the midst of private despair.

Nor was the house at its best. Michael had a genius for destroying the art in little things.

Beside the chair upon which Philip had been surlily directed to wait, there was an oaken chest. The time honoured arrangement of a porcelain chamber stick, brass mounted barograph and card tray had been roughly pushed aside to sicken the eye and make room for a pile of unopened mail and an empty cigarette packet. It was the same everywhere. Mrs. Sedgely's caring hand was not there to set things patiently to rights. Diana had not the heart.

There was general neglect, too. Fallen pine needles strewed the tiles in the hall. The fringes of the rugs were tangled, not lying soldier straight as Diana liked them. Unwound, the long case clock stood mute. The scent of beeswax and bread had given way to a stale, beery smell.

"You've come at a bad moment," Diana's helplessly gesturing hand was caught and held. Philip kissed her firmly on the left cheek.

"I should have come sooner." He placed his hands on her shoulders and looked down at her consideringly.

Diana resisted the temptation to collapse against him. She must pull herself together.

"Fine house," Philip commented briefly to allow her time to recover. "Is there anywhere we can talk?"

There was a fire in the book room's small grate and the kitchen stove was going. The book room's closed door might as well have had "Keep Out" painted on it. Michael was in there. Diana did not want to entertain Philip Strang-Steele in the kitchen. She suggested the garden. There was a little weak winter sunshine, enough to warm the vine conservatory, although there was no heating there at this time of year.

"No, I don't think so," Philip rejected this suggestion with the trace of a smile "Alisdair tells me you have an interesting little library here—your study, I believe. And that your husband has a magnificent modern office at the top of the house of his own—a gift from you, I understand."

"Yes, but . . ."

"So we shall not be incommoding him unduly if we lay claim to your territory, shall we?"

Philip strode to the book room door and opened it wide, signalling Diana to pass through it before him. Diana did as she was bid, propelled into the shooting zone like the ball in a game of hockey. She had no time to decide which player's stick she most detested.

"Ah, Neville," Philip's eyes fastened on Michael. "I've a few things of importance to say to your wife, so I'd be glad if you'd excuse us for a while. I'm afraid our own introduction must wait. Time presses."

Michael left abruptly, slamming the door so that a cloud of smoke fogged the room. It might have been worse.

"You should not have done that," Diana rounded on Philip angrily. "This is *my* house."

"Just so," he pronounced magisterially. "Where may I sit?"

A scratch at the door prevented her reply and Diana went to open it. The orange cat ran in on silent, white tipped paws. He was thin, his coat unkempt but his tail was erect, waving at the tip. Diana, pleased beyond measure to see him, stooped to gather him into her arms. For once the cat did not resist. The intimacy was graciously permitted.

"Sit there, Philip, on the sofa. Excuse me a moment, I must get this animal something to eat."

"Let me," Philip took the cat from her expertly. Their fingers touched and, for an instant, locked together in jubilation over the quarrel they need not now have.

Philip knew all about the orange cat and did not ask its name.

REFUSING COFFEE, DIANA's dragon slayer consumed four cups of very strong tea with three sugar lumps in each.

His battle plans were laid and he ticked them off with the complacency of a card player holding all four aces. About the battle ground, he seemed to know almost as much as Diana herself. Intelligently, he began his summary of the proposed action at the end.

Diana was to be introduced to a temporary but necessary diet of dependence. There was a risk she might find it indigestible. Philip fed the least concentrated doses first.

"Now, Mrs. Sedgely is covered for her hip operation under your company's medical insurance scheme, isn't she?"

Bemused, Diana nodded. Alisdair was a most conscientious double agent.

"Right. Where should she go? The Yorkshire Clinic? Let's get her in there. The sooner she has it done, the quicker her convalescence will be over. In the meantime, my Mrs. Lightbody will take over here."

Diana's squawk of protest was quelled with a glance.

"It's no inconvenience to me. Her sister will fill her place at my house for the time being. Mrs. Lightbody will be paid by me as usual . . . in compensation for the trouble caused . . . and you will pay her whatever you would have paid Mrs. Sedgely. That is arranged."

"Is it, indeed?"

"Yes, it is." Philip brushed aside the implied objection serenely.

"Business starts again tomorrow, although it's a quiet time for English Gardens . . . that's correct, isn't it?"

It was, of course. In January there was little in the way of harvesting or planting to be done by gardeners. The work was all in planning and forward selling. Management functions.

"Good. Alisdair will attend to all of that by telephone and fax. He's as well able to visit your suppliers and retailers from where he is as from here, though," he added, "I know where he'd rather *be*."

"Philip," Diana interrupted him firmly. "Alisdair resigned. I understood that conditions here made it impossible for him to work his notice . . ."

"Quite. Which is why he will work it at a distance on half pay."

Diana was reluctantly grateful. It would be unwise to probe into who was the originator of this scheme.

"Would he help me find his replacement?" she asked.

"We'll see about that later." Philip was clearly anxious to proceed to his next point. "Now, I gather you have, or had, a recording session in Manchester tomorrow? Something to do with a breakfast television programme."

"It's live, actually. But of course, I can't go," Diana started guiltily. She had, in fact, forgotten all about it. Everything was falling apart. "If Yolanda . . ."

"Have you cancelled?" Philip looked up sharply.

"No. Not yet, I'm afraid. I keep hoping Yolanda will come back and everything can go on as normal."

A pitiable delusion. Diana crashed her cup down and bit the inside flesh of her thumb to prevent the tears from coming. It would be some moments before the convulsion subsided and she could speak. Fortunately, she didn't have to.

"Don't cancel. I've been looking at the audience ratings for that programme. Several million in its own area. It's syndicated to Central TV, too. The commercial breaks are a bargain. With you talking about your normal business, the recall factor will be exceptionally high . . ."

Not having the least idea what he was speaking about, Diana stared at him in disappointment. He had written Yolanda off.

"How could I possibly . . . ?"

"If it meant getting Yolanda back," Philip spoke in a dry, precise tone, "I'm quite sure you'd be prepared to do a tap dance in front of the cameras . . . and it won't come to that. Twenty-four hours should do it. Go and pack. One night. We should be back here by tomorrow lunchtime. Oh, and bring the most recent photograph of Yolanda you can find."

Philip's cryptic orders were given quietly, with the absolute conviction of one who has never been disobeyed. Deciding that a contest now would be inappropriate, Diana went upstairs. When she came down with a coat over her shoulders, she found Philip washing up the tea things in the kitchen. Unutterably moved, she watched him complete the humble domestic task in silence. This voluntary subduing of his own power was a subtle kind of bargain. A token service in exchange for submission. He placed the damp tea towel over the bright steel rail of the stove to dry and turned to face her. There was no need to say anything.

Further explanations were delayed until they were both seated in Philip's dark blue Bristol. A motor car of vast proportions and expensive anonymity of style, it was powered by aviation fuel in specially fitted aluminium tanks. Diana saw them when Philip placed her dressing case in the boot.

"Is it quick?" she asked slyly, remembering his defensiveness over the old Bentley.

"Quite quick," he nodded soberly. "People who understand machinery take an interest in it."

Squashed, Diana conceded him the point with admiration.

"Have you told your husband where you're going?"

"Mm. As best I could."

That was not quite true. Diana had knocked on the closed door of his attic study. There had been no reply. Trying to enter, she'd found the room locked.

"Michael!"

Still no reaction. Just the parrot screech of a computer printer. Perhaps he couldn't hear her. Diana scribbled a note and left it face up outside the door, as a child parleying with an alienated parent does. She felt she had run away. There would be all that to face tomorrow. One thing at a time.

Philip's plan, already half executed by the time he and Diana were on the westward bound carriageway of the M62, had a lordly simplicity.

Diana would make a sixty-second film appealing for information regarding the whereabouts of her daughter and offering a substantial reward. The owner of a Manchester film studio had been tracked down at his private address by a fast-acting young trouble-shooter on Philip's main board. Objections to opening the facility on a public holiday had been overcome with the offer of a handsome premium.

Others, too, had been dragged from vinous slumbers, early golf games and family brunches. Philip's Lincolnshire secretariat was busy now reviving dormant lines of communication up and down the country. His personal briefing to Diana was interrupted ceaselessly by the buzz of the car telephone.

"Yes, she's with me now . . . two o'clock . . . No reason to suppose so . . . If we're late, tell them to wait. Don't call me again on this thing."

With the co-operation of the television company's principal media salesman, commercial advertisers had been persuaded to sell slots from their individual schedules, both during the broadcast of the breakfast programme and at intervals throughout the day, to the Strang-Steele Group. A completely personal emergency was admitted and no charity was expected. The slots changed hands at a worthwhile profit to the commercial advertisers. Negotiations for new slots were still in progress.

Diana's appeal would be seen once every fifteen minutes in the designated areas between six and nine in the morning of the following day. Thereafter, the frequency would reduce to every half hour. If there was no news of Yolanda by noon, a provisional plan for nationwide air time would be activated. Total saturation. If a further twenty-four hours' exposure failed to do the trick, a campaign on the continent would go ahead.

"If you ask me, we shall know by tomorrow night at the latest. And, Diana," Philip read her thoughts, "if you mention money to me, I shall find it hard to forgive you."

Jaw clenched, he kept his eyes on the tarmacked ribbon of road winding up beneath them. Diana realised the argument was best postponed. She could never repay him, anyway.

At an average of eight thousand pounds per slot, even allowing for series rates, Philip was ready to spend nearly half a million on the first day. The ability to conceive of such a scheme depended on the power to pay for it. No wonder the rich had few friends. Their potency was crushing.

Diana entertained these thoughts gloomily until the Bristol flew up into the desolate Pennine ramparts which still, in the mind, walled the great province of Yorkshire from its historic enemy. There were fog warnings flashing. Fifty miles an hour, thirty miles an hour. Down to ten in places. Sleet with short, angry flurries of hailstones battered at the windscreen. The glowering moors themselves frowned on this road, punishing the hubris of engineers.

A sign pointed the way to Saddleworth. The Moors Murders. The traffic, relatively light on New Year's Day, was forced to creep slowly past the abandoned farmhouses, the Golgothas of tormented children and their unmarked graves.

To find Yolanda alive, Diana knew she must bear with Philip's patronage. It was offered in friendship, even if it could only be accepted with a tinge of bitterness. Motherhood without omnipotence was nature's nastiest stroke.

"What are you going to do about him?" Philip broke in on her thoughts suddenly.

Diana did not answer immediately. The question was too suspiciously, cunningly broad.

"Look, Diana. I know everything that happened. You mustn't blame Alisdair. I never spend my money blindly and . . ."

"*I* was forbidden to speak of money!" Diana reminded him with heat.

"Yes. I'm sorry. I will express myself better. I like to know what I am doing and why I'm doing it . . . Is that better?"

"Yes. Of course, I understand."

"Well?"

"Michael? Get him to take the best psychiatric advice I can find. What else?"

Philip drummed the tips of his fingers on the steering wheel. The descent into Lancashire had begun now. He pursed his lips doubtfully. This was not a direction he had intended the conversation to take. It surprised him.

"Do you think he needs it?"

"Don't you? How else do you explain what he has done?" Diana turned to look at Philip. It was so obvious, surely?

"I don't explain it. Your husband, it seems to me, is bad . . . not mad. Blast!"

Philip had mistakenly followed signs for Manchester Airport. They were halfway down the slip road. Amid snorts of irritation, a stop was made on the hard shoulder and a map unfolded. A traffic patrol car halted behind them.

"What's up, sir?"

Corrupted by the aroma of influence emanating from the car and its occupants, the constable politely supervised a 'U' turn.

The subject of Michael's delinquency was not touched on again. Had it been, a deeply felt difference of opinion, too soon expressed, might have altered the course of events.

❦ THE STUDIO STAFF were standing by when they arrived in the converted garment warehouse just off Deansgate.

The place, snaked with cable and blue hazed with cigarette smoke, swarmed with cameramen, supernumaries demanded by union rules, weasel hipped men carrying clipboards and make-up women in white overalls. A microwave oven was processing frozen pizza. Diana was offered some.

She nibbled at it, standing up while a number of tall blond girls were paraded for inspection. They were models. Five foot eight inches tall, size twelve with straight hair reaching to the elbow. Stationary and viewed from the back in a Loden coat just like Yolanda's, any one of them could have been her. Disturbed, Diana selected one at random. The successful candidate immediately removed her hair with her Alice band. It was hot under the lights, the girl explained chattily. Diana staggered slightly. Did Yolanda get split ends with having such long hair? the girl wanted to know.

"OK," the Artistic Director shouted. "The rest of you can go home. Submit your expenses through your agencies. You, Zelda . . . Selma . . . whatever your name is, we'll have to work on your walk. No puma stuff."

Philip thanked the rejected half dozen for coming and presented each with a sealed, unmarked envelope. They were well pleased with the contents.

A conference on the script followed and a hairdressing session for Diana. It was four o'clock before shooting began. The Artistic Director found fault with everything, studio time being charged by the hour. Diana, he said, was inexperienced and unaware of her mannerisms on camera. Patently untrue, as her repose was a byword among the television crews who had worked with her. Philip lost his temper.

"Get on with it, man. We're not making *Gone with the Wind* here. And get off Mrs. Neville's back."

Things went more smoothly after that and by nine o'clock in the evening the Artistic Director minced nervily up to Philip and told him he'd got enough to cobble something together. Diana was dropping with fatigue.

"You'd better be sure it's hand-stitched or you'll need a good surgeon to cobble *you* together," Philip growled. Diana placed her hand on his arm. He patted it apologetically.

"I'm sorry," he said. "I don't like not having a choice. But if this isn't done in time for the broadcast tomorrow, we've lost the initiative."

They went to a nearby Chinese restaurant to eat while the film was cut. An hour. It wasn't worth going to the hotel. They ordered shark's fin soup and Peking duck. The sullen faced waiter said it would take forty minutes. Diana excused herself and went to the ladies' room. Ten minutes after her return, the food appeared.

"What did you do? Grease his palm with silver?"

"No, I relied on charm," Philip grimaced with mock ferocity.

Tired and troubled as she was, Diana laughed. He was very good to be with.

They ate quickly and quietly, saying little. Diana's mind strayed to Gilbert's Tower. It might have been years since she was there. Yolanda, she could not think about. It was too dangerous to hope. She was drifting loose.

Back at the studio, the film was still not quite ready. Exasperated, Philip undertook to drive Diana to the Hilton. She had an early start for the Granada studios the next morning. She should go to bed. He would come back to the studio alone to pick up the completed video tape and have it delivered to her room.

He brought it himself at nearly midnight. Expecting a messenger, Diana had left her bedside light on. In spite of that, she had fallen asleep. His knock unanswered, Philip walked in and locked the door behind him. Diana opened her eyes.

"Oh, it's you . . ."

"I've got it. What time do you have to be up in the morning?" He picked up the telephone beside her bed.

"Five. It's all right, the hotel switchboard will call me."

Philip dropped the telephone and began to strip off his clothes with virile efficiency. He kept his eyes from her and Diana watched him in silence. She wondered at what moment she would become afraid or disgusted. Apart from Michael's, she knew no man's body. Philip's frame was revealed to her, tight-muscled and cared for, with long, lean flanks. His chest hair was grey. Composed, he adjusted his shirt on the back of a chair fastidiously and allowed her to look her fill. In the silence which filled the room, they both knew it was the greatest risk he had taken yet, by far. When he turned to her, Diana held out her arm to him, palm uppermost and open. A smile of pure delight touched his eyes.

Sitting on the bed beside her, he offered her his wrist. Diana removed his watch in a final gesture of assent. They were adults and there was no need for very much talk. Philip's hand hesitated on the lamp switch until Diana's closed over it and she extinguished the light herself.

Philip lay on top of her with his face buried between the hollow of her jaw bone and shoulder. Again, he waited tensely for her to change her mind.

"So what do you call this, then, Mr. Strang-Steele?" she asked him at length, smiling in the dark.

"I think, my darling, it would be most convenient to you if we were to call it rape."

"My reputation?"

"Just so."

He made love to her four times during the night. In between whiles, they slept entwined like married teenagers. When the alarm call came, Diana woke immediately, fresh from an eternity of rest. Cradled like an infant in the crook of Philip's arm, she slipped free of his tightening embrace to kiss the pretended morning frowns away.

"Why don't you make yourself useful again?" she goaded him lightly. "You must have slept an hour at least, already."

"I'm an old man," Philip groaned. Veiled by lowered lids, his eyes were glittering slits. Diana knotted her fingers into his steel spring curls and pulled.

"You're a satyr. A prowler in the woods."

He took her again, suddenly and joyously.

Before leaving her, he tipped her chin and looked down into her eyes. The questions Diana read in his own could not be answered until Yolanda was found.

Left with a bare fifteen minutes in which to bathe and dress, Diana did so with tears in her eyes. Unrepeatable happiness is better not experienced. Her mascara ran. She smudged it carefully with her fingertip. It really looked quite good.

❦ AT HALF PAST eight, the breakfast time broadcast was almost over and Yolanda was betrayed.

Her landlady, frying bacon in a quilted house coat, had less than a quarter of her mind on the television set. She always put it on for cheerfulness. Right through the day. It didn't much matter what was on. You had to do something, hadn't you? Too much quiet was bad for people. Creepy. So the spindle-fine woman framed in the picture made small impression at first. Neville, they called her. She was going on about England's forgotten treasures ... some such nonsense. By heck, people like that got some ideas in their heads. Plain barmy. A job of real work ... that's what *she* needed. Her with her walled garden and lily white hands ...

This idle train of thought was suspended by the need to fish a rasher of bacon out of the pan and hang it over the sink to let the fat drip off. "Should've grilled it ... and a lot of extra bother for nothing it would've been an' all."

That Yolanda Neville was a real fusspot about her food. She wanted *fresh* orange juice with her breakfast, if you please, and coffee, not tea. Well, that was extra. She'd had to be told. "Oh, really?" says Miss. "I only mean packet, reconstituted stuff. I don't expect you to squeeze oranges for me, Mrs. Evans. And instant coffee will do quite well. I didn't know it was dearer than tea." So sharp she'd cut herself one of these days.

She was elbow deep in Fairy Liquid suds when her attention was caught by the television again. It was just after the ads. The nice one for Clayton's Crispy Crackers had finished when she saw that woman again. Diana Neville. Her that had been on before. Only she looked different and this wasn't an ad.

"This young lady has a similar figure to my daughter, is exactly the same height and weight ... tan boots ... a coat like this one ... German ... *Junker* label ... inverted pleat at the back . . . black velvet Alice band . . . leather shoulder-bag and a small blue hold-all like this one, here. She was dressed like this when she was last seen in Nidcaster."

There were some more details. A beige handknit jersey, the make of the bag . . . Mrs. Evans stopped what she was doing and turned up the volume. She felt funny all over.

"Anyone who can give information which will enable me to trace Yolanda will receive a reward of five thousand pounds in cash. Please ring this number. You need not give your name. If my daughter is found alive and . . ." Diana Neville's voice broke here. Shame, it was. The landlady found her fund of human compassion expanding. ". . . and in good health, at any time before the end of this week, the reward will be ten thousand pounds . . ."

There was a step in the passage. Mrs. Evans turned the television off smartly. Miss Sly Boots was bringing her tray down. Going job hunting this morning, she was. Wicked. Her poor mother! She should think of the girls her age who had no home. The reward was neither here nor there.

It wasn't as though there were many landladies as would take a stray girl in at Christmas, Mrs. Evans congratulated herself. Too trusting. That's what she'd been. It was her nature.

Mrs. Evans began to dial the number. Good job she'd a memory for things like that. Better not give her name. Not at first. You didn't know where things like that could lead. There was the tax to think of.

🎜 "I'M AFRAID IT'S not over yet." Philip dented Diana's euphoria as he replaced the car telephone. "Have you thought who is going to fetch her away from that place?"

Diana had not. But she could see what Philip meant.

The landlady had already received strict instructions to do and say nothing to Yolanda. She would be contacted again shortly. Meanwhile there were decisions to be made, questions to be answered.

The remaining sixty-second slots were returned to the original advertisers. Of course, they kept the margin they'd made on the sale. Even so, Philip said, the whole exercise had been cost effective. But you couldn't buy trust. Whom would Yolanda trust?

"Could your Mr. Sedgely go?" Philip looked sideways at Diana.

She was iridescent. How much was due to the good news about Yolanda and how much to their lovemaking, he couldn't say. The morning after the first night was always awkward. The need to raise the barriers again. To pretend nothing has changed . . . to give each other a chance to escape. *Leave me now while I can still bear it. While I can still pretend to bear it.* Philip hoped and believed he would not have to bear any such thing.

It was only fifty miles to Leeds now . . . and then Nidcaster. He didn't know what would happen next. He was as much in her hands today as she had been in his yesterday. It was up to her now.

"No," Diana replied to his question. "I suppose Sedgely must know that Yolanda is missing by now. I never told him myself . . . but other people know. But I couldn't talk to Mr. Sedgely about . . ." Diana found she couldn't bring herself to name Michael, "our domestic problems."

"I could go," Philip volunteered.

"And say what? That your son is a paragon of virtue and her father's a villain? You'd never get to first base with Yolanda, I'm afraid. It's my husband she believes in, remember," Diana reasoned.

Leeds, twenty-five miles. Diana noticed the sigh flash by. Tonight would be the first and most painful night of the rest of her life. It would get better. The memory would fade. Love was like that. You could starve it to death.

"Then let him go," Philip said. "I'd ask my mother but . . ."

"No. Please, no." That was unthinkable. Louise was an old lady of respectable parentage. "I hope to God you haven't told her the whole story."

"No, darling. Of course not. This is between the four of us. No one else."

Orphaned as soon as spoken, the endearment dropped between them. Only fifteen miles to Leeds now. Diana looked out of the window at the unloved fields dotted with gimcrack industrial units and tried to imagine she was somebody else, not caught between the rigid tramlines of her own existence.

Philip picked up the telephone and held an obscure conversation with Alisdair. It was about money.

"We'll let him do his own explaining . . . See if there's a branch in Nidcaster . . . Yes, she wants it in cash . . . Briggs can go up and get it . . . tell him to hang on with the car until we arrive."

There was some more talk and then Philip seemed to change his mind. "Look, no. Let's not mess about. Tell them I'll collect it myself."

In Nidcaster, snow was falling from a pewter sky in large, wet flakes. They crossed over the gorge by the East Bridge and joined the near vertical queue of traffic climbing to the market square. A corporation gritting lorry, descending on the other side with air brakes squealing, hurled sand and salt over the Bristol's bonnet.

"It looks as though they think it's going to be bad," Diana commented. They were stuck for a quarter of an hour.

A man wearing an army surplus combat jacket tapped at the passenger door window. It was Ned Garvey.

"Any news?" He mouthed the question. The story of Yolanda's disappearance was now common property. Philip depressed the electric button to roll the window down and leaned across Diana.

"I want to get to Barclay's Bank by twelve o'clock. Is there any way out of this?"

Ned got in the back of the car and guided Philip first to the left through a no entry sign and a series of narrow alleys prohibited to traffic. The Bristol squeezed past the tall, beetling houses with inches to spare. At one point a policeman barred their way.

"Now then, Mrs. Neville," he pre-empted her special pleading and waved them on.

They parked in the market square on a double yellow line. Ned was delighted to be asked to sit in the driver's seat while Philip went into the bank. Local government made too much out of parking tickets.

After a few minutes, Philip returned with a black attaché case.

"You've found her then," Ned said before Philip got back into the car. "That's t'reward, isn't it? Well, I'll be off then. I'm right glad for you, Mrs. Neville. She's a champion lass, is Miss Yolanda."

The last line echoed queerly in Diana's head. *Miss* Yolanda?

Ned had been an early playmate of her daughter's. Messing about in boats. Now she had become the young lady from Gilbert's Tower, a wealthy man's fiancée, a person famous for her absence. Ned had promoted her and let her go. Rather sad. You never knew when your children were grown up till other people told you.

At Gilbert's Tower, a black Austin Princess was drawn up beside the other cars outside the garden door. In it sat Philip's chauffeur, Briggs. He had brought Mrs. Lightbody who was already in the house.

"You'd better go in and get your husband," Philip said bleakly. Clearly he did not intend to accompany Diana indoors. "Briggs will drive him down to Retford with the money."

"Couldn't he drive himself down?"

Philip looked at her. He put his hand up to stroke her cheek but realising the chauffeur could see him, dropped it again.

"I think, for all sorts of reasons, that might not be wise. And you know, if anything goes wrong ... if Briggs is there, at least we'll get some sort of report."

Inside, Diana found Sedgely sitting in the kitchen with Mrs. Lightbody.

There were introductions and hand shakings. Had Mrs. Lightbody found herself a room yet? No, of course not. Diana would see to that in a minute. She was so sorry not to have been there to greet her. Mrs. Neville was not to worry, Mrs. Lightbody said. She had bigger things to think about. Mrs. Sedgely had sent a helpful list of household directions. Mr. Alisdair had handled all that side of things with the Sedgelys. Everyone, it seemed, was becomingly grateful to everybody else. The kitchen looked better already. So did Sedgely. Much more cheerful.

It left Diana with nothing to do but tackle Michael. She found him, to her surprise and relief, at the top of the house in his own study. Dorothy was with him. Would that be the next tug-of-war?

Data spreadsheets were pouring out of the printer as Diana walked in.

"Oh," Michael looked up coolly. "You and the Farm Boy have a good time? Any luck?" Diana regarded him warily. Did he even remember where she had been, and why? It was as if the events of the last twenty-four hours had never taken place.

"Dorothy, dear," Diana turned to the girl. "Would you excuse Mr. Neville and me for a few minutes?"

"Epoch's been trying to contact you."

"I'm sure they have. Perhaps you'd go and telephone them for me and say I'll speak to Mr. Olaff after two o'clock today, if that's convenient?"

Routed, Dorothy left the room with a shrug. There was a challenging sway to her hips. Michael winked at her. Automatically, and from long habit, Diana erased the detail from her mind. His transient infidelities were never mentioned between them.

"Michael, we know where Yolanda is. With any luck at all, she doesn't yet know that we do. Retford. You must go and persuade her to come home." Diana sat down on the edge of a chair facing his desk.

"Why me, for God's sake? I've got to get over to the industrial unit this afternoon to use the mainframe computer ... can't you go?" Michael loosened the knot of his tie and shuffled the files on his desk. "I've got enough on here. I want these figures for the flotation finalised by the end of the month."

"No, Michael. I'm sorry but that will have to wait. You are the only person who can put this right. Yolanda will want to know from you that what you said about Alisdair and me was ... what you call a joke ..." Diana failed to keep the contempt out of her voice.

"Christ! You're a vindictive bitch ..." Michael picked up the files and hurled them into the corner of the room. The pages scattered. "You've always got to have your pound of fucking flesh, haven't you?"

"Would you like me to divorce you, Michael?" She had never intended to say it.

"Good God, no. Fucking Christ! No! Whatever makes you say that?" Michael's face greyed with shock, his features slack. For the first time Diana was able to see how he would age. "You're a miserable old witch ... but I've always loved you." A tic at the corner of his mouth tried and failed to lift it into a smile. His chin wobbled frighteningly.

The responsibility was hers.

All women are mothers of sons in their hearts. Diana no more than the rest could let a man weep or fight the impulse without offering comfort. No promise is too extravagant, from a lollipop to life after death, if only it will chase away the catastrophe of masculine tears. To be the cause of such visible grief stabbed Diana cruelly. She went to her husband and put her arms around him.

Speechless, he submitted to having his tie re-knotted and his jacket put on him.

"Don't, darling. Don't," she said to him.

He went downstairs with her, his shoulder touching hers.

Outside, the snow had stopped though the sky still threatened. Philip, seeing Diana come out of the garden door with Michael, got out of the Austin Princess where he had been sitting with Briggs.

"You'd better get off, Neville, and get back. My chauffeur has the money. Stop in Nidcaster tonight, Briggs, if it gets any worse."

Michael nodded and got into the car. The chauffeur slipped from his place behind the wheel to close the door, but Michael clung to Diana's hand. She disengaged herself gently.

"We'll talk when you get back," she murmured. Philip averted his eyes courteously. Neville's days were numbered.

He and Diana stood together to watch the black car pull away up the narrow lane.

"When shall I see you again, Diana?" Thoughtfully, he did not touch her. The next move must be hers.

"Not soon, I'm afraid. I've a great deal to do." Feeling him stiffen, Diana turned to look up into his face. "Philip, you know I can never thank you enough for what you've done for us ... but my husband needs me."

"I am happy," Philip replied, seeing it was over, "to have been of assistance. I hope all goes well." His words struck like thin whips. He would accept no refreshment but got into his car and left immediately. To linger would compromise her dignity and his. She had made her choice.

What was it, Philip asked himself savagely, that they had done last night in that hotel room? Had she been settling a debt with him? Had he exacted payment? No. None of that. There had been no meanness between them. His flesh was imbued with the memory of her. It would have to serve him.

Diana walked back into the house, a knot of pain in her chest. No tears. There had been enough of those already. She and Mrs. Lightbody spent the afternoon turning out Yolanda's room.

"What does she like best to eat, Mrs. Neville?"

"Short of lobster? Spaghetti Bolognese. *Spagbog*, she calls it." Michael liked it, too.

❧ MICHAEL FOUND HIS journey down the A1 irksome. Visibility was poor and it was nose to tail in the slow lane. Strang-Steele's chauffeur was a taciturn sod. He drove the old limousine as if it had oxen under the bonnet, not a halfway decent engine.

To calm his nerves, Michael chain smoked.

He thought briefly to Diana. It had been a close shave. Out of the blue. Whatever had got into her? She'd never go. She needed him too much, always had. He needed her, of course. But that was different. Strang-Steele? Never. Michael dismissed the suspicion almost before it was formed. That bastard must be a good ten years older than he was himself. Well, thereabouts. He looked as though his cock got frostbite a long time ago. Disinfectant in his veins. No, that was a non-starter. Not Diana.

Still, it had taken the wind out of his sails for a moment. They got difficult, women, at that age. Must be lousy to have your life ruled by hormones. Yes, living with women and their mixed-up insides was no picnic. Bloody martyrdom at times.

"Go on, put your foot down! You can get past this lot."

"I think not, sir. The speed limit is fifty miles an hour." Briggs was imperturbable.

By the time they arrived at the address given to Briggs, Yolanda was ingesting an early high tea in the poppy papered parlour. Sausage and chips. Surprisingly ungreasy. Mrs. Evans was making an effort. Her father's arrival interrupted the meal.

"We've been looking high and low for you, Landa," he said, appearing round the door. "Got a chip for your old man?"

Yolanda greeted him composedly. There must have been a search. It was nice to know. Mrs. Evans would get him a cup of tea if he wanted one, although she hoped she realised it would be extra. Her landlady's favourite word.

"Not when she sees what I've brought her," Michael chuckled. Yes, he would have tea. He supposed there was nothing stronger.

"Unless you want Harvey's Bristol Cream, no. 'Fraid not, Daddy." Michael made a grimace of distaste and agreed to tea.

A fresh pot. It was no trouble, none at all. The kettle was always on in this house.

"She's taken a shine to you, Daddy," Yolanda said drily, observing her landlady's gruesomely girlish performance.

Mrs. Evans' bustle of hospitality gave Yolanda an opportunity to collect her thoughts.

In the first surprise flash of recognition, her father looked strange to her. Against the wallpaper, too bold for the space it covered, the shag carpet with the glazed cabinet holding its population of costume dolls and chromium plated cake baskets, Michael seemed to have an extra dimension. He came from a bigger place . . . a stone dug out of a deeper setting. In the same instant, Yolanda felt herself bedded too shallowly in her new anonymity and Mrs. Evans' boarding house. It was all too near the edge of things. No safety margin.

There were worse things than being found. Her flight had been a reflex. An uncontrollable spasm. And then a revenge . . . but the condition of non-existence had palled rather. A dreadful thing had been done to her. She would never forgive them, never. But should that stop her being who she was? Yolanda Neville was still a workable vehicle for self. Not, after all, a write off.

Suicide? Yes, the idea had crossed her mind. A romantic flirtation only. Death was a suitor with nothing to offer.

Her father, his face, smiling and familiar, was like an unexpected present . . . giving her back to herself. A touchstone of reality. They should be together.

"I was going to write to you, Daddy, actually." Yolanda spread some strawberry jam on half a slice of bread purposefully. High tea was nice once you got used to it, and got it organised. No marge. "Don't you think it would be a good idea if you and I went to London to live? I could get on another course and with that money you have . . ."

A trickle of words swelled to a flood. Yolanda needed quite desperately to talk. Michael let her. It was going to be easier than he thought.

He made no direct admissions. It had all been a storm in a teacup . . . a bit of a balls up. His rotten hangover. Her mother, she must understand, was still an amazingly attractive woman. And Yolanda's bloke wasn't too bad, either. Not for the world would Michael have let Yolanda hear . . . A man was bound to wonder . . . that was something she would learn when she was older . . . Do anything not to have said it. Stupid mistake. And all that. A tear or two winked in his eyes. He dashed them away boyishly with the back of his hand.

"Oh, Landa. You know what I'm like . . . always a bit over the top . . ."

Michael, abject, was irresistible. And Yolanda was homesick. Later she would think of Alisdair . . . unwrap him from his packaging of lies. Could he really be the same? Just now, it was enough to be going home to Gilbert's Tower.

"Come on, sweetheart, get your things before your mother finally does her nut. I promised I'd run you to earth and get you back home. I'm in enough trouble as it is . . ."

Briggs, having quartered the building, decided that guarding the front door was the best way to ensuring that his master's money ended up with the right person. Not that Mr. Strang-Steel had said much. Just that he, Briggs, was to ensure that the money was safely delivered to this Evans woman.

He need not have worried. Michael handed over the attaché case to the landlady. She wiped her hands on her apron before taking it.

"Thanks for all your help," Michael said to her as he picked up Yolanda's hold-all. "Do count it if you want, it's all there. Ten thousand quid . . ."

The landlady opened the case and gazed. No, she trusted Mr. Neville. Having Miss Neville had been a pleasure. No trouble. If only she'd known before . . .

"Oh, Daddy," Yolanda said, stricken. She had been going to write that very evening.

"Doesn't matter, darling. Cheap at the price. Got more than that for *The Folly of Fashion*."

Briggs heard none of this and it was some time before Yolanda knew the truth. Ned Garvey was better placed, however. He gave it as his opinion that Alisdair Strang-Steele's father had put up the brass.

"Aye. So he should an' all. It were 'is son as caused the trouble in t'first place. Fair do's."

That was Nidcaster's way of looking at the facts. Had the townspeople known them all, there would still have been some who blamed the Mummers' Play.

CHAPTER
15

  ANY DISSECTION OF the past eight days was disallowed by Michael. Diana, he said, was far too fond of post-mortems. A morbid streak, he said, which prolonged their quarrels needlessly.

"I try to learn from our mistakes ... it's only so that we don't do the same thing to each other again."

Diana had no awareness of exceptional generosity in her "our"s and "we"s. It was a lifelong habit to assume a share of the blame for their scenes. She may have hoped, long ago, that Michael would in fairness absolve her, but he never did. They were in it together. It took two to tango, as her own mother used to say.

"If we can't talk about it, we can't sort it out, can we?"

But she had said it too often before. Amateur psychology was dangerous and boring ... a flimsy excuse for nagging, Michael said. Quietly, Diana gave up any idea of suggesting psychiatric treatment. It would only cause another row. Michael could never be brought to regard his own behaviour as having any clinical significance. Perhaps it didn't. Perhaps Philip had been right, after all. Badness not madness. That left only repentance as a cure. And no human being, Diana told herself, could administer that medicine ... let alone judge of its effectiveness.

As in the past, Michael's own method of dealing with the more terrible passages of their life together was adopted. A lid was clapped over the smell. Covered, the corpse was ignored. The maggots of memory were left to writhe in secret. When they had consumed the corruption, they themselves would die. That was the unspoken theory. It worked, more or less.

Perceptively, Yolanda elected to assist the process. Within a week of returning home she asked for a flat of her own, underlining the seriousness of her request by applying for a formal interview with Diana in the book room.

"Well," Dorothy said impatiently, "any time will do, won't it? She's got no one in particular coming this morning. If that's no good, couldn't you talk to her tonight, Yolanda? She's going out with Sedgely this afternoon."

"*Mr.* Sedgely," Yolanda corrected absently. "And no, any time won't do. Put me in the diary for eleven o'clock tomorrow and let her know I'm coming. Thank you, Dorothy."

The secretary made a face behind Yolanda's back. She hadn't got time for play acting. With Michael under so much pressure it was all she could do to keep pace.

Yolanda turned in time to catch the last insolent ripple on Dorothy's face, who quickly converted it to a smile. Too late. Yolanda smiled herself and said nothing.

❦ "COME IN, DARLING," Diana greeted her the following day. "It makes me feel terribly important when my daughter makes an appointment to see me. I'm flattered."

Making her case did not take Yolanda long. She had thought it out before. Less than two weeks since, she would not have dreamt of speaking to her mother as she did not. There was a difference.

Her admission to adulthood was no longer a matter of the calendar. Her parents had submitted her to an initiation rite so primitive, so savage, that her claims to grown-up status could no longer be laughed off. Questions of blame or fault were irrelevant. She had been shot through a one-way valve. The accident was, in that respect, irreversible. Diana knew it.

"It is because of that," Yolanda concluded forcibly, "that I know I'm in the way. You and Daddy need to be alone. You can't have three grown-ups living in the house."

Diana did not bother to quibble; she knew what Yolanda meant. Not three grown-ups of broadly equal but shifting status, competing for space and honour. There were no marriages of three.

"And there's Alisdair. He won't come here ... I can't always be going down to Lincolnshire ... I have work to do. He's put his cottage on the market, you know," she added after a pause. "We need a base."

"And what will you do in that base?" Diana queried gently.

"I really don't know, Mummy. Do you think it fair to ask me?"

Diana admitted that she did not. She had lost that right the night she slept with Alisdair's father. Although, of course, Yolanda should never know that. That was what this interview was all about. Decent partitions between one life and another.

"Won't you miss Gilbert's Tower?"

"Horribly. But it's not my house, it's yours. I shall come here often, as a visitor. You and Daddy need ... I don't know ... another honeymoon." Yolanda eyed her mother steadily. It was a lot to say, but not too much. She had earned the right.

"I suspect, darling, that you are more grown up than I shall ever be." Diana gave her a lopsided smile. "Thank heaven. You were a terrible child." And then they both laughed.

The matter was quickly settled. Yolanda wanted an increase in her allowance to enable her to rent a small flat in an acceptable area of Harrogate. Diana said no. Property values had slumped. It was a good time to buy. Mr. Meers was consulted.

Tickled pink, as he said he was, to be handling the affairs of yet another FitzGilbert, he gave the question his best efforts. Diana, he said, could not make a gift to her daughter of such value during her lifetime except in consideration of marriage, not without attracting capital transfer tax. But Yolanda was engaged, or should he say betrothed? A lovelier word by far ... if a wedding date could only be set, the new flat could be brought into the marriage settlement and beat the Revenue. There would be a marriage settlement, wouldn't there?

Diana did not like the idea. It meant involving the Strang-Steeles in a purely personal matter between herself and her daughter. Alisdair should not be asked to commit himself to any dates to save the Nevilles tax. And in any case, the amount involved was comparatively small by Strang-Steele standards. They were not to be troubled over it.

She had not reckoned with Yolanda, who relayed these interesting details to Alisdair.

"She mustn't do that," was his first reaction. "Sheer lunacy.

We can set a date, can't we, Landa?" Alisdair too felt the recent *débâcle* loosened the bonds of his promise.

"If we don't it will cost her forty per cent as much again, or more. I'm not quite sure. But she's very touchy about all this. I really don't know why."

Alisdair guessed. Diana was fighting shy of taking anything further from the Strang-Steeles, even if it should not actually cost them a penny. He sympathised. The God of all good Presbyterian Scots knew that Philip Strang-Steele did not throw his money about, but by Jove, he placed it heavily. What he had done recently on Yolanda's own behalf had been concealed from her. It was a weight that none of them wished her to carry. Least of all her future father-in-law.

"Let me think about this, Landa. I'm sure there's a way round it."

Of course, there was no way around it all. But Alisdair persuaded his father to telephone Diana. He was reluctant to do so but could not say as much to his son, or why. The thought of pushing himself in where he had been so plainly told he was not wanted was deeply repugnant to him. But so also was the pusillanimous payment of unnecessary tax to a wasteful Government. Philip's public spirit overcame his private delicacy. He telephoned.

"Ah, Diana," he cleared his throat. "Er . . . look, couldn't we do something about this? These children of ours seem pretty determined. It's a pity to pay tax for nothing. As I understand it, to fulfill the rules, we'd have to bring the wedding date forward. Well, why not? It needn't stop Yolanda finishing her course. I'm happy if you are. Remember," he pointed out astutely, "in this situation, as in many others, one is acting as custodian for one's own heirs. It's a dereliction of duty to chuck money away they could inherit. Listen, my dear . . . forgive me . . . but are you all right?"

Hastily, Diana assured him that she was. A tremor of excitement fluttered in her stomach . . . the nerves of a dead hope twitching. No. There had been no hope. Just one sublime night. And one day, perhaps when they were both very old, she would tell him everything she had felt for him. If she survived Michael, and they lived that long. But for now, she had chosen the granite path of duty and must walk along it. In a single, irresponsible moment she had shown Michael the way out to freedom. But he had not flown the cage. She must also stay.

As for the matter of Yolanda's flat, the marriage settlement, the wedding date and proper tax avoidance, she agreed. Philip was right. He was about most things. Didn't he ever find this unvarying routine of sagacity wearying to his soul? Eyes dancing, she asked him solemnly, for a joke.

"Not to *mine*, I'm happy to tell you, though it may well daunt the frivolous. Goodbye now. We'll speak soon, no doubt."

They had managed it well. Like the kiss in the Norman meadow, the night in Manchester could be forgotten. Or if not forgotten, stored like a dried flower between the leaves of an old book. Sweet still, but fading.

🌾 YOLANDA BOUGHT A flat overlooking the West Park Stray on Byron Walk in Harrogate. It was the best address in Yorkshire, Sedgely said with surprising cuteness.

"You'll be having your tea at Betty's every day, Miss Landa," he teased her. For was not this the acme of every true Yorkshirewoman's ambitions? Yolanda, enchanted by the thought, laughed. She would like to meet the women of her age who had the time to queue and could afford it.

Her flat, with one big living-room, a double bedroom, sunny kitchen and bathroom was in itself modest enough. It was re-decorated and furnished from the surplus riches stored in Gilbert's Tower's unused attic rooms. The kitchen Yolanda painted herself. Pea green gloss on the walls and orange tile-patterned linoleum. She bought some utility furniture at an auction and, with the bliss of ignorance, painted the chairs lemon yellow, the table bottle green. A second-hand cooker, fridge and washer . . . and the kitchen had a kind of smart rusticity. All for a hundred and sixty-five pounds.

Philip, when he heard, was most impressed. He began to ask after her with increasing regularity. It was a fondness growing at a distance. She must go with them to Provence that summer. He still had not met her.

Yolanda was happy and proud. There is no place of one's own like the first. Mrs. Sedgely presented her with a box full of standard provisions all in nice glass jars. Sugar, flour, mustard powder—many things, and amongst them, a generous supply of pickled red cabbage.

"You'll be glad of that, Miss Landa, whenever you've a bit of cold meat to eat up."

Yolanda eyed her uneasily. There was rather a lot.

On the bitterly cold night before she was to leave Gilbert's Tower, she and Diana had a long talk. Outside, the snow was falling softly and Yolanda had a fire in her bedroom. A special, last night treat.

There was little said that had not been said before. Alisdair and the decisions he must make about their future, where they should live after the wedding, the wedding itself. September would seem to be the most convenient month. Things were in a state of flux, weren't they? So many things almost decided but not quite ... other things, addressed but not resolved.

Diana was helping Yolanda to weed her wardrobe. Some garments were to be thrown away, some packed, others stored or given to charity shops. They came to the Loden coat.

"It's a good coat," Yolanda said, "and I know it seems silly ... stupidly extravagant ... but would you mind awfully if we gave that away?"

"No, of course not, darling. I quite understand. I never want to see it again myself. A reminder of a horrid week. Off it goes." Diana threw it on to the discard pile.

Something about the relaxed atmosphere of these informal rites of passage encouraged Yolanda to say what was on her mind. She and her mother had known a greater closeness during the past weeks than at any other time. It was now or never.

"Mummy?"

"Yes, darling?" Diana continued cushioning the folds of a silk party frock with tissue. "Mm ... what is it?"

"Don't you think there's something, or somebody, else who ought to go?"

Diana glanced up at her in bewilderment. "I don't know what you mean."

"Dorothy. You must have seen it yourself. She and Daddy ..."

"Are very busy," Diana ended the sentence for her frigidly.

Yolanda would never forget the stare her mother gave her just then. It killed the words in her mouth and made goose pimples rise on her forearms. She had gone a step too far.

Diana began to talk about coat-hangers immediately. Then there was hot chocolate. Neither of them normally liked it but they agreed, on a night like this, it was a charming thought. No, a better idea. Damson cordial. Yes, why not? They would drink it up here, by the fire. The bad moment was smoothed over.

Yolanda was shaken, embarrassed by her own clumsiness. After they had kissed goodnight, the coldness in her mother's eyes kept coming back. She had only wanted to help. Knowing Daddy wasn't perfect didn't mean she loved him any less. There was one lasting consolation. At least it meant her mother loved her father very much. Whatever happened, their marriage was safe.

That safety threatened her own happiness but affection mists the eyes. When Yolanda's closed in sleep that night, she dreamed nothing of the future.

❦ AT EPOCH, MERLIN Olaff's vision was unclouded by emotion.

"I wish," he said to Diana when they met in London, "that you had told me about your daughter's disappearance."

"But why, Merlin? There was nothing you could do and your offices were closed."

Olaff dismissed that with a small hiss of aggravation. "Look," he pointed at a map of Greater London taped to his office wall, "you have my private number and I have the number of every single Epoch employee within a thirty mile radius of here. The red pins are for creative staff, the blue for accounts, the yellow for administration personnel. It's like the army here. Leave is a privilege. You get it when it suits. When there's a job to be done, the troops fall in, Christmas Day or not, rat-arsed or stone cold sober."

"But what job could you possibly have done that we didn't manage on our own?" Diana was annoyed. Since when was her private life any business of Epoch's?

"I'll tell you. Crisis management . . ."

"The crisis was personal!" Diana flushed slightly. She had raised her voice. Quite improper.

"Not personal, Diana," Olaff leaned forward in his chair. He was not sorry this had come to a head. It was going to make other things less difficult to get across. "You must get rid of this idea that anything to do with you is personal. Quite the reverse. People are interested in you and everything about you. You stand for ... I don't know ... let's say ... Well, goodness, honesty, purity, peace, a little romance, perhaps ... quite a lot of that, in fact. And, since you are a kind of highly cultivated garden fairy, nothing, but nothing, ever goes wrong in your family."

"It does, however. And it did. What am I supposed to do? Sit idly by and mind my image while my child vanishes from my life?"

"No, Diana. No, of course not," Olaff replied on a less incendiary note.

The last thing he wanted was a titanic row with Diana Neville. English Gardens was not Epoch's biggest client, by a long chalk. But the account brought prestige and interest into the lives of the creatives who worked on it. In spite of the company's prohibition on lavish advertising, some pack design specialists had joined Epoch purely for that involvement. The agency valued them. And the Public Relations Department, virtually founded at her request, acquired other PR clients on the back of that continuing success. Losing English Gardens was not a viable option. Bad strategy.

"Come on," he said, reaching for the refrigerator door, "let's have a glass of this and simmer down."

Diana laughed at the lovely northern expression on his lips, which she herself had taught him. Merlin's panacea for all the world's ills was a glass of Chablis. How alike he and Sedgely were, under the skin.

Olaff was able to explain, then, what his objections to Diana's campaign had been. The juxtaposition of the appeal with her excellent performance on the breakfast time broadcast, arranged by Epoch Public Relations, had belied the witchery of English Gardens.

"You were luminous, Diana. You know, when people talk about the way women in love look ... "

The advertising man was not being deliberately impertinent, Diana knew. Only, as he saw it, professional. Nothing at Epoch was too near the bone for speech. And anyway, she had been in a postcoital, roseate haze. Ravishing as a result of ravishment. Curious that people should sense that, and yet know nothing of it.

"And then your face fades, the silly programme's even sillier tune, and what do we get next? Clayton's Crispy Crackers, followed by you again, looking ghastly. Well, not quite ghastly, perhaps. You could never . . ."

"I can assure you, I felt ghastly."

"It completely rubbished the magic you'd just put over about your company. All I'm saying is we'd have arranged the timing better and . . ."

"Merlin, it worked. It was the very first showing of that appeal that brought in a response. The right response. It found my daughter. Now that's it. No more, please."

It had worked, in fact, exactly in the way that Philip had said it would. Right again. Tiresome man. She really must stop thinking about him.

Olaff subsided.

"Well, OK. Sorry. And I'm glad you got your daughter back. Must have been horrific. But we could have done it cheaper, I bet. You will have paid way over the top."

"I very much doubt that," Diana cut him off. Cost effective. That is what it had been . . . as Philip would say.

The finality in her tone silenced Olaff. None of this was the real point of their meeting, anyway. He went on to talk about the flotation plans. It wasn't Epoch's area of expertise, naturally, but the agency was right behind it. There had been a few column inches in the *Financial Times* about small companies coming to the market. English Gardens was amongst those listed. Who were the brokers? That didn't matter at this stage. What did, was that Michael Neville's name had been mentioned a few times. This wasn't so good.

"Oh? Could you tell me why?" Diana asked sharply. There was something in Olaff's manner that suggested he was leading up to something. He was fidgeting with his pen. Click, click. Very irritating.

Groaning in spirit, Olaff dropped the pen on the table with a clatter. This was all going wrong. Could it ever have gone right?

"Image, Diana. Image. Your husband, I have no doubt, is a very clever man, but he has an image of his own. The wrong one, if I may say so."

"You may not."

There was a moment's impasse. Astounded, Olaff looked at

Diana. He saw the violet flare in her eyes. A danger signal? That was twice she had shut him up. Not too promising.

"Listen, Merlin. My husband has paid for his past mistakes. He has to go on living. It is extremely unlikely that he will affect the marketing side of English Gardens. He has no part to play there and won't have any public profile to speak of. On the other hand," Diana tapped her fingernail on the table warningly, "he will inevitably take an active interest in the financial affairs of the company."

Olaff tried unsuccessfully to interrupt. Diana had taken complete command of the discussion. If only he could make her understand. Neville couldn't change his spots if he wanted to. He was stuck, now, with a seedy wheeler dealer label. The high roller who rolled off. Right into the shit. Tough, maybe. But that's the way it was. He was safe writing financial copy, but that was all. He'd never get a job in a company or financial institution again. It would be dicey for the look and feel of English Gardens if it offered him a haven.

"Michael has skills which I might not find and probably couldn't afford to buy elsewhere. I don't suppose you'd deny the existence of those skills?"

"Oh God, no," Olaff rested his chin on his hand. "We all know about those skills of his."

Merlin Olaff coloured. He could have bitten his tongue off. It was a bad slip and he couldn't cover it up. Diana had caught the careless sarcasm in his tone and assumed correctly that Olaff referred to her husband's embezzlement.

"Mr. Olaff, I rested quiet when you ruined my husband's homecoming for me with a circus of press photographers. You have your job to do. I listened patiently to you when you told me that I put my daughter before my company and that my priorities are wrong. I have stood for it while you told me that I looked, as you say, ghastly . . . a thing few women would tolerate. But my husband's past is off-limits. Below the belt. Offside. Is that language you understand?"

Diana stood up, pale with anger. "My husband's company was once your client. Mine no longer is."

Diana had acted hastily and against her own best judgment. But she couldn't go on indefinitely discussing how best to keep her husband out of sight, as if he were no more than an embarrassing, negative figure on a balance sheet. It was undignified and disloyal.

She terminated Epoch's contract in writing. Michael read the letter over Dorothy's shoulder as she typed it. A couple of polite lines, thanking the agency for what they had achieved in the past; there was no hint of what had caused the breach.

"What the hell's she doing that for?" he demanded of the secretary.

Dorothy shrugged indifferently. Diana had not said.

"Someone ought to tell her you don't rat on business loyalties until you've got something to put in their place."

"Well, why don't you try it?" Dorothy said peevishly.

"Don't worry, I will. Of all the bloody bird-brained things to do."

Diana attempted no defence of her action to Michael.

"Much more of this kind of thing and people will wonder if you're fit to run a public company, Diana. Pull yourself together."

🐾 DIANA'S DAYS AT Gilbert's Tower recovered some of their even tenor.

The winter, severe in the first two months of the year, melted tamely away. A humid, blustery March flattened the narcissus in the orchard and the house overflowed with the casualties. The scent of spring was in the air with hopes of an early, unchecked growing season. There being no sign of frost to nip the peach blossom, Sedgely started to worry about an invasion of aphids and other animal pests. In the seclusion of his potting shed, he peed into quite a few buckets of soap powder solution. Desperate times called for desperate measures.

On April Fool's Day the summer began. Incredulous, Diana saw the outside thermometer rise to eighty degrees in the shade by noon. This must surely be a record, she told Sedgely as he passed her with a laden wheelbarrow of "lovely" stable dung.

"Nowt like," he trumped her. Nidcaster had achieved still greater prodigies of calorific excellence "during t'war."

Mrs. Sedgely had defied Nidcaster's pessimistic forecasts and chosen to follow medical advice instead. Operations, it was traditionally believed by the town's more senior citizens, offered only a slightly better chance of survival than judicial execution. But there Albert Sedgely's wife was, walking about again. It had been "champion" in the Yorkshire Clinic, she confided to her friends. If they had any joint trouble, they should "have it out," at once. Thank the Lord for plastic.

'T were all right for some.

Resuming her duties at Gilbert's Tower, Mrs. Sedgely was surprised to find that Mrs. Lightbody had done very little wrong. Nor had she, but Diana was relieved to see her go, just the same. She had a tendency to talk too much about Mr. Strang-Steele and his ways. Diana found herself listening and disliking herself for doing so. She was like an infatuated schoolgirl, hot for the mere sound of the loved one's name. Ridiculous.

Between herself and Michael there was a precarious peace. He no longer shared her bed, pleading the lateness of his hours. Dorothy, Diana was sure, was a thing of the past. His girls never lasted long.

The girl stayed, however. She made round eyes at Michael, who had ceased to see her. Dorothy had become no more than the engine that powered a shorthand pad and pencil. A part of Diana itched to tell the secretary to leave. Once she had found her with suspiciously red eyes and a crumpled tissue in her hand. It spoiled her pretty face. So pointless, too. Michael took what he wanted and forgot.

Hating to see a harmless young creature hurt, Diana's hands and tongue were tied. A natural reticence prevented her from saying anything. If she did, then her own pain would be exposed. Knowledge of her husband's faults she must, of course, keep to herself. Pride and loyalty. The married woman's unseen veils.

Scheduled for June, the flotation plans were going on apace. Michael spent many days in Leeds with the appointed brokers. Greek Street, a dark, narrow defile lined with towering marble faced buildings, was Leeds's answer to the City of London. Quite exciting. Diana had been once to be formally introduced. The firm's partners had taken her and Michael out to lunch at a nearby Italian restaurant. It was a vast, sumptuous place thronged with would-be customers who could not get a table. The head waiter there specialised in heart stopping rudeness. It was a question of who was "in" and who was "out." Diana was relieved to see that Michael and his stockbroker

friends were "in." There her involvement ended. She wasn't
sorry. This was Michael's world.

To handle the associated publicity, Diana appointed a local
public relations company. They had offices in Harrogate and a
good reputation locally, or so Mr. Meers had said. They had
some big accounts and had grown steadily over the past ten
years. Good signs.

Diana told them nothing of what had caused her to withdraw
her business from Epoch. She waited for the boss, a big, burly,
flint eyed man with hands like rocks, to pounce on Michael's
name. No reaction came other than a grunt and a scratching
noise as a rapid note was made.

Perhaps English Gardens did not matter as much to these
people. Diana felt a twinge of regret for Epoch. At least Merlin
had been open with her. He may have been wrong, but he had
her company's best interests at heart. Diana left the Harrogate
agency's offices depressed. She was sure they would do a thorough job. But would it be inspired? There wasn't the same
meeting of minds. The spark was missing.

English Gardens' shares would be offered on the open market from June 10th. The first day of an account period, as it
happened. Advertisements would appear in the financial press
four weeks beforehand and application forms would be obtain-
able from the brokers. Attention would also be drawn to the
share issue in the amateur gardening magazines, the retailers'
trade press and the distribution industry's journals.

At Diana's own insistence, existing gardener suppliers were
to have the first chance of purchasing the stock. Each would be
sent a special, privileged application form before the sale was
thrown open to the public. English Gardens was their company, she said. They must be given the chance to own as much
of it between them as they wished or could afford. She herself
would retain a relatively small block of shares. It wasn't likely
to represent a controlling interest.

"Are you off your head?" Michael shouted at her. "You're
giving the company away."

Diana said she had Gilbert's Tower free of debt, a little liquid capital and her salary as English Gardens' Chairman. What
else should she need? She had even arranged a pension scheme
for herself. That took Michael aback.

"How very sexless of you," he sneered. "What's the matter?

Are you afraid I might go and dump you in a charitable institution in your old age? Give me a bit of credit."

Warming herself at his feeble flicker of care for her, Diana did her best to belittle her own efforts at providence. She had felt very alone when he was in prison. A pension had seemed sensible at the time. Mr. Meers had recommended it. So had her accountants. Tax free contributions were a bargain, he must see that.

As for the share issue, Diana said that although the company had grown, it was very much a family co-operative. A large part of the appeal of the flotation for her had been to keep it safe and viable for all the people who not only greatly enjoyed their participation but derived a little vital extra income from it. Those people were her gardeners.

"Comparatively few of our suppliers are at all rich, Michael. Most are only averagely well off and plenty are genuinely poor. Did you know that we have two wonderful old boys who let us have the most exquisite rhubarb from a bit of waste ground they squat on? There are a lot like that."

Michael folded his arms and contemplated her in the manner of a schoolmaster freshly amazed by a stupid pupil's obtuseness.

"You really aren't fit to cross the road by yourself, Diana. Has it occurred to you that you could lose your seat on the board? If you behave as you say you're going to, you'll be nothing but an employee of the shareholders."

"And rightly so!" Diana flared at him. "I created English Gardens but it now means too much to a lot of other people for me to destroy it if I am, or am found, unfit to run it. But quite frankly, I don't lose any sleep over it. Neither should you."

Michael rolled his eyes up and then looked down at her through half closed lids.

"Don't patronise me! You've a bad record where old people's money is concerned." She was too angry to regret saying it. She couldn't think why she had. It wasn't strictly relevant. Diana braced herself for a tirade or even a blow. It never came. Michael found this new, passionate Diana wildly stimulating. He grabbed at her and crushed his mouth on to hers, kneading her breast. She struggled and eluded him.

"Don't try and shut me up with that. When I want to talk,

I'll talk! Let me tell you that this flotation also means a bit of extra security for a lot of people who might not otherwise ever think of investing in shares. This is equity in their own company. Something they can understand. Hold in their hands."

They had been standing in the garden and Diana marched into the house, hoping that neither of the Sedgelys had heard their raised voices. That would be too humiliating.

Michael picked up a piece of gravel at his feet and flung it hard, over the orchard wall. It hit a pane of the vine conservatory and cracked it. Diana was a selfish cow. If she threw her company away, what would happen to him?

Sedgely's rage reddened face appeared over the top of the wall.

"There's some bloody vandals about. I'd like to get my 'ands on 'em, Mr. Neville, sir."

Sedgely knew perfectly well who had thrown the pebble. He had also heard most of the conversation. Just what it might mean, he was not sure. But "summut" was up. He'd best have a word with Mr. Alisdair. Bugger it, they were both directors, too.

🦅 ALISDAIR HAD EXTENDED his period of notice by another three months. The same arrangements as before obtained. Although he was offered it, he would not take his full salary or go near Gilbert's Tower. He was unwilling, even, to go into Nidcaster although the staff at the industrial unit missed his grasp of affairs there sorely. The risk of encountering Michael Neville was too great. Everything was done by remote control and telephone.

Naively, Yolanda tried to persuade him to conquer his aversion.

"No, Landa." Alisdair laughed mirthlessly. "He's your father and that's that. But he accused me of both betraying you and insulting your mother. At least he's had the good sense not to attempt an apology. I should have turned it down."

He was paying her a weekend visit in Harrogate. Alisdair still refused to take advantage of Yolanda's greater freedoms and enhanced privacy. He stayed overnight at the Prospect Hotel, opposite her flat on the other side of the West Park Stray. They could flash each other goodnight signals . . . it being too far to wave.

"We've waited so long, we'll wait a bit longer." He lifted the cloak of her hair from her nape and nuzzled it, dizzied by the texture and perfume of her skin. "It's not long to go now."

As well it might, the wedding itself exercised Yolanda's mind. How could she be married from her mother's house, given away by her father, and bring her young husband home to eat his wedding breakfast at Gilbert's Tower unless the dreadful deadlock between these two loved men were resolved?

Asked this, Alisdair said it was quite simple. There was no question of their being married in Nidcaster. Yolanda might choose any other place. Lincolnshire, Normandy, Provence . . . or the Captain's day cabin on an ocean-going liner, for all he cared.

"But it's my home!" Yolanda burst out. "What do I care about any other place? Mummy will be broken hearted."

"I half thought it was my home, as well. But it's no good. I was pushed out and I can't go back."

A pan of spinach and apple soup boiled over on the cooker. Yolanda removed it miserably and dumped it on the draining board. It was difficult to believe Alisdair had actually said all this. He couldn't be so cruel. Couldn't he just forgive a little bit . . . for a little while? Long enough to get married where they had met and where they ought to be on their wedding day?

They ate at the dark green kitchen table. Alisdair tried to distract her attention from their disagreement with various brighter topics. It was no good. Gilbert's Tower was more than an address. It pulled hard at its people with living muscles and ligaments of its own. Yolanda pushed her plate away and broke down in dry, racking sobs.

Alisdair left his chair and put his arms around her.

"Please, darling. Don't do this. I'm truly sorry. I would if I could, but I just can't. My father would never come and . . . "

Yolanda shook him off violently. "What about my mother? She has a right to be hostess at my wedding . . . I have a right to be married from our house."

Alisdair could neither comfort nor persuade her. Yolanda had a stubborn streak. The one that matched his own. He was about to leave her sadly when the telephone in the little hall rang. Yolanda rose to get it.

"It's for you," she said dully. "Mr. Sedgely."

"Hello, Albert." Alisdair was the only one with the nerve to call Sedgely by his Christian name and get away with it. He sounded agitated. "I see. Well, I don't know. It may not mean anything. Could you run into Harrogate, do you think? Well, yes . . . now. I'm going back to Lincolnshire tomorrow."

Sedgely said a few things more. Strong language for him. Alisdair winced as Michael Neville's name was mentioned and glanced up at Yolanda where she leaned against a clothes press, watching him. He hoped she could not hear.

"All right. I'll come now. I'll go over to the Prospect," Alisdair looked again at his fiancée. "Miss Yolanda could use an early night."

He was loath to leave her, he said, kissing her by the door. But Sedgely had something he was burning to get off his chest. Better go and see. He tipped Yolanda's face up, but she turned it away from him.

"Landa, you're surely not telling me you won't marry me if it can't be in Nidcaster?"

"I don't know," she muttered into his shoulder. "I just don't know. I suppose so. But it wouldn't be the same, would it?"

Nidcaster . . . and Gilbert's Tower . . . They were not places you could simply take or leave.

CHAPTER
16

❦ ALISDAIR COULD MAKE very little of Sedgely's near verbatim
report of what he had heard in the garden. Like the audible
side of an overheard telephone conversation, it bristled with
ambiguous clues. The thread of sense was broken in many
places. Which ends tied into which knots was impossible to
say.

"Givin' t'company away, Mr. Alisdair. I heard that as plain
as I hear you," Albert Sedgely insisted, cradling a half pint of
lager. "He's up to summut, mark my words."

"But you say that's what Mr. Neville said to Mrs. Neville."

"Yelling his head off, more like," Sedgely interjected. "I'd a
shovel in my hands and for two pins I'd have knocked his
bloody block off. Talking to Mrs. Neville like that."

"Albert, do you want another of those?" Alisdair indicated
the glass in Sedgely's hand.

Sedgely did not. Foreign stuff. If there was a public bar in
this place, he would go and get himself a decent half pint of
local-brewed bitter. The cocktail bartender offered to get it for
him.

"No tha won't, lad, thanks all t'same. I like to see my beer
pulled for m'self." Otherwise, it seemed, there might be she-
nanigans.

Alisdair was relieved by the interruption. At least it had
deflected Sedgely's attention from the Nevilles' personal relationship.

Already enmeshed in the barbed wire intricacies of the
Nevilles' marriage, Alisdair wanted no further entanglement.
His sole remaining goals were to hand the operational side of

English Gardens over to a competent successor and detach Yolanda from the magnetic power of Gilbert's Tower. With the intuitive, Celtic part of himself, Alisdair was repelled by concentrated malign influences trapped within its wall. For Diana herself, once the re-animator of the place's resident djinn and now the victim of some invading force, he could do nothing. She had opened the gates of her fortress to Michael Neville and all happiness there was laid waste. A contagion. There was no defence against it. Diana had raised no cry for help. It would be a brave man who now went, uninvited, to her aid.

Sedgely was that brave man, Alisdair saw. He asked only for an understanding of the weaponry ranged against him. Alisdair was not able to identify it. He did his best, however, to set the little Yorkshireman's mind at rest. Sedgely, he concluded, had stepped out of his sphere and was out of his depth.

"It's reasonably clear to me, Albert," he said when Sedgely returned, "that by giving the company away, what Mr. Neville meant was that the share price has been pitched too low, in his opinion. And if that is so, it must be because Mrs. Neville wanted it that way."

It all fitted in with the rest of what Sedgely had heard. There was no other logical explanation. Mrs. Neville wanted the shares to be cheap enough to encourage gardener suppliers to buy them. They were to be as unintimidatingly close to post office savings stamps as could be.

"Yes, Albert," Alisdair agreed. "That's it in a nutshell. I suppose Mr. Neville is afraid that it isn't businesslike."

But Sedgely wasn't satisfied. "What were all this business about her losing her seat on t'board, like?"

That too was easily explained. "Well, if Mrs. Neville doesn't keep enough of the shares for herself, she won't in any sense be the owner of the company ... only part-owner with hundreds or maybe thousands of others. They're all voting shares, you see. In theory there's just a chance that the other shareholders won't want her to carry on running things. If that happened she'd lose her job, if you like. But don't worry, Albert. That is only theory. The risk is infinitesimal. Can you imagine English Gardens without her?"

Sedgely placed the half pint pot on the low table before him. "That I can't, Mr. Alisdair. But I'll lay you a pound to a penny there are some as can."

"Listen," Alisdair sighed, wearied now by the circular arguments. "Michael Neville—because that's who we both know we're talking about—is powerless to harm English Gardens, or his wife as Chairman. He is an undischarged bankrupt. That means he can neither buy shares in any company nor sit on any board of directors."

It ought to have been the end of the conversation. Alisdair was sure it would be, but it wasn't. Terrier-like, Sedgely shook the mutilated rat of his doubt again. Its neck was not yet broken. He jabbed an accusatory forefinger at Alisdair.

"Say what you like, Mr. Alisdair, I notice you've resigned. I notice you won't go near t'Tower . . . No, nor t'industrial estate, either. What's up wi' you if it isn't that bugger?" Sedgely fixed him with a glare. "I'll be saying goodnight, then."

❦ ALISDAIR TOOK HIS key from reception and went up in the lift to his room. Heavy hearted, he looked out of the window across the darkened Stray. The top floor of Yolanda's stuccoed building was in darkness, too. He flicked a lamp switch two or three times. There was no answering flash. Asleep, perhaps . . . angry or too sad for these juvenile signals. Damn and blast the Nevilles.

Rebelling at the sight of the neatly turned down bed, Alisdair began to pack his clothes. There was nothing to stay for. No reason to lie in a bed because it was there.

They had all fallen from grace. A demon had got in amongst them, fragmenting loyalties and frightening friendship away. Only Sedgely was staunch. A serge clad Don Quixote, tilting at shadowy windmills because there was no visible foe to attack.

Driving away from Harrogate, Alisdair envied Sedgely's ultimate courage. He was not afraid to be absurd.

❦ DIANA'S OWN INITIAL fears were few.

In the aftermath of her exchange with Michael she had written to the Leeds stockbrokers, reiterating her objectives. She trusted that nobody would take it upon themselves to pervert the intended effects of the share issue. English Gardens was first and foremost for its natural members. The gardeners. Of course, signs of support from pension fund investors would be welcome. But grabbing and stagging by speculators was to be discouraged.

She typed the letter herself, marked it confidential and kept no copy. She took great care not to question herself regarding this secretive correspondence. No, she was not afraid of Michael. She could not afford to mistrust him. It was just that she had responsibilities that belonged to her alone.

The stockbrokers received the letter on the day of Michael's discharge from bankruptcy. They were taking him out to lunch to celebrate. They showed him the letter and laughed. Ladies, bless them, were extraordinarily successful at starting businesses, these days. Feminine projects enraptured the market time and time again. Something to do with "green" consciousness. A backlash against hard-edged things that happened on the news. A burying of heads in the sand. Or the soil, in this case. But when it came to peddling her dreams on the stock market, Mrs. Neville, like all the rest, still needed slick, sophisticated hands to guide her.

Oh, she could buy and sell. They had to hand it to her. Money in exchange for goods or services. Simple stuff, though, when all was said and done. Just what any market woman knew. But launching a thousand, insubstantial little hopes, and winning hard cash in return—that was different. *Pension fund investors*, indeed. They should be so lucky! *Grabbing and stagging*. That was a good one. Pigs might fly.

Before they left the office, a soothing reply to Diana's letter of the sort dictated by men in suits, was drafted.

"That do the trick, do you think, Neville? Keep your good lady calm?"

Michael read it and threw it back at the typist. She hated him. "Perfect. She's a sucker for a soft answer is my wife."

A finished visual of the company prospectus was produced. The garden gate logo on the front cover, a scattering of pictures representing packing stations and print shops on the inside spreads. Some of the freeholds had been acquired. They were assets. As yet, the copy was just grey lines. Michael would write that himself.

"We've sent a colour photocopy to your wife."

"Oh, Lord," Michael rolled his eyes up comically in mock despair. "You might have spared me that."

"Have a heart, Mike," there was a splutter of protest. "She

is the Chairman. We can't keep her quite out in the cold. Usually it's the Chairman's wife who gets to frig about with the look of these things."

There was a moment's nervous silence as Michael brought his cold fury at the comparison under control. The thrust had been unintended. The man who had made the blunder ran his finger around the inside of his collar. His was a junior partnership of recent date. The others covered it up with *bonhomie* and the clink of bottle necks on tumbler rims. Gin and tonic. Michael Neville was their sort. A man's man. A thoroughly good chap . . . streetwise. There but for the grace of God went all honest City men. Anyway, he was off the hook now. Free to make a new start.

"Good luck" and "Happy days." Those were the toasts. You couldn't keep a good man down.

❦ A TABLE HAD been reserved at the Italian restaurant. Michael's group were hustled to it with the head waiter's unique combination of obsequiousness and impudence.

"I see the *signores* have come prepared to enjoy themselves. Much of the gin and tonic, no? And why not? It is Friday. For a first course I recommend to you the langoustine." The man scanned the five faces before him. Encountering no disagreement, he scribbled on his pad. The weather was warm and the langoustine were hanging on. The most expensive *antipasto* on the menu. "With it, you will want two . . . no, three bottles of the Chianti Classico. The white. It is very good. Then we see . . ."

They drank a lot of wine. Under its influence Michael disclosed some of the details of his discharge from bankruptcy. His assets had realised sufficient to pay his creditors a total of thirty-three pence in the pound. It was a jolly good show, that, his companions agreed. And of course, his bankruptcy had not itself been technically criminal. It was quite a separate matter from the fraud. Otherwise the application for discharge would have been turned down flat.

"I dare say my known association with English Gardens might have swayed the powers that be in my favour, too," Michael went on. "Distinct smell of roses, you might say. Or bloody peach blossom."

There was some muddled talk of which kind of fruit blossom actually had any perfume. Escalopes of veal came. Nobody could remember ordering them. They were eaten but not tasted. The head waiter made sure there were fresh glasses on the table and kept them well replenished with Barolo.

"Anyway," Michael waved his hand expansively, knocking his glass to the marble floor. "Doesn't matter what it smells of. 'T isn't dog shit. Thash what counts."

"I suppose Mrs. Neville must be terribly pleased," said the soberest member of the party. It was the one who had offended before. He was keen to make up lost ground. "It means you can be appointed to her board."

"My wife," Michael slurred, "doeshn't know . . . *yet*. A nice surprise for my good lady. Eh?"

After innumerable cups of thick black coffee, Michael declared himself fit to drive. Of the four stockbrokers with him, three were in no condition to judge and the junior partner dared not.

The parking meter on Greek Street showed Michael was into penalty time. There was a ticket stuck under his windscreen wiper. Extracting the car from between two others, he reversed it into the headlights of the one immediately behind. There was a tinkle of broken glass and the bumper was slightly dented. Coming along the street at that moment, the owner of the damaged car shouted.

It was nothing much. An exchange of names, addresses and insurance companies would have been enough. Michael never heard the shout and put the car into first gear. He shunted the vehicle in front. Grunting with frustration, he ignored the outraged owner of the first car, gesticulating wildly at the window. The man was in the way. Wouldn't move. Finally, Michael rolled down the window.

"Piss off, cunt."

The man fell back and watched the Rover shoot forward. He got the number.

Michael drove back to Nidcaster at an average speed of ninety miles an hour. He neither saw the flashing blue lights nor heard the sirens.

❦ DIANA AND YOLANDA were together in the kitchen at Gilbert's Tower when Michael's car screeched to a halt outside the garden door.

It was about half past four in the afternoon. Mrs. Sedgely had left and Yolanda, whose unexpected visit had delighted her mother, was about to carry a tray of tea out to Sedgely and some potential suppliers who had come to visit the garden. Diana planned to join them a little later. Yolanda wanted to talk.

"Oh, look, here's Daddy now." Yolanda saw him come through the garden door. "Shall I make a cup for him?"

She got no further. Michael entered the house and brushed past his wife and daughter, jostling the tray in Yolanda's hands. He said nothing but strode on through the kitchen with a set, glassy expression. Diana stared after him in bewilderment. She had no time to collect her thoughts before there was a hammering on the door. She went to answer it. Two policemen and a policewoman stood there, blocking out the light. They seemed very tall. Diana recognised one of them. From Nidcaster police station. Unfriendly looking, they towered over her. Diana tried to readjust her brain, like winding a film on in a camera. There was something wrong with the last snap. Where were the smiles?

"Is your husband at home, Mrs. Neville?" The voice reached her ears across a yawning canyon of disbelief. Once, this had happened before.

"Yes. But . . . he just . . ."

Like all things that happen very fast, to the eye, the action was slowed to a series of jerking stills. The two men and the woman standing on the doorstep advanced. There was no permission asked. No explanation given. No apology. It seemed as if they would walk through her. Or over her. Diana stepped back, no feeling in her feet. Swept aside like a cobweb.

She saw Yolanda standing there, still with the tray in her hands. The image was unconnected with thought. Myriad half formed questions swarmed in her mind. Could they do this? Just walk into her house? What was it about? Should she have somehow blocked them off . . . refused them entry? What was happening . . . was it happening at all?

The policeman disappeared into the kitchen passageway. They never asked her the way. Where were they going, anyway?

"Has your husband had anything to drink since he came home?" The policewoman had stayed behind.

Diana looked at her, helpless and humiliated. She didn't

know what the girl was talking about. It was some sort of trick. There was a right answer and a wrong. Which was which?

"No. I told you . . . he only just . . ."

The policemen reappeared. They had Michael between them, held by the elbows. He shook one of them off. Dorothy followed in their wake, waving her hands as if she could have done something with them, had there been time.

Yolanda, Diana noticed, was no longer there. The front door banged. Gone.

Later, Diana realised she must have asked the policemen where they were taking her husband. Not why. She didn't want to ask them that. Dorothy told her. She had been there when they arrested him. Drunken driving. Diana could pick him up from Nidcaster police station in about an hour and a half. The time it took to conduct tests and to charge him.

It was Yolanda who had shown the greatest presence of mind.

The visitors could have caught no more than a glimpse of her father and only at a distance. They were walking at the southernmost limit of the orchard. Too late to shield them from all knowledge of the incident, Yolanda made light of it. He father had some colourful friends, she said, distributing cups of tea in the vine conservatory. Always in bother with the police over something or other. Usually motoring offences . . . sometimes rowdiness in pubs. That sort of thing. They often ran for cover at Gilbert's Tower. Her mother was so soft, she'd probably shelter a mad axe murderer. One day she'd get herself into trouble.

There were hypocritical murmurs of sympathy. Nobody believed her. It hardly mattered. Everybody knew what to pretend to believe, at least till they were off the premises. Thin lipped, Sedgely flashed Yolanda a look of gratitude. T'lass had got it up top. He'd give her that. For all t'good it would do.

Disciplined as ever, Diana came out of the house to chat with her guests. Yes, the strawberry crop looked like being early this year. The heat was fantastic. No sign of a break in the weather. What happened in a drought? she was asked. Were English Gardens suppliers regarded as commercial growers by the Water Boards, or not? There had been a battle royal about that. It was still ticklish . . .

"Well, that were a bloody disaster," Sedgely said frankly, after they were gone. "What were it all about?"

Diana told him. Her words were bland but tongues of violet flame leaped in her eyes.

It was the violation she could not forgive. Hostile footsteps in the house . . . strangers' voices. They had trampled over her to get to Michael. Honest citizen, tax paying householder . . . it had gone for nothing. Gilbert's Tower, the place of safety, had been overrun. Diana, Lord of the Manor of Leypole and great-niece of Theadosia FitzGilbert, was affronted. The pride of place boiled in her blood like volcanic lava. Molten and deadly. It was Michael she blamed.

None of this was said but Sedgely read it on her face. But his time was not yet. He looked at the turnip watch.

"I'll collect his nibs in t'van, shall I? Be about finished with him now, I reckon."

"Thank you, Mr. Sedgely, but no. The walk will do him good."

Yolanda walked back to the house with her mother, engulfed in the crackling aura of anger that surrounded her. It would be impossible now to talk about Alisdair, her wedding, her father. A small thing had changed the shape and substance of bigger things. It was as if a glowing electrical element had been thrown into a bowl of live fish. The cinders were unrecognisable. She would need to think again.

"Well, now," Diana said on a high, strained note, "you came for a chat. So let us chat. We will have something to drink ourselves. The sun is sliding down the sky."

Yolanda considered her mother's words. Repressed hysteria? The offer was declined. "No, Mummy. No. It will wait. Daddy will be home any minute." Yolanda found she did not want to use that term of filial affection, suddenly. But it was a lifetime's habit. There was no other. "Look, has he got a key? Wouldn't you like to come back to the flat with me and have a bite of supper there?"

Shuddering inwardly as she spoke, Yolanda anticipated a rebuff. There were no thanks, she had learned, for supporting one parent against the other, even in the interests of both.

"No, darling. Thank you. It's kind of you but I must stay here."

Diana waved her off in the Volkswagen at the garden door

and then went to sit on Mercury's fountain parapet. It had been like a burglary. She must stand her ground and defend what was left.

🐾 MICHAEL DID NOT return to Gilbert's Tower till the following lunchtime. A night in the cells, said the desk sergeant, in response to Diana's telephone enquiry, would cool him off. He was a bit lively, like, at present. Mrs. Neville was not to worry, they'd take good care of him. Nothing like a station brew-up. The old lags loved it.

That was the kindly Nidcaster way of saying that Michael had been noisy, abusive and obstructive. The normal courtesies had been resumed. Diana blushed for shame. It was the third time Michael had dragged their name publicly through the mud.

She made a tour of the garden under the stars with the orange cat trotting at her heels. They were re-marking their territory together. Wiping out the usurpers' spoor. In all her troubles, Diana had never felt abused by the police before. Michael had brought her to this.

It was a bitter thing, Diana discovered, to have sent away the man who loved her out of an arrogant, self-deceiving sense of duty to one who did not. How very proud she had been of herself. How supremely virtuous she had felt. Life had held a hand out to her and she had spurned it. What reward had she expected? A cold and lonely pedestal, perhaps. Instead she had got a seat in the village stocks.

She scooped the cat up. For the very first time it nibbled at her ear lobe. Diana buried her face in its fur. Would it consent to sleep on her bed? she wondered. She wanted somebody close.

🐾 IN THE MORNING, Diana was up early. There were so many chestnuts to pull out of the fire. She began at the top of the list. She dialled Philip Strang-Steele's number in Lincolnshire. Once she heard the ringing tone she wanted to drop the receiver. It was too early. She licked her lips. What was she going to say to him, anyway? The instrument refused to separate itself from her hand. It was as if she was clutching an icicle. Burning and sticky.

Mrs. Lightbody answered.

"Oh, hello, Mrs. Neville. You're an early bird, I must say. Mrs. Sedgely's coping all right, I hope ..."

Pleasantries could not be avoided.

"Now hold on, I'll get Mr. Strang-Steele for you. He's about finished his breakfast."

She had not even had to ask for him. Mrs. Lightbody's feet tapped away. It was a good line. Wild thoughts of hanging up occurred to her. No use. He would only ring her back.

"Diana?" It was Alisdair's voice.

"Oh," Diana responded blankly. "Alisdair. Actually, it was your father I wanted to speak to."

"I'm sorry, he's gone to Australia. Flew from Heathrow yesterday. Is there anything I can do?"

Australia. It might as well be the other side of the moon. Diana's heart, which had fluttered so high behind the cage of her ribs, swooped down to her diaphragm. She felt a wave of nausea.

"No," Diana answered him slowly. "It's nothing, really. Well, it's a form to do with the marriage settlement ... I needed to ask him about it. That's all. I suppose it will wait. When's he coming back?"

"Hm ... Well, not for a while," Alisdair hummed and hawed. "A few weeks, at least. He's gone to look at some land for sale in the Hunter Valley. The old man's interested in it. Said he might go himself, for a change. I could give him a message when he telephones but ..."

Diana got out of it as quickly as she could. It was her own fault. Philip Strang-Steele had taken his disappointment like a man, and moved on. There was nothing she could do. She had been a fool to think there was. The moment had come and gone for her.

Dorothy arrived and with her, the post. Among the letters was the one from the stockbrokers. Diana read it first. There was something about the superficial, slithering phrases that she did not like: "anxious to reassure ... years of combined experience ... excessive manipulation rarely desirable ... chips fall where they do ... best efforts ... don't hesitate to contact ..."

Two paragraphs and a line. Less than eighty-five words in all. The signature block was that of the firm's senior partner but the signature itself was not. His secretary had received instructions to "pp" everything for him if he wasn't back in time for the last post. He hadn't been. He went straight home in a taxi, cursing Michael Neville. He was a terrible influence, that man. The stockbroker had forgotten all about his letter to Neville's wife.

So there it was, signed with the neat, legible lettering of a girl who reads little, writes less and has nothing to hide. Unquestionably, a fobbing-off letter, Diana decided. And a pretty poor attempt it was, too. It wouldn't have deceived her three years ago and it certainly didn't now.

The layout of the company prospectus, which had been sent under separate cover with a second class stamp, impressed her even less. Dull. And why a photocopy? Surely she was the one person entitled to see the original. The copy, said the covering letter, would obviously be written by Mr. Neville . . . there could be nobody better qualified for the job. "Debatable," Diana wrote in pencil in the margin.

Her first impulse was to go at once to Leeds and confront these gentlemen in their offices. No appointment, no forewarning. She was already halfway up the staircase, hoping her best summer weight coat and skirt were spotless, when she stopped. It wouldn't do. There was a language barrier. She had no phrase book.

She remembered when she had first met these people, how they had frozen her out with their talk. "Earnings per share . . . rights issues . . . founder's shares . . ." And those were only the words she could remember. Many more made no memorable, comprehensible pattern in her brain at all. She had asked for explanations, translations. They only pretended to explain what they meant. Diana had been made to feel stupid. And then rather cross. These people, like others she had met, were guarding their little field of knowledge with code. She hadn't been found eligible for the code-breaking manual.

She went back downstairs again to the book room and told Dorothy to stay there. The girl was avid with curiosity about yesterday's happenings. Diana did not indulge her.

"Stay there and mind the telephone, Dorothy. I shall be busy upstairs for a while . . . with my husband."

That was a nice touch. Diana was amazed at her own dexterity. Dorothy, of course, had no idea where Michael was. She would assume he was at home.

In Michael's office there were three filing cabinets. One held material concerning his work for financial journals. Three files for each of the journals. Cuttings, Correspondence and Records of Payment. Nothing there. The next cabinet contained all the files on the English Gardens flotation and the last one was personal files. She might just have time to go through one or other of those thoroughly. But probably not both.

Since the source of her disquiet was English Gardens, it seemed best to tackle that one first. Diana took the first file over to the desk by the window. If she kept standing up to look through the dormer, she could see him coming down the lane. In fact, she could see as far as the parish church yard and the station signal box. He would have to pass both. As an added precaution she opened the window. Then she would be able to hear when the garden door opened. There would be time, even then.

These are *my* files, she told herself, feeling like a thief. She started on the first one, turning the pages quickly. All in order. She glanced out of the window. Sedgely was coming down the lane. Putting the first file back in the top drawer she went on to the next. There was something wrong somewhere . . . but where? Noticing her own fast breathing, Diana stopped and counted to ten. This was ridiculous. Of what should she be afraid?

Three hours or so passed in this way without result. A lot of the correspondence concerned valuations of the company's assets. There were letters about the merits of the unlisted securities market. That suggestion had been rejected by Michael. A full listing was possible, so why not go for it? Counter arguments. Figures . . . examples . . . costs.

The kitchen door must be open because she could hear Dorothy talking to Mrs. Sedgely. Diana looked out of the window again. Sedgely perched on the fountain parapet, sucking his pipe. The church bells swung and blotted out sound. There was a woman who lived in the lane crossing the railway line. She'd better hurry up. There was a train on the viaduct. One day there'd be an accident.

Diana got out the first two files in the top drawer of the filing cabinet marked "Personal." Banks and Bankruptcy. The door was kicked open and Michael walked in.

He folded his arms and leaned on the door jamb. Diana sat completely still.

"Well, well. First Dorothy the ghost and now Diana the sleuth. Been enjoying our conference, have we? Got through a lot of business, have we?"

He walked towards the desk and picked up the unopened files. "How much of these have you read?"

"Nothing," Diana said truthfully. "I went through the English Gardens stuff first."

Michael concealed his satisfaction at this news with very little effort. He had the mother and father of a hangover. He could scarcely recall the list of the charges against him. Assaulting a police officer was one . . . all pretty piffling stuff. He'd lose his licence, of course. But then, by the time the case came up, he'd have enough to pay a chauffeur if he wanted one. And now this. What a dangerous fool Diana could be with her instincts and suspicions. Always acting against her own best interests. Well, no harm had been done.

"Oh, I see. Did the English Gardens stuff first, did you? Quite right. That's my girl. Unerring sense of priorities, haven't you?" Michael hiccupped and apologised. Not in his prime any longer, he said. Couldn't shift as much alcohol these days.

"I don't like the prospectus," Diana rapped out. There was something odd about Michael, he wasn't nearly angry enough. It couldn't possibly be because he had nothing to hide. Could it?

"Don't you?" he replied, equably enough. "Hey, be a good girl and let me sit down at my own desk. We'll get the bloody prospectus changed. You do it. Get your muckers at Epoch on to it. They've got two weeks. That's if they'll speak to you. Shouldn't blame them if they've forgotten your name."

Biting back a retort, Diana prepared to leave him.

"Hey, I'd really appreciate a sandwich. Send Dorothy up with it."

Diana sent Dorothy home. Michael could make his own sandwich.

Upstairs, Michael locked his filing cabinet and the door of his study. He spent the rest of the day deeply asleep.

Sitting alone in the book room, Diana bit the loose flesh at the base of her thumb till it bled. For the moment, she could think of nothing else to do. They had gone too far down the road to turn back now. English Gardens needed Michael. And because the company was all she had left in life, she needed him too.

After a while, she sat up straight. This was no way to behave. It was all such utter nonsense. She had Yolanda and Alisdair too, of course. And Philip. Whatever was over and done with between them, he would always be a friend. Michael? Yes, well . . . she would say something quite definite to him this time. What she had thought of as forbearance was nothing but weakness. Her will had been rotting away.

❦ THERE WAS AN electric storm that night.

Diana was one of those who never surmounted a childhood terror of thunder and lightning. She lay awake with the curtains undrawn, watching the sky tear apart, flinching each time the room flooded briefly with unnatural white light. The house had a lightning conductor on top of the tower. She clung to that thought. The noise was like the rending of linen, magnified many times. A great crash to the rear of the house made her sit up in bed. She dared herself to find out what it was.

At that moment Michael appeared at the door of his dressing-room with pyjama jacket on and a towel round his waist.

"You all right?" he said. "I'll come and kip with you if you like, scaredy cat."

Diana was nonplussed for a moment. The left-over rag of affection from their early days waved like a flag of truce. Shivering with fear, Diana refused it. They had not talked terms.

"No. I'm all right. Go away." She pointed at the dressing-room door. Her arm shook. Michael turned on his heel and retreated wordlessly. She would certainly pay for that.

Making her protesting limbs move against their will, Diana slipped on a dressing gown and went out into the corridor. The north side of the house was blind, pierced only by the long staircase window. Beneath there was nothing but a cinder strewn area where visitors' cars were parked. Beyond was the main York road, which crossed the Leypole Bridge. A tall elm tree, cloven by lightning, lay across the road. The trees!

Diana ran down the stairs and unlocked the front door. She had nothing on her feet. The thunder seemed more distant now, the lightning less frequent. She picked her way painfully through the gravelled parterres till she reached the orchard gate. The oldest peach tree had once been struck, or so Sedgely said. It had an iron crutch now and a cramp in its fork. It started to rain in fat, sluggish drops. A movement reflected in the nearest glasshouse's glazing made her scream. It was only Sedgely.

"What are you doing here? You frightened me."

"I come to comfort trees a bit," Sedgely admitted tranquilly, shining his torch in her face. "I've been round. There's none of 'em hurt. High strung they are, though, some on 'em. Like me. Here," Sedgely produced a spirit flask from the recesses of his baggy gardening jacket. "Have a nip of this."

They had quite a few "nips" in the vine conservatory, out of the rain. Diana sat curled up in a basket chair with her feet underneath her.

"You'll be a rich woman in a few weeks now, Mrs. Neville," Sedgely ventured.

"I don't really think so ... unless something quite extraordinary happens. Then we'll all be rich," Diana laughed. "Nice, but not likely. Not overnight."

"Your husband'll make summut on it, though. That's 'is game, isn't it?"

Diana explained carefully about Michael's impotency as a bankrupt. Sedgely was a director. He had a right to know.

"Aye," Sedgely sucked his pipe. "That's what Mr. Alisdair said. And that chap, Cedric Lafontaine. I had a word with him, an' all."

He glanced sideways at her, watching for her reaction. He'd as good a right as any of them to speak to the company's bankers. It was just that he never had before. That silly Cedric had treated him like the village idiot. It was better like that. Never let 'em see t'spots on your dominoes.

The penny of comprehension dropped with a rattle inside Diana's head. She had held the answer to the doubts which neither she nor Sedgely could admit to each other in her hand that morning. The bankruptcy file.

"Why did you ring Cedric Lafontaine up, Mr. Sedgely? I never do if I can avoid it," Diana asked him cautiously.

"I've three thousand pounds saved. I thought I'd put it into t'company's shares, like ... as long as things go on as they have," Sedgely took the pipe out of his mouth and pointed the stem straight at Diana's chest. His meaning was plain. "I wanted to know what that young whippersnapper thought to it. He's one who reckons to know. It's a fair bit o' brass."

Diana laughed softly at Sedgely's carefully qualified confidence in the young banker. "He is a whippersnapper, isn't he? But he thought it would be all right, did he?"

"He said he could see nowt wrong wi' it," Sedgely replied gnomically. "No bad thing is this rain. We've been wanting it."

When the rain stopped, Sedgely escorted her back to the house chivalrously.

"Nay, Mrs. Neville. You should have put summut on your feet. I'd lift you if it wasn't for me leg."

❦ IN THE MORNING, Diana had the indelible impression that Philip Strang-Steele had come through Michael's dressing-room door and spoken to her during the night. Something perfectly ordinary and domestic. A word of reassurance about the storm. She woke happy, ready to go to him. The realisation that he was not there and never had been came with painful slowness and wet her cheeks with tears. A dream.

❦ "HAVE YOU, OR have you not, become unbankrupted, or whatever it is they call it?" Diana faced Michael across the breakfast table.

"Is it bloody likely, Diana? Ever since I got out of that sodding place I've been too busy representing you."

Quite clever of her. Michael went on mopping fried egg from his plate with a piece of bread. She hadn't read the file, of course, because Diana never lied.

For her part, Diana acknowledged the truth of what Michael said. There was something in it. He had been neglecting his own journalist's work to handle the flotation of English Gardens.

"Just tell me, Michael. Yes or no."

"No, then. No, no, no! Is that good enough for you?"

It was a nuisance, Michael thought. He never liked telling barefaced lies. For one thing, it was dodgy. But women were like the fucking police. They forced you into it. They thought that this was a black and white world, which it bloody well wasn't. The footwork would have to be re-choreographed. The bottom line would be the same.

"Satisfied?"

Diana didn't answer. She supposed she would have to be. If she tried to check up, it might blow the whistle on the general soundness of English Gardens' management. Cause trouble. Epoch had warned her against doing anything like it. Not at this stage.

The slice of humble pie she had chewed in Merlin Olaff's ear had been no more than a sliver and he had sprinkled it generously with sugar.

She was not to look at it, he said, as any kind of a climb down. There had been a misunderstanding. It happened in the best regulated families. Diana's attitude was entirely understandable. Epoch was as glad to welcome her back as she graciously said she was to re-employ them. It would be a wonderful thing for the agency to say that they'd seen English Gardens right through from the first spark of imagination to public limited company. That was rare. Nobody need ever know about their little spat.

The prospectus? No problem. Diana was to send what she'd got now down by way of Bob's private and unofficial Red Star system. Cheap, efficient, unfailing. Nothing like private enterprise, was there? There'd be a fresh visual sent up by the same route the very next day. The Epoch studio would work all night if necessary.

As for Michael. Well, he was a reformed character, wasn't he? Working his socks off for practically no reward, all to promote a squeaky clean little company that even a left wing saint could invest in. That was right, wasn't it? The triumph of good over evil. Forgiving wife pulling together with repentant husband. Family life. There was less than a month to go. The PR boys would get busy. Don't anybody rock the boat.

Outside the public relations industry there are few, if any, who understand its almost sinister power to convince. It begins with the consultancy's systematic self-hypnosis into a kind of mediumistic trance. The voices that come out in the shape of articles, photographs, and stage-managed interviews bridge the gap between the client's daily reality and a daydream transformation of the facts. Believing your own PR, Epoch's departmental head had said, was the first essential. When the agency staff believed it, the client would ... and the public would follow along. That's what happened.

Looking at the cuttings which came in the post every day from Epoch, Diana began to see Michael as others did ... or were being led to see him. A good looking, irrepressible whizz kid. A man who'd been led astray by fast company and his own restless brain. Somebody who'd done his bird cheerfully and put the time to good use. And now he was back in the bosom of a supportive family, leading his wife's good cause from the front. "Neville as English Garden Gnome," teased one headline in the *Investor's Chronicle*. "An innocent flutter for those who believe in the healing power of the soil," the *Penny Share Guide* said.

True, all true, thought Diana. Through, of course, what she and Michael had once had together was now only an artfully rouged corpse propped in its coffin. From now on, it would be a question of keeping up appearances for the company's sake.

THE PRIVILEGED SHARE issue to existing "members" was an unqualified success. The entire allocation was taken up. Some of the parcels were tiny. The brokers had received cheques for less than a hundred pounds in many cases. Moved to see the familiar names, Khan, Garside, Garvey, the "Rhubarb Brothers," as Alisdair called them, and many others, Diana wrote a personal letter of gratitude for their support to each and every one.

Father Murphy was presented with a parcel as Diana's gift. His support for English Gardens, she told him, was through the back door (his and hers, via Sedgely's), but none the less valuable for that. Damson cordial—she was careful to give it that unincriminating name—had seen her and Sedgely through fair weather and foul.

"Well, well," he accepted beamingly. "So I can tell me bishop to go play with himself because I'm a man of independent means ... and all on account of me little damson tree."

Hastily, Diana begged him not to rush into things. Sometimes Father Murphy picked up odd phrases without having the least idea what they meant.

On June 10th, applications for the remaining shares were in. The issue was fully subscribed. Most amazing of all was the very large block purchased by a gentleman said to represent an offshore investment trust. Channel Islands. Half a million pound's worth. The brokers were staggered. An astonishing vote of confidence, they said. It just showed you. The "green" share was where the equity market was going.

Michael, of course, had bought nothing. Verifying this with Lafontaine Frères, who as issuing house were receiving the cheques, Diana was relieved. He had been telling the truth. The sponsoring brokers were merely suprised. Neville had missed a trick. Not yet his old self, evidently. Still, they imagined he'd discussed it with his wife.

The shares traded briskly during the next fourteen days. At the end of the account period they had more than trebled in value. Excitement was running high. It demonstrated, City commentators said, the impact of personalities on business confidence. Diana and Michael Neville were a magic partnership. Still, it was a bubble. There would be tears before bedtime.

In their St. Mary's Axe chambers, Mr. Lafontaine senior couldn't help getting a rise out of his nephew.

"There you are, Cedric. You can do arithmetic till you're blue in the face. Guts and imagination—you've got to add those into the sums." He began to hum "Take a pair of sparkling eyes."

Lafontaine Frères, Cedric said huffily, would have been dead and buried long ago if it had relied on hunches for a living. On the contrary, his uncle baited him, banking was all about hunches, flukes and freaks. And Mrs. Neville was the prettiest freak he'd seen in a while.

Diana was upset. The thing was out of control. She sent a round robin to all her "member" investors. They should hang on to their shares and not panic. They had bought at the right price. Their shares were voting shares. If they succumbed to an understandable desire to take a profit, they would lose the right to vote at shareholders' meetings. For the most part the gardeners remained steady and didn't sell.

When the speculation fever died down the shares found a rational level. But not before the Channel Island investment trust, which was no more than a brass plate screwed to a St. Peter Port terrace house, had made a great deal of money ... without Michael Neville's nominee having to produce a penny piece. The buyer didn't have to pay up till the end of the fourteen-day account period. If he sold at a figure above the purchase sum within that time, he was home free. A successful stag.

With the profits, Michael's nominee bought a hefty block of English Gardens shares, at the latest and lowest price since the issue. This time, to keep. A classic transaction.

"You know," Alisdair handed Yolanda the *Sunday Telegraph*'s report of the whole English Gardens affair, "I hate to say it, but this thing has an unsavoury flavour. It reeks to high heaven."

They were reclining in the Gilbert's Tower boat in the shade of the trees. Yolanda had persuaded him to go to Nidcaster, much against his will. It was so hot and the flat didn't even have a balcony. Nobody, she said, need ever know they were there. Her parents never went down to the boat house. The water was so low in the river, they could scramble along the bank from the bridge.

Yolanda took the paper from Alisdair's hands languidly. The wedding thing was still unresolved. They'd more or less decided to put it off indefinitely. Perhaps, Yolanda thought privately, she ought to let Alisdair go. They could agree about so little these days. Why was she sitting under the walls of her own family's home like a stranger? He was making her choose between them. Alisdair was so supple in some ways but so hurtfully rigid in others. Now he was carping at her parents' success.

"Where's the stench? Daddy seems to have done pretty well by English Gardens, whatever you may think of him." She swotted a horse fly and screwed her face up at the blood on the paper.

"I know. That's the problem. English Gardens . . . OK. But I can't get rid of this feeling that he means your mother harm."

"Oh, no, Alisdair. No. My father does some incredibly awful things but he doesn't really mean to hurt anyone. He just doesn't *think*. Don't you see, he's just a buffoon?"

Yolanda started to replace bottles and plates in the cool box. "There's some salmon left, if you want it."

Alisdair shook his head. Yolanda's idea of what was enough to eat was beginning to outface even his appetite. The Sedgely influence.

"And remember, he does do his best to put things right. He

made a complete fool of himself at Christmas but it cost him a packet to find me."

Alisdair was not even surprised. She had said something like it before. Michael Neville's effrontery had no limit. Yolanda's slow disillusionment was heartbreaking to watch. At this rate, it might take years.

Ned Garvey skimmed past in the kayak he kept for policing the river on busy days. Droplets from the paddles flashed in the sun. He winked and called out, "By heck, Miss Yolanda. Your Mum's in t'big time now. I've queues on 'em at t'landing stage, all wanting a boat to take down to gawp at Gilbert's Tower. What's it worth if I don't tell them you're t'Crown Princess?"

"I'll kill you if you do, Ned Garvey!" Yolanda shook her fist at him and grinned.

That was the trouble with PR, Alisdair grumbled. It could get out of hand. Epoch had over cooked it.

CHAPTER
17

❦ JULY 15TH WAS the day set for an extraordinary meeting of
the English Gardens shareholders.

The agenda listed only two items of any significance. The
directors were to be confirmed in their positions and a proposed amendment to the company's articles of association was
to be read. If adopted, it would enable English Gardens to pursue the business of general distributors. This would cut out the
high cost of subcontracting to people like Fernley.

Diana was not attracted by this but realised it was probably
the only way to ensure the long term vitality of her company's
founding inspiration. It was her idea. It was ironic, she commented to Alisdair, that because what his father had called a
"romantic notion" was now so successful, she was forced to
face up to becoming a very unromantic businesswoman. At
least the gardeners would be protected from the bathos of bottled sauce and rolls of lavatory paper.

There would be a requirement, too, for proper company offices. A public company could not be run from the book room
at Gilbert's Tower. Michael obtained estate agents' brochures
for office suites in Leeds, York and Harrogate. Leeds was the
favourite. Diana wouldn't have it.

"Why on earth should I drive into Leeds every day to run
the company I've been running perfectly well from Nidcaster
for the past four years? Have you been on that road in the rush
hour?"

More than that, the company's natural home was Nidcaster.
The country town background was something her gardeners
felt comfortable with. So did she.

"They'll carry on coming to see us here. You can't imagine the Rhubarb Brothers having anything to do with a place on the ninth floor of a tower block in Leeds, can you?"

Michael could not, and a very good thing too, he said. They would be far too busy to be mollycoddling old-age pensioners or cooing ecstatically over a few sticks of rhubarb.

"Grow up, Diana. Suppliers are just suppliers. When their stuff's good enough to sell, you sell it. When it isn't, you tell them to get lost."

"When that happens, Michael, I will not be here."

"Have it your own way." Michael terminated the conversation.

During the past few days he had put a stop to any contentious discussion with the same phrase. Diana attributed it to her new policy of plain speaking and direct confrontation. Michael, it seemed, was beginning to understand the limits of his authority. On that basis it would be possible to pull in harness. He seemed to want a job with her company. He could have it and let her do hers. General policy over internal and external relationships was definitely her area. If he kept out of it, they would get along. A workable arrangement.

More space was, however, becoming an urgent necessity. Diana was prepared to compromise. She went to see the old FitzGilbert linen mill.

It stood beside the river where the gorge flattened out to level ground. There was a weir and traces of the old mill race. Water had powered the looms until the latter years of the mill's life. Basically eighteenth century with Victorian extensions, like Gilbert's Tower, it was part brick, part stone. It had stood empty for close on ten years until it was acquired jointly by a co-operative of small craft businesses, all hoping to catch passing tourist trade. Sheepskin slippers, wooden salad bowls . . . that kind of thing.

Roughly repaired with rags stuffing some windows, it was clear that the fabric was decaying. The craft venture had not been an outstanding success. Rumours in the town said the co-operative was about to call it a day. If the building weren't sold—and who would buy it?—it would be abandoned to an unequal fight with wind and weather until rotting timbers and falling masonry made its demolition compulsory. There were plenty of old people who remembered working in that mill . . . and some not so old, neither. Another bit of history gone.

Diana asked Mr. Meers to approach the co-operative discreetly. Would they be willing to sell? The answer came back, a heartfelt "yes." The co-operative members would be very glad to salvage something from the wreck of their hopes. Two independent valuations were obtained and the difference split. Diana could buy the building for seventy thousand pounds.

"Mind you," cautioned Mr. Meers, "it needs an awful lot doing to it." The wall fronting the river was sliding slowly into the water. It would want underpinning. The entire refurbishment would take months.

Diana was jubilant. If Gilbert's Tower could no longer be the company's regular headquarters and registered office, the old mill was a very good second best.

"Say we'll buy it, Mr. Meers. It's bound to be lucky for us."

Carrying out his instructions, Mr. Meers felt that whereas "luck" had smiled on English Gardens so far, it was going to take some downright, hard headed common sense to keep it moving ahead. He'd bought a worthwhile block of shares and sold half when the price hit its peak. The rest he retained in the expectation that Michael Neville, whatever his faults, would see that they rose steadily in value. Diana had given him full credit for the flotation, and a resounding success it had been.

Telling Michael of her agreement to buy the mill, Diana did not expect an enthusiastic response.

"You're off your rocker. Let me tell you, Diana, you'll never run this business from there."

"And you stop addressing me like a badly behaved dog or you'll find yourself without a job."

Although the most aggressive thing she had ever said to him, it was quietly spoken. Diana didn't want to quarrel with him. The public belief in them as a mutually complementary couple, carefully fostered by Epoch, was too important now. If news of a breach leaked out, the share price might well fall again drastically and take a lot of little people with it. Within her marriage, as she saw it, it left Diana small room for manoeuvre.

The prisoner of her own success, she would have to keep on smiling and waving from behind the bars.

* * *

❦ THE ANNUAL GILBERT'S Day pilgrimage took place a day before the shareholders' meeting. Michael had wanted to take himself to a cricket match at Headingley to keep out of the way of these religious junketings. Diana protested vigorously. People would expect to see him. And while neither the pilgrims, the Monsignor nor any of the other clergy might have anything directly to do with English Gardens, everybody was an opinion maker in their way. The Nidcaster *Bystander* always sent a reporter and so, last year, had the *Yorkshire Post*. The connection between the company, the house, the yearly event and their name was inseparable. The Nevilles must be seen to present a united front.

Feeling he had little to lose at this juncture, Michael capitulated. As host at the pilgrimage luncheon, he succumbed to habit and mixed business with pleasure.

"You've a rare opportunity here, Monsignor, to dine with a publican and sinner," Michael quipped winsomely at the gaitered grandee's table. It wasn't until the pudding stage that the mellowing cleric confessed to owning a small but shapely share portfolio. Now, would English Gardens add the exciting, maverick touch? What did Mike think? By the end of the afternoon, the Monsignor was in contact with his brokers by means of the book room phone.

Michael slapped the new shareholder heartily on his well-tailored, broadcloth back and offered him a second, very large brandy, man to man.

"You could do worse than come to the meeting tomorrow," he said.

"How's that?" the Monsignor replied in a mock *mafiosi* tone. "Something going down?"

Michael chortled appreciatively and they talked classic gangster movies until Diana saw that she had no option but to invite the Monsignor to supper. It was a pity, because she was tired and tomorrow was a very big day.

❦ ALISDAIR SPENT THE last hours of the day cooling his heels at Heathrow, waiting for a delayed Quantas flight. When the jet finally touched down to disgorge its passengers, Philip was not among them. Alsdair swore. His father had let him down. The next arrival from Sydney was not expected for another eighteen hours. It would be too late then for him to intervene at the shareholders' meeting. Not that Alsdair had been able to adduce a single plausible reason for Philip to do so. Now Sedgely's jitters had landed his young codirector with a three hundred mile drive back to Yorkshire all for nothing. A pointless expedition from start to finish.

🐾 THE MEETING WAS held in a conference suite at the Prospect Hotel in Harrogate. The meeting room itself was very large, embarrassingly so, Diana thought.

"Surely this number of people will never come?"

She was standing in the doorway of the adjoining room with Mr. Meers and other directors. Alsdair had consented to be there only if Michael was kept out of his way. Diana was not told this, only Yolanda. She had waylaid her father in the foyer and was keeping him busy in the bar.

"It's terribly expensive and tiring to travel these days and after all, it's just a rubber-stamping session."

Diana had thought sufficient of the rubber-stamping session to commission a new dress from Bessie Brown. Quite understandably, Mrs. Brown considered the first outfit she had made for Mrs. Neville to have been a crucial factor in deciding the destiny of her client.

"Ee, it did all right for you, that apricot job, didn't it?"

"Well, I certainly got the money to start English Gardens in it, Mrs. Brown." Diana did not deny it. "Now I need something to make me look as if I'm up to carrying it on, but please, no square shoulders or straight skirts."

The dressmaker provided a flame coloured dress in silk tussore. It had a severe, shirtwaist bodice and a long, full skirt.

"You'll want a fresh white gardenia for the collar and some very high heels. Practise walking in 'em. You don't want to totter."

"But this is the New Look, isn't it, Mrs. Brown?" Diana remembered her mother wearing something like it when she was very young, after the war.

"It's back," Bessie Brown said firmly. She knew what was best. "You'll look like a firefly in that get-up."

"Don't you think it's a bit dressy for a business meeting?" Diana had swished the skirts wistfully, watching the light ripple on the folds. They were faintly shot with purple. Just like real flames.

"It's an evening do, isn't it? Now let's not have any nonsense, Mrs. Neville, love."

At seven thirty, half an hour before the scheduled commencement of the meeting, the chairs provided for shareholders had all but filled up. A sea of faces. Some were familiar, many more unknown. Watching from her vantage point, Diana saw the Monsignor arrive in a wonderful Al Capone hat. Catching sight of her, he waved his agenda paper jauntily.

"Did you see who that was?" Diana turned to Sedgely. "Aren't people kind?"

"Well now, not entirely, Mrs. Neville." Father Murphy came up for a word before taking his seat. "They call him Blue Chip Billy, ye're aware . . ."

Diana could believe it, and laughing over this lemon flavoured drop of clerical gossip prevented her from seeing Philip Strang-Steele enter the room and take his seat directly behind the elegant priest.

Philip's brokers had managed to scrape him some English Gardens shares together at the previous day's closing price. He had missed the Quantas flight and travelled a nightmarish route, changing planes in places like Bangkok, Karachi, Baghdad and Sofia. He'd lost count of the airports he'd seen.

At five to eight, Mr. Meers indicated that the directors should take their seats at the baize covered table facing the body of the room. It was raised on a platform, a foot or two off the ground, with a row of microphones. There was a momentary cessation in the buzz of conversation while the impact of Diana's appearance was absorbed. "Ah!," "Ee!" and "Oh!" The verdict seemed favourable and Diana silently blessed Bessie Brown. She really did know.

Michael came striding down the middle of the aisle. Smiling and self-assured, he nodded to those he knew and disclaimed the scattered claps by lowering his head and parting his hands abruptly, palms down. Like a conductor cutting an orchestra dead. It was cleverly done. The applause had never had sufficient impetus to grow into anything significant but Michael seized the moment and manipulated it to his advantage. It looked to most people as if he had modestly shunned an ovation. He sat in the front row on the seat reserved for him, Yolanda, tanned in white linen, beside him. They were a handsome family.

Proud of them both in spite of herself, Diana smiled before bending over the notes she had made for her short speech. That would come later.

Cedric Lafontaine rose and invited an executive of his bank temporarily to chair the meeting until such time as the directors, who had of course stepped down, should be re-elected to the board.

"I have little doubt, Ladies and Gentleman," the bank executive intoned, "that this can be achieved in the time it takes to count a show of hands. I take it that will be acceptable to the meeting?"

There was no demur at that. A show of hands it would be. The undesignated appointments were to be dealt with first.

"Will anybody propose Mr. Albert Sedgely as a Non-executive Director?"

A number of people stood up waving agenda papers. There was a shriek from one of the microphones and an engineer hurried forward to silence it. Meanwhile Father Murphy and Major Garside indulged in a jocular contest for the honour of proposing Sedgely. The other competitors fell back into their seats.

"Thank you . . . er, Major Garside. Thank you. Will anyone second the motion?" The microphone interrupted again but Father Murphy won the consolation prize. He got a stop watch out of his pocket in the way of modern clergymen about to sermonise.

"Thank you, Mr. . . . ah . . . *Father* Murphy," the banker said hastily, advised in a whisper by Diana. "Most kind. May we have a show of hands?"

Albert Sedgely was returned to office by a triumphantly unanimous vote. Most who knew him stuck up their hands out of respect and affection. Those of the Nidcaster contingent who had sometimes smarted under the ascerbity of his tongue saw that Sedgely was out of reach. There would be no taking him down a peg or two now. Abstentions would be noted and repaid. The rest voted in his favour because there was no reason not to.

"The motion is carried."

The rest of the re-elections went in much the same way. Alisdair was re-appointed as a Non-executive Director. A new

Technical Director would be presented to the shareholders for endorsement at the annual general meeting.

The interest of the meeting lay not in the composition of the board but in the future direction of the company.

"And finally, Ladies and Gentlemen, to conclude this section of the agenda, will somebody please propose Mrs. Diana Neville be reappointed as Chairman and Managing Director?"

Michael shot to his feet. Everyone could see him and although there was no shortage of shareholders who would have been happy to propose Diana, everyone gave place to her husband.

Some were unaware that as a supposed undischarged bankrupt he could not be a shareholder and was therefore not eligible to make the proposal. Others in the room more practised in these affairs simply thought he wished to make a laudatory speech in praise of his wife's leadership. Unnecessary but very proper, all the same. They settled back to wait it out. Two or three other men in the room adopted a more attentive posture.

Diana looked uncertainly at the executive who was still in the chair. Did he know this was going to happen?

She leaned forward to see the faces of her fellow directors. All re-elected except her. Cedric Lafontaine shrugged. Alisdair followed suit and looked away. Diana had seen him do that before. Secretive and pleased. She must be wrong. Sedgely was glaring at some point above Michael's head. Mr. Meers was expressionless. Diana was left to answer her own question. Some sort of surprise verbal bouquet? A technicality had been overlooked ... Or was this to be the fulfilment of her undefined dread? Whatever it was ...

"Mr. Neville, you wish to speak to this motion?" the temporary Chairman asked. Lafontaine had given him only a cursory briefing. Cedric himself was struck dumb.

Michael nodded sharply. He snapped his fingers at the engineer squatting nearby. The youth sprang forward with a microphone.

"Indeed I do, Mr. Chairman," he turned away from the dais and addressed the body of the room. "My wife, as you all know ..."

"This man has no right to be heard!" It was Philip. He was on his feet, waving his agenda paper. That voice! Diana's eyes found him and focused. In front of him the Monsignor fanned himself with his fedora and smiled in Michael's direction. The promised entertainment was beginning.

"The meeting must know . . ."

"Please address your remarks through the chair," Mr. Meers ordered fussily. He had never seen Philip Strang-Steele before.

Diana could not believe she was seeing him at all. Things were confused.

". . . has been the guiding spirit . . ." Michael held the microphone near his mouth, his glance slipping from one side of the room to the other. Watching for snipers, ". . . of a phenomenal, one might say an accidental . . ."

"Mr. Chairman, I protest in the strongest possible . . ."

Philip had no chance against Michael's amplified voice. People around him urged him to sit down. There was muttering and scuffling. Diana was poised on her chair like a porcelain doll. Paralysed. Whatever the argument was, she had no right, she understood, to take part in it. She was not the Chairman of English Gardens. Not even a director yet. She had little more voice here than Michael. Surely he should have none? But like it or not, he was using it.

". . . success by peradventure is no qualification . . ." Michael was undisturbed by the squall of dissidence at the back at the room, ". . . for active participation in the more demanding . . ."

The man standing up at the back couldn't really be Philip. Against all reason, she hoped it was not. He was in Australia. He was making things worse. She didn't want him to witness all this. Alisdair had said nothing. Philip was standing up again.

"This man is *not* a shareholder . . ."

"Through the chair, if you please . . ."

"Let the man speak . . ." Someone else had got to his feet.

"So rude . . ." A woman's voice, this time.

It was not clear who was supporting whom. Diana looked about her desperately. What were the rules? Through it all Michael went on speaking, his back turned to the platform. As far as Diana could make out, he was urging the meeting to vote her clean out of office. She heard herself repeatedly damned with faint praise. Over and over again, phrase by traitorous phrase.

". . . a talented amateur . . . magnificent effort . . . no

disrespect . . . Would always be held in the highest esteem . . . Well-deserved rest . . . showing signs of unbearable strain . . . possible advisory role . . ." Michael's voice rose in controlled increments, just enough to cover the rustle of agitation. He was letting her reputation down like a tyre.

Momentarily and illogically, Diana covered her ears, ashamed that Philip was listening. Was it really for this she had sent him away?

The rustles became rumbles. People craning their necks. A chatter of words, staccato and shrill, ricocheted from the walls.

"Shame!"

"Hear, hear!"

"The bastard!"

"Bound to say he could well be right . . ."

"Bloody shambles."

"But she's his *wife*, isn't she?"

Nothing put Michael off his stride. The temporary Chairman was helpless. Mr. Meers thumped the table. A waste of time.

Diana's jaw had dropped slightly. She no longer seemed to have anything to do with this. Out of her hands. Her fate was being tossed about the room like a rag doll. A severed head paraded on a pike. No pain. Like a wound under water.

Philip had left his place and was moving, unseen by Diana, down a side aisle. Now he bounded up on to the platform. He snatched up the microphone from in front of her. So close . . . she could touch him. But he scarcely seemed real. He never looked at her. Just a man, doing a job. He turned his back, blacking out and blinding her to what lay in front.

Odd things came back into Diana's mind. Straws in the wind. *Have it your own way*, Michael had said. Why not? The condemned woman's last requests. No reason to oppose them. Nothing had mattered to Michael at the end. She felt sorry for Epoch. Their work was in shreds.

"Michael Neville is an undischarged bankrupt," Philip roared, "with a record for fraud."

"That is libel." Greville Goodwynne had been lying in wait, lost in the crowd. "A baseless allegation. My client will sue."

So that was it. But why Greville Goodwynne? Oh, yes. She had rejected him once. Revenge. He had waited till now. Alisdair was leaning back, balancing his chair on two legs. He reached behind Meers and touched Diana on the elbow. This was it. They had flushed Michael out in the open. His lips shaped the words. In the uproar, Diana only half understood. Nothing now could be saved.

"What is so baseless, sir?" Philip threw down the challenge. "The fraud or the bankruptcy?"

They were silent, now, in the room. Michael stopped speaking as if on a cue. Attention had shifted to Goodwynne. He gave them facts, figures, and dates.

"My client is now the Chief Executive of the Guernsey Worldwide Opportunities Investment Trust. The Trust has acquired a majority shareholding in English Gardens." The lawyer sat down. His part was done.

For a moment the meeting was stunned. It took a moment before a groundswell of murmurs, sucked back like the sea, crashed back on the platform party's beach. Accusation and counter accusation. Who had known? Who *should* have known? Who had checked? Nobody, it seemed. Faces floated before Diana. Why hadn't she told them . . . warned them? She must have known. A good thing . . . or a bad thing? What did she want to do now? Would she step down? She would have to, wouldn't she? If it came to a fight, it wouldn't be a matter of hands in the air, but votes on each share. Ballots and counting. Her constituency was weak.

Diana couldn't answer. The questions came too fast. The noise was too loud. Her mind stuck on Michael. Worldwide Opportunities Trust. How like him that was. And he'd grasped the opportunity right under his nose. Philip's back was still turned. Why was he here?

Michael had begun to speak again. Calling for calm.

"Ladies and Gentlemen, I think we should hear what Mr. Neville has to say." It was Meers. Diana heard him, though no one else did.

In the midst of the uproar she saw Sedgely lower himself cautiously from the platform. His bad leg. What she could not see, because of the protective barrier of Philip's body, was where he had gone. Oblivious, Michael continued making a noise with his mouth. An alarm siren which no one could switch off. Yolanda got up unnoticed and tore the microphone lead from the power source. Her father's voice fell away. He hurled the piece of useless equipment at the engineer's head. It missed.

"You bloody little sod, you," Sedgely screeched. He was beside himself. "I knew you were a wrong 'un from the word go."

Coming to life, Diana moved from her seat. She was in time to see Sedgely fall. Michael's bunched fists worked like pistons. His right crunched into the old man's jaw, the left into his solar plexus. One, two. Spinning away from the blows, Sedgely caught Michael's flying right foot in the thigh. He hit the floor, tangled. A ventriloquist's dummy, inhumanly dapper.

People at the front saw it all. The word was passed back.

"What happened?"

"It's Albert Sedgely . . ."

"Who's he?"

"He's collapsed."

"No, that man hit him, didn't you see?"

Diana knelt down beside him, her skirts spread around her. Sedgely was deathly white. Pink looking spittle bubbled on his lips. He didn't move and there was blood oozing from a trouser leg.

"I think he's dead," Diana whispered to herself. *My God, we've killed him. Mrs. Sedgely . . . where was Mrs. Sedgely . . . ?*

"Silly old fool . . ." Michael started to bluster. Somebody grabbed him and thrust him aside. Father Murphy, in fact.

"That's enough, Michael."

"Get him," someone else said.

Turning round in a daze, Diana saw Philip with his arm around Yolanda. Her face was turned into his shoulder.

Michael had his back to a wall. He was trembling violently, trying to light a cigarette. Alisdair did it for him, avoiding the other man's touch.

The doors at the back of the room were open and people were leaving. Others were talking. Shouting. Waving their arms.

"An ambulance is coming." A man forced his way through the crowd in the aisles.

Yolanda disengaged herself from Philip. She looked down at her mother. "What about the police?" she said.

"Bandy-legged chap in gaiters is doing that."

It made as much sense as anything else.

None of them except Alisdair looked at Michael again. He

was rubbish to be cleared out of the way. Meanwhile he must be kept where he was. Isolated, like toxic waste.

The police were called by the Monsignor, which caused some delay. Fazed by the title, they thought him some sort of joker. He had to ring three times in all. After an eternity of twenty-five minutes they came and took Michael away. It was handcuffs, this time.

Diana wondered, as women do in a crisis, where they would all sleep. The day, even this day, would come to an end. No. It would go on for ever. Philip lifted her from the ground. Floating, she never felt his arms.

❦ SEDGELY WAS NOT *quite* dead. He had a badly bruised jaw bone, a hairline fracture of the pelvis and a compound fracture of his bad leg. There was some internal bleeding, but it stopped. He was shocked, by far the worst risk at his age. He was admitted to intensive care in the District Hospital. Diana and Mrs. Sedgely sat up in a corridor all night.

"Nay, Mrs. Neville, love. Don't go blaming yourself. Sedgely were always a foolhardy man."

"But it is my fault . . . if only you'd both never met me . . ."

"Now, now. None of that."

Throughout the long hours of plastic coffee cups and men in white coats going by, Mrs. Sedgely sat bolt upright, feet together, eyes dry. Diana could do no less. The standard of behavior had been set.

She sat quiet, painting the blank, boring hospital walls with blood in her mind. Patterns of anger, hate and death. Looking down at her dress, she wondered why tragedy always found you wearing the wrong clothes. She said she was cold, which she wasn't. A nurse brought her a blanket. A doctor should see her, the nurse said, and treat her for shock.

"No. I'm just cold. Please, just leave me alone."

Alisdair came to see them at about three in the morning. Michael was at Harrogate police station. He would be charged in the morning. Grievous bodily harm, very likely. Unless anything changed. Philip had taken Yolanda home to Gilbert's Tower. They were together there. Philip was trying to get her father a lawyer. Greville Goodwynne had fled.

"It won't be easy, Diana." Alisdair took her on one side.

"Nobody likes this sort of crime. Mr. Meers will instruct counsel, but it's a question of who we can get. How's Albert?"

Sedgely was holding his own. Stable, they said. Or very nearly. Fantastic, considering his years.

"Please, Alisdair. Why should you do all this for me? You and your father? Poor Yolanda ... how can she ever ... ? Why don't you take her and go?"

There were so many people to fear for, so many things to regret. Diana was not able to establish any order for anguish. Michael. She was responsible. He was hers, and her fault. Why had she not protected them all?

Alisdair was tempted to say that everything would work out for the best in the end. But whilst Sedgely's life hung in the balance, that would be premature. Diana was about to be parted from an evil by Philip Strang-Steele. It would please him, he said to his son, to see her permanently free. It could be arranged, he said. Cash was the key.

☙ BAIL WAS SET at a sum that was unreadable in either figures or words. Every nought on the end separated it by another light year from reality.

There should have been no bail at all. But counsel wore the judge out not so much with the inventiveness of his arguments but the length. "First offence of this kind ... unpremeditated ... knee-jerk reaction under unbearable stress ... seriously considering a not guilty plea ... unlikely to re-offend ... if genuine offence there had been."

A few files full of statistics reduced the prosecutor's will to live, never mind fight.

There was much else besides. Psychiatric evidence was heard. More stress at the moment might render the defendant unfit to stand trial. Was that merely possible or actually probable, asked the judge. Perfectly probable, the expert witness replied. Observe the prisoner's persistent habit of cracking his finger joints. A brand new nervous symptom.

In fact, it was the judge himself who indulged in this distressing aid to concentration. Ruffled, his lordship desisted and Michael instantly got to work on his knuckles. Counsel grasped this unexpected gift. He was beginning to run out of steam.

Did not his lordship remember the notorious case some

years ago, the lawyer entreated him, when in remarkably similar circumstances, a miscalculation was made? The accused had been an inveterate joint cracker, if memory served.

His lordship gave in. That man had hanged himself in his cell. There had been a stink. Sighing deeply, the judge named his price. Whoever came up with that sort of money wouldn't take any chances about presenting Neville for trial.

"It astounds me, Mr. Neville, that you have any friends left," the judge addressed Michael directly. "But since you do, I will place my trust in the amount Mr. Strang-Steele has to lose."

Michael evinced no surprise at his benefactor's identity. Strang-Steele must be more of a sucker than he had thought. Sweet on Diana. *She'd* come through with the goods.

❦ DIANA WAS VERY angry with Philip.

"I don't want him out . . . *ever*. He's nearly murdered my friend, destroyed my life and ruined my company, too. I don't want him here, I'm afraid of him. Don't you understand? Why have you done this to me?"

"You will eventually see," Philip answered her temperately. "At the moment things are not entirely predictable. But I do promise you this, he won't come near you again."

Apart from Sedgely and Alisdair, they were all at Gilbert's Tower together. Louise had come and spent long hours with Yolanda. Talking and talking . . . about the past and the present.

"When somebody you love does something terrible to somebody else you love," Yolanda appealed to Louise, "what should you feel?"

"You feel as you do, my dear child, and think as you ought. Love is good in itself, the unworthiness of its object does not alter that." Louise was ironing bed linen, Mrs. Sedgely having gone to the hospital. It was a pleasant occupation for someone who couldn't see very well, she said. "Smoothness is as pleasing to the fingertips as to the eye."

"I thought your eyesight was more than adequate, *Grandmère*," Yolanda twitted the old lady gently.

"That is what I allow them to think, my child. But you and I . . . we are friends, no? With men it is different," she went on, anticipating Yolanda's next question. "Excessive frankness is gauche."

Distracted from thoughts of her father, Yolanda laughed. Louise was happily scorching the pillow slips. Such an agreeable, good housewife smell, she remarked. There was nothing like the enjoyment of simple things.

That is what it had come down to, hour by hour. Yolanda hung on to the belief that something could be retrieved for her mother. Her future looked uncertain.

"A flat headed girl," Louise reported to Philip. She meant "level headed," of course.

Philip stayed close to Diana. She accepted his presence without question, at first. On her return to Gilbert's Tower he had put her to bed. Yolanda had gone to the hospital to relieve Mrs. Sedgely and Louise made herself busy elsewhere in the house.

"No, I don't want to go in there," Diana stopped at the door of her room. It was the room next door to it that bothered her. Michael's dressing-room.

"All right, I'll get your things. Tell me what and . . . where to find them." He emerged with clean night things, tooth and hair brushes. "Where are we going now?"

She led him to the tower room and Philip helped her off with her clothes. He brushed her hair and she let him.

"Do you want something to eat?"

"No, just something to drink."

Philip came back with a glass of Cognac and some water but Diana had fallen asleep. She lay on her back with one arm hanging over the side of the bed. He put it under the bedclothes, kissed her forehead and went away. He couldn't stay with her, he had too much to do.

Mr. Meers was summoned to Gilbert's Tower. He was shocked by the previous evening's events. He felt so badly, he said. He had never dreamed that Michael Neville was an unreformed crook, after all.

Philip cut him short. If Meers was admitting to having been a supporter of Neville's, it was not his concern. He didn't even know that. Diana would deal with him in her own good time. No, Mrs. Neville was seeing nobody at present.

"I have another task for you, Mr. Meers. Prepare Mrs. Neville's petition for divorce. We will need something for her

husband to sign, acknowledging service of the petition and in-
dicating his immediate, unconditional consent to all the terms
of an accompanying deed of separation, which you will also
prepare. He is never to see, or attempt to see, her again. Nor
is he to make any kind of financial claim on her. Is that clear?"

"Perfectly," Meers replied huffily. "But I must tell you that
I really can't accept instructions in a matter like that except
from my client's own lips."

"I assure you," Philip sat on the lawyer, "those instructions
will be forthcoming."

Philip handed over a sheaf of manuscript notes. The basis of
the petition. The whole squalid story laid bare. "Make the best
of it. Now, if you'll excuse me ... No. There is one more
thing. Try and get the court's permission for us to take Neville
down to my house in Lincolnshire. As you'll appreciate, he
won't be wanted here."

That interview concluded, Philip next rang his brokers. The
share price of English Gardens was showing a change. A slight
dip against yesterday's price. Evidently, Philip thought, the
gossip mongering had yet to take full effect.

"I'll buy any that come on the market."

The price rose by the end of the day but Philip continued to
buy. Whatever had gone on in the background, the stock market saw no reason to stop trading in the shares. None at all. A
bit of a roller coaster, English Gardens. What was going on
there?

Epoch were ordered to spread appropriate rumours. Some
uncertainty about the future management of the company. Mrs.
Neville was ill. Maybe just the faintest whiff of a takeover ...
that should keep things nicely buoyant.

Olaff was overcome. "Who are you? Oh, I see. Can I speak
to Diana?"

"No, not at the moment. She's *hors de combat*," Philip parried. "Speak to my son." Epoch knew Alisdair. "And Cedric
Lafontaine." The affair must be kept under wraps.

Mrs. Lightbody was fourth on the list. She was to pack her
bags and go to the Sedgely house and make things comfortable
there. Briggs would bring her. They were both to report to Gilbert's Tower first.

In the book room, Dorothy was fielding calls and piling up

memos and messages for Diana. Who was this strange man patrolling the house? Yolanda explained.

"I can't deal with half these things, Mr. Strang-Steele," Dorothy was on the verge of despair. "Where's Mr. Neville?"

"In jug. Give those things to me. I'll see what I can do with them."

He couldn't do much, not understanding what to him were small quantities and vast prices. Completely insane. It was Yolanda who stepped into the breach. She was surprised how much she knew. Nearer home there was a problem. The walled garden was in a messy, transitional stage between crops. The work there couldn't wait. Thinning the grapes and the peaches. Yolanda solved that as well. Alisdair's old college sent someone to help.

When Diana got up the following day, she was surprised she still had a business to run. "But what about me? I mean, can I carry on or not?" she asked Philip.

"Who's to stop you? There's nobody here. But we're coping. Why don't you go and see Sedgely?"

Sedgely was in theatre, having his leg set. They were going to have to take the old steel plate out and replace it. Nobody, including his wife, would be allowed to see him till much later. He might walk again. No reason, on the face of it, why he shouldn't. But on the other hand he might not.

Diana burst into tears then and said she didn't know how she could live with herself in the future. A wheelchair would be Sedgely's death warrant. It might have been better if he'd been killed outright.

"Let's try and keep a sense of proportion, dearest," Philip urged. "Mrs. Sedgely may not agree with you. Half a Sedgely is better than no Sedgely."

This unfortunate witticism brought on a fresh paroxysm of grief. Philip had not meant to be callous. He really must try and keep his own optimism in the background and not go racing ahead. Gloom was an unavoidable stage on the path to better things. He ought not to be parsimonious over the time allotted to it.

"If they can't do a decent job of patching Sedgely up locally, I shall personally escort him to where they can reassemble him from scratch. Cubic centimetre by cubic centimetre. Fellow's a hero."

Diana was not cheered. She hoped they locked Michael up and threw away the key. Really, she thought, she deserved the same fate. Philip went away with a spring in his step to let her grieve in peace. All this was a part of the process. Michael Neville and all his works must be washed out and swept clean. Tears were the best possible detergent, Philip thought. He had an unreasonable confidence that things would work out and that Sedgely would mend.

The petition for divorce temporarily supplanted Sedgely in Diana's mind. Meers brought it in person and explained its content. They talked in the book room where the orange cat sat in the pending tray licking its paws. Diana was brusque.

"You've taken rather a lot on yourself, Mr. Meers."

Meers glanced shiftily at Philip, who stood at Diana's side. Something in the tall man's expression dissuaded him from attempting to exculpate himself at Strang-Steele's expense.

"Then I must apologise if this petition does not represent your wishes, Mrs. Neville. I hoped to anticipate them as some small recompense for my . . . lack of judgment regarding your husband's fitness to . . ."

"Never mind, Mr. Meers. We have been guilty of the same error. Where do I sign?" Diana wrote her name firmly between the pencil crosses. The step should have been taken long since.

Philip witnessed her signature without the ghost of a smile. It was only one item in a projected sequence of unrelated events. It was essential to think and act in those contradictory terms. Philip, who was, after all, the son of Louise and the father of Alisdair, had no difficulty in reconciling mental chalk with mental cheese.

With Diana, an immediate reaction set in. She alternated between listlessness and over anxious activity. She walked in and out of the house, lifted telephones and put them back down again. She stood outside the door of Michael's study for half an hour but never went in. Eventually, she sat down on the floor. She was still there at suppertime. Louise found her. After that, Diana was watched closely for signs of nervous collapse. She got up in the middle of the night, unable to sleep. Her footsteps, coming down from the tower and creaking on the old landing floorboards, awoke Philip. He followed her down the main staircase and made her drink tea. Then Yolanda, hearing the noise below, came down herself.

It was suggested by Philip that Diana should come down from the tower. It was too far away. Diana exploded.

"Too far away for what? I don't need feeding and changing every four hours. No more babysitting, please."

Relieved, in a way, that he had outstayed his welcome, Philip said he had affairs to attend to. He would go home but might he, for the moment, leave Louise? Any breakages and despoliations, he offered, would be paid for in full.

Diana laughed. Of course Louise must stay as long as she wished. Anything irreplaceable could always be locked up.

"Don't think me ungrateful, Philip, but I can't get a clear picture of anything with you so close."

Philip thought a tactical withdrawal at this point ideal. It fitted in perfectly with the final arrangements for Neville. He'd delayed signing the bail documents long enough. It should have been done immediately after the hearing but Philip had managed to fudge things for a couple of days. Then at the last moment, Diana seemed unwilling to let him go. What if Michael came back? What could she do? Couldn't Alisdair come and be with them?

"In a day or two, yes. Just now I need them. Neville won't come back. If he does, call the police. You do not have to have him in your house, Diana," Philip finished crisply, kissing her cheek.

"I wish to God I never had," she groaned. "Now I'll have to go through it all again."

PHILIP DID NOT intend there to be any repetition of the Nevilles' past.

Michael was collected by himself and Briggs in the old Austin Princess from Armley gaol. He was taken in silence to Lincolnshire. The car had security locks on the doors. Expecting to be taken home, Michael sensed some sort of trap. Whatever its purpose, he had no intention of sticking around to find out.

"Look, Strang-Steele, I don't know what all this is about, but I need a slash."

"That is inconvenient, Neville. Out of the question, I'm afraid."

Briggs handed a urinal bottle over his shoulder. Michael ignored it.

Arriving at North Barkwith, he was taken to a unoccupied

staff flat. Alisdair was already there. Michael was allowed to relieve himself in a bathroom that had no windows.

"Sit down, if you please, on that chair." Philip indicated a straight chair in an otherwise unfurnished room. "My son will tell you a number of facts. Facts that are quite unconnected to these documents I have here."

Michael was alert, intent.

"I will begin by listing the documents. Your wife's petition for divorce, together with your acknowledgment of service. Various other papers connected with the termination of your marriage, which you will find self-explanatory. A share transfer certificate. Your signature on this will convey to me all your Guernsey outfit's shares in English Gardens for a consideration amounting to their value at last night's close of business price."

"You bloody, bribing . . ."

"A fair price is hardly a bribe, Neville, is it? I'm offering you nothing at all. What you do, you will do entirely of your own free will."

It was Alisdair's turn to speak.

"Two miles due south of here there is a small private landing strip and a hangar. It used to be a club. If you were to walk there—it would take you approximately half to three-quarters of an hour—you would find a light aircraft there. It belongs to a small aviation company specialising in crop spraying. A one man band. The fitter, who is also the pilot, is often to be found there carrying out checks and minor repairs. He likes to hop across to the Continent when he can afford the fuel. That happens very infrequently. Just lately, he's had a windfall. He likes company, too."

"You pair of unprincipled fuckers," Michael got up from the chair.

"Do sit down, won't you?" Philip invited him smoothly. "Try to think, Neville. As clearly as you can."

Michael sank his head in his hands. He could go somewhere else and start again. If he stayed in the UK he'd go to prison for years. Probably to a good old-fashioned nick. No second bite at the "programme participant" cherry. If he took the chance these two pompous pigs were offering him, he could never come back here again. Either way, his wife and his daughter were lost to him. The final de-balling.

"You get to fuck my wife, and I get to fuck off . . . is that it?"

"You are becoming muddled, Neville." Philip retained perfect command of himself. Alisdair would have very much liked to hit him and probably would if his father had not been present. "This suggestion of a deal is quite inappropriate. It is a creation of your imagination. You have been acquainted with a string of unrelated facts. How you act upon these is for you to decide. Possibly you will dismiss what you have heard as having no coherent meaning. No bearing on your situation."

"Cash, passport, destination?" Michael demanded. "What guarantees do I have?"

"You express yourself very strangely, Neville. For a man who must report to the police on a regular basis and eventually stand trial. The only guarantee that affects you is the certainty of fair treatment before the law. Of course, there is no guarantee that poor Mr. Sedgely will live. His condition is considered precarious."

"You'll be charged with murder if he dies within a year," Alisdair interrupted his father. "Does that make anything clearer?"

"I didn't ask you sods for a lecture. I asked you about money, travel documents and . . ."

"You are a resourceful man, Neville. Whenever, after a long term of imprisonment, you need these luxuries again, I'm sure you will find them available. For the moment, you are our guest."

Michael knew he would get no more from them than that.

On the way from the disused flat to the house, Alisdair kept up a running commentary on the features of the estate. The loose boxes in the stables, he mentioned, all of which were now offices, faced south. This had been the preferred orientation of housing for valuable horses. Interesting, wasn't it?

There could be no doubt in Michael's mind as to the direction he should take.

He was left to dine alone, waited on by a crop haired, monosyllabic young man with tattooed hands. A portrait of "Biggles" on one and the "Red Baron" on the other. Michael's hosts, unfortunately, had a prior engagement. They hoped he would enjoy his meal and sleep well. He must help himself to the contents of the sideboard decanters . . . and anything else.

After he had eaten, the tattooed youth showed Michael to a ground floor bedroom suite. It had been furnished for the convenience of visiting Strang-Steele Group executives and had originally been the morning room. The use of the colour television and shower were solemnly demonstrated.

"The french window opens as well, sir. But lock it last thing, and take the key out of the lock, won't you, sir? Mr. Strang-Steele's mustard keen on security."

He began opening drawers in a fussy, valetish way. This and his sudden garrulity were at variance with his earlier demeanour.

"Looks as though the last bloke left something," he said. "Just a moment, sir, I'll get you a fresh cake of soap."

Michael examined the contents of the bureau's top drawer rapidly. A folder contained cash in several currencies and a passport. Julian Smart. He bore a passable resemblance to Michael himself. Not bad. Occupation: agro-chemist. Not so good.

When the tattooed manservant came back with the soap, Michael had gone. The youth closed the french windows and, locking them, left himself by the front door.

Approximately thirty-five minutes later, the navigation lights of a light aircraft could be seen from an office in the old stable block's hay lofts. The pilot waggled the wings.

"I hope Smart's not going on holiday shortly," Alisdair remarked.

Philip poured himself a small whisky and said that forgetful men suffered many inconveniences. He also said that chaps who embarked on rescuing princesses in moated granges must expect some expense. Law breaking was quite another matter, but honest knights were easily duped.

Not normally a very demonstrative man, Philip clapped his arm around his son's shoulders.

"We must prepare ourselves to feel very foolish indeed."

CHAPTER
18

❦ THE ABSCONDMENT OF Michael Neville was soon common knowledge. Speculation was rife. Would all the bail money be forfeit? Surely not, it was thought, if Neville were caught in time to stand trail. Poor Mr. Strang-Steele had been taken for a hell of a ride.

In Nidcaster, public and private sympathy savoured freshly of lemon. A fool and his money were soon parted, they said with knowing shakes of the head. There was one born every minute ... especially outside Yorkshire. An agreeable, if self-evident fact. It quite took the edge off Michael Neville's escape. The wastage of other people's money, like the spillage of other people's blood, had a certain mysteriously redemptive effect.

More to the purpose, Neville's come-uppance, whenever and wherever it came, need not sully the town's scrubbed civic doorstep. A place that specialised in ice cream, boat trips and effortless fecundity of an horticultural kind could dispense with the ghoulish attraction of murderer and martyr alike. Good, clean family fun was the basis of trade. Sensationalism, along with waxworks and whelks, the *Bystander* loftily prosed, belonged in seaside resorts. There were no horror shows wanted here by the gorge.

Nidcaster's Mayor and Aldermen sent a "get well" card to Sedgely. The message inside advised him robustly to put his back into living. There'd be a seat on the Council for him, it was hinted, if he cared to survive.

Diana, becalmed at the eye of the storm, was left severely alone. For once Nidcaster forbore to comment. What old Miss

FitzGilbert would have thought, no one could guess. Her ghost was invoked repeatedly, however, as the only way of expressing solidarity with the present day chatelaine of Gilbert's Tower. Some sufferings were deemed too deep and distinguished either to witness or discuss. As fast as was possible, the townsfolk politely turned their backs. Not so much as a quizzical "Now, then?" was addressed to Diana. She understood. She had been placed in quarantine pending further developments. A question mark hovered over Gilbert's Tower. All hoped devoutly that Michael Neville, like a visitation of plague, had done the worst that he could and moved on. Time would tell.

"My guess is he's slipped through our fingers for good." Alisdair tried and failed to look regretful on a visit to Sedgely.

"Aye, well," the patient grunted, "he would since you spread 'em so wide. You were taken in good and proper. You and your dad."

Alisdair observed the foxy glint in the Yorkshireman's eye with a degree of misgiving. How much did the old fellow guess? It was Sedgely's perspicacity that had brought his father home from Australia in the first place. Until Alisdair had agreed to contact Philip there, Sedgely had pursued him relentlessly. He knew a villain when he saw one, he said. Goaded day and night, Alisdair gave in. Lack of hard evidence troubled Sedgely not one whit. If cornered, Michael Neville would show himself up in his true colours, Sedgely insisted. And he had.

Even so, Diana's husband might still have got away with it, had it not been for Sedgely's own drastic intervention. He had very nearly paid the price of his persistence with his life.

"I'll be sorry, Albert, if you don't get your revenge." Alisdair tested the ground a little further.

"Nay, Mr. Alisdair, lad. You know me better 'n that. He's gone and I 'ope it's for good. Best thing. Debt's paid in full."

Alisdair was prevented from asking what this extraordinary statement could mean by the approach of an exasperated nurse.

"Now, Mr. Sedgely, we've been fiddling with our drip again, haven't we?" The nurse placed her hands on her hips.

The needle, which Sedgely had removed from his arm at the start of Alisdair's visit, hung loose by the bed. He didn't hold with saline solution. "Saline *dilution*," he called it. It was weakening his blood.

"I 'ave, lass. Can't speak for you." Sedgely reproved the nurse's plural language of caring. "I suppose thee'll fiddle t'damn thing back in again. I've enough ruddy watter in me to sink a battleship."

Sedgely succumbed to the ministrations of the nurse with a bad grace. He was proving a very fractious post-operative patient. By turns impish and rancorous, his vitality signalled a speedy recovery. It was also playing havoc with ward routines and tempers.

"Now I want a word with you," Sedgely wagged his forefinger at Alisdair, disregarding the wretched nurse's attempt to re-attach that hand to the saline supply, ". . . before you go. Try and get Mrs. Neville to leave off coming to see me so much. Wearing 'erself out, she is. She's no need to blame herself. What's past is past. She wants to be concentrating on getting t'Tower spic and span for when you and Miss Landa get wed. No point in putting that off. No point at all. And speaking of Miss Landa, I'd like a word with her an' all. Tomorrer morning 'll do."

Of course, whatever Sedgely wanted, Sedgely had to have.

❦ WHILST SEDGELY, IN his own inimitably cryptic fashion, informed the daughter of his heart where her best interests lay, Philip wrestled with his conscience.

Looking at it coldly, he had done nothing wrong. He had happened to notice the useful alignment of a few accidental circumstances . . . and perhaps tweaked them a trifle. Was he truly to blame for another man's carelessness over his passport? The trip to collect an emergency consignment of pesticides from Holland was perfectly genuine, too. He was not Neville's keeper, only his sponsor. So many small things had conspired to promote Philip's intent and limit his guilt.

Tramping moodily up and down his pea and bean fields, Philip reached an estimate of his own actions with which he could live. He had tempted a man to do wrong, knowing he could do nothing but. Having no actual responsibility to close the gate, he had left it invitingly open. It was no worse than that. Any punishment due to Neville he would take with him wherever he went. Banishment saved the tax payer the expense of imprisonment ... cost effective retribution which would spare Neville's innocent family more public agony. He, Philip Strang-Steele, had nothing whatsoever to gain.

Satisfied with his portrait of himself as a disinterested social benefactor and finding himself in the nineteen acre spinach field, Philip hitched a lift on a tractor and went back to the house. Two weeks had gone by and Diana had not heard from him in all that time. There was no news of Neville either, Scotland Yard said, through the medium of the Wisbech police. He could be lost in the stews of Dar-es-Salaam by now, they said. It was out of their hands. Interpol had all the details. They would follow it up, the Chief Constable implied, whenever international manpower resources could be spared from vastly more significant crime.

"Not promising, then?" Philip managed to sound resigned.

"It's drug runners," the policeman replied candidly. "They're more of a career catch for these foreign flash Harrys."

Expectations of bringing Neville speedily to book were not high. He had a fifteen-day start on the law.

Philip directed his thoughts to Gilbert's Tower. After some uncharacteristic dithering between this pin-striped poplin shirt or that, he had the Bristol brought round and drove there at once. Before his reward could be denied him, he reasoned, it must first be claimed. Decent intervals, considerate delay ... faint hearted excuses made by cowardly suitors. The time now was ripe.

On the way up the A1, Philip reviewed his arsenal. A glance in the wing mirror reflected a reasonably picturesque ruin, he believed. Of course he was dull and had never shown as a wit, but there again, he was amply supplied with funds. If that failed to seduce, as it conceivably might, then Philip feared he would find himself at a loss. At least she owed him an outright rejection. Let Diana tell him herself, in so many words, that she could not love him, and neither wanted nor needed him. She should not have an easy time doing it. He owed himself that.

Bringing his vehicle to rest outside the garden door, Philip was exhilarated. Any minute he would see her again and, in an hour or two, know where he stood. Whatever her verdict, it would be better than dangling like a half hanged man, choking on hope.

"I didn't want to ring you," Diana greeted him with a dry peck on the cheek. "We seem to have depended on you far too much . . . and now this dreadful business of Michael skipping bail. Where on earth can he have gone? Why have you thrown such an obscene amount of money away on us?" It came out in a rush.

"Well, now," Philip stood on the doorstep, arranging his features, "I might get over it better if you allowed me inside."

Overcome with confusion at her unintentional rudeness, Diana took his arm and drew him indoors. Mrs. Sedgely appeared from the rear of the house, smiling broadly.

"We're right glad to see you, Mr. Strang-Steele, sir. Madame love's upstairs having her rest. Mr. Alisdair 'll be in to 'is tea soon and Sedgely's going on as well as can be expected, like. Miss Landa's just gone off to t'ospital and won't be back to 'er supper till late. You'll be having yours here, I expect. It's nowt special, mind."

Having delivered her summation of the combined Neville and Strang-Steele affairs, Mrs. Sedgely retired to the kitchen and clattered things in loud celebration. That was all that was needed, pot and pan seemed to say. A bit of male company for Mrs. Neville. Help take her out of herself.

In the drawing-room, Diana motioned Philip to a chair almost awkwardly. She did not sit herself but moved about the edges of the room, shifting books and flowers. The company of somebody to whom she owned too much was disquieting. She had taken from him until she was ashamed to take any more.

"Philip, I don't know what I can say to you. I do wish you hadn't done this," she looked at him reproachfully. "I feel that you own me."

Glad of the opening, Philip was quick to explain that Diana's feeling had a foundation in fact. It was not the most auspicious of introductory courtship speeches.

"I should like to talk to you about that. One way and another, during the past few weeks I have acquired a controlling interest in English Gardens. Now . . ."

The look of astonished betrayal in Diana's eyes faded a little as Philip described what he had done and why. She paid him close attention.

"It was only a temporary rescue operation, I assure you. Not a predatory raid. When people were losing their nerve and selling, I bought. That way confidence came back. Now the situation's stable, I can start releasing those shares back on to the market in unsuspicious dribs and drabs, but . . ."

"If you do," Diana finished for him, "we will always be vulnerable to another raider . . . another Michael?"

"Quite. On the other hand, if you let me absorb English Gardens into the Strang-Steele Group, I can protect the company and spare you the tedium of broadening the trading base of the company into general distribution. You don't really want to squander your life on cans of baked beans, do you, Diana? No poetry in that."

"But it's no longer up to me, is it? You'll have to ask the other directors and shareholders. I'm not a director. Michael saw to that."

Philip looked down his nose and pursed his lips.

"I should take no notice of that. A no-ball, a mis-deal . . . the whole affair. Company lawyers of the kind I employ will arrange matters to suit me. And that means to suit you, my love."

Holding his arm out to her, Philip coaxed her to come and sit near him. She was wild and shy with him.

"That's better," he said. "I don't care to conduct business with a moving target."

All this businesslike kindness was very long drawn out. Diana was not personally happy with the proposals. How could she work for a man she had slept with and no longer did? Relegation from bed to a boardroom in bondage to the Strang-Steele Group. That's how it sounded. This was too economical a recycling of the waste fibres of love. A travesty of what might once have been. Philip *deared* her and *darlinged* her without tiring. Incongruous words for a takeover bid.

Not quite knowing how to get around to his point, Philip outlined the many advantages to English Gardens that membership of the Strang-Steele Group would bring. All excellent stuff for a corporate wooing. But somehow, he noticed, he was missing the mark with Diana.

Philip felt uncomfortably young. A rising sensation of

knobbliness, thick throated inarticulacy and an adolescent itch on the skin. Trapped in a groove, he kept on talking of massive resources, economies of scale, and immediate uplift in the share price, freedom from fear of the future.

"But not freedom from you, Philip. I and my company would be yours, lock, stock and barrel."

Feeling his hands and feet grow larger by the second, Philip took a deep breath. There was no help for it now. He'd best say his piece and be off.

"I am patient, determined and rich," he avowed with startling bluntness. "Lacklustre qualities, perhaps, but dependable. Sufficient, I hoped, to persuade you to consider another kind of merger on the strength of them. I dared to think that by now you might be convinced of my devotion . . . Diana, I'm not an articulate man." Philip paused, searching her eyes. "And since I see," he went on in a monotone, "that you do not love me and cannot, therefore, accept me, I will not oppress you with a distasteful inventory of my feelings for you."

This was insupportable. "Please don't say that, Philip."

"You are right. I deserve it. I have interfered with your life, intruded in your home and your marriage . . ." Philip elongated his face lugubriously as he continued to condemn himself in harshly unjust terms. It wasn't strictly fair, of course. It was all made to sound as if these were Diana's own accusations. It seemed to be working. Having nothing to lose now, Philip played on this theme. "I have even, er . . . pestered you with attentions which must have been unwelcome."

Diana flew at him and pressed her hand over his mouth. That he should repudiate their single act of lovemaking, all the gentleness that had been between them and which her memory cherished, hurt her indescribably.

"I can't bear you to say these things to me. Stop it at once. It's wicked and cruel of you."

Philip's eyes sparkled above his gag. Diana stormed at him for minutes together. She said everything he wanted to hear.

"I would do anything for you. But how can I, when you never stop doing everything for me?"

"You wouldn't leave Neville for me," Philip freed himself.

"You didn't ask, not exactly, and I couldn't. Not unless he left me. I was stuck, don't you see?"

"Yes," Philip held both her hands rigidly. "I did see. Not at first, but later. That's why I came back to try again. Now will you have me, Diana?"

A lengthy discussion ensued. It was all the usual thing. Revelations of doubts and confusions, an unearthing of misunderstood signals and the wonderment caused that love should ever be mutual or arise from the mere accident of once having met.

They found themselves awed that *they*, simple pinpricks of being, had been selected by chance to be stars in a constellation of two. Diana and Philip, forty-three and fifty-three respectively, traced the origins of their attraction with just as much narcissism as the hero and heroine of any youthful romance.

"Oh, but Philip, we can't. I mean I can't . . . not with all this hanging over me. And remember, I was married to Michael for more than twenty years." She sat on the arm of his chair and held his face between her palms. "And what will the children say?"

"I suppose they may very well jeer at us." Philip seemed delighted at the prospect. "Do you realise, the first time I had you in my arms, we'd met to prevent them marrying?"

There was more in a similar vein, fit only for the ears of the parties. Sentimental recollections threatened to outface the ordinary rules of good taste. Credit was also given to Louise's gothic machinations. She had wanted this and been right to want it—never an easy admission to make regarding the desires of a parent, no matter how old or exotic.

But Diana could not long be distracted from the single fly in the ointment. She had been marked out for misfortune and, by association, disgrace. It was an ignominious dowry and not one she could simply lay down. Whoever took her would also get this. People, she feared, might drop Philip if he married her.

Unhampered by false modesty or a courtier's tongue, Philip laughed that to scorn. Very few had been granted the opportunity of taking him up in the first place, he said. Moreover, he pointed out with forgivable smugness, the happy and beautiful wife of an innocent man with financial clout was likely to arouse the judgment of envy . . . not morals.

Diana looked only mildly disapproving at the unblushing enumeration of these unfair advantages. She relaxed against his shoulder, and was too late to spring quite away from him before Louise, stealthy in soft soled Italian pumps, was upon them. Her vision was poor but there was nothing wrong with her ears. And a moment's pause at the drawing-room door had served to forearm her against any attempted discretion.

"Charming," she said, "utterly charming. But you had better go out to dinner," she added in a managing tone. "One love affair at a time, if you please. You must take your turn. My grandson's marriage takes precedence."

Diana didn't know quite how it was that she came to be helping Philip reassure his mother that they had no intention of stooping to the selfish vulgarity of a double wedding.

"And I haven't even said I can or I will yet, *Madame*."

"I should hope not, *chère* Diana. That would not be quite *comme il faut*. In the case of a second marriage, the refusals should occupy an interval of approximately four hours or until bedtime, whichever is the sooner. Longer would be pretentious."

It was impossible not to laugh and agree.

Conferring matriarchal kisses on her son and Diana, Louise bound them to secrecy. Diana's Decree Absolute was not through yet, for one thing. A more settled prognosis regarding Mr. Sedgely ought to precede any announcement of happiness arising out of his pain.

"We must see our way clear, as far as we can. And from now till September, my Yolanda is queen. Once she is married, then you may proceed."

Philip said Diana must be allowed to make her own decisions, particularly in her own house. Diana hushed him, and said Louise was quite right. And really, she had not yet said yes. In all the surrounding circumstances, wouldn't it be just too opportunist to marry?

The nuance in the language was too much for Louise. She wanted to know what opportunities were for, if not to be grabbed. *Taken*, Philip corrected austerely. Ladies did not grab. Not English speaking ones, at any rate.

While Diana changed her dress and Philip telephoned the Tsaritsa, Louise, left in sole possession of the drawing-room, fumbled for her spectacles.

"We old ones," she addressed Aunt Thea's portrait, "must ensure that all is ordered with dignity. A marriage between our two houses is serious business. It will not have escaped you, *chère Mademoiselle*, that it has been long in the planning. When it is done, we may both of us rest."

🦋 SEATED IN THE first floor *salon* at the Tsaritsa, at the very table where Philip had laid eyes on Diana for the second time, she gave him her formal and final answer. Of course, it was "yes."

"Mr. Neville has had his twenty years, Diana. I don't say whether or not he deserved them, but we have only one life, my darling. This is not a rehearsal."

Misery, Philip persuaded her, had no rights. No prolonged ceremony of self-denial or wearing of long faces was due.

That clinched it and Philip ordered champagne. They held hands across the top of the table and beneath it, sat with ankles entwined. Highly improper behaviour, both would have thought, if they had considered deportment at all. Many eyes were turned on them. Some were soft with nostalgia and others stark with jealous suffering. But lovers are pitiless people and drinking their wine, Diana and Philip were insulated from any looks, murmurs or gestures that were not entirely their own.

Only the arrival of a platter of perfect peaches, some amber, some crimson—the first of one crop and the last of another—aroused Diana. They came from Gilbert's Tower. Philip weighed them in his palm and smoothed their bloom with his thumb.

🦋 BY THE MORNING, Diana had changed her mind. Perhaps it was the peaches. They represented the home she had fought for and saved. How could she leave it? Gilbert's Tower clung and would not loosen its grasp. It was all too much, too soon.

"I must take advice, Philip," she told him on the telephone, "about the company merger, and other things, too. May I have a little time?"

"My dear," he gruffly informed her, "the world waits on your pleasure." He rang off abruptly.

Not knowing whether to laugh or cry, Diana promptly did both.

"Foolish woman." Louise contained her bitter disappointment at hearing of Diana's Janus faced reply to her son's proposal. "She will lose the best husband on offer in the whole Common Market." Which was small comfort to Philip. To herself she added, "Oh, this house!"

CHAPTER
19

❦ THE WEDDING OF Yolanda and Alisdair did take place in September as originally planned.

More angry, perhaps, than anyone else with her father, Yolanda had taken some persuading. To get her wish to be married from Gilbert's Tower in such a way, against such a background of treachery and violence, she felt, would tarnish the day. She and Alisdair could get married in a registry office anywhere . . . or just live together somewhere. Who needed an empty show?

In their separate ways on different occasions, Louise and Sedgely strove to revise these opinions. On one point they concurred. Yolanda was told that she had always been right to consider the place and the style of her marriage important. An enterprise not begun right could scarcely end well.

A wedding, Louise lectured, was not staged solely for the principals, but to make a fitting end to the not inconsiderable labours of the people who'd had the trouble of bringing them up. As vital, Yolanda should realise, to a mother's well-being as a live birth itself. Louise was unconscious that she spoke not only of Diana but also herself.

Sedgely preferred blackmail to reason.

How could Yolanda think of disappointing him after all he'd been through? Nidcaster needed a wedding, he said. Aye, and English Gardens did too. Summut positive for a change. 'T weren't all a matter of fattening the share price. The thing had a soul that were crying out for nourishment, as well. The father's part, Sedgley snorted, would be played by himself. He would give her away.

"Not that tha wants any giving, mind, but I fancy I might walk again if it were a matter of getting up t'aisle."

Not a day later, Louise said that the best place to embark on life's journey was from home, in good shoes. There was a fair amount of salty folkloric wisdom of that sort handed out. Old Provençal sayings, Louise claimed. In fact, she made them up as the needs of her dialogue with Yolanda suggested.

Yolanda compared these arguments ceaselessly. In the end, it was Alisdair, now living alone at the Harrogate flat, who made an end of debate.

"Do you want to marry me or not?" he blew up. "Because if so, I will make the decision. Wherever Michael Neville is not, I am ready to go. No alteration there, you'll agree. That being the case, we'll be married from Gilbert's Tower."

He said a good deal more. Yolanda must pull herself together for everyone's sake. There was no longer any obstacle. Diana was not to be troubled with this imaginary controversy. She had enough on her plate. The thing must be settled between them right now. Today. Messing about was stressful to all. Enough of the past had been spoiled, why should the future suffer? Yolanda did still want to marry him, didn't she?

Yolanda said yes, in a very small voice, and then rallied, to Alisdair's pride and relief.

"On one condition. That you don't abuse my father again in my hearing or anywhere else for that matter. However bad he has been, he's not here to defend himself."

"Ha!" Alisdair barked sharply on hearing this sensitive truth. "How right you are. You've got yourself a deal there, darling. My lips are sealed."

Wisely, he said no more. It was enough that Yolanda had allowed herself to be guided for once. Alisdair went off to the industrial unit with air cushioning the soles of his feet, an invisible laurel wreath encircling his curls. A man in love with a wilful woman likes to think he can dominate her just now and again.

Pondering Alisdair's blissful departure, his kisses still damp on her neck, Yolanda felt the last of her doubts disappearing. A little carefully managed crossness was very invigorating. Her fiancé understood that one needed, just occasionally, to be ordered to do what one wanted. Gilbert's Tower it must be.

"September the twelfth, Mummy, if you don't mind," Yolanda instructed her mother with mannerly firmness.

She sat behind the desk in the book room, from where she was running the day to day affairs of the business during the long vac. Real life commercial experience. It would count towards her diploma. From the day after the cathartic shareholders' meeting, she had slipped so naturally and effortlessly into her mother's shoes that nobody thought it odd. The problem now was how she could be spared for her course which recommenced in October.

"Are you going to give me a shorthand note of whom to invite, Landa?" Diana teased. "Do you think you can trust me to get this thing right?"

Straight faced, Yolanda said she was certain she could. Hadn't Diana founded English Gardens all by herself? Amused rather than irritated, Diana set to work. There was just enough time to get the banns read.

The Vicar's sparse Sunday morning congregation soon spread the word. Before Nidcaster's Yorkshire puddings were out of the oven, the town's keenest intellects had digested the news. Summut special had better be done. A bit of a do.

" 'T isn't a matter of sycophancy, or owt of that sort," said the Mayor to his wife. "I've got to think of the good of the town. If that there refurbishment at t'owd mill goes ahead, there'll be a score of jobs there for a start. Maybe more. To win commitment, you've got to show it."

The Mayor masticated a forkful of beef, pleased with the big time, political flavour of this thought. "How do you think them Geordie geezers in Sunderland got the Nips to put up a car factory on their patch? I'll bet it cost 'em a packet in *sake* and bows."

The headmaster, the editor of the *Bystander* and selected local worthies were barely through with their trifle when called to the phone.

The Mayor put his case to them squarely. They could kill several birds with one stone. Put on a bit of a spectacle to mark t'occasion of t'marriage ... it would round off t'tourist season nicely. Relations with Gilbert's Tower and English Gardens would be cemented and public charged for t'pleasure of looking at t'show. Now that'd give Blackpool illuminations summut to go on with ... and it were a bit of tradition, an' all.

Irresistible arguments. The details were thrashed out in the chamber next day. Tasks were in the process of delegation and publicity arranged just as Diana was ringing Epoch in London. Her daughter's marriage, she told Merlin Olaff, for reasons she was sure he could imagine, was to be a low profile affair for family and friends. A quiet country wedding. He was invited, indeed, very much wanted, but the press most emphatically were not.

Nidcaster, however, with its genius for the back handed compliment, decreed otherwise. The FitzGilbert wedding (for that is what it was called during the run-up to the event) was to do everyone a bit of good. Diana was helpless to prevent it. And in truth, she was touched that in spite of everything, she and her family should still be of note in the town.

There were to be fireworks and the Lord only knew what else. There was a lot of hammering going on in closed boat houses and sheds along the water front. And in the lane there had never been such a late planting of window boxes or beating of rugs in the yards.

❦ THE DAY WAS near enough to the anniversary of Diana's first coming to Gilbert's Tower.

It dawned with a vapour of low lying mist that might herald autumn or great heat to come. There were no guarantees at this time of the year. Outside, the vine conservatory wore a striped skirt. An ingenious, circular marquee extension fitted out with buffet and bandstand with a sufficient supply of gilt chairs. It wasn't very big, enough for seventy people or so. Indoors, the caterer's headquarters was already set up in the kitchen. The bride's breakfast would be carried up to her room on a tray. The rest of the household would have to catch what they could.

Awake early, Diana looked from her window and ran up the sash. She had got over her aversion to Aunt Thea's room and in Michael's old dressing-room much of her own wardrobe was packed. The doors were kept locked. No one was to know. Except Mr. Meers, of course. He had received his instructions. There would be more to this day than anyone could possibly guess.

The phone rang by her bed. Diana caught it up quickly,

mouth dry, afraid even now to hear Michael's voice. *Oh, wherever he is . . . Don't let him spoil it . . . Not now.*

"All set?" It was Philip ringing from the Prospect. "Can I do anything?"

He was always the practical, unoffendable friend.

"Have you changed your mind about anything again . . . yet?"

"Now, Philip, don't fluster me. I'm the bride's mother. Entitled to respect for my nerves. I must think only of hair-dos and food. Good heavens! It's only six o'clock. I hope you haven't rung Alisdair."

Philip reassured her. Alisdair was to be left until half past nine and delivered to the church at twenty to twelve. They talked for a while, contented to have so many small things in common. Quite enough, Diana thought, for the present.

"Will Sedgely be all right, do you think?"

"You leave that to him."

Sedgely had been removed to a private orthopaedic convalescent centre. There he had worn the physiotherapists out. He laid his own timetable down. He had a certain distance to cover on a certain date. September twelfth. No wheelchair, no walking frame. The supervising specialist had attempted to dissuade him from this incautious ambition. Sedgely had sent for his suitcase. The clinic was obliged to give in. The exercise programme was stepped up. The Moss Bros assistant sent to fit Sedgely for a morning coat swore he'd had to measure the peppery old party on the run.

Sedgely was now at home. Unbeknownst to Diana, he was already about and, in between trying on his grey topper at alternate angles, was limbering up for his feat.

"I 'ope, Albert Sedgely," his wife admonished, sipping her tea, "you'll be satisfied with yourself in time to give me a chance at that mirror."

Not long afterwards, the whole town was astir, sampling the air with experienced sniffings and reviewing the portents. For tradesmen and café owners, it was more than sufficient that the heavy dew had vanished. A dry, warm day for t'wedding and a crisp, dry night for the fireworks. The forecast in general was good. It should bring a lot of folk into Nidcaster to spend their money. Others were not so sanguine.

In dark, narrow ginnels off the market square, pinafored

Cassandras with nothing to lose stood on their doorsteps gossiping gloomily while down by the river there were similar mutterings. A coterie of elderly men in guernseys and gumboots, Nidcaster's regulation waterside wear, were dressed to do nothing but prophesy doom. It were all very well, t'Council spending folk's money . . . but what if nobody came? They were going at t'thing bull headed. The sky might be cloudless now, but t'ducks were looking like rain. Any mistakes with the Mummers' Play and nature exacted her price, proposed one ancient triumphantly.

"Nay, lad," chorused the others. That were going too far. Sedgely's bad leg were enough. This were Yorkshire, think on, not some benighted foreign dump.

More practical people were busy.

The wooden grandstands on the forest side were in place. So were the rafts in the river. Workmen were scrambling all over the place, banging in a few last minute nails. Mrs. Garvey's café was putting on a wedding day tea, plaice and chips, bread and butter, blackberry pie with real cream and a bottle of ale. Six quid a head and a free seat in a boat when you'd eaten. Beat that for value.

Ned was still locked up in his shed, putting the finishing touch to his present. Gilbert's Tower would have t'best craft on t'river. A sleek gondola job with the FitzGilbert crest on the prow.

While a hairdresser unloaded her gear at Gilbert's Tower, ready to perfect the ladies' *coiffures*, Father Murphy was hard at work in his study. There had been no trouble getting permission to preach the address. Nidcaster's vicar knew a refusal would put ecumenism on the line. And Murphy was a longstanding family friend. The hospitality of the pulpit could not be denied. Fifteen minutes was the limit for speechifying, though. A rule of the parish. Father Murphy serenely ignored it.

Bessie Brown arrived next at the Tower to attend to the bride and her gown. Meanwhile, Bob at the station was patrolling the platform, readying the place for the arrival of London based guests. He nipped out dead heads from the hanging baskets, curbed straggles of late summer lobelia, fretted overall with watering can and broom.

"Stand still, Miss Landa, love, do." Mrs. Brown gave the

bride a small shake. "I've only a half dozen to go now. I don't know. You young people have been ruined with velcro."

There were forty-eight silk covered buttons to do up Yolanda's dress. It was oyster coloured wild silk, cut low and square at the neck, with elbow length sleeves, a seed pearl embroidered pointed stomacher and a train of moderate length. Straightforward eighteenth century elegance, Bessie Brown had called it when showing her sketches. No puffs, frills or flounces. No need with a figure like Miss Neville's. And there was to be no veil, hat, coronet or wreath. Nothing to mask those shoulders or compete with the shine of her hair. That was to be dressed into a butter gold crown with a single, long ringlet falling down. Absolute simplicity.

A magnifying glass or X-ray eyes were needed to appreciate how expensively complicated Mrs. Brown's notions of simplicity were. Between the dress itself and the lining, the blue stain bows which decorated each seam were concealed. The embroidered wheat ears, executed in gold and cream thread had real pearls for the grains. These were contributed by Louise. Survivors from an old necklace, too elaborate and out of fashion to re-thread. There were enough left to incorporate in the wheat ear patterned lace, made by a craft group locally, for the narrow edgings to neck and to sleeve.

"Why wheat, though?" Yolanda had asked.

"Fertility, dear. You want babies, don't you?"

Yolanda was tempted to reply she'd like sex first but kept it to herself. No girl with pretensions to street cred owned up to virginity these days.

When Bessie Brown had finished, Louise and Diana joined Yolanda. Louise, chic in royal blue ribbon lace with some absurd little item perched on her hair, kissed Yolanda through a wide meshed, spotted veil.

"Philip told me to give you this." Louise produced the pearl necklace with diamond clasp that she had once ill advisedly persuaded Diana to wear. "It was worn by his first wife, and belonged to my mother. Now it is yours to wear and pass on as you please. So are these." Louise snapped open a small leather case in her hand. "My wedding gift."

"Oh, *Grandmère!*"

Yolanda was unable to say more about the pair of ear-rings Louise took from the case. Two blue tinged diamonds suspending a pair of matched beige drop pearls. The bells began pealing in a mad jangle of joy.

"You will wear them, no?" Louise yelled. "Now I must be off to the church. These last moments you should spend with your mother. That is necessary."

Yolanda thanked Louise above the noise with a lump in her throat and turned to Diana who was closing the window.

"Oh, Mummy. You gave all your jewels up. None of this would have happened if you hadn't . . ."

"Sh. A lot of things would never have happened, perhaps. We don't know. But I have no jewels to give you, Yolanda, so I'm glad Alisdair's family have. I haven't given you anything yet, have I?"

Yolanda mistook her mother's meaning. "Oh, but of course you have. This dress, the wedding . . . all this . . ."

"No, darling. Those things are your right. My duty and privilege to provide. A present is different. Mine to you comes later today. I just didn't want you to think I'd forgotten, that's all."

Yolanda didn't answer but sat down on her bed to stroke the orange cat, who lay in a nest of tissue paper. She got up at once, remembering her dress. Something ought to be said. Thank you for everything, perhaps . . . or about Daddy. No, not that. Her mother must be feeling desperately lonely today. Yolanda decided to play it safe and remarked on her clothes. A bias cut yellow *grosgrain*, to neck, knee and wrist. Very clever and supple with a plainest of pill box hats to match. No handbag. Yolanda had no bridesmaids and her mother would take her bouquet in the church. Whatever Nidcaster said, it was still a very quiet wedding.

Yolanda and Alisdair would miss the firework display. It was a pity, in a way, but they would be long gone on their honeymoon by the time it started. Only Alisdair knew where. Would Diana feel up to managing the company while Yolanda was away? What was going to happen afterwards? Where would they live? The flat was really far to small for the two of them. Diana said not to worry. That might all be a lot clearer by the end of the day.

A sound of car doors slamming and a familiar voice forestalled any question that Yolanda could ask. Diana breathed a sigh of relief. In her nervousness, she had nearly given the secret away.

"I must leave you now, darling. Mr. Sedgely is here. I know you'll be happy." Diana's hand went to her mouth. She bit at her thumb as she always did under stress. "I'm wearing purple mascara. I can't possibly cry."

"And the bride's mother wore woad," Yolanda joked just in time.

"I don't think even ancient Britons wore warpaint for weddings," Diana smiled gratefully, eyes swimming.

Yolanda walked to her wedding, after Sedgely had had a few moments alone with the bride in the drawing-room. As substitute father it was his right to administer the steadying, ceremonial mouthful of brandy and to say the ritual words.

"Now you're sure, Miss Landa. There's no need to go through with it if you don't want. T'expense is nowt. It's insured. Change your mind if you like, love. Forget all t'fuss and think of yourself. You're only one as counts."

Keen to exercise his privileges to the fullest extent, Sedgely stood in danger of overdoing it. He painted the blackest pictures of marital disharmony about which he personally knew nothing. Mr. Alisdair were a sound enough lad . . . very nearly good enough . . .

Yolanda got Sedgely to his feet and out of the house. Down the steps, along the terrace and out of the garden door. The cord to raise her train was not needed. The householders in the lane had carpeted the cobbles with rugs. All the way to the church. There was everything there, from faded old Persians to bright floral Axminsters. People thronged in the doorways and leaned out of the windows. Camera shutters clicked.

"Give us a smile, Yolanda, love . . ."

"Can't you go any faster, Sedgely? You'll have t'lass late at this rate."

"Now you can't tell me t'Princess of Wales looked any better nor that."

The walk took four minutes, just twice the usual time. But they got to the altar on the dot of a quarter to twelve amid gasps. The bells ceased abruptly and Sedgely allowed himself to sit down. That'd shown them.

It was Alisdair who came nearest to fainting. The spun sugar princess beside him told him, in a whispered aside, either to get a grip or take his suicide pill ... in a very unfairytale way. The colour came back to her bridegroom's cheeks. This was Yolanda, all right.

❦ THE WEATHER STAYED fine, the service went well and the town was filling up nicely.

The wedding breakfast was conventionally grand with wild salmon in aspic, lobster, and hot roast saddle of venison. None of your mingy afternoon tea sort of weddings like they had in the South. The *Bystander's* editor made an approving note. As a man who had travelled, he knew. There was no nonsense here about standing around with a curry puff. It was a proper sit down, knife and fork carry-on. No dodges. Mrs. Neville was doing them proud.

At a quarter past three there was a clearing of top table throats. The string quartet scraped to a halt and a spoon or two was banged. Sedgely got up for the last time that day and announced that although in temporary *loco parentis* to the bride, he'd nothing 'tickler to say. Young Mrs. Strang-Steele were a beauty as any fool could see ... and she'd a head on her shoulders, which might be less obvious to the generality of folks.

A splutter of sophisticated London laughter greeted this rustic sally, which Sedgely rightly ignored. The bride's good sense were amply demonstrated by the fact she'd married t'man who was best for her. Like himself, Mr. Alisdair, you might say, had had a hand in bringing her up and had got his reward today. Sedgely did not begrudge him. He wasn't going to blather on, he said, but hand them over to someone with more right to talk.

Sedgely's brevity earned him a round of thunderous applause. He resumed his seat, beetroot faced, as Diana rose from hers. Philip drew out her chair for her and touched her hand briefly under the table.

It wasn't usual, Diana said, for a bride's mother to address her guests. Nor would she have done so, but her wedding gift to her daughter and new son-in-law was not something she could place in their hands. It had been a last minute decision, she said, and she hoped her friends would sympathise with her whim to do in their sight what would soon be generally known. But she was getting ahead of herself. Diana paused to let the ripple of anticipation die down.

She said a good deal in praise of her daughter and of Alisdair. Both had stood by her during difficult times ... of which her guests were aware. Without the friendship of them, the Sedgelys and the Strang-Steele family, there was no doubt that today's pleasant event would not have occurred.

"This house," Diana seemed to abandon the former thread of her speech, "was given to me when I needed it. So, it seems to me right to pass it on in my turn to one who can make fuller use of it than I ever could—my daughter, Yolanda Strang-Steele."

It caused a sensation. Yolanda's wonderful mouth formed the roundest, most perfect of "Oh!"s. Philips flung himself back in his chair and stared up at Diana.

"You've made yourself homeless."

"Hm," Diana replied for his ears alone. She slid her eyes sideways at him and sucked in her cheek.

Louise was astounded. First, the best man she was ever likely to meet ... Now her house. Had Diana gone mad? Alisdair, his grandmother noted, was quite *boulversé*. Surprises did not suit the Strang-Steele constitution.

Diana went on to say something of her great-aunt's regret that Gilbert's Tower should lack a real family to shelter ... a young family needed space and so forth. There were claps and "Hear, hear"s ... a subterranean buzz of comment. Diana Neville to leave Gilbert's Tower ... a turn-up for the books. Merlin Olaff was horrified. From a public relations man's standpoint, it was rash. He should have been warned.

"What's going on?" Gholam Khan's Begum asked him in Pathan. She had finally plucked up the courage to come. Hearing the news she began to ululate, a thrilling sound in the throat. Gholan told her to stop. Terminal generosity in this country wasn't a subject for congratulation. More of a medical matter.

"And," Diana continued calmly, "as some of you may know, the Lordship of the Manor of Leypole vests in me. It is an interesting detail that the title is separable from the freehold as long as it goes with a square foot of land on the Manor. I now deed to my son-in-law the square foot of conservatory quarry

tiles on which his chair rests, together with the nominal fief-
dom of Leypole.

"In the fullness of time, I dare say," Diana smiled at Louise,
"title and freehold will be reunited in one of my grandchildren."

It was left to Philip to propose the health of the bride and
the groom.

"Long life," and "good luck," roared back the good natured
acclaim ... though just how much more luck they could possibly expect was open to dispute, as Alisdair said when he replied to his father.

He dilated at length on his mother-in-law's generosity and
imagination. As Lord of the Manor of Leypoole, he would
never sit in that chair in the hall by the fireplace at Christmas
while she lived to take his place. In fact, he went on a touch
too long. Yolanda tugged at his sleeve and whispered discreetly that it was usual to pay some passing regard to the
bride's perfections. Quite so. Had she a list?

"Start with my patience and go on to my hair," Yolanda
hissed. "Then work down from the top."

Alisdair did so, sitting down to a kindly burst of applause.
He'd not done bad for a bridegroom, Sedgely beamed. By
gum, what a day. He could scarcely take it all in.

Louise was in full flood with a most elegant fit of weeping.
In a similar if less histrionic state, Mrs. Sedgely left the mar-
quee to cast around for a particular kind of stone. Certain West
Riding patterns had better be drawn on the top front doorstep.
The kind her own mother-in-law had made in front of the ter-
race cottage which had been her and Sedgely's first home.
Foolishness, maybe. But you couldn't take chances with luck.
Happen Mr. Alisdair had learned his lesson about that.

As Alisdair leaped over the magic design on his doorstep
(though it was never admitted as such), holding Yolanda tight
in his arms, the very last ticket for the firework display was
sold. Nobody's rheumatics were foretelling rain and the ducks
were seen to be working the waterside crowds in their usual,
fair weather formation.

❦ ALISDAIR AND YOLANDA were seen off in a flower filled carriage at the station, their destination still unknown. The guard's
van was stuffed full of their luggage. It wasn't a convenient

way to leave but Bob had earned his share of the action. They were to be gone until Christmas time if they wanted.

Yolanda clung tight to her mother at the last. "Oh, Mummy, what have you done? You'll stay, won't you ... and live with us?"

"Certainly not, my darlings," Diana laughed at the moment's wholesome hesitation which warred with the anxiety in her child's voice. "What kind of gift would that be? Take Gilbert's Tower and be happy there. I shall be gone by the time you get back. Come on now, no tears and no questions. It's all for the best."

Walking back down the lane beside her, Philip was silent. Glancing up at him, Diana saw he was overcome, managing the customary set of his features with difficulty. She took his arm and did what she never normally did ... prattled. Every other emotion, she knew from experience, is extinguished by a blanket of boredom.

She thought she might make Yolanda Chief Executive of English Gardens when the bridal pair returned, she said. And shouldn't he think of handing over some Strang-Steele Group responsibilities to Alisdair now? She was sure he could handle them ... though of course it was none of her business.

Philip was still formulating his answer when they were parted by Major Garside's wife. Could Diana dine with them the week after next?

The party was a long way from over. Forty-five bottles of champagne had already been drunk, a statistic the *Bystander's* editor recorded with glee. He was keeping tabs on the empties. Nidcaster readers liked t'nitty gritty. Mrs. Neville to leave Gilbert's Tower. Well, well. A bit of a scoop there. He cursed old technology ... hot lead and overtime. Still, a special edition would sell.

At dusk the Mayor asked Diana if she would kindly consent to inaugurate the firework display. Merlin Olaff encouraged it. First-rate PR stuff. Unimpressed, Diana declined, pleading tiredness, shyness ... or anything else that would do. Really, she had had enough for one day.

"Come on, my dear," Philip urged unexpectedly, with a glance at the Mayor. "All you have to do is put a match to a rocket and I want a go in that gondola."

The lantern lit craft was poled to the midstream raft. Helping her up, a man thrust a microphone into Diana's hand. A public address system. In the gloaming, the spectators were barely visible.

"There you are, Mrs. Neville. Just say a few words, like. Then I'll set t'whole shooting match off."

The Mayor introduced her as the hereditary Lord of the Manor of Leypoole, on to whose former lands the corporation was glad to welcome its visitors. While he went on with an exposition of municipal niceties, Diana turned anxiously to Philip. This was all wrong. She had given the Lordship away. And now the Mayor was misrepresenting her position on Alisdair's wedding day.

"Not at all," Philip whispered. "Didn't you read the deed? He doesn't accede to your throne till midnight tonight. But Diana, what *then*?"

"I thought I might come and live with you, actually," Diana cocked her head on one side. "That a good idea?"

Philip was momentarily struck dumb. How slow he had been. "So you gave up . . . That was the reason . . ."

"Hm. So I'd have nowhere to run back to . . . I love it, you see."

"Ahem," the Mayor interrupted this colloquy, having completed his oration. "Ready, Mrs. Neville?"

Diana lifted her hand with the microphone to adjust her hat bringing it level with Philip's mouth.

"Just a minute," he said, "I think this lady has asked me to marry her and I'm going to say yes."

"Warrabloodyballsup," muttered the public address system man. He went unheard above the noise from the crowd. Whoops of laughter and cheers. There was no silence for Diana's speech. The thing had got off on its own. There had been a change in the air . . . an extra injection of hydrogen molecules. Atmosphere. Better go with the flow. Words were inaudible above the din. Diana nodded at the Mayor and the English Gardens' logo flared into blazing life. The gate with *Y* and *A* intertwined.

"What an unforgivable blunder." Philip coloured richly under cover of darkness. He was very embarrassed.

"You'd best wave, love," the Mayor mouthed his suggested improvisation. "And you an' all, sir," he squinted at Philip. He looked a bit of a gent and might do.

"Let's have you kissing 'er, sir," a man with a camera appeared alongside the raft. It flashed as Philip swept her into his arms. With the news already climbing the gorge, the raft was suddenly inundated by well-wishers, their boats crowding the sides. Ecstatic, Louise emerged from the gloom, was hoisted aboard and seen to be minus a shoe. Somebody fell into the water. It was Diana who noticed.

"Rescue him, please!"

It was all getting quite dangerous.

While the night-time sky whistled and popped with starbursts of candy floss colour, Philip extricated Diana. They drifted away unnoticed in Yolanda's new gondola. But not for long.

"Now then, Mrs. Neville," Ned's loud-hailer blasted their ears. "Don't go scraping that paintwork. Hang on, I'll come and give you a tow." He hadn't yet heard.

The parish church clock struck midnight as Diana walked back through the garden door at the Tower with Philip, breathless and laughing. They had been mobbed, jostled, shoved and embraced. It was all a glorious, spontaneous, magical muddle . . . not Diana's style really, and not Philip's at all. In the garden at least it was quiet. But there was none of the old silent greeting now. No moist, thin lipped butting of feline tooth and whisker on Diana's leg. This house was no longer her home.

In the town, pub and shop tills were still ringing. The police were taking an independent, Nidcaster line on the licensing laws. The whole thing had been a right, rip-roaring success. One lost nipper, now found, and two emotional lads in the cells. That was the count.

The *Bystander* press was at a temporary halt. Late news . . . and yes, red ink.

Philip presumed on his daughter-in-law's hospitality and slept in the tower room—or rather, lay awake there. Diana came in to him an hour or so later.

"I can't get to sleep on my own."

"I was a bit hurt that you tried," Philip made room at his side. "If you've nothing particular on, we'll get married next week." The Decree Absolute was through.

"I do need a roof," Diana said. She had opened her hand and lost everything to gain a new life. "And you."

Then he murmured wonderful things to her in French, which are permissible for a proud man to say in that tongue.

Miles away, sailing south down the Rhone on a freshly fitted river barge, Yolanda conceived her first child. At Gilbert's Tower, Louise was excitable and kept waking Marie to remind her of things she hadn't forgotten. They were leaving next day.

Sedgely composed himself for sleep with meditative calm. A reign of a sort was over. Mrs. Neville had chosen her own time to go. And her own way ... the transcendent mark of a leader. By heck, she'd looked liked a Plantagenet queen on that raft. Mrs. Sedgely agreed.

A roving sentinel on the moon silvered tops of the garden's perimeter walls, the orange cat ordered his unknowable thoughts. Left-over lobster claws had something to do with them, no doubt, but not all.

Epilogue

WHAT SEDGELY CALLED a "straight edge" was only a temporary illusion. Things would keep on happening at Gilbert's Tower, in Nidcaster and the greater world outside.

Philip and Diana were not in fact married until just after their children's return from Provence. It was an absolutely private, civil ceremony at the Mairie in Rouen. Tired of the glare of publicity, they both wanted it that way. Louise provided a family luncheon at the Manoir des Evêques. The Sedgelys were invited but would not come. Sedgely refused the invitation with dour humility. He had gone far enough in the world. Any further and he might fall over the edge. It was too late for him to go risking his health in foreign parts. Mrs. Sedgely loyally agreed with him, though privately, she wouldn't have minded the jaunt.

Their wedding present to the senior Strang-Steeles was a fine old Leeds pottery tea service. The real thing. It made Diana weepy, because she knew it was Mrs. Sedgely's pride and joy. The accompanying gift of a year's supply of pickled red cabbage made her laugh, however. Apparently, this was to be renewed every year of Sedgely's natural life. Not quite so amusing but to be taken in good part. Diana never dreamed that it was *Mrs.* Sedgely who had hit on this brilliant scheme for clearing her cellar.

Diana and Philip embarked on a period of travel. Florence, New York, Vienna, Copenhagen, Rome. Looking and listening to all the things which Michael had despised and Philip had never had anyone to show. In the late spring, immediately after the birth of Yolanda's baby, due in May, they would charter a yacht and cruise in the Melanesian seas. The first Christmas of the new order of things, both couples would spend alone. Alisdair and Yolanda, Diana insisted, were to enjoy Gilbert's Tower at that season, for once at least, on their own. For her, it was a part of letting go.

While Philip took his bride from one capital to another, to concerts, museums and galleries and got her portrait painted, things were jogging on in Nidcaster in a more pedestrian way.

The refurbishment of the old mill was well in hand. The same supervising architect not only created a nursery apartment in the rooms over the kitchen in the Victorian wing at Gilbert's Tower, but opened up long forgotten rooms in the medieval tower itself. The spiral staircase was half blocked with fallen masonry and this was cleared away and made safe. It meant there would now be direct, under cover access to the boat house and a new landing stage was built. Ned's beautiful gondola would be worthily housed. It could be used for taking business guests direct from house to mill in fine weather.

Already Ned had orders for something similar from all over the country. He was training and recruiting craftsmen, teaching himself as well as them as he went along. Yolanda Marine, the new venture is called. No one gets away with tittering. Ned still carries a bit of a torch for her.

The old espalier pear outside the book room failed to blossom that year. Yolanda was glad Diana was not there to see it. An old friend gone. To balance against that was Yolanda's pregnancy. "Textbook." She quoted the consultant obstetrician to her mother over the telephone.

"And how do you feel, darling?" Diana probed. "Are you sure you want to have it at home?"

Philip, who was standing beside her at that moment in their hotel suite in Venice, grimaced. The whole thing terrified him. He had lost Alisdair's mother that way.

"The midwife say's I'm blooming . . . I feel hugely, importantly *big* . . . And yes. I must have he, she or it at home. How are you two?"

At the end of April, Philip heard of a yacht that might suit them berthed in a New Zealand marina. There was time to get there and back a week before Yolanda's expected confinement with a day or two to spare. Even so, Philip swallowed his wish to have her with him and suggested Diana go on ahead to Gilbert's Tower. But she would not leave him. Every word that he said, every small thing that he did from brushing his teeth for exactly six minutes, to lavishing bank notes on beggars when he thought she wasn't looking . . . All that was too adorable to miss. No breath that he took was without its value to her.

The result was, they missed the birth of their granddaughter entirely.

It happened because Michael rang up. Yolanda was tidying her overflowing desk in the book room at the end of the day and picked the telephone up when it rang without the slightest premonition. Alisdair was out for the day. It was probably him.

"Gilbert's Tower, Yolanda Strang-Steele speaking," she answered formally. The working day was not quite over.

"So you did it then," Michael's voice replied, eerily matter of fact. "When was the wedding? Poor old Landa . . ."

Unable to say anything, she stood there with the receiver clamped to her ear, mind moving slowly through a morass of glue.

"Landa! Landa? Are you there?"

"Yes, I'm here," she managed to say. "Where are you?" It must be some distance, she thought. There was a satellite blip and a sort of echo.

"Papua New Guinea. Me and another bloke are setting up something here. Fantastic place. I wish you could see it. Why don't you come out? I've got a power boat for going round the islands . . . You should see my house . . ."

He went on long enough for Yolanda to work out what she should say and what she should not. As little as possible. When he let her speak, she said she was well and so was her mother. Everything was going on normally. That is, things had been sorted out. Nothing much had changed. No, she couldn't come out. She was too busy. She and Alisdair had their hands full. No, she'd had to give her course up. Involved in the business. What was his address?

Michael was not willing to give her that. Not at the moment, he said. Was Diana there? No, she was not. No, not on holiday. Just away . . . on business. She was sorry. She had to go. Alisdair was waiting.

The mention of her husband's name got Michael off the line very fast. Not that Yolanda realised that. She was breathing hard when she put the receiver down. There were tears in her eyes, though she couldn't think why. Shock. A pain doubled her over. Or it would have done if there had been anywhere in her middle that would bend. Again. The baby.

Yolanda did not panic but made her way slowly upstairs to Aunt Thea's room, now hers. She lay down on the bed and got her breath back. The doctor's surgery number was scribbled ready on a card by Alisdair's side of the bed. She reached for it, waited a little, and then dialled the number.

There was a ghastly rush of warm water from between her legs. Like peeing herself. The lovely new chintz covered eiderdown was soaked. She could have killed Daddy for that. It was all going wrong. She thought of rolling off the bed and getting herself to the window. Mr. Sedgely was probably still pottering about outside. No point. What could Sedgely do? The surgery answered, thank God. Yes, someone would come when they could. Meanwhile, keep on with the breathing. It was early, wasn't it? According to the notes.

An hour and half later, the midwife turned up to find Yolanda alone, still fully dressed and already dilating.

"Where's your husband? I thought you were having a monthly nurse."

"I am but she doesn't come till next week."

They got through it somehow. A bit messy and alarmingly quick. Alisdair arrived home from Lincolnshire, where he'd been, to find himself too late to do all the things he had learned about and was looking forward to performing. He was disappointed and horrified in retrospect at what might have happened. But Yolanda was all right and his tiny red daughter was bellowing like a miniature Guards sergeant major. She had everything she ought to have, the midwife assured him, handing him the struggling bundle. She just wanted a drink. Premature? Barely. And as Yolanda said later, well enough cooked. The trouble was that although perfectly serene before, Yolanda could not feed the baby. Her poor breasts were in hard, strangulated knots.

"Relax, dear," the midwife ordered. "You're much too tense. Very strung up."

She had some formula in her car, fortunately. And the week before, Yolanda had rather contemptuously bought a couple of feeding bottles. Alisdair had to sterilise them and mix the feed, turn and turn about throughout the night. Yolanda must rest, the midwife said. There was to be no getting out of bed just yet.

"How many future multi-millionaires feed their own babies? I was led to believe there were some perks," Alisdair muttered to himself at five in the morning. Every three hours, regular as clockwork, the little one was. In between whiles, he dozed, sitting up on the bed, resting his back on the headboard beside Yolanda's sleeping form. His daughter reposed contentedly in his arms . . . until the next bout of feeding frenzy. Like a young shark.

"You had a baby yesterday evening," Alisdair remarked to Yolanda's waking face. "I don't suppose *you* remember . . ."

"Vaguely," the yawning mother replied. "Is she all right?"

"She's the greediest, ugliest heiress I've ever seen," Alisdair crooned. Maternal indignation brought Yolanda's milk in at once.

She never told Alisdair what had precipitated the birth. He would not understand that in a sad, small part of herself that would always be there, she was glad she had spoken to her father.

Philip and Diana arrived days later to find the nursery already occupied and everything running on oiled wheels. They were surprised and concerned. But the minutest covert inspection of both baby and mother revealed nothing to criticise. Louise came next, without Marie who was, in her mistress's words, *inutile* with babies. She herself could hardly be persuaded to relinquish her great-granddaughter. Monthly nurse, father, mother and grandparents were all regarded as somewhat inexperienced and having a lot to learn.

The first mutual descendant of Philip and Diana was christened Titania Diana Louise Theadosia FitzGilbert Strang-Steele. A dreadful encumbrance for the poor child. But as Sedgely pointed out, that was the whole point of names, to keep them to yourself. They'd probably call her Tania at school . . . which they did, the minute she joined the local playgroup. The rest could be her own secret. No need to go shouting it about.

The orange cat, who spent far too much time in the nursery to suit Nanny, seemed to bear his name theory out. Titania, once she could talk, called him *Cat*. Her very first word.

Yolanda admitted the unflattering fact. But that was a year later.

Diana and Philip resumed their travels once the christening was over. By November they were temporarily settled at the Manoir—where Louise was rarely in residence owing to supposed responsibilities to her great-grandchild at Gilbert's Tower.

That Christmas, they did go to Nidcaster and up to now, every subsequent one. As Alisdair always vowed, Diana is made to preside over the very merry little Christmas court there as she did in the past. She doesn't even pretend to object. The welcome she gets from the town, the family and their guests would make that ungracious. She always has a new dress for the night of the Mummers' Play. One year Paris, the next Bessie Brown. There's nothing to choose between them so far, though Diana thinks Paris is slipping.

The first year they were with them, Philip presented Diana's portrait to his son and daughter-in-law. It hangs now over the chimney piece in the drawing-room. Aunt Thea has joined the other ancestors in the dining-room. There have been no wailings or hauntings, no creakings or self-moving furniture to suggest that she resents the demotion. Diana's will come eventually, when Yolanda's image follows hers into the place of most recent honour.

The firework display has become an annual affair although, very sensibly, it has been moved to Guy Fawkes night. More commercial. Alisdair opens it. Diana refuses point blank to attend. The event belongs to "The Children," she says. It was started for them and the first one jealously opened itself. Philip recalls that particular scuffle with rueful pleasure.

In the second year after Tania's birth, Sedgely became Alderman Sedgely and in due course was elected Mayor of Nidcaster. He adorned the office with kingly simplicity, adding several excellent suits to his wardrobe. The dandification of Sedgely tended to obscure his growing political sense. A nudge here, a grant there and Sedgely arranged Nidcaster's civic affairs pretty well to his taste.

Nothing is perfect.

Louise died before her second great-grandchild, Sholto Philip, was born. She departed this life casually, in her sleep one night at Gilbert's Tower. One of those expected things that takes everyone completely by shocking surprise. She was squeezed into Father Murphy's sole remaining burial ground plot. She had been as happy at Nidcaster as anywhere else and her family were there. So Louise's fragile French bones were laid in good Yorkshire earth.

On the day of the funeral Father Murphy preached a sermon about Ruth, mothers-in-law ... It was all arse about face. Appropriate somehow, nonetheless. Not a dry eye in the house. On the domestic front, Louise was sent off in splendour. Mrs. Sedgely saw to that. Roast York ham and Earl Grey. There was even champagne. It was the sweet end to a plotter who had not plotted in vain.

Philip found it impossible to spend as much money as he wanted on a slab of marble. Diana supplied the playful inscription:

> *For her own breakfast she'll project a scheme,*
> *Nor take her tea without a strategem.*

The quotation was ascribed to Goldsmith ... probably wrongly. Never mind. It was the agreed descriptive label that Louise carried with her to Paradise. Her whole family knew she would have been proud of it, too.

Father Murphy stroked his chin. What was this impious jingle? But pseudo-Irishman and true Yorkshireman that he was, he recognised a trade-off when he saw one. He'd got one of t'FitzGilbert crowd at last. And with Aunt Thea resting in the churchyard, as Diana said, they'd established a foot in both camps. As he grew older, Father Murphy began to think Louise's grave *was* Theadosia FitzGilbert's. They had been rather similar people.

Alisdair inherited the Manoir and lets it to his father at a pretty fair market rent. Business is business. Louise's property in Provence was also taken out of the Group ownership and kept for general family use. A holiday place. Ramshackle and wasteful. It was allowed to stay that way. Marie lives there permanently now.

People ask Diana if she doesn't long for a house of her own. She says that Philip is roof, hearth and walls to her—unlike Gilbert's Tower, he is maintenance free. Nor could any house ever claim her as that one had done.

From time to time, Michael's voice is heard again on the telephone. It's a jolt, every time. Yolanda and Alisdair take the brunt of it. Michael is always somewhere different doing something new. Full of bravado and talking big. It always has to do with money. It is both his raw material and his product. Yolanda suspects he meets with increasingly little success. His calls, always made when least expected, come at roughly seven to ten month intervals. From Peru, it was once . . . the next time, Taiwan, where he did not last long. The young Strang-Steeles say nothing to their parents. It did happen once, however, when they were there. It was Philip who took the call. It made him go grey in the face.

All of them wonder just how Michael's life will end. There are separate and private imaginings. About soup kitchens, a park bench for a bed. Death in an alleyway or a ditch.

A spectre in the family cupboard, the subject is rarely mentioned. Philip sends money secretly to a numbered account in Switzerland, having a shrewd notion that the man is practically destitute. Yolanda keeps the Harrogate flat empty when she could let it . . . thinking some day her father might need it. Michael knows nothing of his grandchildren and if Alisdair has his way, he never will.

It is a sad business. All the more so, the Strang-Steeles think, because they are happy. So on the deficit side, there is unearned, undeserved guilt. It is Philip who feels it most keenly, wondering always if he did the right thing. A glance at his wife reassures him.

If she half guesses, now, with what speed, cunning and daring her liberation was planned, it's the one thing she never discusses. Philip Strang-Steele is a reticent man.